THE ICE BALLOON

JENNY BOND

A catalogue record for this book is available from the National Library of Australia

Cover created by DAMONZA

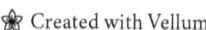 Created with Vellum

For Chris, for telling me to write a book

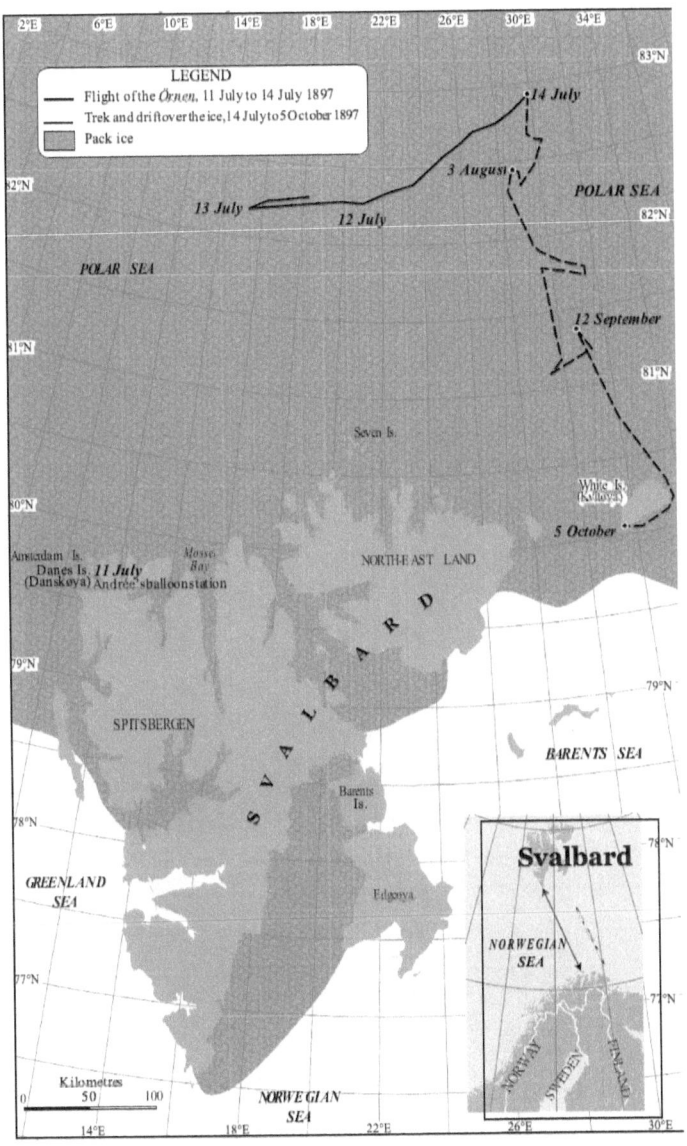

PROLOGUE

Albany Express, Albany, NY 16 January 1896

A PERILOUS EXPEDITION

The proposed polar expedition by balloon is beginning to assume shape. The balloon will be made in Paris, Engineer Andree, of Stockholm, will be in command, and Dr Ekholm, of the University of Upsal, will be the meteorologist of the expedition. A photographer named Strindberg will take snap shots on the way.

The air ship will have a capacity of 4,500 metres. It will be made of silk of several thicknesses, made waterproof and varnished so that it will be absolutely impermeable. The cost of the balloon, all told, will be about fifty thousand francs. The constructors have agreed to accompany the expedition to Spitsbergen to look after the inflation of the balloon and direct the preparations for the departure. The air ship is to be finished by May 11. The acids, the materials necessary for making hydrogen gas, and the shed to be put up to shelter the balloon during the process of inflation, will be carried to

Spitsbergen from Sweden by a vessel of the Royal Navy. The ascension will take place at one of the islands of Norskoearna, a little archipelago northeast of Spitsbergen, about 650 miles from the pole.

The balloon will carry three guide ropes, weighing altogether 1,000 kilogrammes. One of their uses will be to diminish the speed of the air ship, so as to enable the travelers to govern it to some extent. By start- ing from a station so near the pole, the aeronauts will be able in a few hours to get beyond the latitudes that have been reached so far by any expedition. A number of photo- graphs will be taken, giving an exact idea of the regions over which the party will be taken by the caprices of the wind. The guide ropes will hold the balloon at a height not exceeding 200 metres.

After passing over the pole the travelers expect to reach civilization on the other side, or at least a locality where they will have a chance to be sighted by a whaler.

According to the calculations of Dr Ekholm, it is probable that the expedition will remain at least fifteen days in the air, and that during this period the balloon will travel a distance of over 3,000 miles. A collection of 2,000 photographs is expected.

How the men plan to protect themselves for fifteen days from the intense cold that they will encounter in mid-air in the regions of eternal winter is not even suggested. It does not seem possible that any amount of furs would suffice. To sustain life upon the ice, where it is at least possible to secure some shelter, is extremely difficult, as experience has taught; in the frail car of a balloon, where the men will be constantly exposed to the intense cold of the open air, it must seem impossible. It looks as if this expedition will result in the sacrifice of several human lives and nothing more.

PART ONE

THE FIRST ATTEMPT

ONE

STOCKHOLM, SWEDEN
AUGUST 1895

AN UNCOMFORTABLE SILENCE settled over the Strindberg drawing room. Nils looked to his older brother Erik for a reaction, but none came. His mother sat speechless in her armchair and his father stared stubbornly at a spot on the wall. Finally the quiet was broken by twelve-year-old Tore.

'It will be a marvellous adventure, I should think.' Nils smiled at him in gratitude. 'I mean, it's the chance of a life-time really, and Nils will return a hero.'

'If he returns,' Erik mumbled under his breath. He took a long, pointed drag on his cigarette.

Nils shot him a hostile glance. Erik returned fire. 'Go to bed, Tore, it's late,' his mother said quietly.

'But the first men to reach the North Pole! Nils will make history. Don't you see?'

'Tore!'

Nils ruffled Tore's hair. 'Off to bed with you. I'll see you in the morning.' With that Tore walked out and closed the door with theatrical force behind him.

Their father turned to Nils. 'Do you have time to reconsider?'

'I've given my word and I don't want to reconsider. Andrée is an accomplished balloonist and engineer. He's a member of the city council. If you'd heard him speak at the Academy you wouldn't be worried.'

'Andrée is insane, a mad ballooning zealot,' Erik interrupted, his voice so loud that Rosalie flinched. 'Travelling to the North Pole in a balloon? Is he serious? Are you serious? Even the American Greely thinks he's round the bend. And John Wise, Andrée's ballooning hero, disappeared over Lake Michigan fifteen years ago.'

The brothers glared at each other until the deadlock was broken by the sudden sound of frantic activity in the entrance hall. In a few seconds Sven, looking dishevelled and smelling of beer, entered the room.

'Sorry I'm late. What did I miss?' the twenty-one-year-old chirped, straightening his tie.

'Stop grinning, you idiot,' Erik blasted. 'What did you miss? Well, Nils is going off to kill himself, that's all.'

Sven's brow furrowed and he looked quizzically at his mother. 'What's he shouting about?'

'Never mind, darling,' she said calmly. 'Nils will tell you all about it in the morning. I think you should hop on up to bed now.' Rosalie led her son to the door and gave him a soft kiss on the cheek. Sven complied.

Thanks to his size and demeanour Erik had been nicknamed 'Viking' by his family and friends as a child. He took after his father, Oscar, in this regard. A mere sixteen months his brother's senior, Erik saw himself as Nils' protector, and Nils resented it bitterly.

Neither could give way to the other on any subject, no matter how trivial. Their determination to outdo the other drove their teachers to distraction and their mother to tears – yet they were the truest of friends.

Nils sighed impatiently. 'Greely has no experience with balloons and his expedition ten years ago ended with twenty of his party dead.' His voice was rising. 'What does he know about successful Arctic exploration?'

Erik sneered. 'And how is Andrée going to fund this flight of fancy? Apart from you, dear brother, who's foolish enough to invest money or time in this madness?'

'The King. He'll do anything to ensure Sweden's is the first flag planted at the North Pole.'

'How many of you are going, Nils?' his father asked. 'Will it be just the two of you?'

'No, Papa. There's a third man, Nils Ekholm. He's a meteor ologist. Quite a well-known one, actually. He and Andrée are old colleagues.'

Their mother now joined the debate. 'But why you, darling?'

Nils sat down on the arm of his mother's chair and took her hand. 'His concerns are partly practical, Mama. Andrée needs someone young and fit and healthy, someone who'll be able to endure the conditions. And my scientific training will also be very useful to him.'

Nils spoke with characteristic modesty. He was a highly trained and well-regarded physicist, assistant to Svante Arrhenius, one of the world leaders in his field of Greenhouse Law. Andrée would benefit immensely from Nils' expertise.

'I'll be recording wind pressure and direction, the movement of ice floes and other meteorological data,' Nils explained evenly. 'I hope to return to Stockholm with information that will advance the university's research.'

Rosalie nodded, alarm still evident in her brilliant blue eyes.

'Andrée has also heard about my photography, Mama. He wants to document the entire expedition on film. Who better to do that than me?' Nils' final remark was punctuated with a wan chuckle.

He neglected to tell his mother that it was not in fact Andrée who had approached him. Nils had met with the adventurer after his speech at the Swedish Academy of Sciences in February not only to congratulate Andrée but also to offer the man his full support. Rosalie smiled at him thinly, then stood and left the room. Nils looked after her but said nothing. He checked his watch then cast an eye to the clock standing at the far corner of the room. He was stunned to see it was only eight o'clock.

Erik did not seem persuaded by his brother's speech and gave a loud huff as he sat his broad frame heavily on the sofa.

Out of sheer frustration, Nils turned on him. 'You've made your mark in your career, brother. Your expertise is needed in America and I'm sure you'll be able to establish an extremely prosperous livelihood for yourself there. I'm an excellent scientist, but I have no head for business. This is my opportunity to establish myself and make my mark.'

Erik stood abruptly and strode to the window. He parted the curtains and looked out onto the street. When he eventually turned, there was a wry grin on his face.

'Well, if this fool's errand has any chance of success, Andrée will need you along. You're the most capable man I know, brother.' Erik grabbed Nils' hand and shook it. Then, without warning or precedent, he pulled his brother to him and wrapped him tightly in a bear hug, overcome with pride in Nils' courage and the fear of losing him. He couldn't stop Nils from becoming his own man; Erik was just disturbed by the means he had chosen to achieve his goal.

Nils was shocked and surprised at this display of brotherly admiration. This had been a remarkable day, indeed.

'You don't need to do this,' Erik said. 'I'm leaving Stockholm . . .' He trailed off, unable to express what he hoped. Erik was aware that he cast an extremely large shadow, but how could he convince his brother that there were other, more sensible means of stepping out of it?

Nils nodded, understanding the gist of his brother's faltering argument. His silence was enough to show Erik that his plans were not going to be altered.

Their father began, 'To be frank, Nils, I never thought I'd see you involved in such a foolhardy scheme. Erik's always been pig-headed and the first to put himself in harm's way. Sven's determination to leap at any opportunity frightens me silly and Tore is reckless by nature. But you've always been the sensible one.' Oscar took his son's hand. 'I can understand what you hope to achieve and I wish you the best of luck. But my word isn't the last. I'm sure your fiancée will have an opinion.'

In the heat of the dispute someone had been entirely overlooked. Nils turned and smiled at the dark-haired young woman sitting in the corner. He looked at her expectantly. Her heart raced but she hesitated to speak until she could restrain her words.

'I need air,' she said, standing. She smiled politely at Nils, Erik and their father and strode from the room.

TWO

The discovery of these objects in this desert place, these lifeless
things, which swiftly carried the thoughts to their former owners
and the uses to which they had been put, gave birth to an
irresistible impression of the opposition between life and death.
Here, then, had men, warm-blooded and with a will to live, been
compelled to cross the threshold of the kingdom of omnipotent cold!
They had lived here – and perished.
– Knut Stubbendorff, 1930, *Andrée's Story*

KVITØYA, NORWAY
SEPTEMBER 1930

THE JOURNALIST STEPPED TENTATIVELY off the sloop and onto
the bleak, snowy tundra. An appropriate place to die,
Stubbendorff thought as he stared at the desolate scene. He
was more than tired and the shadow of a headache lay
behind his right eye. He brushed his white hair from his
brow as he took in his surroundings.

What had begun as an adventure for the twenty-five-year-old a week ago, a change in the daily tedium of local news and obituaries, had soon become a chore. Engaging a seaworthy boat equipped with a wireless, negotiating costs and times with drunken, simpleton sealers and surviving the rough night journey to the Norwegian no-man's land had quickly managed to turn the exploit sour.

Squinting his pale blue eyes against the intense sunlight, he looked out at the Arctic Sea and the cloudless sky. Stubbendorff was unsure what he would find here, probably just the grim pickings left behind by polar bears and the *Bratvaag* expedition two weeks before. The original assignment had been to intercept the *Bratvaag* on its return journey to Norway and interview the geologist Dr Gunnar Horn about the discovery. But delays due to bad weather meant that the rendezvous was missed. Horn's booty was in Norway, soon to be in the hands of the Scientific Commission in Sweden, and Stubbendorff would have to make do with merely documenting his visit to what had overnight become the most renowned and remote graveyard in the world.

He walked steadily with his companions – a photographer, new on staff at the *Aftonbladet*, and the captain and six crew from the *Isbjörn* – in the direction of a rocky ridge that ran from east to west along the length of the small island. At the summit of the ridge a pole, held in place by three guywires, had been erected. Below it was a rocky mound built from loose stones, a makeshift memorial constructed by Horn and his team. Before Stubbendorff had travelled fifty paces from the beach, he was rewarded. At the foot of the ridge lay a sledge, various articles of clothing and a collection of everyday objects one would use at a camp site – utensils, a compass, a saucepan and a knife. Trapped under the ice for more than three decades, these items had been exposed by a hotter than usual late summer sun and a rare absence of snow. The journalist wondered why they had been left by Horn. Perhaps the discovery of the two bodies preserved in ice had proved a distraction.

Stubbendorff halted and surveyed the scene. He had not expected anything like this. One could simply place three living men into the picture and have it take on new life. Everything remained exactly as he imagined the trio left it. His assignment suddenly took on a different meaning. If they knew they were doomed, why and how did they keep going? They must have persevered with a daily routine right until the end, he thought. It would have been understandable to the reporter if the three of them had taken a short walk into the Arctic Sea. Surely, this would have been an easier solution to their predicament. The intensity of their will shocked him. When Bergman had informed him of his assignment, Stubbendorff had viewed it as nothing more than an escape. Time seemed to move so slowly in the offices of the *Aftonbladet*. The clock resting on the wall above Bergman's door inched so agonisingly that at times Stubbendorff believed it had stopped. The undertaking was also an easy way to gain some credibility at the newspaper and, if he was lucky, a little of Bergman's good favour. But for the three dead men, the ice had captured them and Kvitøya had become their prison. Yet, from what he saw around him, they had refused to surrender. A lump formed in his throat and threatened to choke him.

An adolescent boy from the crew bent over and drew a small axe from a muddy puddle. The lad raised the implement above his head, a gesture of mock violence in an attempt to amuse his older colleagues. 'Don't touch anything. Leave it where it lies until we've photographed and documented everything,' Stubbendorff ordered.

The boy dropped the axe in surprise. Stubbendorff hastily produced a notebook and pencil from the pocket of his coat. He hoped this uncharacteristic order would make the *Isbjörn*'s dim-witted crew think twice before pocketing any souvenirs. The boy's thoughtless joke provoked an inexplicable anger in the reporter, who was usually immune to sentiment. Besides, he wanted a record of everything.

He loosened his scarf as he felt beads of perspiration forming on his upper lip. The polar sun was hot but the gravity of the task was also beginning to weigh on him. If he was not present, he thought, the crew would take what they liked and sail back to Norway. He was not a geologist, archaeologist or historian. Certainly he was not an adventurer. Yet he felt he was the only man here who could comprehend the immensity of what had been found and the colossal responsibility that would have to be shouldered.

As he meticulously listed objects half-embedded in the ice, a cry came from the north side of the ridge. 'Herr Stubbendorff, over here! We've found something.' Once he had made his way over the ridge, he saw four crew members staring down at a bone in the mud, about fifteen inches long.

'It looks like a leg bone, thigh perhaps,' Stubbendorff said. 'I wonder how Horn missed this?'

'Whose do you think it is?' someone asked.

'I haven't the slightest idea.' He cleared his throat. 'Perhaps it's the third man, Frænkel. Or perhaps it's part of Andrée or Strindberg. I'd say the bears have had their way with the bodies. It will be the job of the Scientific Commission to work out who's who.'

The men turned to Stubbendorff for direction. 'Let's get this photographed, shall we?' he said. 'If Horn missed this, then there's more than likely other . . .' – for the first time in his life the writer was lost for a suitable word – 'debris.'

'I doubt if anything was missed, Herr Stubbendorff,' the *Isbjörn*'s captain, Anton Hallen, said.

'What do you mean?'

'The ice. My guess is that what's-his-name . . .'

'Horn.'

'Yes, Horn couldn't get everything out of the ice without causing damage. It's been two weeks. The ice has melted even more since he was here.'

Stubbendorff nodded, thinking it a reasonable explanation.

Over the course of the long day, as the party moved around the island, the bones of the lower half of a body were found. The bears had made a mess of the entire camp, scattering the skeleton all over the island. As each bone was found, it was laid solemnly in its correct place like a morbid puzzle piece.

Stubbendorff, with his shirtsleeves rolled to his upper arms, quietly moved around the skeleton, gently adjusting and repositioning the bones as new ones were prised from the ice, uncovered and presented for inspection. He was no student of biology, but the journalist believed the majority of a torso and lower body had been found. If this man was Frænkel, he would have been twenty-seven years old when he died, Stubbendorff thought. Just two years older than the reporter.

As he fastidiously arranged and rearranged the bones, stepping gingerly over the remains, he thought about the three men and what they had accomplished. Their fearlessness and spirit had made them national heroes. Strindberg had been just twenty-five, like himself. Stubbendorff couldn't help comparing his own achievements with that of the explorer.

He thought back to the moment his life had become

charted on this course. The instant he saw Bergman open his office door, a telegram clasped in his pudgy fingers, and walk towards his desk, Stubbendorff's first instinct had been to hide or run. But he remained inert, staring at the keys of his typewriter, his stooped shoulders forming a protective cave.

'The publishers want a return on their investment,' Bergman had explained. 'This paper funded a large chunk of that expedition thirty years ago in return for exclusive rights. At the time, they got nothing. The odd message from a carrier pigeon, but nothing truly newsworthy. Now the camp has been found, they're looking to finally cash in.'

The assignment had seemed like an entertaining diversion. The reporter was familiar with the details of the Andrée expedition. It was one of his father's favourite bedtime stories and the tale of the ill-fated men had captivated Stubbendorff as a child. But now he realised the project had taken on a greater personal significance that he was struggling to define.

As the day began to grow cold, Stubbendorff called a halt to the search. 'We're losing the sun. Let's head back to the boat and crack on in the morning.' He wrapped the bones in a tarpaulin, secured it firmly with rope, picked up the bundle, threw it across his shoulder and made his way back to the beach. Stumbling on a piece of half-buried driftwood, Stubbendorff fell to his knees.

As he was about to heave himself to his feet, he caught sight of a figure under the ice. Stubbendorff bent lower, his face only inches from the ground. It was the head and upper body of a man lying on his left side, his left arm bent upwards, with the hand beneath his head. The dead man was frozen fast to the ground. Stubbendorff stood, unable to take his eyes off the man. He has lain there undisturbed since death touched him, Stubbendorff thought.

He called to a few members of the crew to help him. After breaking through the frozen tomb, they removed several layers of clothing, revealing the skeleton. But it broke apart as Stubbendorff was trying to carefully excavate the body using a small spade. A knot formed in his chest. The journalist closed his eyes before speaking. 'Wrap the bones in a tarpaulin and take them back to the boat.'

The man's skull was last to be exhumed. It lay alone in the trench that had been created by the dig.

'Leave it,' Stubbendorff said quietly. 'I'll take it.'

He stared into the empty eye sockets as the sun set behind the horizon. Was this a courageous or a stupid man, Stubbendorff wondered. His immense undertaking had amounted to nothing, just bones in the earth. A life lived, prematurely snuffed out to become food for the bears. As he walked towards the boat with the skull secured under his arm like a football, he was reminded of Shakespeare's Danish prince, weighed down by the burden of righting a wrong. Once on board he locked the skull and bones in a chest in the captain's cabin, returned to his own small cabin and fell asleep.

Stubbendorff woke and looked at the time. It was approaching seven. He had slept for ten hours. An intense hunger gripped him and he walked briskly to the galley. Everybody else had already breakfasted, so he satisfied his appetite with a chunk of bread doused in treacle. He downed a cup of black coffee laced with sugar then headed up to the deck.

The weather had changed. Yesterday's sun and heat had given way to a damp mist and what looked like a snowstorm heading their way.

'Good morning, Herr Stubbendorff. Awake finally? You'd never make a sealer. I've been up at dawn for the past thirty years.' Hallen gave a throaty chuckle and lit his cigarette. 'Even after the day we had yesterday, I was still wide awake by—'

Stubbendorff cut him off. 'What do you think about this weather?'

'There's a storm on its way, that's for sure. You know, until yesterday, to be honest, I thought this island was a myth made up by drunken sailors,' the captain said. 'No one has been able to sail to Kvitøya for the past fifty years, I'd wager – hidden for all that time by thick fogs and surrounded by ice.'

'So this hot spell isn't likely to last?'

'That's right. I'm surprised it's lasted this long.'

Stubbendorff walked to the starboard side, leant over the rail and stared at the island. A thousand thoughts raced through his head. Bergman would be beside himself waiting for word of what had been found. He wanted an article worthy of the front page: some scandal, perhaps a little controversy. But such an article would not do Andrée and his men justice. It seemed to Stubbendorff that after more than thirty years their camp had been exposed for a reason. The ice had melted for a purpose.

Andrée, Strindberg and Frænkel must have had wives, mothers, sweethearts, perhaps even children. Living all these years not knowing how the men's story ended would have been torturous for their loved ones. For Stubbendorff it was simple. These three remarkable men deserved a memorial. If he left now, all that he sailed away from on Kvitøya would remain buried under the ice for another three decades, or at least until the extreme polar weather allowed another brief respite. The crew had collected only a portion of what might be found.

He turned back to the captain. 'We should keep searching the island and gather as many items as we can before the weather turns. Will you please instruct two of your crew to build a coffin for the remains of the man we found?' The captain nodded. The rest of the men followed Stubbendorff off the sloop and into the rowboats that would transport them the mile to shore.

Stubbendorff heard squalls in the distance, visibility worsened and the journalist noticed a storm signal had been hoisted on the *Isbjörn*. He quickly made his way around the island and signalled to the scattered crew to head back to the beach and the awaiting rowboats. There had been a steady flow of found objects and bones to the *Isbjörn* all day. Stubbendorff had requested that everything be placed in his cabin. The crew seemed amiable enough, but he noticed they were sloppy and careless; already a number of items had been broken. They did not comprehend the importance of this grisly treasure hunt.

That evening following supper Stubbendorff began the immense task of classifying everything that had been hastily dumped in his cabin. He then numbered each item and described it in detail in his notebook before placing it with other related items. After several hours Stubbendorff checked the time. His watch read eight o'clock, but he knew it must be later, the sun had set hours ago. He tapped the face. It was broken. Damp was the culprit, he thought. The watch had been a sixteenth birthday gift from his mother.

He cautiously stepped over the objects covering almost the entire floor and sat cross-legged on a small, bare spot in the middle of the cabin. He drew in a deep breath, closed his eyes for an instant and suddenly became aware of an overwhelming tiredness, a stinging in his throat and a dull ache in his lower back. He scratched his chin through his sandy whiskers and realised he had not telegraphed the *Aftonbladet*. Bergman would be mad with anxiety. Stubbendorff decided he would relay the news at first light. He raised himself to his feet and resumed work.

THREE

I have seldom, if ever, experienced a more dramatic, a more touching succession of events than when I began the preparation of the wet leaves, thin as silk, and watched how the writing or drawing, at first invisible, gradually became discernible as the material dried, giving me a whole, connected description written by the dead.
– Knut Stubbendorff, 1930, *Andrée's Story*

KVITØYA, NORWAY
SEPTEMBER 1930

STUBBENDORFF SET about opening a rectangular sheet-iron box that the crewmen had pulled from the ice-covered rocks. He had left this find until last: its weight told him that it contained something significant. The lid had rusted shut. He cautiously edged his penknife around the rim until the top came free.

Inside, the reporter discovered four books and a number of loose documents wrapped tightly in oilcloth and bedded in straw. They were stuck fast together. Even after ten hours in his stuffy cabin they were only just beginning to thaw. He could not yet open the books but guessed by their sober leather bindings that they were journals. If these were the diaries of Andrée, Strindberg and Frænkel, a thirty-three-year-old mystery might be solved.

He took his knife and gently eased it between two leaves of paper. One of them shattered as would a thin pane of ice. They have been buried so long, Stubbendorff thought, they have become one with their environment. Fearing the books would be destroyed if he proceeded, and wary they might turn to pulp if he retreated, Stubbendorff closed his penknife and scowled in frustration.

He imagined there would be an expert in Stockholm who would know what to do, perhaps a diligent archivist with small spectacles who could tell precisely the correct temperature at which the journals should be thawed. Working in the gloomy bowels of a museum, using peculiar custom-made tools, he would meticulously separate each page from the next at the exact moment to guarantee its preservation. There was no such man on this boat.

He yawned deeply, squinting his eyes until moisture sprang from them, then he took up his knife again. He worked for the next twelve hours and through painstaking trial and error discovered that at a certain point in the thawing process the documents were firm yet still pliable enough to ease apart with his knife. He rigged up a makeshift drying apparatus in his small room – two parallel pieces of twine hanging twelve inches from the ceiling and travelling across the cabin's length. As each leaf became free, he laid it carefully across the strings to dry. He soon had five such drying lines hooked up, forcing him into an uncomfortable stoop.

His editor in Stockholm was forgotten. He did not stop to

eat or sleep – not for a good many hours. An urgency had overcome him, one that he did not stop to question.

He was eventually roused by a succession of firm knocks at his cabin door. Hallen was shocked to be greeted by a man who appeared many years older than the one who had boarded the Isbjörn less than a week before. Hair uncombed, beard unshaven, red-eyed, Stubbendorff stood before the captain, speechless.

'The weather isn't going to shift. There's no point waiting any longer. I don't want to risk getting iced in,' Captain Hallen said. 'I've wired Tromsø and told them we'll be heading back straight away.'

Stubbendorff regarded him, bleary eyed.

'You've had some telegrams. Two from the *Aftonbladet* and another from the Scientific Commission in Stockholm.'

Stubbendorff took the telegrams and stared at them blankly.

'Are you not well, Herr Stubbendorff?' Hallen peered over the journalist's shoulder, surveying the disarray of the berth with astonishment.

'I'm sorry, captain, I've been working all night. It's a pity we have to leave now, but I completely understand. I'd thank you, captain, to send a little food immediately. Could I also trouble you to send someone to wake me in two hours?' Stubbendorff closed the cabin door sharply and threw himself down onto his bunk.

We rose and I cooked a little food – cocoa and condensed milk and biscuits and sandwiches. At 4.30 o'cl. we started and now we have

drudged and pulled our heavy sledges for four and a half hours.
The weather is pretty bad: wet snow and fog, but we are in good
humours. We have kept up a really pleasant conversation the whole
day. Andrée had talked about his life, how he entered the Patent
Office, etc. Frænkel and Andrée have gone ahead on a
reconnoitering tour. I stayed with the sledges and now I am sitting
writing to you. Yes, now you are having evening at home and you,
like I, have had a very jolly and pleasant day.
– Nils Strindberg's journal, 31 July 1897

Stubbendorff was woken a few hours later, and as the sloop rolled and heaved he began to read what he had so carefully salvaged. Two of the books were purely scientific. They featured meteorological readings, charts, diagrams and other data. He could tell by the different hands that one belonged to Frænkel and the other to Strindberg. He flicked through these hastily, not able to make sense of their contents.

Another of the books was Andrée's own diary. Much more than a log of the expedition, it detailed every triumph and disappointment the three men had faced.

Although Stubbendorff knew the story of the expedition, it had been told to him as a tale of adventure and the bold daring of three courageous men. Now he learnt the precise details of the journey.

Within only a few hours of the *Örnen*'s launch on 11 July 1897, the balloon 'began slowly sinking into a winding curve'. The men threw overboard as much ballast as possible but due to the heavy fog the *Örnen* refused to rise any higher than a few feet, bumping its way so persistently along the ice that Strindberg and Frænkel became seasick.

Despite this, Andrée's spirits remained high. 'Is it not a little strange to be floating here above the Polar Sea,' he wrote. 'To be the first to have floated here in a balloon. How soon, I wonder, shall we have successors? Shall we be thought mad or will our example be followed? I cannot deny that all three of us are dominated by a feeling of pride. We think we can well face death, having done what we have done. Isn't it all, perhaps, the expression of an extremely strong sense of individuality which cannot bear the thought of living and dying like a man in the ranks, forgotten by coming generations? Is this ambition?'

Stubbendorff sighed heavily and shut his eyes briefly, contemplating Andrée's query. He read on. By the early morning of 14 July the *Örnen* had come to a rest. The three decided to set off across the drifting pack ice on foot in an easterly direction towards Franz Joseph Land where a large depot for the expedition was situated. After more than a fortnight of pulling heavy sledges loaded with supplies they had drifted west with the ice more quickly than they had marched east. 'This is not encouraging,' Andrée wrote. 'But we shall continue our course to the east some time more, as long as there is a bit of sense in doing so.'

Soon the explorers chose to head west towards Seven Islands, where another depot lay.

But this destination was never reached, according to Andrée. Inadequately supplied and combating injury and illness, the party eventually and inadvertently drifted, at the beginning of October, onto the first land they had set foot on since departing. The island was Kvitøya. Andrée's final coherent entry, dated 7 October, read, 'Morale remains good. With comrades such as these, one ought to be able to manage under practically any circumstances whatsoever.'

The reporter closed the diary and walked to the small porthole in his berth. He rubbed his neck as he strained to see the horizon but the fog was too dense. Stubbendorff grabbed the final notebook and looked at the first page, which read, 'The Ruminations and Imaginings of Nils Strindberg, July 1897'.

The journal was exactly what the title suggested: a vessel for the young explorer's ideas and feelings, his fears for the present and his dreams for the future. Strindberg described a strong camaraderie with his two colleagues, how after ten hours of tramping through knee-high snow they rested and 'chatted, ate and drank' and were in 'the best of humours'. They seemed an eccentric band of explorers who found amusement with one another in the most extraordinary of circumstances. Strindberg mocked Andrée regarding the quality of the bear he killed for their supper, saying it was 'as tough as leather galoshes'. The trio had even packed formal attire, top hats included, for when the time came to disembark victorious.

Stubbendorff was left with the impression that the three men rarely disagreed. Jokes were shared and birthdays and national holidays celebrated during the three months they spent together. Sensing early in their journey that the expedition was doomed, they never allowed their individual doubts to cloud the others' outlooks. Strindberg was happy to be in the company of such steadfast men.

But what gripped Stubbendorff more profoundly were Strindberg's reminiscences about family life in Stockholm. Stubbendorff was an only child and found the childhood antics of Strindberg's older brother Erik and younger brothers Sven and Tore captivating. Strindberg explained that it was 'Erik and Sven who always led their play, usually something to do with Vikings and dragons.' If teams were involved, 'Tore and I never had a chance against Erik and Sven, but we didn't complain. There was too much laughter.' Their boyhoods seemed so foreign to Stubbendorff, who thought seldom of his youth, and rarely with mirth.

The boys were encouraged to learn and excel by their parents and one another, and were given free rein to do so. Strindberg recalled the 'dreadful concerts that our parents insisted we stage for their acquaintances where Erik would sing and Sven, Tore and I would play violin and piano'. From his writing it seemed that, apart from his decision to join Andrée, Strindberg could not recall an instance in which his mother or father had questioned any choice he had made.

Stubbendorff thought of his own mother, who had worked tirelessly to control her son, fearing any departure from her authority would incur the wrath of God or, more seriously, her fellow churchgoers. In the years immediately following his father's death Stubbendorff had battled against this. He had placed his elbows prominently on the table at mealtimes, refused to attend church, played with the children with whom his mother had forbidden contact and never said 'please' or 'thank you'. The boy broke the rules with an intensity of purpose Fru Stubbendorff had never imagined possible in a child and it made her furious. She would beat and berate him for the smallest infraction of her rules. The contrast with the Strindbergs' childhoods could not have been more pronounced and it made Stubbendorff ache. He hugged the pages to his chest for an instant, then read on.

Much of Strindberg's diary was a general record but he had also written a series of love letters to his fiancée, Anna Charlier. Strindberg had poured his soul into the letters – that much was obvious to Stubbendorff – but none of them hinted at his bleak fate. Just the opposite – they were light-hearted, casual, even jocular. He described the balloon trip, how they were 'travelling so beautifully that it is a pity that we are obliged to breathe as that makes the balloon lighter'. He related to Anna how he fell into 'the soup' with his sledge, but his one concern was for 'your portrait – my dearest treasure during the approaching winter'. Strindberg instructed his sweetheart to 'push on with the wedding plans even though I will be home slightly later than anticipated'. And he never failed to reaffirm her place in his heart. 'I long for the scent of your hair and to be lost in the dark pools of your eyes once more,' he wrote.

The intensity of Strindberg's regard for this woman, the strength of his feeling, was evident in every neatly formed letter. Stubbendorff had no frame of reference, no understanding of what such love looked like. He closed his eyes tightly, struggling to recall a moment when his mother and father had laughed, hugged or even given each other a familiar glance in his presence. They had been strangers living in the same home, raising, quite disparately, the same child.

Charlier had never read Strindberg's letters and perhaps she was never meant to, but it troubled Stubbendorff that a courtship so singular had ended in tragedy. He wondered why Strindberg had joined Andrée, why he had left this woman. Strindberg had been an idiot, he thought. He had deserved to die.

But this diary was the story. Bergman would love it.

However, as he closed his eyes and drifted towards sleep his body and mind relaxed. Stubbendorff realised he knew very little about the complexities of love. By the time he awoke, his ruthlessness had evaporated like a dream.

FOUR

TORQUAY, ENGLAND
SEPTEMBER 1930

She woke with a gasp and sat up straight in bed. Her husband was asleep beside her and relief coursed through her body. She put her trembling hand to her chest and found she was sweating. With her dark hair pasted to her head and her nightdress clinging to her back, she made her way down the hall and into the bathroom.

Anna stared at herself in the mirror as she felt the cool water drip from her face and onto her chest. She was panting, her large hands trembling. What had brought on such a nightmare after all these years?

The first bad dream had come the evening Nils announced that he'd joined the expedition. She pictured the scene in her mind's eye. She remembered how composed she must have appeared as her fiancé explained the scheme to his bewildered family.

It hurt all the more because the two had been trusted friends throughout their entire relationship. When Anna and

Nils had first met, she had been immediately attracted to his open face and relaxed, unfussy nature. Even before their romance had begun, he always greeted her with a smile so warm and sincere it ferried her blissfully through the rest of her day. Responding to her every thought, comment or query with genuine interest, he didn't seem to notice she was a woman, treating her as his equal. Likewise, he discussed his studies, work and friends with great candour. As they strolled along the winding streets of Staden mellan broarna on Sunday afternoons, he would unburden himself of his worries about his career. Anna's offers of advice gave her a feeling of importance and authority. The two became confidantes. Love came later.

It was not only the prospect of losing Nils that terrified her – it was her harsh exclusion from his decision. Never before had Nils been so callous and she was uncertain how she should best respond. He had proposed and she had accepted, committing herself to a journey. Now he had changed course without considering her. Frustrated at her powerlessness she could do little else but leave the room.

When Anna returned, Nils was alone. He sat on the settee, head between hands, cigarette between fingers. As she entered, he looked up at her, and in his light-blue eyes she could read an apology. He stubbed out his cigarette before speaking. 'I'm so sorry. I have no excuses, only cowardice and greed.' He saw her puzzled look. 'I didn't know how to tell you. This was the wrong way, and I'm so sorry.'

'How are you greedy?'

'I want everything. I want to marry you and I want to go.' He was plainly distressed.

'That's not greed.' Anna took his hands and sat. He buried his face in the sweet-smelling folds of her dress. 'You have never been denied anything. You have been made to believe you are your own master, that you can accomplish anything that you work towards. This is what makes you the man that you are, but—'

'If you say you are going to end our engagement, I will write to Andrée immediately and withdraw from the expedition.' This was no ultimatum, she knew. There was no malice in his voice.

'My feelings have been hurt,' she said, 'as insignificant as that seems after what you told us tonight.' Nils hugged her tightly and kissed her hard on the forehead. He returned his head to her lap as a child might, grateful for her mercy. In this position they sat for a few minutes before Anna spoke.

She had the power to stop his departure. One tear was all it would take. Anna stroked her fiancé's hair. His reluctance to discuss his plans told her that he did not want to be stopped. She also understood that, no matter how mad the scheme seemed to her and to his family, Nils believed it had merit. Perhaps it was just as he had explained earlier – he saw scientific value in the expedition. However, she suspected Erik played a role in his brother's commitment to Andrée.

'You have to go. I can't be responsible for your regrets and I will not break off our relationship. I know you will return to me.' She struggled to keep her voice level, to prevent any tremor. 'But don't ever keep anything from me again.'

That night was the night the dreams began.

As the *Isbjörn* sailed into Norway's Tromsø Harbour, it was met by two men-of-war, the *Svensksund* and the *Michael Sars*. With flags lowered to half-mast, the hulking convoy dwarfed the sealing vessel as it was escorted to Nemak Pier. A forest of blue and yellow lined the foreshore, and the crowds were held back by barricades.

Stubbendorff stood on deck and watched the grand spectacle he was partly responsible for creating. He had wired Bergman and the commission with news of his findings. He was sure the former was behind this display. It would make a great front page.

He lit another cigarette as he watched a suited man and a companion board the *Isbjörn* from a small rowboat. It was Bergman and a photographer. Hallen promptly led them to Stubbendorff.

'Wonderful job! Wonderful job!' Bergman vigorously patted his employee on the back. 'I was worried when I hadn't heard anything from you for a couple of days, but this is amazing. A thirty-year-old mystery solved and who is responsible? Sales will skyrocket.'

'I'm very pleased that you're happy.' Stubbendorff had hastily prepared an article with the headline 'Conversations with the Dead' before the sloop arrived in Tromsø. It was a melodramatic recreation of the explorers' final days – somewhat sensationalist, but nothing that would offend the families of the dead. It was just the sort of trash he knew Bergman wanted.

'Happy doesn't describe it, Stubbendorff, my friend. Starting from Monday I'm moving you to the main news desk. A greater piece of reporting I have never seen.' As he said this, Bergman gave the young man an envelope. Glancing inside, Stubbendorff reckoned it must have contained at least one hundred kronor.

'Thank you, sir,' he said coldly as he stuffed the package into his pocket. 'They were extraordinary men, you know.'

Bergman nodded vaguely, looking out at the crowds.

In little over a week, it seemed, the entire nation had gone Andrée-mad. The timing worked perfectly for Bergman, Stubbendorff thought. The other two bodies had been in the hands of the Scientific Commission at Tromsø Coast

Hospital for a fortnight. All that Bergman had had to arrange was for the bodies to be transferred the mile or so back to the quay on the day the *Isbjørn* was due to arrive. The impact would be greater if all three men arrived together, just as they had departed. Stubbendorff himself was to be a pall-bearer, at Bergman's insistence. He shook his head and smiled wanly at the thought of it all. There was a part of him that had once admired the big-voiced, barrel-chested editor, but not any longer.

The crew of the two warships formed a guard of honour and the caskets were carried onto a podium from which a number of dignitaries delivered speeches. Stubbendorff was deaf to the proceedings, his gaze focused on the three coffins draped in the Swedish flag.

He had decided to quit his job at the *Aftonbladet*. He was glad of the one hundred kronor in his pocket – that would keep him going for at least a year if he lived frugally. As he stood in the sun, willing this pomp to end, he felt sweat running down his back and squirmed uncomfortably. He looked towards the crowds and wondered if Anna Charlier was among them.

When the speeches had finished, Bergman directed those involved to hoist the caskets and move towards the hearses.

A volley of gunshots prompted gasps from the crowd. Children's hands muffled their ears. As military drums beat a sombre death march, the ill-fated explorers were carried slowly along the dock to three waiting hearses. The black carriages glinted in the warm sunlight. Helping to carry the casket of the man he had discovered on Kvitøya, Stubbendorff was transported from the scene by the steady pulse of the drums. In his mind he travelled back to Kvitøya and thought of the men waiting to die in their frozen hell, tried to imagine himself in their place, the terror they must have felt. Would each second stretch out into an agonising blow to the spirit or would every tiny increment of time be relished like the final tasty morsels on a plate?

The spell was suddenly broken by Bergman moving swiftly in and out of the crowd, directing the photographer to secure the best vantage point. After twenty-five years in the newspaper business this was Bergman's long-awaited moment of glory. The sight of such a graceless man bobbing and weaving expertly through the assembled throng brought the shadow of a grin to Stubbendorff's face. There was a grim comedy to the situation.

The coffins were loaded onto the hearses and Stubbendorff watched as they began their measured journey to the hospital, followed by a horde of patriots. A profound sense of loss and guilt washed over him as the parade trickled gradually from sight. Finding the explorers' camp, sorting through their possessions and reading their journals had given Stubbendorff entry into another world, but now it was gone.

'Here he is, Herr Borg. This is Knut Stubbendorff.' Captain Hallen's cry interrupted his thoughts.

Stubbendorff turned to see a well-dressed man in his fifties striding towards him, smiling broadly as he extended his hand.

'Good morning, Herr Stubbendorff, my name is Elling Borg. I am president of the Scientific Commission. I would like to thank you for your efforts.'

Hands were shaken and pleasantries exchanged.

'I understand from your telegram that you managed to recover a great deal from the Andrée camp. The commission would like to take possession of the artefacts now, straight away, if you please. We are returning to Stockholm with the bodies as soon as possible. We also need to interview you, at a later date, of course. In Stockholm.'

'Yes, of course. Everything I found is in my cabin.' Stubbendorff searched his pockets for the key. 'Why don't I head back to the boat now and clear out my kit, then you can have free rein. I wouldn't want to get in your way.'

'Thank you for your help. We very much appreciate it. We'll be in touch when we've sorted through the artefacts.'

The men shook hands, said their goodbyes and Stubbendorff made his way back to the *Isbjörn* with a bounce in his step that soon sped up to a trot, then a jog, until he was almost running. Once in his cabin he locked the door and reviewed the room's contents. He was out of breath from the run and the apprehension that now sat like a brick in his chest. He had neatly placed all the objects in wooden crates. But the pages from the journals remained on his bunk in four neat piles secured by twine. He positioned three of the books on top of the crates, along with his own notebook, in which he had documented the findings. He cautiously slid the pages of Strindberg's diary into his own satchel and left the *Isbjörn*.

FIVE

TORQUAY, ENGLAND
SEPTEMBER 1930

'It says the bodies are going back to Stockholm for burial, travelling by warship, apparently. They'll be back there by the end of the month.' Anna's husband sat at the breakfast table, leaning over the day's newspaper. 'They'll be getting a state funeral. Not bad.'

With her back to the table Anna stood at the stove and rhythmically stirred the porridge. Her eyes were fixed on the wooden spoon and the rivulets it made in the steaming beige mass. She had not slept well last night and had got up before it was light. She had scrutinised the article several times, searching for the names of the people she once knew and loved, before she had heard her husband's footsteps in the room above.

When the dreams had started up again three nights ago, Anna was at a loss as to the reason. After the first recurrence she had waited until her husband had left the house then rummaged through the blanket box at the end of their bed.

She produced a wooden box with a hinged lid. Then she had sat, legs folded, on the bed for the entire morning, taking in the box, its sanded surface, the daisies engraved into its lid and her initials, expertly carved into one corner. Anna knew exactly what was in the box. She took an inventory in her mind. Yet she could not open it.

That same afternoon she ventured into town the long way, along the seafront. She needed fresh air and as she walked she inhaled the cool, salty breeze deeply. She hoped sunlight and exercise would cure her of the anxiety she had confronted in her sleep the night before and the shadow of sorrow that remained. But when she turned onto the high street, she was faced with a horror she had not expected and her private speculations about her troubled subconscious were laid to rest. In the centre window of the tobacconist, the front page of the *Daily Mirror* hung prominently. Its headline put an end to any errands she hoped to complete that afternoon. After buying the newspaper, she walked briskly to a bench overlooking the harbour and began devouring the print. There were photographs of Andrée, Frænkel and Nils on the day they departed from Spitsbergen. There were images of the men with the balloon and there was also a single shot of Nils. It was one he had sat for on his twenty-first birthday.

As she examined his neatly carved features and the hint of a smile evident on his lips, she found herself recalling the touch of those lips and the sound of his voice. She wished she could hear his musical laugh again, and willed the likeness to speak. A wave of nausea swelled in her stomach and she realised she was sick with disappointment. Don't be absurd, she thought, and placed the folded newspaper in her bag before moving on with her afternoon.

But walking home she began to think about an expression of which the English were fond, about the past coming back to haunt you. Was that what was happening? The most shattering decision of her life had been granting Nils his independence, giving him the freedom of his own ambition. She had made a great sacrifice, allowing him to go – even greater than he knew. When it became apparent the expedition had failed, Anna would replay the evening scene in the Strindbergs' sitting room many times, Nils' head resting in her lap as she pondered her choices. She had successfully rewoven many events in her mind over the following years, darned the holes in the fabric of her memory. She had never shared the details of that evening with anyone. Even Erik remained ignorant of her conversation with his brother in the Strindbergs' sitting room that night and her decision to let him go. Fearing they would hold her responsible, and unable to confront her own culpability, she severed all ties with them shortly after hope was lost. Those years immediately following his departure were a haze of guilt, regrets, anxiety and grief.

The porridge began to bubble more furiously and Anna became aware of her husband's voice. 'Well, no doubt Andrée and his men deserve it. And a proper Christian burial will be a comfort to their loved ones. I suppose you can remember it all. By the sounds of things it was quite a big deal when they left,' he said, seeking a response. 'You were in Stockholm then, right? It must have been a big deal, in all the papers?'

She stared into the saucepan. 'Of course. I remember it very well.'

'But a balloon. It was a daft plan from the start. It's a wonder they made it as far as they did.'

'Yes, I suppose so.' Anna ladled the porridge into the bowls and placed them on the table. As they ate their breakfast, they said no more on the subject.

❄

Once Gil had left for work, Anna retrieved the box from her bedroom and carried it downstairs to the kitchen. An hour passed before she was able to open it. Inside were keepsakes of her other life. Letters Nils had written to her, ticket stubs from galleries, concerts and exhibitions they had attended together, and a number of photographs. She held an image of herself and Nils, taken for their engagement, close to her face.

She laid the items out on the table side by side and examined them closely. She gently traced his writing with her index finger, believing she could feel the shallow indentations his pen had made in the paper. Taking a ticket for a recital in her hand, she held it to her nose and inhaled, desperate to reclaim a scrap of the past. Even though time had rendered the memorabilia odourless, she summoned up Mozart's Prussian Quartets and swayed gently to the music in her mind. Her plump lips broke into a blissful smile.

For a moment she was there, sitting beside her fiancé in the fifth row of the university theatre, nodding her head in time to the music. Out of the corner of her eye she could just distinguish Nils' long fingers tapping on his knee. Anna ran her hands over her thighs and felt the soft folds of her lavender skirt and, as she listened, thoughtlessly caressed the thumbnail-sized lilacs embroidered there. She had made the dress herself, very quickly, with the guidance and encouragement of her more adept sister. Herr Strindberg, the handsome violin teacher with whom she had become friends, had asked her to accompany him to the concert, and she had nothing suitable to wear. Anna had fashioned the dress herself while the more skilled Gota had created a lawn of pretty flowers on the skirt. When it was completed, Anna was disappointed. The dress had been hurried and it fitted badly – but Gota's embroidery was faultless.

Anna took in her surroundings, the small theatre and the

other members of the audience. She guessed they were chiefly in their twenties, students mostly. Nils suggested, if there was time, that she might like to have supper with him after the concert. Gota had advised her to take any opportunity to prolong the evening and their time together. Anna had not eaten since lunch and was aware of her gurgling stomach, hoping it did not annoy the other concertgoers.

The chirping of a bird drew her out of her memories. She dropped her hands by her sides, opened her eyes and caught her reflection in the mirror that hung on the back of the kitchen door. At fifty-nine her face was much fuller than it once had been. Her jawline was no longer distinguishable and her chin had an unfortunate habit of losing itself in her neck. There were lines on her brow and at the corners of her eyes, and an army of grey hairs had invaded her chestnut mane. Standing up and moving closer to the mirror she smoothed her moss-coloured dress over her hips. While she had kept her figure, she thought, the clothes she wore now were shapeless and lifeless, nothing like the creations Gota had fashioned. She suddenly felt old and very lonely and so far away from Stockholm.

SIX

STOCKHOLM, SWEDEN
MIDSUMMER, JUNE 1894

ANNA AND GOTA stood side by side on the edge of the dance floor watching the couples merrily glide across its smooth surface. The warm air and the dancing made Anna's skin clammy. As she pushed her hair off her sticky brow in irritation, she noticed Gota laughing.

'Anna, you look a sight. Your face is red and your wreath is limp. Your hair looks as if you've been caught in a rain storm. Perhaps we should go home. No one else will want to dance with you looking like that.'

Gota's frankness never failed to dismay Anna, but in the spirit of the festivities she removed the wreath from her head and looked closely at the daisies, which had only that morning been so fresh and vivid.

'They have seen better days, haven't they?' She looked at Gota and laughed. 'It's been a lovely evening, but I suppose we should get home.' The sisters had joined the celebrations early – maypole festivities in Stortorget, followed by dinner with Anna's employers and now, dancing by Riddarfjärden. Anna's feet ached blissfully and her head was light from the few sips of vodka her sister insisted she drink.

For her sister's entertainment she returned the wreath to her head at a comical angle. As she did so, another prospective dance partner appeared in front of her, taking her unawares.

'Excuse me, ladies.' The gentleman offered an abrupt bow to both women, but addressed himself solely to Anna. 'I hope you'll not leave yet. I'd like to introduce myself. My name is Erik Strindberg. Would you give me the honour of allowing me to partner you in your final dance?'

Earlier in the evening Gota had pointed the same man out. She had whispered in her sister's ear, 'He's the most handsome man here and the most refined. You know he's an architect. He's been looking this way often. I do hope he asks me to dance.'

'He looks rather brutish and his laugh is too loud,' Anna replied shortly.

Fru Strindberg, Erik's mother, had employed Gota as a dressmaker and Gota had visited the Strindberg home on a number of occasions for fittings. Afterwards she had exhausted Anna with descriptions of the lavish furnishings and the lady's fine manners and deportment. She also mused endlessly about Erik Strindberg, the most attractive of the lady's four sons. Gota had hoped Erik would be here this evening. His mother had told her they were not going to the country as usual. Her youngest son had come down with a nasty bout of chicken pox.

Erik stood waiting for a reply. Anna looked once more to her sister, but Gota's plump face gave nothing away. Would she be angry? Not wishing to offend the young man, Anna answered, 'Thank you. I would love to. I'm Anna Charlier.' After all, it was only one dance, she reasoned.

'Anna Charlier from Skåne County.'

'Yes.' Anna was astounded. 'How did you know?'

'From everything about you,' he remarked confidently as he took Anna's hand and led her into the centre of the dance floor.

The tune to which they danced was a vigorous, lively piece. Anna was surprised by her partner's grace. He was large and Anna had assumed he would be ungainly. But he moved lithely and she was thrilled by the weight of his hand pressed assuredly into the middle of her back. The ease with which he weaved and manoeuvred her among the other couples on the crowded dance floor was exhilarating. That evening Anna had danced with many partners. Some of the young men were friends from university and others were strangers – but none of them had Erik's certainty.

When the music ended, Erik once again gave a brief bow. 'You're a very good dancer and you have a glorious smile, Fröken Charlier. Would you like another dance?'

No man had ever spoken to Anna with such candour. She didn't know whether to feel shocked or excited. 'I would love to, but my sister was hoping to leave. We've had a very busy day and it's four o'clock already.'

'But the sun just rose half an hour ago. The day is just beginning and anyway,' he said, pointing to Gota, who was executing a particularly energetic jig, 'your sister doesn't look the least bit tired.'

They laughed.

'You could stay a little longer and allow me to escort you and your sister home. She could act as chaperone. I'm from a very good family,' he explained. 'We are quite well known in Stockholm.' Erik's blue eyes brimmed with hope.

Anna realised that, despite her sister's obvious attraction to the man, she had developed a fondness for Herr Strindberg herself. Gota had been right – he was the most handsome man at the gathering.

Anna found his broad face warm and inviting and his physical presence appealing. While his assuredness was disconcerting, she also found it refreshing. She was flattered too that such a distinguished gentleman would notice her.

'That would be most generous. But I believe I would like to rest for a while. I'm really very tired.'

'Of course. Take a seat and I'll get some refreshments.'

Erik soon returned and, while they did not dance again that morning, they did converse on a great many topics. Taking the lead just as he had on the dance floor, Herr Strindberg was confident and articulate on each subject they discussed. Later that day, as she was attempting to justify her actions to Gota, Anna had described his opinions as robust. As they had sat by the lake, many people passed by who were acquainted with Erik and his family. They all offered midsummer greetings and then moved on. Each time Erik would explain to Anna the exact nature of their relationship to himself and his family. Anna feigned interest. At no time did he ask about her interests or background or occupation or, indeed, mention Gota, whom he had met before. He rarely even looked Anna in the eye. Did he think he knew about her by the mere fact that she was from Skåne County?

Was he attempting to impress her, the country girl? It took very little to impress Anna. She came from a humble family. The two-room apartment in which she now resided in Stensbastugränd was next to a brewery. Even during summer's hottest days the sisters shut the windows tight to keep out the stink of hops. They were only a notch above the working poor but, thanks to Gota's fine tailoring skills, nobody knew it.

The band began to pack away their instruments as Gota approached.

'Shall we allow Herr Strindberg to escort us home now?' Gota was panting and her cheeks flushed. 'I've just been playing sardines. It was great fun.'

Anna flinched and looked quickly to Erik. His composure had not diminished.

'Sardines is a schoolyard game, Gota,' Anna admonished. 'You've got your dress dirty.'

'Anna is such a prig, Herr Strindberg. You'd think she was the older sister,' Gota said as they began the walk home. 'Sometimes I wonder if she knows what fun is.'

Erik smiled respectfully at Gota as he took Anna's elbow and led her in the direction of Staden mellan broarna. At times Gota was forced to walk behind them along the narrow streets. Anna's height made it possible for her to keep up with Erik's long stride, but Gota's short legs meant she was forced into a trot for most of the distance as she struggled to stay within earshot. While Anna was pleased the situation would make it more difficult for her sister to embarrass her further, she knew it would drive Gota insane.

During the twenty-minute walk to Stensbastugränd Erik did not draw breath. As they passed by the graveyard on Trångsund, Erik rattled off a history of the two sculptures flanking its entrance. As they strolled down Västerlånggatan and spotted Hemlins booksellers, Erik listed a number of recent purchases, alphabetically, in order of the author's surname. Anna merely nodded gravely.

'You know Stockholm so well, Herr Strindberg,' Gota babbled. 'You'd make a superb tour guide.'

Of course he knows Stockholm, you ninny, Anna thought. He's lived here his whole life. What's more, he's an architect. No one would know the city more thoroughly. She wanted to gag her sister, whose flattery was only serving to make an uncomfortable predicament unbearable.

As they walked, every word he said only served to

increase her annoyance. He seemed to assume she was completely ignorant of the city in which she lived. When they reached Järntorget and her apartment building came in sight, Anna quickened her step. It was a relief to reach the door of her building.

'Thank you, Herr Strindberg,' Gota began. 'Thank you for seeing us home and thank you for sharing all your wonderful insights about the city.'

Please stop, Anna willed her sister.

'It's my pleasure, Fröken,' he replied. 'Now if you don't mind, would you leave your sister and me alone for a minute or two?'

The request shocked both women. Gota's resentful brown eyes turned to her sister.

'I can assure you that I don't intend anything untoward,' he said pleasantly but firmly.

Anna indicated with a faint nod that she was fine to be left alone. She was impressed with how well Herr Strindberg had handled her sister. It was more than she had ever been able to accomplish. Gota offered an affected, if reluctant, farewell and left the two alone on the street.

Anna scanned the empty pathway, waiting for Erik to speak. The city would just be going to sleep, she thought. The sun already had a bite and it was only seven. How hard it worked in the summer, she pondered, another fifteen hours before it could rest again.

She turned to Erik. He looked at her but did not speak.

'Thank you, Herr Strindberg. I've had a very pleasant time.'

'Indeed, as have I. You are very lovely, Fröken Charlier. I would very much like to call on you again. I would be very happy to meet your father whenever it suits.'

'My father and mother are both deceased. I only have my sister with me in Stockholm.'

'I'm sorry to hear about your parents. If your sister would like to chaperone an outing, I'd be happy for her to be present. Perhaps a concert or a picnic at the Bergianska trädgården? The gardens are lovely at the moment.'

The thought that Anna would not want to see him again had apparently not crossed his mind. He was handsome and privileged, from an influential family. Most women, especially at twenty-two and in her position, would be eager to pursue such a match. Could she overlook his self-importance? Could she tolerate his arrogance? More importantly, did she like Erik Strindberg enough to provoke the wrath of her sister, who had already said she found him handsome?

Anna was certain Gota was standing on the other side of the street door, her ear to the wood, waiting for her response.

'I'm sorry, Herr Strindberg. But I don't think I can meet you again. I am extremely busy with my work. I rarely have time for social engagements.'

His face grew dark with disappointment and Anna immediately regretted her terse reply. She'd taken his words and actions for conceit, but she realised now that his behaviour this morning had been driven by a desire to impress her and win her favour.

Anna opened her mouth to speak, but Erik held up his hand to stop her.

'Thank you for your time, Fröken. I'll trouble you no further. I regret if I have distressed you in any way. It's just that … I like you so very much. Good morning.' Erik looked at her directly for a few seconds before shaking her hand briefly and making a hasty departure.

Anna stared at his broad frame as he retreated, willing him to stop. If he does, she thought, I shall call him back, give him a second chance. He did not. As he rounded the corner, she felt a pang of regret, and stood in the street a minute or two, not quite ready to face her sister.

Later that morning Gota scolded her, pointing out that Erik may have been the key to their futures. Despite Anna's pleas that she had been prompted by concern for Gota's feelings, her sister could not be pacified. If she were ever afforded the opportunity to embark on a courtship with Erik Strindberg, she said, she would never be so stupid as to turn him away. Anna's foolishness was beyond comprehension. Once the lecture was over, Gota stormed out of the apartment, still lamenting her sister's thoughtlessness. Anna sat alone at the table, dismayed and bewildered.

SEVEN

STOCKHOLM, SWEDEN
JULY 1894

ANNA SAT EXTREMELY STILL in the hushed room, terrified to move for fear of being scolded. She wished she had positioned herself differently. Her back was growing stiff, but it was too late. To suggest any movement would invite the anger of her two young students. Anna could hear their breath choked with concentration.

'I believe my portrait is just about finished,' thirteen-year-old Johanna Larsson said cheerfully. 'All that is left is my signature.' The girl signed her name with a dramatic flourish and stood up from her stool. She wiped her hands free of their charcoal smudges, pushed her spectacles up the bridge of her nose and removed her smock.

'Oh, mine is not,' Kalle Larsson complained. 'Please don't move till it's finished, Fröken, and don't talk to her, Johanna.'

Johanna walked to the window. She straightened the ribbon in her hair and looked down at the street. Placing her hands on her waist, she hummed quietly and twirled her body from side to side, enjoying the way her skirt fanned out around her legs.

'Mother said our new violin teacher is beginning this afternoon.' She looked to her audience for a response but Kalle was too absorbed in his portrait to speak and Anna was trying to remain still for him.

'At two o'clock,' she added with a musical lilt, more in an effort to draw their attention than to convey information. 'Mother said he is a student at the university studying something or other. I don't believe she mentioned his name. He tutors in the summers. He came to the house last week when we were visiting the museum. I wish I could have met him. I do hope he's handsome. If he's a student, he's bound to be young. Our last violin teacher was a horror. Don't you agree, Fröken? She looked like a troll.' Anna did not speak but shot the girl a sharp rebuke with her eyes. Johanna giggled. 'Fru Bruse. She was always so crabby. Not a bit of fun.' She pushed her spectacles higher on her nose.

Anna had not known the new tutor was beginning that day. Fru Larsson had asked her in June whether she knew of anybody who might be suitable. Anna did not. That was all she'd heard. She secretly agreed with Johanna about Fru Bruse, though. She had been a most ill-tempered woman. As Anna instructed the children in piano, she was often required to accompany the violinists during their lesson. Fru Bruse always made these sessions particularly unpleasant, treating Anna and the children with equal disdain. Johanna and Kalle's progress had suffered noticeably – and it was Anna who was chastised when the children played badly at musical afternoons hosted by their mother. Anna hoped Fru Bruse's successor would be a more agreeable character.

She stood abruptly and took a turn around the room. Kalle groaned as he had not yet finished.

'You are too young to be speaking of these matters, Johanna,' Anna said. 'Now, shall we review your portraits?'

The girl ignored Anna's request. 'Girls get married at my age all the time in the country. Isn't that true?'

'That's a different situation. You're fortunate there's no need for you to marry so young. You'll have your choice of suitors when you're old enough. Now gather your portraits.'

Anna had been raised in a farming family herself but did not want to go into the details of country life with her young charges. Anna and Gota had not attended school, but were tutored by their mother. The only other children they came in contact with were those who attended church each Sunday. Anna thought about this often, her sheltered upbringing, and whether, in fact, she and Gota would even be friends if they weren't sisters. When her daughters argued, Sofia Charlier would tell them to be grateful for each other's company and stop bickering. Although time and experience had taught Anna to tolerate her sister's moods and lofty notions, she had never been able to understand them.

Their father had attempted to marry his girls off to the sons of local farmers when he was prematurely made a widower. Albert Charlier had hoped they might bring their new husbands to live on the farm so that it would remain with the Charlier family after his death, even if not in name. It was not to be. A flock of healthy, honest, clear-eyed young men had been paraded before Anna and Gota for inspection. None attracted the attention of the sisters. Their earnest faces and sturdy frames only served to amuse Gota, who would fall into fits of unrestrained giggles once the prospective spouse had departed. Anna, on the other hand, worried quietly about her future.

Despite his theatrical outrage Albert was a soft-hearted man who would not see his daughters unhappy for the sake of a piece of land. Moreover, their mother had attempted to instil a refinement in Gota and Anna that was absent in most country girls. Albert reasoned, in the end, that he would be ruining his late wife's good work if he were to marry them off to the well-intentioned but ignorant sons of farmers.

When Albert Charlier died, the farm was taken over by his brother. The girls' uncle was willing to support his nieces for as long as they wanted to stay, but the sisters preferred to leave. Nothing was holding them in Åby. Their uncle gave them a generous amount and this, combined with payment for the family's piano, which Anna sold, helped the sisters begin a life for themselves in Stockholm. Gota began work as a seamstress and Anna took classes at the university in music, art and literature. Gradually she began to establish herself as a tutor to the children of middle-class families. She was pleased when she was employed by the Larssons as governess to Johanna and Kalle. After two years she was often told by her employer that she was a part of the family. The children treated her like an older sister and Fru Larsson often invited her to social engagements as well as musical soirées held at the house. But Anna never managed to feel comfortable in Fru Larsson's company. She felt that she was viewed as more of a project than an employee by Fru Larsson, who was as determined as a mother to see Anna married. Anna had never revealed her true pedigree to the Larssons and it worried her. She suspected the young men at Fru Larsson's tea parties and recitals would not want a farm girl for a wife.

Unlike her sister, Anna had no great urge to be married. At her age it would be a wasted effort to search out a suitable match. Although she had always hoped to have children of her own, she was extremely happy at the Larssons' and despite Gota's pleadings had no desire to change her present situation. Gota, on the other hand, had made it her life's work since her sixteenth birthday to secure a husband. But, as Anna often noted, she aimed too high. Despite Gota's pretty face and buxom figure, a working-class woman living next to a brewery could not hope to win the favour of a gentleman such as Erik Strindberg. Anna's own success in this regard remained a pleasant mystery.

Lost in her thoughts, Anna stared at the portraits of herself. Both were very different, but each a fair likeness. Johanna's was meticulous. Every detail of the portrait was exact, but the work was superficial. Kalle's, although it had taken more time, was less scrupulous, but to Anna it was his drawing that had more depth. His heavy lines and the smudging of the charcoal had captured a darkness which Anna found intriguing. A more thorough examination of the portrait was interrupted by her young charges.

'Anyway, who would want to marry you, now or ever?' Kalle teased his sister, laughing. 'You wear spectacles and your face is covered in freckles. Marriage is something you need never worry about.' Johanna threw a cushion at her brother, hitting him in the face. This only served to increase his satisfaction. Anna stepped between the siblings before Kalle could return fire.

'It's such a lovely day. Shall we take a walk in the park?'

'But we must be back by two,' Johanna interjected.

'We must not be tardy,' Kalle said in mock seriousness. 'We must not keep Johanna's future husband waiting.'

At a quarter to two the trio returned. They washed their hands and Johanna asked Anna to brush her hair and retie her ribbon. By two o'clock the three were waiting in the sitting room for the arrival of the new tutor. The children's violins lay on their laps but no ring at the door was forthcoming. Anna checked the clock. It was five minutes past the hour. Johanna repositioned herself on the settee to greater advantage and Kalle took a book from the shelf. After a further five minutes Fru Larsson bustled into the room.

'No sign of our violinist yet?' Anna shook her head.

'That's strange. He's never struck me as the unpunctual sort. I'm sure there's a very good reason.' Fru Larsson spoke as if she knew the man.

'May I ask the gentleman's name, Fru Larsson?' Anna said.

'Herr Strindberg. Nils. He's the son of Oscar and Rosalie Strindberg and a student at the university. Studying something scientific, I believe. A very bright young man who plays the violin beautifully. Herr Larsson and I were invited to a number of his recitals when he was younger,' she said with a satisfied, unbecoming smirk.

Anna's heart began to pound. 'The Strindbergs are quite a well-known family in Stockholm, are they not?'

'Indeed. A very fine family. There are four sons – Erik, Sven, Tore and Nils. I feel rather privileged to have secured Nils as the children's tutor. I should think my familiarity with his family may have aided my cause. He's an extremely accomplished young gentleman.'

At least it was not Erik, Anna thought. But having his brother in the house could be equally uncomfortable.

At twenty minutes past two the doorbell was finally sounded. Johanna straightened her posture and pushed her glasses up her nose. Kalle replaced the book on the shelf. Anna heard Hilda's footsteps. There was a brief mumble of voices and then the maid entered the sitting room. 'Herr Strindberg has arrived.' She stated this fact as if it were an accusation. Over her two years at the Larssons' Anna had learnt that Hilda did not appreciate tardiness. Herr Strindberg had already made an enemy. Once lost, Hilda's favour would be difficult to regain.

'I am terribly sorry for being so late,' the young man said as he entered the sitting room. 'My watch is broken and I was in the laboratory, you see.' Hilda raised her eyebrows in disbelief. 'Now I look a sight. I ran the entire way. And I've made a dreadful first impression. I'm sorry for babbling like an idiot.'

His humility caught the room off guard. 'Please don't concern yourself, Herr Strindberg,' Fru Larsson said, springing to her feet and taking his hand. 'It's so good to meet you again.' Anna and the children stood, awaiting introductions.

'Come in and meet my children and our governess. This is Johanna, and Karl.' Strindberg shook the children's hands. Johanna attempted a coquettish curtsey.

'And this is Fröken Charlier, our governess.' Anna smiled and took the young man's hand. He gripped it firmly and shook it vigorously.

'I'm sure we shall very much enjoy working together, Fröken Charlier.' He held his violin case aloft. 'I believe you play the piano? Rather well, from all reports. I hope you do not embarrass me.'

'Rest assured, Herr Strindberg, that will not be the case,' Anna said. Strindberg grinned and looked around the room.

'Hilda,' Fru Larsson said. 'Would you mind bringing us some afternoon tea – some lemonade for the children too, please.' Hilda nodded, her face austere.

'Please, don't go to any trouble on my account,' Strindberg said. 'Hilda, if my tardiness has kept you from your duties, I apologise.'

'I can probably spare the time,' said Hilda. 'You look quite hot. A glass of lemonade would do you the world of good.' The maid left the room, offering a rare smile to the guest.

'I do apologise for Hilda, Herr Strindberg. She's been with the family for years. She believes, I fear, that she is the lady of the house and we' – Fru Larsson indicated those assembled in the room – 'only exist to make her life easier. But she does seem to like you.'

Strindberg laughed merrily and the group sat down. Hilda soon returned with afternoon tea and lemonade. Anna was startled by the ease with which Strindberg spoke with all, children and adults alike. He engaged Johanna and Kalle with tales of his younger brother Tore, relating in humorous detail a number of misadventures in which his sibling had become embroiled. The children were delighted and begged Strindberg for more. He promised them another story on his second visit. He chatted to his hostess about mutual friends and family acquaintances and then conversed with Anna about her time at the university and her studies, listening with rapt attention as she spoke.

Anna couldn't help comparing Nils with his brother. Physically, Nils was shorter and of a slighter build. She considered him quite handsome. His features were finer and more delicate than Erik's and his hair was a darker shade of brown. He wore a thin moustache. The brothers' eyes, though, were of the exact same shade of blue – crystal clear and vital.

In character the brothers seemed completely unalike. Content with his companions and interested in Johanna and Kalle's often inane chitchat, Nils seemed to have an endless supply of good humour. Anna was struck by his disregard for convention and by the familiarity with which he spoke to his companions. She realised part way through the conversation that at some point he had begun to call her by her Christian name. It didn't bother her. On the contrary, she welcomed his lack of formality.

For many years, working in the comfortable homes of

comfortable families, Anna had diligently refined her manners until they were suitable, mimicking the behaviour of others and studying their conversation and conduct. But in less than half an hour she was suddenly relaxed – foolishly so, she thought. Embarrassed by her own frivolity, she glanced at Fru Larsson, fearing her disapproval, but she needn't have worried. Fru Larsson had been disarmed as well, enjoying Strindberg's company.

Anna realised finally that it was this young man's modesty that separated the brothers. Nils wore his confidence discreetly; Erik wore his like armour. While Nils chatted amiably with the children, Anna found herself thinking more and more of his brother and their encounter only a few weeks before.

'Well, my young mariachis, shall we play?' Strindberg's voice summoned Anna from her thoughts. Johanna and Kalle looked confused. 'Don't worry, that's just what they call musicians in Mexico.'

'Have you been there, to Mexico?' Kalle enquired eagerly.

'That's for another time. Let's get to work.'

Fru Larsson excused herself from the room. As she passed the governess, she flashed her another satisfied grin. It became clear to Anna that the hiring of Nils Strindberg was, in part, motivated by a desire to see Anna suitably attached.

'Anna, would you accompany us, please?' Strindberg removed a pile of crumpled pages from the case along with his violin. 'Handel's Trio Sonata in G Minor. Do you know it?'

'I'm not familiar with it but I'm sure I'll be able to struggle through.' Anna smiled and placed her fingers confidently on the keys.

'My, what big hands you have,' Strindberg said.

Anna placed her hands hurriedly in her lap. It was a reflex, but she knew it would seem silly to her mocker. The only aspect of her appearance that had ever displeased Anna was her hands. They were large and muscular. Gota called them 'peasant hands'.

Kalle laughed. 'All the better to play with . . .' Strindberg and Johanna laughed too, and after a moment Anna joined them, helpless to resist.

When the quartet regained their composure, they readied themselves and flattened the pages on the music stands. Then, much to Hilda's irritation, music filled the house.

EIGHT

STOCKHOLM, SWEDEN
AUGUST 1894

As the days of summer passed, Nils became a fixture in the Larssons' house. One violin lesson each week soon became two, and then three. By mid-July he would more likely be found at Gåsgränd 6 than at any other address in Stockholm. While Johanna and Kalle were becoming increasingly competent at the violin, a healthy friendship was also growing between the tutor and the governess. By August their association had moved beyond the house and they began to meet on a Sunday. They would usually visit a museum or gallery and then take a walk in the park. Occasionally they would go cycling or embark on a hike in the country. Anna found herself speaking more freely with her companion than with anyone else she had known. Even Gota was not permitted access to all of her sister's thoughts – she was so prone to judge and criticise.

Although Anna and Nils were friends, and nothing more, she was careful to keep this new relationship from her sister.

Anna was happy with the friendship just as it stood, but Gota would not have comprehended that.

While Anna was able to conceal the existence of Nils Strindberg from Gota, she was unable to hide the burgeoning friendship from Margrit Larsson. 'It seems Herr Strindberg has taken quite a shine to you, Anna,' she chirped one morning, and on another occasion she whispered in Anna's ear, 'I have noticed that you and Herr Strindberg are spending a great deal of time together. Have you met his mother and father yet?' One afternoon not long after, Fru Larsson called for Anna. 'My dear, it's obvious an attachment has formed between yourself and Herr Strindberg. What do you think is the best course of action?'

'Pardon me?'

'Well, in the absence of your father, would you like my husband to speak to Herr Strindberg on your behalf?'

'About what? I'm sorry, madam, but I'm not sure of your meaning.'

'Anna.' Margrit sat next to her on the settee and took her hand. She smelt of scent. Gardenias, Anna guessed. It was overpowering. 'Has Herr Strindberg informed you of his intentions? Has he spoken of marriage?'

'Herr Strindberg and I are not in love, madam. We're friends, that's all.'

'Marriages have been built on less, dear.'

'I appreciate your concern. But I have no desire to formalise our attachment. I believe Herr Strindberg would agree.'

'Are you sure of that?' Fru Larsson asked, smiling. 'He seems a very devoted suitor to me. Has he never made any advances towards you?'

'No!' cried Anna, mortified. She was certain Nils had no romantic feelings for her, distracted as he was by his work and his studies. Come September, when Nils returned to university, he would more than likely disappear from her life.

Fru Larsson smiled again, but when she spoke she sounded a little impatient. 'Really, Anna, this has been going on long enough. The next steps need to be taken. Your relationship should be formalised. I don't wish to see you compromised.'

As soon as she could, Anna made a hasty retreat, and from then on she tried to avoid being left alone with Fru Larsson, making excuses for her often swift departures as she bustled the children out of the room. She did not wish to discuss the matter with her employer any further – and yet once the question had been raised she kept revisiting it, turning it over in her mind.

Margrit Larsson seemed to see marriage as the end to all means as much as Gota did, Anna thought. Since they were girls, Gota had prattled on about the most efficient method of securing a husband. She was seeking out a mate, plain and simple – someone who could promise her a secure and reasonably happy future – not a soul mate. If she were fortunate, affection would develop at a later, indeterminate date, but she would never pass up an advantageous match because she was not in love.

Anna thought of Gota's fury when she had rejected Erik Strindberg out of concern for her sister's feelings. She had always thought of Gota as selfish, yet Gota had been genuinely outraged at what she had given up for her.

Sometimes, on her walk home from the Larssons', she imagined herself married to Nils, the mistress of a fine home, with a fine husband and fine children. Anna had seen enough of Margrit Larsson's comings and goings, duties and entertainments to picture her own life as a middle-class wife. It seemed quite a pleasurable existence, especially if you were the wife of a kind, intelligent, courteous man. Perhaps Anna was asking for too much, wanting love and admiration as well as respect and affection.

She also began to wonder if she had judged Nils' feelings correctly. Fru Larsson seemed to think he harboured an attraction to the young governess, and Anna worried that perhaps she had misled him in some way. She was uncomfortable letting their relationship go on without clarifying their mutual expectations, but it was impossible to raise the subject without sounding predatory.

She had kept her relationship with Nils a secret from her sister because Gota 'wouldn't understand it', and she had told herself repeatedly that Margrit Larsson would not be able to comprehend the nuances of their friendship. The truth, she now realised, was that she herself did not fully grasp the nature of their relationship.

Anna had become used to discussing her inner life with Nils, and it was difficult to agonise over a problem like this alone. One day she could bear the uncertainty no longer and decided to speak to him about their friendship. It was Sunday afternoon and the couple had just left the Museum of Natural History.

Nils took her arm and they made their way to the cafe in the park. Anna smiled and then began, timidly, 'Our outings, what do they mean to you?'

'What do you mean?' Nils asked.

'Well, people are beginning to wonder where our outings and so forth are heading,' she told him.

'By people, do you mean Margrit Larsson?' Anna nodded sheepishly.

'That woman has always been a busybody. Margrit Larsson invents scandal for her own amusement.'

'Regardless, I am interested in . . .'

'My intentions?'

'Not exactly. This is so awkward. I'm sorry . . . I'd like to know how you feel about me. That's all.'

'That's a reasonable request,' Nils said. 'I like you enormously, Anna. You've become extremely important to me. And, if I'm honest with myself, my reasons for being at the house so often have little to do with the musical education of Johanna and Kalle.'

She felt the colour rise in her cheeks. 'Thank you for your candour. I enjoy spending time with you as well.'

'As I've never been in love before, I can't vouch for the authenticity of my feelings. But I believe I may be. In love with you, that is. I do find myself wanting to kiss you quite often. So perhaps, if you're agreeable, we should begin courting. Is that the correct term?'

'Oh . . .Yes, I believe it is. Goodness.' She stopped and abruptly sat down on the grass. Nils joined her, smiling. He lay down and placed his hands behind his head, looking up at the sky through the trees.

It was a peculiar proposal, she thought, but it seemed sincere. She glanced sideways at Nils, who had closed his eyes. He was a scientist, a rationalist; she couldn't expect anything more romantic. Perhaps Gota and Margrit Larsson were correct – perhaps this was all she could hope. Perhaps the notion of a great romantic love was a myth, something that only happened in fairy tales.

She definitely had feelings for the young man lying by her side. She cared for him, valued his opinion, enjoyed his company, but was it love? Nils is offering respect, trust and genuine affection, she reasoned. How can I require anything more? Would it be futile to ask for anything more?

Nils rolled onto his side and propped his head up in his hand. 'Well, what do you say?'

She stared at his eager, honest face for a second before she answered. She had no desire to hurt him.

'Well, yes, I suppose so. I suppose we should begin courting.'

'Excellent,' he cried, springing to his feet and pulling Anna to hers. 'Will you attend the photographic exhibition with me? That will be an excellent opportunity to meet my family.'

'Exhibition?'

'I'm sure I invited you. No? Well, I entered a few of my photographs in a competition. They're being exhibited next Saturday at the palace, when a winner will be judged.'

'Really? I'd be honoured to attend. Thank you.'

As they strolled on towards the cafe, Nils took Anna's hand again and looped her arm through his own. He squeezed her fingers contentedly as he did so. With this small gesture of affection their attachment entered entirely new territory.

NILS STRINDBERG'S JOURNAL, 3
AUGUST 1897

This morning as I was sitting in the tent attempting to light the Primus I recalled the evening Tore and I went camping in our garden. He was only about ten, but he pitched the tent with little effort and invited me to join him for the night. I was reluctant at first, it was March and the nights were still fearfully cold, but he was so filled with excitement it would have been heartless to disappoint him. He heated a little soup from the kitchen over the Primus that Mama and Papa had given him for his birthday. After supper we laid on our backs under the stars and I told him the names of the constellations. As he was going to sleep he told me it had been a grand night for brothers.

NINE

STOCKHOLM, SWEDEN
SEPTEMBER 1930

STUBBENDORFF STOOD outside the house on Lilla Nygatan. He was unsure of what he should say or how he would explain his actions. He rang the doorbell.

An attractive young woman opened the door and smiled warmly at him. She was dressed in what he thought might have been a bathrobe. The garment was secured around her waist with a tie. The fabric was light and delicately patterned.

'Hello. I'm Knut Stubbendorff. I telephoned yesterday and arranged to meet Herr Strindberg. Is he at home?'

'Of course. He's expecting you. He's waiting for you in his studio.' The woman opened the door and Stubbendorff entered the Strindberg family home. In the entrance hall he removed his hat and coat and, as he did so, took in his surroundings. It was not a grand house, by any means. On his return from Tromsø the reporter had spent days in the newspaper's archives attempting to discover as much as possible about the family. Based on the distinguished professional and public careers of Oscar the patriarch, now deceased, and his surviving sons, Stubbendorff was expecting a home of more imposing stature. But this house was inviting and snug. It was late afternoon and a fire crackled and cast a warm glow in the sitting room. He could see it through the room's open door.

The woman took his coat from him and placed his hat on a shelf. Her hair was loosely fixed in a braid that hung just below her buttocks and her feet were bare. She could only be Strindberg's wife, he thought. Noticing his bewilderment, she smiled encouragingly and gestured for him to follow her along a hallway. Her tread was gentle on the threadbare burgundy runner. Stubbendorff's eyes ran from her narrow feet up the backs of her long legs to her buttocks. The fabric of her gown was nearly transparent.

Then her head turned. Stubbendorff had been caught; there was no doubt about it. Her eyebrows rose only a fraction before she turned back. He felt the heat rise in his cheeks.

As he followed the woman down the hallway towards the back of the house, he was amazed by the number of paintings crowded together on every available inch of wall space. In the colourful, artistic jumble he noticed Kandinskys next to a Carl Larsson next to what he believed was a portrait of August Strindberg by Edvard Munch. It struck Stubbendorff that what he was viewing was the most democratic gallery in the world. The works of great artists were hung adjacent to those of nobodies. From his inexpert perspective many of the hangings looked incomplete, rough drafts of something more brilliant to come.

Sculptures littered the surfaces of hall tables and cabinets. Many of the forms were unrecognisable, indecipherable.

Others were busts of men and women. Like the paintings, some appeared to be unfinished or imperfect.

The house was cluttered, without a doubt, but its effect on Stubbendorff was transfixing. As a newspaper reporter his work was edited and cut to fit on the page. During his first months on the paper he had watched in alarm as his words were scratched and reordered into a form he no longer recognised. Descriptive passages intended to engage the reader were seen as superfluous and indulgent. Each mark, every cross and slash from Bergman's red pencil, was as a mortal wound. He had learnt too readily, he thought in hindsight, to be economical with his writing. But it was survival. Evolve or perish. It concerned him now that he had given up so easily, suppressed his imagination. This house, in all its creative mayhem, was the loveliest he had ever entered.

The woman tapped softly on the studio door, where a metal engraving hung reading 'Do Not Disturb. Explorer at Work'. A brick of a man promptly opened it. He was sporting an almost comically lustrous black moustache. It appeared to cover both his top and bottom lip, leaving one with the impression of a frolicsome Affenpinscher. Dressed in a white coat speckled liberally with paint, the man stretched out his similarly speckled hand and waved Stubbendorff into the room. His appearance momentarily boggled the journalist, who had almost expected the eager thirteen-year-old boy from Nils' diary to open the door. Stubbendorff had come to know that young fellow very well and was looking forward to meeting him. It was somehow shocking to find him grown up.

'Good afternoon, Herr Stubbendorff. Please, Agneta, some tea and a little something to nibble also.' The woman moved away swiftly as Stubbendorff was shown into the spacious studio. He snatched a final glimpse before she closed the door behind her. 'She's very beautiful, no?' Tore said. Stubbendorff nodded. 'Agneta is my housekeeper, secretary, one-time muse, sometime model. I could not do without her.'

Stubbendorff nodded again, hoping to appear more sophisticated than he felt.

The artist invited Stubbendorff to sit down and led him to a tattered settee in one corner of the room. Stubbendorff was still examining the room, delighting in the space, when Strindberg began to speak, wasting little time on preliminaries.

'I'm most grateful to you for contacting me, Herr Stubbendorff. We, I mean my family, had discussed travelling to Tromsø to be there when Nils arrived. But such hoopla! We wanted no part in those festivities. Rather ghoulish. But I'm eager to talk to the man who visited the scene of my brother's death.'

Stubbendorff shifted uncomfortably. 'I participated in the ceremony with the greatest reluctance. I had no idea what the newspaper was planning. And I have since resigned my position.'

'A man of principle. Delightful! I suppose the *Aftonbladet* want their share of the pie. They've been waiting a long time. But enough about those vultures. Tell me about your trip.'

Agneta returned with a tray of tea and small slices of buttered toast. Tore rose and helped her lay out the crockery, and Stubbendorff gave the young woman his most worldly smile.

'I hope you have a lovely afternoon,' she said. 'Let me know if you need anything else.' She brushed past Stubbendorff. She smelt of soap and he quivered in the breeze of her departure.

Tore sat down once again. 'Where were we?' he said. 'Ah yes, your trip.'

Stubbendorff did not know where to begin. 'It was an

incredible experience. I felt privileged to see it all. Their camp was as they left it . . .'

'Frozen in time, as it were.'

'Yes, exactly. And it was as if I had somehow been chosen to restart the clock.'

'You are a writer, yes? You wish to tell their stories?'

'No, it's not that.' Stubbendorff took a sip of tea. He wanted to explain himself clearly. 'I found their diaries. It was clear that they were three men of extraordinary potential. I found your brother's diary particularly moving. He spoke very highly of his family and seemed to love you all so profoundly.'

'He was a person of considerable intellect, talent and charm,' Strindberg said. 'I loved him most dearly. I was the baby of the family and my brothers Erik and Sven treated me as such. Nils, on the other hand, treated me as his equal. I loved him for seeing more in me than everyone else did. This was his workroom.' He circled his arm above his head. 'I can't imagine working anywhere else.'

Strindberg stood abruptly and walked to a table by the window. It was crowded with small sculptures like a miniature, jostling dance floor. He took up a single example of his work and brought it to Stubbendorff to examine.

'I made this when I was at the Academy. It's not an exact likeness, but it's how I remember him.'

The figure was of a young man in shirtsleeves. His trouser legs were rolled up to just below the knee and he was sitting on the banks of a lake. His head was thrown back in profuse laughter and he was holding a small sailing boat in his hands. The expression of utter happiness on the face seemed to Stubbendorff to transcend reality.

'My tutors did not appreciate the style. But I found the process quite cathartic.'

'It's very good.' Stubbendorff stood so he could examine

the sculpture more closely. 'I've only seen a few pictures of your brother but from what I've learnt from his writings, I think you've captured his personality very well.'

'I like to think so. When my first wife saw this, she told me I'd transformed my brother into a god. The last time I saw Nils, I was thirteen and I idolised him. I suppose I'll always see him through the wide eyes of a boy.' There was a brief pause. 'He was a marvellous musician as well, you know. The violin. He could have made music his career. He was exceptionally gifted. Much better than I ever was.'

'Yes, he mentioned playing the violin in his diary. The two of you practised together for hours, didn't you? And his fiancée, Anna Charlier, was a pianist, I believe?'

'She was indeed. That's how they first met. She was a governess to a local family and Nils tutored the children in the violin.'

'Do you know if Anna Charlier still lives in Stockholm?'

Strindberg placed his teacup on the table very deliberately and cleared his throat. 'No, no, I don't think she does. I know many people who know many people in Stockholm and I'm sure her name would have cropped up if she still lived here. There were no parents, but I think perhaps she lived with her sister.' Strindberg removed his spectacles and pinched his eyes in an effort to bring the name to mind. 'It's on the tip of my tongue. Gota!' he said triumphantly after a moment. 'We saw Anna less and less after Nils left. She took his disappearance extremely hard. I haven't heard from her since those days. Why do you ask?'

'There were a number of letters in your brother's diary that he wrote to Anna Charlier during the expedition. I thought she might like to read them.' He allowed Strindberg to consider the idea. 'They were of an extremely personal nature, quite lovely, really.' Stubbendorff hesitated before saying, 'I kept his diary from the Scientific Commission.' He found himself ashamed, preparing to be admonished by his host.

Strindberg chuckled. 'Don't worry, my boy,' he said. 'Matters of the heart should be of no concern to the Scientific Commission. If you can find Anna, she has every right to read her correspondence, even if it has been delayed thirty years.'

Strindberg patted Stubbendorff's shoulder heartily before returning to his tea. Stubbendorff felt as though Strindberg was giving him his blessing.

'Would you like to read the journal? I have it here.'

Strindberg's expression became grave. He placed his head in his hands and sighed loudly. When he straightened, Stubbendorff saw his eyes were moist, glistening with tears. 'No. It was personal and he would never have wanted his little brother reading his private thoughts. What's done is done, as they say, although there are a few things I wish I could go back and change. Sometimes, when you're young, your emotions can overrule your better judgement.'

Strindberg withdrew a crumpled handkerchief from his pocket and blew his snub nose loudly. 'Would you like to see what I'm working on at the moment, Herr Stubbendorff?'

'Yes, I would. Very much.'

Strindberg went quickly to an easel on which a large sketchbook stood. He mimed a drumroll before turning the easel. The page the sculptor showed Stubbendorff was blank.

'The city council has commissioned me to sculpt a memorial for my brother and his two companions. Of course I agreed, but now I'm having trouble. Blocked. My love for Nils is proving an obstacle. I'm having extreme difficulty designing a sculpture that honours the three men equally. My attempts so far have been too general and a tribute to none.'

Stubbendorff was confused and flattered that Strindberg

was confiding in him. 'Perhaps you should look at the expedition rather than the individuals? Remove the personalities from the equation,' he suggested.

It was as if the force of this idea slapped the artist in the face. He literally seemed stunned. When he finally spoke, it was with renewed vigour.

'That's an excellent suggestion, Herr Stubbendorff. Perhaps I'm trying to incorporate too much. Perhaps I should pare it back, make it simpler.'

The young man nodded in agreement, a little perplexed at Strindberg's reaction. He checked his watch, then remembered he had not yet had it repaired.

'I'm glad I could be of help,' he said, and stood to leave. 'My watch is not working. May I trouble you for the time?'

'It's nearly five,' Strindberg answered, and laughed. 'You remind me of my brother, Herr Stubbendorff. His watch was never working. He either forgot to wind it or he wound it too far or forgot to remove it when he was bathing. Before too long he stopped getting it repaired and joked that his salary didn't stretch that far. Yet it remained on his wrist.'

'Mine stopped when I was on Kvitøya. I've not had the chance to get it fixed. I live in fear of being late.'

'Being unmindful of time was part of my brother's unique character, I believe.'

'How so?'

'He never hurried. He was supremely composed in almost every situation. But most important to a younger brother, he always had time for me.'

Stubbendorff moved towards the door. 'It's getting late. I should leave you to your work. I look forward to viewing the finished piece.' He smiled as he said this, indicating the empty page in the sketchbook.

The men walked the length of the house, along its cluttered hallway, without speaking. When they reached the door, Strindberg gripped the writer's forearm. Stubbendorff could feel his strong, callused fingers pressing into the flesh just below his elbow. The men were the same height. They locked eyes. The younger man could feel the warmth of Strindberg's breath on his cheek.

'If you do contact Anna, Herr Stubbendorff, please let her know I would like to see her. I said something a long time ago that hurt her greatly. I would like to make amends.'

Stubbendorff lifted his head in enquiry.

'It was just a boy's thoughtless lashing out,' Strindberg said, but he could not disguise his shame as they said their goodbyes.

Out on the sidewalk Stubbendorff was unsure what to do next. He looked both ways along the street and noticed a small cafe on the opposite side. He walked there quickly, his stocky legs barely able to keep pace with his intent. Once seated with a cup of sweet, black coffee, he produced a tattered notebook from his satchel and hastily scribbled an exact transcript of the meeting.

TEN

PHILADELPHIA, PENNSYLVANIA, UNITED STATES
JULY 1876

'PLEASE START, MR ANDRÉE,' John Wise said.

Andrée positioned his knife and fork carefully in his hands and turned the utensils over several times between his fingers without removing his gaze from the plate. Wise watched him a while, intrigued. Finally he said, 'For goodness' sake, you're skin and bone. Begin!'

Andrée obeyed. The men did not speak until Andrée's head straightened and he had cautiously laid his knife and fork across his plate. Wise nudged the platter of beef with the back of his hand towards his guest. The young Swede served himself a second helping and had finished it before Wise had completed his first. Andrée drank two large glasses of cold water while he waited.

'You haven't had a square meal for a while it seems, Mr Andrée.' The young man shook his head and grinned bashfully. 'Why is that?'

'I have no money. I volunteered my services at the Swedish Pavilion as the consulate had no vacancies. I'm the janitor.'

'And you arrived in Philadelphia in May?'

He nodded.

'Then how have you been living for the past two months?'

'Frugally,' Andrée answered.

Wise was in equal parts amused and disturbed by the pallid young man's candour. 'Take it from me, Mr Andrée, you don't look well. You're gaunt and hollow-eyed. If you don't take care of yourself, you'll surely become ill. Then this entire endeavour will be wasted.'

Andrée was indeed gaunt. He couldn't recall the last time he had seen himself in a mirror, but when he ran his hand over his face he felt it. Living in the dank basement of a lodging house, which he also maintained in return for board, had not been conducive to good health. 'Why have you come to Philadelphia, Mr Andrée? I hope you haven't come all this way just to see me.'

'I'm interested in ballooning, of course. But I'm also an engineer. I've come here to learn as much as possible from the Exposition. I can worry about my health when I return to Stockholm. I appreciate your concern, Mr Wise, but I'm here today to discuss ballooning with you, if you wouldn't mind.'

Wise was struck once more by his young guest's directness. He did not know whether he would have been so bold with a gentleman three times his age and with three times his experience when he was just twenty-two. It was clear to the American that Andrée found small talk irritating, a frustrating obstacle to his main goal.

Wise glanced at the thermometer on the wall. It was approaching one hundred degrees in the house. He suggested they sit on the porch – it was about that time in the afternoon when a breeze usually picked up.

Once they were seated outside, Wise asked, 'How can I help you?'

'On the steamer, coming to America, I read a book called *The Laws of the Winds*.' Wise indicated with a brief nod that he was familiar with the book.

'It struck me that balloons, even if not dirigible, could be used for long journeys if they were to catch a favourable current. It occurred to me that a balloon might possibly cross the Atlantic.' Andrée looked to Wise for a response.

'The same idea occurred to me twenty years ago, Mr Andrée. But it came to nothing. Although it exists, locating that great elusive river of wind that runs from west to east over the Atlantic is more difficult than it seems. Launching a balloon into it is even more difficult. When I attempted it, I was fortunate to crash-land in New York. If we'd gone down over the ocean somewhere between here and Europe . . . well, that would have been the end. I gave up my dream of a transatlantic crossing years ago.'

Andrée's brow wrinkled in consternation. Wise had flown balloons in sunshine, hail, snow, thunderstorms and hurricanes. He had been stuck on chimneys, smokestacks, lightning rods and church spires. He had been dragged through rivers and lakes, over garden plots and primeval forests. His balloons had whirled like tops, caught fire, exploded and fallen to the ground like stones. He had more than four hundred ascents under his belt, and had never sustained an injury. He had decades of experience in the field. Yet now he was suggesting that it could not be done, that a transatlantic crossing was too dangerous.

'You're up there at the mercy of the wind,' Wise said. 'And believe me, she's not a compassionate mistress. If there was a way to control the balloon, steer it with any degree of accuracy, then the chances of success might be greater.

'If you're familiar with my innovations with drag lines,

then you'll know that the altitude of the balloon can be managed. That's the first step. The ability to float above or below the current is crucial. Mr Andrée, I can tell you how to make a balloon, how to fill a balloon, how to launch it, how to rise and how to descend. But I am getting too old to take the next step. I shall leave that up to you.'

Andrée was quiet, his eyes fixed on the trees that bordered Wise's property, dancing in the westerly wind. Wise was concerned he had disappointed the boy.

'Would you like to accompany me in an ascent? I'm taking my niece up next week on Independence Day.'

Andrée was surprised by the invitation but accepted readily. It would be his first ascent.

Wise paid Andrée's train fare from Philadelphia to Huntington, Pennsylvania, where the balloon was to be launched. Andrée joined Wise for the filling of the balloon and lodged that night in the older man's spare bedroom. The following day, on the hundredth anniversary of American independence, Andrée, Wise and Jemima, the aeronaut's niece, travelled together to the field where the balloon was waiting. Andrée estimated one hundred people were assembled to witness the launch. Wise's niece, dressed as the Goddess of Liberty, was hoisted into the basket and, holding her torch aloft, was photographed by newspapers.

Following a brief speech by Wise concerning the importance of the day and the national significance of aeronautic travel, the adventurer joined Andrée and Jemima in the basket. The anchor was lifted and the securing ropes cut. While the Goddess of Liberty waved farewell, a gasp was heard from the crowd as the envelope began to collapse like a rag to the ground. The balloon failed to launch.

One week later an intestinal complaint forced Andrée to return on the first steamer to Sweden, where, over the subsequent month, he was nursed back to good health by his mother.

ELEVEN

STOCKHOLM, SWEDEN
SEPTEMBER 1930

Stubbendorff approached his childhood home. He stood at the door for a minute or two taking in its shedding paint, unsure what had brought him to Prästgatan that morning, what had drawn him back to the building where he had spent the first sixteen years of his life. A knot tightened beneath his diaphragm. He stood there a moment longer, looking up at the second-floor apartment. When he eventually entered the building and began climbing the stairs to number four, it was with dread and remorse.

The woman who answered his knock was a faded version of his mother. His mother's ghost. In the nine years since Stubbendorff had seen her, she had aged decades and become smaller. Her skin was lined and almost transparent. 'I saw you from the window.' The woman gestured briefly over her son's shoulder. 'I was wondering if you'd come up.'

'May I come in?'

The woman walked into her apartment, leaving the door open. 'Close it and lock it. Please.'

Stubbendorff did as he was instructed and passed down the narrow hallway into the sitting room. The room was just as he remembered, although prints of Jesus and the Virgin took the place of the family photographs that had once hung on the wall. Likewise, religious statuettes were prominent on every surface. A large crucifix hung over the mantel.

He sat down on the settee without being invited. He remembered sitting on the same settee as a child. The fabric was threadbare. His mother remained standing opposite him. The room seemed smaller to him. The foreboding presence of God combined with the looming spectre of his mother was stifling. Stubbendorff removed his coat and draped it carefully across his arm.

'How have you been, Mama?'

'Quite well.'

'The apartment looks the same.'

His mother nodded curtly.

'May I have a glass of water, please?'

His mother left the room without speaking and walked into the kitchen. He could hear her opening the cupboard and turning on the faucet. She came back holding the glass far out in front of her. 'Thank you,' he said, rising to take it. The water was tepid and the glass smelt of soap. Stubbendorff took one sip and then placed the glass on the end table next to him.

'I'm sorry not to have visited sooner.'

'It's been ten years.'

'Nine.' Stubbendorff knew immediately that was a childish, prickly response. 'But I'm sorry. It's been a long time.'

'It has,' she confirmed. 'But I've had my faith and my work at the church.'

'That's good. It's good to keep busy. I'm glad that you have a purpose, a higher calling.'

She said nothing in response and seemed unwilling to sit down. As Stubbendorff stood and walked around the room, affecting interest in the pictures and religious knick-knacks, he tried desperately to think of something they could talk about – a shared memory, anything – that might engage her.

'Have you read about the discovery of Salomon Andrée's camp?' he finally asked.

His mother shook her head. 'I don't read the newspapers.'

Stubbendorff noticed there was no radio in the room either. Had she cloistered herself completely from life, he wondered.

'I was sent there, to Kvitøya, by the *Aftonbladet*. I found some things that belonged to the men, their possessions . . .' But Stubbendorff could tell his mother wasn't listening. Still standing, her distracted gaze was fixed somewhere behind him. 'May I see my room, please?' he asked.

'Hmm?'

'My room. I'd like to see my old room.'

'Be my guest.' A note of scorn whet her tone.

His bedroom adjoined the sitting room. As Stubbendorff stood in the doorway scanning the space – the metal-framed bed with its thin, bare mattress, the narrow wardrobe with its poorly aligned doors – he became a boy again. This room had been his sanctuary, his retreat. It was in this room, lying on his bed, that he was finally liberated. He'd read books of his choosing then hide them in the bottom of an old toy chest. Sometimes he'd read school texts, usually history or guides to foreign languages. He read quickly and possessed the remarkable talent of being able to retain information almost word for word. He would often write adventure stories in the vein of Scotland's R. M. Ballantyne and the

American Harry Castlemon. He hid these also in the toy chest.

When he announced to his mother at the age of fifteen that he wanted to be a writer, she had argued that he could never make a living that way. How did he intend to support her? He had compromised and decided instead to pursue a career in journalism, as a stepping stone to a successful life as an author. Stubbendorff had begun as a cadet at the *Afton-bladet* three days shy of his sixteenth birthday. Before he knew it, he was celebrating his twenty-fifth birthday. During the intervening years his dreams and confidence had been eroded by Bergman and his own indolence.

'I gave all your clothes to the church some time ago, if that's what you want.'

He turned, startled. His mother was standing directly behind him, her hands clenched in front of her bosom. He nodded.

Stubbendorff went to the toy chest at the foot of his bed, knelt and opened the lid. It was empty. 'Were there any papers here? Did you find any notebooks?'

She shook her head.

'I used to write stories, in notebooks, and I put them in this box. Are you certain you found nothing?'

'Of course I'm certain,' she said bitterly. 'What do you think I am? Stupid?'

'I must be mistaken.'

'You must be,' she responded without emotion. 'Is there anything else you wanted?'

Stubbendorff sat on the box. He looked up at his mother, who had positioned herself in front of her seated son. There was neither compassion nor warmth in her cloudy grey eyes. What had he hoped would be the outcome of this visit, he wondered. He'd hoped he might be forgiven for his curt exit from her life. He'd hoped that with maturity and experience he'd be able to view his mother in a different, more charitable light. He'd hoped to find his notebooks. And he'd hoped she'd be proud of her only child.

'No, nothing else. I should be going.' Stubbendorff walked to the front door. 'It was nice to see you again, Mother. Is there anything I can do to help you?'

'Not a thing.'

'I have a little money . . .'

'No, thank you.'

'If you change your mind and need anything or . . . I live above the cafe on Triewaldsgränd.'

'Goodbye, Knut,' his mother said before closing the door.

As he walked down the stairs to the street door, he wondered what his mother might have done with his notebooks. Perhaps she had thought them rubbish and carelessly thrown them in the bin or, realising they were the work of her estranged son's imagination, burnt them in the stove. He hoped that neither was the case.

TWELVE

STOCKHOLM, SWEDEN
SEPTEMBER 1894

WHEN ANNA HAD TOLD her sister about Nils, her response was firm.

'You've already ruined one opportunity. I'm not going to let you make the same mistake again.'

'You mean Erik.'

'Indeed I do.' She grinned. 'Now I can have him all to myself. I have a way in now, don't I? If you don't chase Nils off as well, I mean.'

Now, on the day of the photographic exhibition, Gota darted around the room incessantly, committed to transforming her sister's appearance into something remarkable – a vision no man could resist. Her figure, she reasoned to Anna, would make up for any deficiencies in her personality.

There was not sufficient time for a new dress to be made but Gota had done an excellent job fashioning one of her own dresses into something suitable for her sister. As Anna was ordered about the room – *sit down, stand up, tilt your head this way, stand straight, breathe in a little* – she struggled to keep Gota's kindness and generosity in the forefront of her mind. She was grateful the event was being held in the afternoon. Gota's creation was a testament to her talent but, as skilled as she was, a fairy godmother she was not. She would never have been able to fashion an evening dress on such short notice.

But it was more than Gota's fussing that unnerved Anna. Even though Anna had suggested she meet him at the palace, Nils had insisted on collecting her. She had argued that this had not been their habit in the past. Nils joked that escorting one's partner from her home was the custom when you were courting. Margrit Larsson would have it no other way, he added. Nils had never seen Anna's home and she had never told him about her meeting with Erik in June. Both circumstances filled her with dread.

As Gota was pinning her hair, she decided to confess, and beg her sister's cooperation.

'Gota, I've never told Nils that I met his brother. Would you mind not bringing it up?'

'Ah, what are you planning?'

'Absolutely nothing,' Anna replied, surprised. 'I just didn't mention it because I thought it might be awkward.'

'But Erik will be attending the exhibition, no?'

'Yes, he will. I'm praying he doesn't say anything either. I know Nils has told his family about me. Perhaps Erik has forgotten me.'

'It's highly likely. A gentleman of his standing and looks would have women lining up.'

Anna accepted this affront as a ray of light. Perhaps their meeting by the lake had been merely one in a series of such encounters for the extremely eligible Erik Strindberg.

'You're probably right. I'm worrying for nothing.'

'Well, you're giving yourself airs if you're worried. Would

you like me to attend with you, as a chaperone?' Gota stopped work and leant over Anna's shoulder, catching her eye in the mirror. 'Then I could act as a distraction. Wouldn't that be wonderful, Anna? If Erik Strindberg fell in love with me. Then we could have a double wedding.'

'You sound like Johanna Larsson. Nobody's getting married. Stop all this make-believe.'

Anna shooed her sister away and moved to the full-length mirror. Even though the dress was pink, a colour Anna disliked, she was delighted with her sister's creation. Gota had removed the frills that had once cascaded down the skirt and shortened the sleeves slightly. Anna marvelled that such an indelicate personality could craft such a wonderful, perfectly suited dress. Gota had, despite Anna's urgings to the contrary, also lowered the neckline, arguing that high necklines made Anna look like a goitred giraffe. She did add, however, that one of Anna's finest features was her décolletage and it should not be hidden. Anna's hair was piled loosely on her head. Glossy curls framed her face. Gota had also made a starched pink bow from the same fabric and nestled this deep into the knot high on Anna's head.

The sisters sat at the kitchen table waiting for Nils to arrive. Anna adjusted the position of a stunted vase stuffed with daisies that she'd placed at the table's centre. She was disappointed the arrangement did not do more to improve the room's appearance. The air was warm and Anna hoped Nils would be on time. He was usually late. If she sat in the room for much longer, she was certain she would begin perspiring, but at twelve o'clock promptly there was a knock at the door.

Nils took Anna's hand and kissed it softly. He moved swiftly to Gota and did the same. He chatted with Gota as if they were old friends, which pleased her sister greatly. Anna was grateful Nils' animated conversation provided limited opportunity for her sibling to speak. To Anna's amazement and relief, Nils did not seem to notice the size of the room or the stink of hops in the staircase as they descended to the street.

Standing in the gilt-lined gallery of the palace, with a row of twelve elaborate crystal chandeliers lighting the rectangular expanse, Anna could hardly believe she'd been in her shabby flat less than an hour before, and marvelled at the change in her surroundings.

Nils guided her around the gallery and introduced her to his photographs. Five were images of Stockholm – Skeppsbron Quay at sunset, the Christmas markets in Stortorget, Norrbro at dusk, the statue of King Charles XIV on Slussplan caked in ice and Maria Magdalena Church on All Saints' Day. The final photograph was different. Taken in the Larssons' sitting room, it showed Johanna and Kalle standing by their music stands, violins held to their chins, laughing wildly. 'It's beautiful, Nils. I had no idea you'd taken this. Johanna will be so pleased to have her photograph on display at the palace. We must bring them.'

'My aim had been to photograph them practising,' Nils said.'But the more I insisted on them taking the moment seriously, the more they laughed. Cheeky beggars. They were impossible. They made appalling models. But once I developed the photographs, I realised they, like the others, captured a moment. An infuriating one, but a moment nonetheless.'

'You'll definitely win,' she whispered. For a moment she felt truly happy. She was enjoying being here with Nils. He was talented and attentive and amusing and she did not feel at all out of her depth. 'Anna, my family has arrived. Come with me and I shall introduce you.'

And suddenly she was drowning.

Before Nils could say another word, a striking matron draped in emerald silk stepped forward and took Anna's hand. 'What a pleasure it is to meet you, my dear. My son, in his absent-mindedness, has told me so little about you – except of his immense regard, of course. I'm looking forward to getting to know you. What a lovely dress. You look an absolute picture.'

The group laughed politely at their mother's pun. Anna had never before been the recipient of such an effusive greeting. Fru Strindberg went on to introduce the other members of her brood.

'Unfortunately, my husband could not join us. He has been called away to Gothenburg on business. But here comes my eldest, Erik. He bears a remarkable resemblance to his father. The two could be interchangeable.'

Erik approached Anna and took her hand. 'It's a pleasure, Fröken.' His expression gave away nothing. Erik's hand was warm.

'It's lovely to meet you as well.'

'My brother speaks of you often. He has grown very attached to you, in fact. And it's no wonder.'

'Thank you, Herr Strindberg.'

'You work together, yes? At the Larssons'. That's where you met?'

'Yes, it is.'

'It's a wonder your work allows you any time to socialise. I'm sure the life of a governess can be rather challenging.'

Anna nodded.

'Fortunately for my brother you were able to spare a little of your valuable time.'

He was hurt, Anna realised. His feelings were hurt. Erik

Strindberg remembered exactly who she was: the woman who had wounded him. And, she supposed, her attachment to Nils was the salt.

She opened her mouth to speak. She wanted to explain her actions. She had never intended to injure him. But this was not the place.

Nils directed his brothers around the gallery, showing them his photographs. The four were so at ease with one another, Anna thought, though they each seemed so different. Tore bore the strongest resemblance to Nils, both of them compact and lithe, swift of body and mind. Sven was most like Rosalie and the most striking of the four. His willowy build and his height brought to mind a crane. He followed his brothers through the room at a far more sedate pace, but with an exactitude that was absent from the hurried gait of Nils and Tore. Finally, she looked to Erik. He shared Sven's height but was broader of frame. Gota would consider him the most fetching man in the gallery, and many would have agreed with her. Anna noticed the reaction of young women as he passed by, struggling to catch his attention, whispering behind their fans to one another. Erik ignored them all, focusing only on his brothers and the photographs.

Anna remained with Rosalie. 'My dear, who made such a lovely gown? It's so simple but so elegant. It's perfectly suited to the occasion.'

'My sister, madam, whom I believe you know. Gota Charlier.'

'Ah, really? I should have made the connection. She's a fine seamstress.' Rosalie looked gravely into Anna's face. 'How strange,' she went on, more cheerily. 'I can't see a family resemblance.'

'People say we're very different,' Anna said.

Rosalie nodded thoughtfully before placing Anna's arm

through her own and setting off down the gallery.

As they walked, they spoke of Anna's work as a governess, her attachment to Nils, and the photographs. Never did Rosalie Strindberg condescend or attempt to intimidate. No further enquiries were made about Gota or her background once Anna had mentioned her parents' death. Rosalie declared that the sisters' decision to build a life in Stockholm was a sign of strong character born of a good upbringing, a quality she admired greatly. Anna was aware she was not a suitable match for a Strindberg male. But she was treated by the matriarch of the family with absolute respect. It buoyed her spirits.

They strolled on and Rosalie squeezed Anna's arm in a gesture of familiarity. 'In the absence of your own mother, my dear, please allow me to act as a kind of surrogate, if you will. If there is any guidance you require, I would be overjoyed to help. I've lived in a house full of men for more than twenty-five years. I'm so thrilled there will finally be another woman around.'

Rosalie Strindberg had the face and mannerisms of a girl. Her eyes were lively and she skipped from one subject to the next with abandon. She laughed spontaneously and was generous with her attention. Anna recognised these traits in Nils. But Rosalie was also commanding. She moved around the space deliberately, her long neck stretched, her chin held high, her eyes skimming the tops of heads to a place more interesting beyond. Rosalie's honey-coloured hair was twisted into a complex knot at the base of her head and a small circular hat was angled at the crown. The glorious peacock's tail feather that adorned her headpiece only made her more formidable. Anna saw these qualities reflected in Erik.

At two o'clock the audience was assembled, gathered around a lectern at one side of the gallery. The ten entrants were positioned on either side. Anna stood by herself, to the back of the crowd. She could see Rosalie Strindberg on the opposite side of the semicircle, speaking to an equally smartly clad woman. Tore and Sven stood nearby. They leant against a wall, talking quietly. There was no sign of Erik.

'Hello, Fröken. Are you enjoying the afternoon?' The voice behind her made her turn. Erik must have left the gallery and circled back in through the balcony.

'Yes. Yes, I am.' Then, mustering her courage, she said, 'Thank you for not indicating that we'd met before.' She looked up into his blue eyes. 'I was foolish not to tell Nils about it. I'm not really sure why I didn't.'

'When Nils told me he'd lost his heart to a beautiful governess named Anna Charlier, I guessed you hadn't told him about our brief encounter by the lake. Whatever your reasons for keeping it from him, I didn't want to embarrass you or upset my brother today.'

They said no more for a few moments. The audience, which had been hushed in preparation for the announcement some minutes before, began to speak at a louder volume when the proceedings were delayed. Anna was aware of Erik's coat sleeve brushing her arm. She drew breath in anticipation of speech, then exhaled slowly. She found herself craving conversation with Erik but was too fearful to begin.

'Your dress is very pretty.' Erik's voice was even and he looked straight ahead. 'When I saw you this afternoon, I couldn't quite believe you could manage to look even more lovely than you did when we met at the lake.'

'I seem to recall that I looked somewhat dishevelled by the morning, or perhaps that was merely the way I felt.'

'You were yourself – natural, untroubled, playful.' Erik looked at her and smiled kindly. 'It pains me that you were unable to consider my proposal.'

She was at a loss. A thousand thoughts streamed through her mind. Erik was correct. She hadn't considered his proposal. She had been thoughtless and insensitive. What must he think of her? She wanted to explain, to tell him about Gota, how she feared hurting her sister. If they could begin again, would they? It was too late. She was committed to his brother. Her arms hung loosely by her sides in a posture that would seem, to the impartial spectator, very much like hopelessness.

Anna did not see Erik move, but she felt his large, warm hand seek out her own. He held her fingers gently, then, when she made no gesture of objection, his hand encompassed hers entirely. She looked to him, uncertain, but found only assurance in his gaze. Her heart pounded and an unfamiliar sensation of longing and exhilaration flowed through her entire being. She closed her eyes for an instant. With their hands concealed by the folds of her skirt and the press of people observing the ceremony, they stood, in a state of petrified intimacy until the formalities concluded.

The round of applause broke their clasp and Anna walked hurriedly from the gallery and onto the balcony as spectators jostled to congratulate the winner. Leaning against the wide stone balustrade, Anna stared out at the harbour, beyond the city, struggling to compose herself. Tears filled her eyes. She shut them tight, holding back the flood. She gasped loudly then moved into a more sheltered corner. Why had she compromised herself so? How was she to disentangle herself? Although Erik was often on her mind, it was not until this afternoon, the afternoon of their second meeting, that she truly understood her feelings towards him. Each outing, each meeting with Nils, had strengthened her feelings for a man she had met once. As her friendship with Nils had grown, so had her desire for his brother. What was lacking in her relationship with Nils had merely bolstered her feelings for Erik. Why couldn't she love Nils? Admiration, affection and obligation, she now realised, were barely enough. Nils had held her hand on hundreds of occasions, yet his touch had never excited her as Erik's had. Embarrassed and ashamed, she buried her face in her hands.

'Anna! There you are.' When she looked up, Nils stood before her, holding up a gold medal proudly. 'Why didn't you wait to congratulate me?'

'Everyone wanted to talk to you and it was so hot in there. Congratulations, I'm so proud of you, Nils. I told you there was nothing to worry about.'

'You look a little flushed. Are you feeling well?'

'Of course. It was just crowded in the gallery and we were waiting for so long.' She had to distract him, had to speak calmly, rationally. 'How are you going to spend the prize money?'

'Photographic equipment. I feel as though the time I've devoted to my hobby has been justified. It's borne fruit.' She could hear the excitement in his voice. 'I want to take it further. It could be more than a pastime. This medal proves it.'

He hugged Anna unexpectedly, tightly, like a wrestler. 'The judges said they were extremely impressed by the photograph of the children. That's what I'll do, where I'll take my work. Portraiture! You could be my model. How would you like that?'

'Of course. I'll do anything I can to be of help.' Anna was trying hard to match his enthusiasm.

'This has been a fine afternoon, has it not? You've met my family, who I have it on very good authority all adore you. You've had tea at Stockholm Palace and I've won a gold medal and twenty-five kronor.' He took her hand, drew her closer and spoke softly into her ear. 'But what would make this afternoon perfect, absolutely perfect, would be the opportunity to kiss you.'

Margrit Larsson would say a woman should not allow herself to be kissed until a couple's commitment had been sealed by a proposal of marriage. But Nils did not adhere to convention and Anna, overwhelmed by shame, would do anything possible to purge herself of the guilt that had only minutes before devastated her. She moved closer to him and he placed his arm around her waist. His other hand gently brushed her cheek. When their lips met, it was with a harmony that Anna had not anticipated of her first kiss.

He clutched her more tightly and his tongue skirted the inside of her mouth. This she had not envisaged, but the sensation was so natural, so comfortable that she concealed her surprise. Anna found the experience pleasurable. She allowed her own tongue to enter his mouth and, in doing so, prompted from him a muted groan. He pressed himself tightly against her body, thighs locked against hers. She pushed his coat back and her arms encircled his torso. Her hands explored the length of his back. When they broke off, they hugged for some minutes. He told her that he loved her and she said the same.

'We should go back inside. People will be wondering where we are,' Nils said quietly, although he did not let her go.

Anna nuzzled more tightly against his shoulder and closed her eyes. She had hoped kissing Nils would erase her indiscretion with Erik. It had not, and it was all she could think about. The desire she knew she had aroused in Nils, his pleasure, did nothing to blot out the stain on her conscience. Anna raised her head and saw Erik standing in the doorway to the gallery. He studied the scene for a moment before an air of total despondency drained his handsome face. His hushed retreat into the gallery drew her heart with him.

THIRTEEN

STOCKHOLM, SWEDEN
APRIL 1887

As Andrée hurriedly rose from his desk in his cramped office, he knocked his chair backward. It hit the dark wooden floor with a crack. He moved around the desk and offered his hand.

'I am honoured to meet you, Herr Nobel. I wasn't expecting you.' This was only partly true. As chief engineer at the patent office Andrée was keenly aware there had been some difficulty in renewing Nobel's patent for dynamite.

'Of course you weren't,' the older man said abruptly, ignoring Andrée's outstretched hand. He was speaking more loudly than necessary and Andrée couldn't quite identify his accent – no doubt the result of his colourful life and broad travels.

'I was just passing and thought I would clear up this business personally. There's no point having letters travelling back and forth, back and forth.' Nobel waved his cane wildly to illustrate his point. 'Waste of time.'

'Absolutely. I'll do anything I can to be of assistance.' When Andrée had assumed the position of chief engineer, the thirty-three-year-old had made it a priority to check the validity of all patents. He had discovered that Alfred Nobel's licence had not been renewed every seven years as the law dictated. Andrée wrote to Nobel immediately but after eighteen months correspondence had ground to a halt.

Andrée had known who this man was as soon as he saw the towering figure standing in the doorway. Alfred Nobel had been a hero of his for many years. Chemist, inventor, entrepreneur and fearless risk-taker, Nobel had been a model for Andrée's own life and career. The gentleman removed his fur-trimmed overcoat and hat and thrust them both in Andrée's general direction. He pulled out a chair and sat down, thumping his cane on the floor heavily between his lanky legs. He nodded his head once, sharply. It was an indication that Andrée should take a seat as well.

'I was granted the patent for dynamite in 1867, Herr Andrée, and not once in two decades have I been asked to renew the licence.' Nobel spoke firmly but not rudely.

Andrée would have liked to point out to Nobel that his own lawyers were not assuming any responsibility for the error and were now ignoring his requests to have the matter rectified. Instead he said, 'That was an oversight on the part of my predecessors and this office and I offer my sincere apologies, Herr Nobel. However, the law states that patents must be renewed every seven years or they expire.'

Nobel leant forward on his cane and peered at Andrée. 'Correct me if I don't understand you fully, but are you saying that in the last thirteen years anyone, off the street, could have applied and been granted the patent for dynamite?'

'Yes, that's exactly the case.'

'You are remarkably calm, Herr Andrée. This could have ended very badly, very badly indeed.'

'I'm aware of the possible consequences,' Andrée said. 'But that has not happened and the next step is to correct the error immediately. I'll have my secretary bring us the correct paperwork and some tea.' Andrée had cleared up many such oversights in his two years with the patent office. He despised loose ends and slapdash work.

He left the office briefly. When he returned, holding a tea tray, the paperwork was under one arm. 'Here we are. Shall we get started on these forms?'

Andrée poured the tea, sat down and began asking Nobel a series of questions, writing furiously as Nobel dictated his answers. When he was finished, Andrée looked over each page.

'We're done. I need your signature on each page, sir, and then you're free to leave, patent renewed.'

'Thank you, Herr Andrée. You've been most efficient. I only wish your forerunners had been as competent.'

Andrée smiled. All animosity that had remained in the office vanished and Andrée scrutinised Nobel as he read and signed each page. The chief engineer was devoted to his career and had forgone all social relationships, including women, in his pursuit of excellence. But at no time did he view this abstinence as a sacrifice. Andrée was aware his co-workers thought him aloof and unfriendly, even odd. But since he was a child, he'd been focused on one goal – greatness. What could he learn from this man sitting on the opposite side of the desk? There was an opportunity here that Andrée would not allow to escape. 'If you have time, sir, there's another matter I should like to discuss with you.'

'Yes, proceed.'

'I founded an organisation last year, an association of inventors. Swedish inventors. I hope to raise the profile of such people in this country, provide a forum where they can have their questions answered regarding patents and so forth, and debate new ideas and concepts with one another. I was hoping you might lend your name to such a cause. Your endorsement would definitely aid our growth.'

'How interesting.'

Thus began a meeting of minds that lasted more than three hours. The men held different opinions on almost every topic – science, technology, religion and politics – but by the end of the marathon Nobel had agreed to speak at the next meeting of the Society of Swedish Inventors, being held the following month.

A buoyant Andrée escorted Nobel out to the street and his waiting carriage. They shook hands heartily before bidding each other farewell.

FOURTEEN

STOCKHOLM, SWEDEN
AUGUST 1895

ANNA SAT on a granite bench in the pretty courtyard that led from the Strindbergs' kitchen. The cool from the granite penetrated her skirt to the backs of her thighs. She found it a welcome relief after the stifling atmosphere of the Strindberg sitting room. The late summer sun was setting in the clear sky and igniting the white stone of the courtyard into a brilliant flame. She shut her eyes against its glare.

Anna was finding it hard to hold back her tears. Nils had proposed marriage in June, on midsummer eve, without mentioning the expedition. She had accepted his proposal blindly. Now he was going off and leaving her.

Anna heard the door open and close and a hand caressed her neck from behind. She thought it unusual for Nils to be so affectionate, comforting. But enjoying the sensation, she kept her eyes closed and dropped her head forward. Warm breath at the nape of her neck made her shiver and he began rubbing her shoulders. Anna thought the soft pressure wonderful. She gave an audible sigh. Placing her hands on his, she let them rest there a moment then slowly pulled the strong hands down, over her shoulders, and threw her head back. They kissed.

Alarmed, Anna jumped to her feet. 'Erik! What do you think you're doing?'

'Do you expect me to believe you didn't know who it was? Are my brother and I so similar?'

'Of course I thought it was Nils. Do you think I would have knowingly let you touch me, kiss me? If anyone had seen us . . .' Anna was furious.

'I saw you were upset when you left the room. I only wanted to comfort you.'

'Of course I was upset. Everybody in that room was upset.' Her voice was louder than it should have been in the confined courtyard. But the truth was that she had needed to be comforted at that moment and Erik was the only person in the house to recognise it. 'What did you think I was going to do?' she asked more calmly. 'Abandon Nils and run off with you? Even if I wanted to, I couldn't do that to Nils.' Anna had never spoken with this degree of candour to anyone. 'I can't believe he proposed marriage when he intended all along to leave me – and so soon!'

'Nils has never really thought about the consequences of his actions,' Erik said. 'He gets engrossed, obsessed with an idea or scheme . . . He doesn't consider the effects on others.'

'Why are you defending him?'

'He's my brother. I can't help that he's an idiot as well.' They offered each other a half-hearted smile. 'Proposing when he did was wrong if he intended to join the expedition. But it was probably something he did impulsively, caught up in the romance of midsummer . . .You shouldn't doubt his intentions.'

There was a long pause as Erik looked down at his hands.

'Why did you accept his proposal?' he asked.

Although Anna had spent midsummer eve with Nils, she had been thinking of Erik. He had left Stockholm to travel in France for the summer. She felt his absence everywhere. While he was gone, she would often close her eyes and recall the afternoon of the photographic exhibition and strive to conjure the thrill of his presence. No matter how she scolded herself, she was powerless to resist this temptation.

Many times recently she had felt like an outsider watching her life from afar. Many times she had considered the actions of this person confounding and absurd.

'It seemed the only thing I could do.'

'Do you love Nils?'

'In a way.' Anna placed her hand lightly on his. She hoped he would understand the meaning of this small gesture.

'Marry me, Anna. Marry me and come to America?' Erik spoke softly but his voice was eager. 'I love you, Anna. I have since I first saw you. And even though you've never said the words, I believe you love me . . . are in love with me.'

It took a few moments for Anna to compose her response. She had no desire to injure either Erik or Nils. What Erik said was true and the urge to flee to America with him was strong. She loved him with an intensity of feeling both terrifying and exciting. He would devote his life to her happiness. But she had travelled too far with Nils to turn back. Nils was kind, generous, humorous. She was easy and content in his company. While she was angry and hurt that he hadn't allowed her a voice in his decision, to break off their engagement would be to punish him senselessly. And it *would* punish him. Nils was more fragile, seemed less equipped to cope, than his brother.

If she had never met Nils, if Nils had never existed, she wondered what course the past year would have taken. Would she have pursued Erik once she realised her mistake?

Would she have made a happy and lasting marriage with him? Probably. But Nils *had* been born, she had met him at the home of the Larssons and it was merely an awkward twist of fate, an uncomfortable coincidence, that he was Erik's younger brother.

'I am going to wait for Nils. I'm sorry, Erik. I can't deny there's an attraction between us. You're handsome, intelligent and very amusing and I very much enjoy being with you.' She stood and waited a moment, gathering her resolve, finding the strength to leave this man. 'But I can't hurt Nils and I don't think you want to see him hurt either. I do hope we can remain friends. Goodnight.'

As she stepped over the threshold back into the kitchen, a window closed quietly above her head. Preoccupied with her thoughts, she did not hear it. Erik peered up at the second storey of the house, but no lights were visible.

FIFTEEN

STOCKHOLM, SWEDEN
MIDSUMMER EVE, JUNE 1895

Nils clutched Anna tightly around the waist as they danced. They had eaten before sunset, slept, and now, at four in the morning, they held each other closely on the open-air dance floor by the lake. As Nils guided her this way and that, Anna felt weightless. She nestled her head against Nils' neck and could detect the lingering smell of summer strawberries on his breath. The early-morning sun was warming as he kissed the pink flesh of Anna's cheek. She had never been happier.

Midsummer eve was Anna's favourite celebration. The carefree air that pervaded the city was wonderful and, during the dark of winter, it was the distant remembrance of food, family and flowers that acted as a reassuring beacon.

'Did you put your flowers under your pillow, Anna?' Nils whispered in her ear.

'Of course not. What a silly superstition.'

'But what of your future husband? How will you know who it is if he doesn't come to you in your dreams?'

'I think he has come to me already,' Anna replied mischievously and placed her lips lightly on Nils'.

They danced on and on, smiling and laughing. If she did not know otherwise, Anna thought, she would have said she was in heaven. The lake, sunrise, cool breeze and the recollection of strawberries all combined to effect one blissful combination. Anna could not imagine herself happier.

Suddenly the band stopped. The musicians scrambled to collect their instruments and place them back in their cases. Others did not bother. They rushed from the bandstand, instrument in one flailing hand, case in the other. Anna looked to Nils in confusion, but he just closed his eyes and held her even tighter.

With her face pressed firmly to her partner's shoulder, Anna scanned the other people on the dance floor. She saw panic in their eyes and became suddenly conscious of water at her feet. Women hitched up their skirts and ran to higher ground, others were hoisted into the arms of their partners and carried to dry land, but Anna and Nils were rooted to the timbers of the dance floor. She tried to break free from her partner's grasp, but he was unaware to the commotion and the rising water. He merely grinned again and nuzzled his face into her hair. Soon the pontoon broke away from the shore and floated haltingly toward to middle of the lake.

From the bank a crowd of people shouted to them to jump and swim to shore. Anna pushed Nils away but found she was unable to detach her feet from the wooden platform. She bent over, trying to free her feet from her shoes, but the pontoon rocked and she fell. Nils helped her and held her close. He whispered in her ear reassurances they would be safe. As the water reached their thighs, they clasped each other closely. Deaf to the screams of onlookers, Anna relented and slowly passed under the water, locked in Nils' arms.

The sun, penetrating the water, lit up Nils' face as they sank, casting on it a holy radiance. Anna's chest was becoming tighter but, staring into Nils' serene blue eyes, fear seemed to elude her. Wrapped in her lover's strong arms she placed her head on his shoulder and closed her eyes.

Anna woke. She looked around the dark bedroom, trying to gauge her whereabouts. She touched her chest and forehead. She was sweating and her long hair was pasted to her face. Wiping it away, she turned her head to see her husband Gil sleeping peacefully beside her. Beyond him on the bedside table she could just make out the time on the alarm clock. It was a quarter past three.

Anna threw back the bedclothes and walked quickly to the open window. Drinking deeply of the cool night air, she gradually calmed and relaxed her tense body.

Sitting on the window seat, closeted by the heavy curtains, Anna shivered slightly. She should change out of her saturated nightdress before she caught a chill, she thought. But the effort would be too great. Since learning of the discovery on Kvitøya, she had been a shambles. The recurring nightmares were only a part of it. Perhaps, she thought, she had not been functioning for the last thirty years. The ever-present desire to escape had become almost overwhelming.

'Hey, my sweet,' Gil said, swatting aside the heavy fabric of the curtains. He sat beside her on the window seat, 'Can you not sleep?'

'I had a bad dream.'

'Can I get you something? A glass of water?' He touched her face tenderly and then, more anxiously, her arm.

'You're chilled to the bone. Come on, let's get you your dressing gown.' Dressed in only pyjama trousers and a singlet, Gil walked swiftly across the room and retrieved both their robes from the back of the door. He was a large, ungainly man who moved slowly and with purpose. Gil's careful, deliberate movements always managed to relieve her, set her at ease.

He placed the robe across her shoulders and snuggled her tightly in his arms. Although her body was warming quickly, her face still stung with cold. The sensation reminded her of the bitter cold of Sweden. She sighed.

Anna could feel Gil's body sag, his head heavy on her shoulder. He was falling asleep, she knew. His shift at the hotel ended at midnight and she didn't feel him crawl into bed until half past. Wrapped in his bulky arms, feeling the heat he generated and his warm breath on her cheek, Anna closed her eyes tightly, relishing the moment.

Stubbendorff lay in his small bed staring at the crack that ran the length of the ceiling. He lit another cigarette and wondered what time it was. How long had he been lying there awake, thinking of the drama in which he had become embroiled?

After his visit with Tore Strindberg he had felt both heartened and disappointed. His brief glimpse into the artist's world had invigorated and inspired him - but he was no closer to locating Anna Charlier. He wondered if she knew that the camp on Kvitøya had been found. The discovery had made worldwide news. She would have to be a hermit not to know, he thought.

He rolled onto his side and saw the pages from Strindberg's diary on the floor at his bedside. He had now scoured each entry so many times he was able to visualise and recall each page and its contents. That small book, that watermarked, brittle piece of history, was the cause of his sleeplessness. The three men had died on Kvitøya, but the story was not finished. It would not be over till Anna Charlier held the diary in her hands., read the letters that Stubbendorff knew by heart. He could not rest until he had given it to her.

He went over what he knew. Anna was still living in Stockholm when Nils had departed. As far as Stubbendorff could tell, there had been no ill feeling between them. In fact, Nils had written joyously of their upcoming nuptials and their future together. She seemed part of the family, entrenched in their lives. It is strange then, he thought, that she simply disappeared as Tore had told him. One would have imagined she might have found solace within the family.

There were few leads Stubbendorff could follow. He had already spoken with Tore, the Nils wrote most lovingly of in his diaries, who had no clue as to Anna's whereabouts. Although his final comments about Anna had been intriguing. How had he lashed out all those years ago? Erik Strindberg had moved to America immediately following the expedition's departure and Nils' father had died many years ago. Next Stubbendorff would try Sven Strindberg and his mother, and, of course, Anna's sister, Gota, if she could be found. He stubbed out his cigarette, repositioned the pillow beneath his head and began to read.

SIXTEEN

STOCKHOLM, SWEDEN
APRIL 1895

'Do you remember me, Herr Andrée?' Alfred Nobel stood in the same doorway that he had eight years previously. He had aged, there was no doubt about that. His hair and beard were whiter, he relied more heavily on his cane, and time had etched the lines on his face deeper. But the voice was identical and it echoed in the untidy office.

'Of course, Herr Nobel. How good it is to see you again.' Andrée grabbed the man's hand and shook it vigorously. Nobel, in return, clasped Andrée firmly by the arm. 'I am certain your patents have been renewed. I saw to them personally.'

Nobel stepped into the room and looked about. The desk was bare, mounds of files littered the floor and boxes had been stacked neatly in the corners of the space.

'My visit is not due to expired patents, my friend. But it seems that I am fortunate to have caught you. Are you leaving your position?'

'Yes, this is my last week. I'm leaving on quite a long journey next year and I need to make preparations.'

'Don't be modest, Herr Andrée – may I call you Salomon?' Nobel laughed. 'I've read about your scheme in the newspaper. In fact I've followed your career rather closely since our last meeting.'

'I'm honoured.'

'I was in America in February during your lecture to the Academy of Sciences and I was sorry I couldn't attend. Thank you for the invitation.' Andrée nodded as Nobel carefully took a seat. 'But I was sent a transcript. Your speech was excellent, most persuasive.'

'Once again, I'm honoured that you think so.' Andrée was genuinely pleased. He thought about his meeting with Alfred Nobel often, and Nobel's subsequent appearance and speech at the Society of Swedish Inventors. It had been reported in the *Aftonbladet*. His attendance had caused membership to swell. Andrée felt deeply indebted. But he had assumed a man of Nobel's calibre would not have given an employee at the patent office another thought.

'May I speak frankly?' Nobel asked, and Andrée nodded assent. 'I've been advised to get my affairs in order – ominous words. My doctors seem to be of the opinion I may not be long for this world.' Nobel stood and moved to the window, carefully avoiding the documents strewn on the floor.

'I have no children, Salomon. My brothers and nephews will inherit my company. But I would like to help you.' Nobel gestured towards the other chair.

Andrée took a seat.

'I view myself as a citizen of the world. I've lived in many countries and I've visited even more. Travel has made me wiser and richer in numerous ways. My dear friend Victor Hugo once called me Europe's wealthiest vagabond, but it seems in my old age I'm becoming sentimental. I would like to offer Sweden a gift in return for all it has given me.'

Andrée was dumbstruck, guessing what Nobel was about to propose.

'Your expedition has merit and I believe you have merit also. Embarking for the North Pole in a balloon – some would call it ludicrous. I would call it courageous and pioneering. No man has managed the feat by any other form of transport. I'd like to back you, fund your flight.'

While Andrée had calculated the cost of the expedition, he had not given the fundraising a great deal of thought. He assumed industrialists, royalty, people of note would share his confidence in its success. 'I'm very grateful. But there are worthier causes in which you could invest. I have no doubt I'll be able to raise the funds.'

'Don't be naive, Salomon, and don't expect donors to flock to your support. The wealthiest people are the least generous with their money. I know this to be true as I'm one of them. My advice to you is to beg, borrow and steal anything that you can. I'm guilty of all three.'

Nobel produced an envelope from the inside pocket of his coat. It was a bank note for twenty thousand kronor, more than thirty times Andrée's annual salary.

Andrée shook Nobel's gaunt hand. 'I'm certain your investment will be rewarded,' he said.

By the end of the following week, a week that Andrée dedicated to meeting with financiers and company leaders seeking donations, he was less certain of his ability to raise funds and confounded by the frequently voiced opinion that his expedition was doomed to failure.

Andrée penned a further note of thanks to Nobel, at the close of which he mentioned – quite purposely, Nobel's secretary thought that fundraising was moving unexpectedly slowly. Within three days another bank note had arrived, the sum of which was sixty-five thousand kronor – half the estimated cost of the expedition.

Stubbendorff drifted in and out of sleep until the sunlight put paid to his efforts. Once the aroma of coffee floated up through the floorboards from the cafe below, he pushed the covers back and got out of bed. He washed, dressed and was glad when he was out of the door of his apartment. The most valuable item he currently owned was safely in his satchel. He bounded down the stairs to the street. Even following his restless slumber, he was filled with the energy of possibility. He had three leads and he was determined to follow them all as far as possible.

'Good morning, Knut. This is most unusual. I never saw you so bright and early when you were employed. Where are you off to?' The other patrons laughed at Ivar Skarsgård's jibe as he passed a cup of coffee across the bar to his tenant.

'Nowhere in particular.' Stubbendorff was used to his landlord's banter.

'You certainly aren't dressed for a job interview. Should I be worried about the rent?'

'Not at all.' Stubbendorff drank his coffee quickly, then, along with payment for the beverage, slid a further ten kronor across the counter.

'That's a generous tip. Who's died?'

'I've come into a little cash. That should take care of my lodgings for the next three months. You need not worry about my fortunes, Ivar.'

'But I do worry, Knut. These can only be ill-gotten gains. A horse race? A dog fight? Will the police be pounding down my door?' Skarsgård roared with laughter for the sake of his audience. His customers immediately joined him.

'You think so little of me. It was a bonus from my employer. A show of his appreciation for my efforts at the newspaper.' There was mischief in Stubbendorff's tone.

'Ha. Now I know that's not true. You're the laziest bastard I've ever known.'

'I've turned over a new leaf, Ivar. I'm a changed man.'

'How so?'

On his way towards the exit Stubbendorff stopped and turned. 'I don't exactly know yet,' he said. It was the first time he had ever managed to render the little toad behind the bar speechless.

'I cannot help you, Stubbendorff.'

'The information I need is not for the newspaper. You don't need to worry. This is a personal matter.'

'No, absolutely not.' The young man from the civil registry stood up from his desk and took Stubbendorff's forearm firmly. 'You must go. If Frost sees you here, I'll lose my job.' He led Stubbendorff to the door.

'Be reasonable, Markus. Two names, that's all. I give you my word I won't bother you with anything else ever again.' Stubbendorff placed his hands together in a position of prayer and summoned his most winning smile.

'Do I need to remind you, Stubbendorff, that you nearly cost me my job and my reputation? You quoted me off the record. You gave me your word then and it meant nothing. Frost was livid. I was on probation for three months. And I was to be married. For three months I lived in fear of being fired.'

'Markus, you may be employed by the Church of Sweden, but I know you're not a monk.'

'What are you talking about?' the young man said guardedly.

'Do I really need to remind you, Palmgren, of the evening of the sixteenth of July, 1929? Who kept that particular incident out of the *Aftonbladet*? It wasn't Frost. But I'm certain I'd be able to track down . . .' Stubbendorff closed his eyes, pretending to scan his memory for a name he had forgotten. 'Fröken Maria Olander. I believe she'll be quite easy to find if I drop by her usual haunts. She was very pretty, I seem to recall. How much was it again that she stole from you while you were still sleeping? Seventy-five kronor? Money that you won on a horse race? Fröken Olander has probably spent it by now, but I'm certain she'd be happy to explain her side of the story to Frost. I'm not sure how the church would react to such a scandal. They'd probably want to keep it quiet; fire you, of course. Or perhaps they'd prefer to make a public example of you. That's more in the church's style, isn't it?' Stubbendorff then added a final nail. 'Did you just mention you were recently married?'

Markus Palmgren was unable to speak. He was too busy weighing up whether the anger of his wife, his boss or his god was more severe.

Stubbendorff smiled at him, genial now. 'Why don't we call it even? I've left the newspaper. Look into these two names and you'll never see my face again.'

'Who? What names?'

'Anna and Gota Charlier. That's all I have.' Stubbendorff handed Palmgren a piece of paper on which he'd scrawled the women's names.

Palmgren nodded, slid the note into his trouser pocket and returned to his desk.

That afternoon Skarsgård called to Stubbendorff from the foot of the stairs. 'Knut, I'm glad I caught you. I have a letter for you.' He waited as the writer descended.

'The fellow who dropped it off, he looked very nervous. Didn't even stay for a drink. Is he an informant? Something shady going on?'

Stubbendorff rolled his eyes. The writer's casual reticence irritated Skarsgård. He threw the envelope across the counter. It landed on the floor.

'A sandwich, please, and a cup of coffee,' Stubbendorff said, offhand, before picking up his letter and retreating to a seat by the window.

Written in heavy upper-case letters on the envelope were the words *KNUT STUBBENDORFF: CONFIDENTIAL*. Fool, Stubbendorff thought. No wonder Skarsgård's curiosity had been piqued. He opened the envelope and scanned the contents of the letter.

Gota Elin Gustava Charlier (born 3 March 1869), married William Neve on 13 October 1913

William deceased (18 November 1924) Neve's occupation – butcher

No children on record from the marriage

Gota Neve née Charlier, last address Munkbroleden 32 Occupation – seamstress

Anna Albertina Constancia Charlier (born 25 July 1871) Occupation – governess

Last address – Stensbastugränd 21

Skarsgård set the sandwich and coffee on the table. Stubbendorff folded the paper and slid it back into the envelope.

Aftonbladet, Stockholm, Sweden 3 May 1896

ANDRÉE'S DARING VOYAGE

The Andrée balloon expedition is now assured up to the point of departure. The kindness and scientific spirit of King Oscar II, added to assistance given from other quarters, have enabled the leaders of the expedition to purchase a balloon and the equipment they require.

It is a distance greater than one thousand kilometres from the point of departure to the North Pole. Andrée expects to cover the distance rapidly, if he can fly his ship into a current of air which moves directly north. Meteorologists regard his faith in the phenomenon as foolhardy, but having lived in that cold region for some time, his belief may be warranted. Propelled by the wind, Andrée is confident the pole and its surrounds will be reached in a startlingly short time. In forty hours, in fact, they hope to attain their objective and land for observations. After this they will set out for civilisation, but at a more leisurely rate. Finally in fifteen days at the least and two months at the most, Andrée, Strindberg and Ekholm will descend to British North America with the balloon in excellent condition and the party safe and sound.

SEVENTEEN

STOCKHOLM, SWEDEN
MAY 1895

THE KING WAS SEATED behind his monument of a desk when Commander Ehrensvärd of the Royal Navy entered his privy chamber. Ehrensvärd stood opposite the monarch for some time before Oscar raised his head and slid the document he had been examining pointedly across the desk. Oscar leant back in his chair and stroked his grey beard slowly as Ehrensvärd quickly ran his eyes over the paper. He had read the same page thoroughly only the day before.

'Sit.' The King gestured towards a chair. 'What's your opinion?'

'Andrée is extremely persuasive, extremely persuasive in his arguments.'

'Did he persuade you?' The King eyed his adviser critically.

'No. I would advise against offering any support to Andrée, financial or political. His plan strikes me as . . .' Ehrensvärd thought for a few moments. 'Ill-conceived.'

'Really? That's interesting. I found his plans, as outlined in his lecture, comprehensive.' At sixty-seven Oscar II was still as politically astute as he had been when he took the throne almost a quarter of a century before. Commander Ehrensvärd had been in similar scenarios before with the King. He knew Oscar would exhaust every avenue of argument before making a decision.

'Comprehensive, yes – blindingly so. But highly unrealistic. He's a dreamer, sir. He has some experience with balloons, nine ascents in his air ship, the *Svea*, but very little with the Arctic wilderness. He is a patent officer, Your Majesty.'

'That's true,' Oscar said. He rose from his chair and walked slowly to the window. 'But as he said, men have been attempting to conquer the pole for generations, all using the same methods – ships and sledges. These have failed. An air balloon might just be the answer.'

Ehrensvärd stood and turned to the King. 'With all due respect, Your Majesty, I fear he's dazzled you with the detail. Travelling to the North Pole in an untested aircraft carrying the amount of equipment he listed . . . sledges, photographic equipment, berths for three men, provisions for four months, a boat, a tent, arms and ammunition—'

'Ehrensvärd,' the King interrupted, 'I believe your position as commander of the Royal Navy may prejudice you against aircraft and their capabilities.'

'I hope not, Your Excellency,' Ehrensvärd replied. 'I take my role as King's Adviser very seriously. My advice is derived from looking at a matter factually. I fear Andrée's lecture aimed to tug at the patriotic heartstrings of the audience.'

'But the standing ovations, one from the Academy and a second from the Anthropological and Geographical Society.

These are learned men, Ehrensvärd – are you suggesting he hoodwinked them all?'

Ehrensvärd laughed politely. 'Of course not, Your Majesty. I believe they may have been carried away in the moment. To be first to reach the pole – this is an achievement Swedes have been striving towards for decades. I admit that to be victorious in this race would be truly glorious. It's the stuff that can unite a nation for generations. However, a failure – a gigantic failure of the type I predict – would make Sweden a laughing stock. To throw your wholehearted support behind such an expedition could be disastrous.'

'The problem is, Ehrensvärd, I'm a gambling man and even though the odds are stacked against him . . .' His voice trailed off. 'But six days! Six days, from Spitsbergen to the pole. They would be home in a month. My god, Nansen is out there now and has been for a year. There's no time to lose. If Andrée embarks immediately, we might still be in with a chance. Nobel has given him eighty-five thousand kronor.'

'So I've heard. But if you'll forgive my callousness, Nobel is dying. He can afford to be reckless. I've sailed to the region, seen the ice and the conditions. It cannot be done, sir.' Ehrensvärd looked at his sovereign squarely. 'I guarantee, it cannot be done.'

The King nodded and returned to his desk. 'Giving him nothing would be an unspoken refusal of my support. If the expedition does succeed . . .'

Ehrensvärd finished his ruler's thought. 'It would damage your reputation. I agree. Andrée would speak out in the press and you would be the nay-sayer who failed to back the great Swedish undertaking. My solution is this – a token. Donate a token amount to Andrée's expedition and publicly announce your faith in the endeavour, in moderate terms. Then, whether he succeeds or fails, your reputation will remain untainted.'

'Hedge our bets, in other words.'

'Exactly. Thirty thousand kronor. The amount is large enough not to be considered meagre, but it is not excessive.'

'It seems like the safest route to take.' Oscar sat down. 'That will be all. Thank you for your time.' Ehrensvärd turned but was halted by a final enquiry from the King. 'You believe strongly that there is no chance the expedition might succeed?'

'Unfortunately, yes. I feel for the men who are to accompany Andrée on this mission, whoever they might be.' He bowed curtly before leaving the chamber.

June 5, 1896

    Lilla Nygatan, Stockholm

    Dearest Anna,

    Best wishes on your birthday, my beloved. I know you will be presently in Mölna. Mama told me of her plans before I departed. I am tortured by the thought of missing the festivities and my heart cries out in protest, but I am certain Mama, Papa and the boys will do everything in their power to make your twenty-fifth birthday memorable. Rest assured, darling Anna, you are all that I think about.

    Your next birthday and the next and every one after we shall spend together. I have vowed never to be absent for another. Hopefully, by the time Erik gives you this letter, we will have reached our destination and landed heroes in the wilds of Canada or Alaska or Siberia. Andrée has hopes to land in San Francisco! With good fortune on our side we might even be returning home. Just think of that!

Have a marvellous day with the family in the sunshine. I can taste the strawberry cake as I write this message.

My comrades and I shall give you a fourfold hurrah in honour of your birthday.

All my love, Nils

EIGHTEEN

MÖLNA, LIDINGÖ, SWEDEN
25 JULY 1896

'IT IS BLISTERING. Don't you agree, Herr Strindberg?' Gota twirled her parasol coyly, a sparrow attempting to gain the attention of a crane. Anna wished her sister would cease this pantomime.

'It is indeed,' Sven replied, finishing his glass of lemonade quickly. 'And unfortunately my brother is waiting for me on the court. Please excuse me, Fröken.'

He turned to Anna and clasped her hand in both of his own. 'I'm extremely pleased that we're all here together. It's just the sort of weekend Nils would love. We shall talk more after my game. I don't think I'll be very long. I'm playing Erik.'

Gota responded with a brief curtsey before Sven ran to the court.

'He's charming, charming. A little thin, perhaps, but that can be taken care of. Lovely black hair, and those blue eyes . . '

'Sven plays the field quite a lot, Gota. He's a wonderful fellow, but I'd advise against setting your sights on him. I have the impression he's not interested in settling down.'

'Oh, Anna. You're always so cautious. Every man wishes to settle down with the right woman.' Gota walked closer to the court, as if the force of her spinning parasol was propelling her into a cheerful trot.

Anna poured herself a glass of lemonade and watched the match from the refreshment marquee. Erik was an excellent player and the power behind his strokes made him rather formidable on the tennis court. She knew that Nils had never bettered him. But Sven's flexibility and long limbs made him a worthy opponent for his brother. No matter where on the court Erik forced the ball, Sven seemed able to reach it and then return it with accuracy across the net. Sven was a sight to see running, in full flight, legs stretched, arm extended, racquet seeking out the ball. With Tore acting as umpire and ball boy and unofficial commentator, heckling both siblings joyously, the match was an entertaining distraction for Anna on her birthday.

In Nils' absence Rosalie had insisted on organising the celebrations. A weekend tennis party and picnic were planned and Rosalie had rented a house for the family in Mölna on Lidingö. It was the same cottage the family had vacationed in since Erik and Nils were children. Anna's petitions to cancel the celebrations failed in the face of Rosalie's immense enthusiasm. But when the party had arrived the day before, Anna was comforted to find the house was small and modest.

It was a little wooden cottage with a wide balcony, painted in the palest shade of blue Anna had ever seen. The rooms were light and the beds ample. No staff were on hand and Rosalie herself was handling all domestic matters during their stay, including the cooking. This revelation provoked

howls of laughter from her sons and husband. Rosalie apologised to Anna because she had to share a bedroom with her
sister. Anna politely explained that she had spent every night
in the same room as Gota since her birth.

That morning Rosalie had made a great fuss of her at
breakfast. Champagne was opened and gifts presented. Sven
had crafted a small birch-wood box. Carved into its lid were
three daisies and, in the bottom right corner, her initials. The
sheet music to Debussy's 'Valse romantique' was presented to
her by Oscar and Rosalie. Rosalie placed another gift in front
of her as well, a generous length of navy-blue linen. Gota
gushed over its superior quality.

Following his initial offering of good wishes Erik was
reticent during breakfast, tearing his bread, spreading it with
marmalade, cutting his cheese and sipping his coffee with
slow and deliberate movements. He did not look at Anna
even once.

When breakfast was done, the group dispersed to prepare
for a morning of tennis. Anna was last to leave the conserva-
tory. As she was stacking her gifts into a manageable pile,
Erik returned to the sunlit room. He stood in the doorway,
hands in pockets.

'I have something else for you.'

'You shouldn't have gone to any trouble.' When Erik had
failed to produce a gift earlier, Anna had tried to suppress
her disappointment. All of a sudden she felt quite elated.

'What I have is not from me. Nils wrote you this before
he left.' Erik removed a letter from his trouser pocket. 'He
asked me to give it to you on your birthday. I wanted to wait
until everyone had gone. Tore and Mama would have wanted
to read it or at least be informed of its contents. I believe
that's why my brother asked me to deliver it. I shall leave you
alone.'

He handed her the envelope and left the room. Anna

returned to her seat and placed the letter on the table in front of her, too frightened to read its contents. She had been caught in a deception. Nils was in this very room watching her, judging her actions, reading her thoughts. She found herself drawn to Erik in the most confounding way. In truth, Anna thought, part of her fascination with Erik was that the attraction could not be explained. The appalling fact was that she thought about him constantly, replaying endlessly his every action and word in her mind. The night before, knowing he was sleeping in the adjacent room, she had lightly touched her palm to the wall, hoping to sense his presence. Anna drained her coffee cup. The dregs were cold and bitter.

The contents of Nils' letter made her reflect, harshly, on her behaviour here in Mölna, and she resolved to act more solemnly in the absence of her fiancé. Nils' sweet words and his thoughts of the future shamed her. This, she knew, was not his intention. His letter was entirely guileless. He remained blithely ignorant of her feelings. Now, watching the antics on the tennis court, Anna allowed herself to relax a little. The heat of the mid-morning sun combined with the frivolity of her companions soon cheered her. The match eventually became a sort of farce, with both Erik and Sven too exhausted from laughter and heat to play on. They each declared themselves the winner. When they shook hands at the net, they locked arms and hugged, then proceeded to attack Tore with as many balls as were at hand. The three brothers were soon standing by Anna, guzzling large amounts of cold lemonade.

'Mother can't even make lemonade well,' Tore said loudly.

'What are you talking about?' Sven replied, distorting his face into a comical grimace. 'I like my lemonade tart.'

'You wouldn't say that if your mother was here, and not in town buying tonight's supper,' Anna interjected.

'Oh no. Another opportunity to be poisoned! And at your birthday dinner, Anna. I lay blame at your pretty feet,' Sven said.

The three of them laughed and then Tore challenged Sven to a game. Gota, who was just making her way over to the group, swiftly performed a showy about-face and returned to her seat in the shade by the court.

Erik placed his empty glass on the table and cleared his throat. 'Are you enjoying your birthday?' He spoke again before Anna could answer. 'It's been fantastically good weather . . . This has been our holiday spot since we were children. Nils and I found that the best place for fishing is in that inlet over there.' He pointed over beyond the trees. 'But that's not so good for swimming. Too shallow. We usually just go to the beach to swim. The water is lovely and warm this time of year. We should do that tomorrow – all of us, of course.' He stopped abruptly and poured himself another glass of lemonade.

'I'm most appreciative to you all. I wouldn't have done anything like this if it weren't for your family.'

'I have a gift for you as well,' Erik said.

Anna's breath quickened in surprise and anticipation. Her eyes glimmered at the prospect.

'It wasn't the right time at breakfast, and there was Nils' letter . . .'

'Of course, I understand.'

'In hindsight it's a rather stupid gift. I shouldn't have chosen something so personal. But when I saw it, it reminded me of you, and I must have been feeling daring at the time . . . I'm not feeling as courageous now that it's time to give it to you.'

'I'm intrigued. But if you're uncomfortable, please don't feel obligated. I'm certain there are other more suitable young ladies you could surprise with a mysterious gift.' Anna smiled at him.

'There are no other young ladies, Anna. Don't tease me.' She was immediately ashamed of her foolish flirting. It was out of character, more like Gota than herself.

Erik took her hand and led her up the lawn to the house at a swift pace. When they reached the balcony, he asked her to wait outside while he went inside to retrieve the parcel. Anna leant against the balcony railing. The air was thick with summer but a relieving sea breeze was picking up from the south. She hoped for an afternoon rain shower, but when she looked into the sky all she saw was blue.

When Erik returned, his hands were behind his back. 'Close your eyes and put out your hands,' he instructed. She complied.

'Happy birthday, my beautiful girl. Open your eyes.' She did so.

A small square package wrapped in lavender rice paper was perched in her palms. Erik was grinning like a child.

'Open it.'

'It's such lovely paper. I daren't tear it.'

She carefully untied the string and handed the paper to Erik. It was a small black box. Anna opened the lid and its tiny hinges gave a pleasing squeak. She stared in amazement at its contents. A silver heart, about the size of a fifty öre coin, lay brilliantly against the velvet interior.

'Do you like it? Here, let me put it on for you.' Erik eagerly removed the pendant from the box and fixed it around her neck. The heart lay flat against her chest, resting slightly below her collarbone. The metal was cool on her warm skin.

'It's heavy.'

He smiled, contented.

'It's beautiful, so beautiful. I'm speechless, Erik.'

She began to cry. Erik put his arm around her and led her to a bench around the corner of the balcony. As he rummaged in his pockets for a handkerchief, Anna gulped air, trying to stop the sobbing. She was torn, utterly torn, and she could see no way forward.

'Here, here.' Erik wiped her face. 'If I'd known my birthday gift was going to have this effect, I'd probably have thought twice. What's troubling you?'

'What a mess,' Anna said. 'What are we to do, Erik? For an instant I'd forgotten Nils. It was just you and me, here, together. But that can never be. Nils will always be between us. I've promised myself to him, and you're his brother. Can't you see it's hopeless?'

Erik took her face in his hands and kissed her gently on the lips. 'Stop crying, my love,' he said, and wiped her face again. It was their first kiss.

Anna's eyes were raw with emotion and an unspeakable wave of relief coursed through her body. Without recognising the signs, this had been what Anna had been waiting for the last two years. She rested her head on Erik's shoulder as he wrapped his arms around her. They both looked out to the garden beyond. After a few minutes, when he was confident she had settled, he spoke.

'I don't know what's to become of us or this situation, Anna. But we need to be honest and you need to make a decision.' His tone was reasonable but firm.

'I thought I had made a decision.'

'Perhaps not the correct one.'

They sat together, still and quiet. The sun made Anna's eyes sting. She closed them and relaxed, exhausted, into Erik's arms. She could hear the steady beat of his heart, then further away the agreeable drone of worker bees and the buzz of flies. Anna could hear the high-pitched chirp of wagtails and the rustle of dead leaves as the birds searched for bugs and worms beneath the shrubs that bordered the balcony. In the distance she could just make out the irksome cry of a lone gull and the lively hoots and laughter of Tore and Sven, carried by the breeze up the hill from the tennis court.

Anna looked into Erik's face. She reached upwards and kissed him on the mouth. Her gesture took him by surprise, but it was not impulsive. He tasted of salt, sugar and lemons. She licked her lips when she pulled away and nestled back into the crook of his arm. He drew her more firmly to him as Anna absently fingered the ornament on her chest. Occasionally his hand would stroke her arm, or his fingertips would explore the flesh around her ear or her hair or her neck. He kissed her softly on the forehead. Each gesture was unexpected and pleasurable. She pressed her face tightly into his chest and felt his chin resting in her hair.

'Anna, are you here?' Sven and Tore could still be heard in the distance, but Gota's voice was coming from the balcony. Erik and Anna immediately broke apart and stood. Gota rounded the corner.

'Ah, excuse me for interrupting,' Gota trilled without missing a beat. 'You two disappeared without a trace. I thought I'd come and hunt you out, make sure you were safe and sound. But you seem to be taking care of yourselves quite well.'

Erik stood frozen, his chest heaving. Anna's lips were plump and red, her neck flushed.

'That's a lovely pendant you've got there, Anna.' Gota advanced for a better look. 'From Herr Strindberg here, I presume.'

Anna nodded.

'What a thoughtful birthday gift. You're such a lucky girl.' Gota's eyes darted quickly from her sister to Erik.

Anna's eyes did not leave her sister but, beside her, she

saw Erik's posture relax. He cleared his throat and took a step forward. Before he could say anything, Gota spoke.

'Oh well, I must get back to the others. Sven and Tore are having such a wonderful time. You should come and join us when you're able.'

With that, she casually left. They could hear her humming blithely as she made her way towards the tennis court.

Erik took Anna's hand, but she pulled away and moved to the railing. 'This has to end. No more. I can't bear it.'

'Come with me to America,' Erik said. 'The family will understand – if not immediately, then eventually, and Nils will recover . . . You don't know him like I do, Anna. He's resilient, and if he knew—'

'No. I'm engaged to marry your brother. How can you speak so callously? His letter this morning . . . it would crush him. He trusts me, loves me. I can't deceive him any longer. This has to be the end of it, Erik.' She reached for the clasp of the necklace.

'I refuse to allow you to dictate the terms of this relationship. This is just the beginning. You love me, I know it. I am positive of it.'

'You are mistaken.' Anna calmly placed the pendant in Erik's hand and walked away.

Later that afternoon it began to rain. The group was forced under cover. While the men played chess on the balcony and Rosalie busied herself in the kitchen, Anna and Gota sat in the parlour. They had offered to help prepare the evening meal but Rosalie insisted she was enjoying the chance to have the kitchen to herself. Anna had chosen a novel from the shelf and her sister was busy with her needlepoint. Anna's eyes rested on the pages of the book, blindly skimming the black text. Uncharacteristically, Gota had not mentioned the incident that morning. She could not have mistaken what she saw. Anna and Erik had been caught red-handed. Their silence when Gota walked out onto the balcony would only have confirmed her suspicions. Anna knew her sister well enough to know she would not let this subject rest. It was only a matter of time before she brought it up. Anna decided it might be wise to broach the subject herself.

She laid the book on her lap and sighed. 'I'd like to explain what you saw earlier.'

Without looking up from her needlepoint, Gota said, 'And what did I see?'

'Erik and me.'

'Hmm?'

'Erik and me together.'

'Well, it's quite obvious, Anna. I can see exactly what you're playing at. I understand your actions. They make complete sense,' she said brightly, her fingers quickly guiding the needle back and forth through the fabric.

'I beg your pardon.'

'If Nils doesn't happen to return from this ridiculous expedition, then you'll have the other brother readied and waiting. It's a marvellous scheme.'

'No, that's not it at all,' Anna said. 'How can you even suggest it?'

'It's logical,' Gota replied, as if speaking to an idiot. Her eyes returned to her needle and thread.

'That's the last thing it is. I'm engaged to marry Nils.' Anna was at once furious and astounded by her sister's assumption.

'Of course you are, but—'

'Wait, let me finish, Gota.' Anna stopped to choose her words. 'I love Nils, but I find myself compelled to seek out

Erik. I can't explain it. Believe me when I say that I've tried.'
Close to tears, all she wanted was for her sister to understand her actions, offer a comforting word, a soothing touch.

'Well, I can't blame you. He is superbly handsome and
charming. So accomplished as well. Did you see him play
tennis? And an architect! You know he'd be very well off. I
commend you on your choice.'

Tears welled in Anna's eyes. 'He's not my choice. Nils is
my choice. I've told Erik that a future for the two of us is
hopeless. I'd appreciate it if you'd view this morning's events
as a terrible blunder on my part and never mention the incident to anyone. It would devastate Nils.' She was near
hysteria.

'Shh, shh,' Gota cooed. 'Everyone will hear you.Well, of
course I won't say a word. If that's what you wish.'

'That's what I wish.' Anna left the room, unable to tolerate
her sister's company any longer.

NINETEEN

STOCKHOLM, SWEDEN
AUGUST 1896

ANNA SAT NERVOUSLY IN THE STRINDBERGS' sitting room. Erik had left to collect his brother from the station and Tore was frantically swathing the entrance hall and dining room in blue and yellow banners and other homemade decorations. Miniature balloons hung like Japanese lanterns from the ceiling and an elaborate diorama of three small clay men planting a Swedish flag in cotton-wool snow had taken over Rosalie's buffet. Since learning of his brother's return, Tore had dedicated every waking hour to ensuring Nils' recent excursion was viewed by his family as a triumph. This was often difficult in the face of Erik's harsh cynicism and the press's constant criticisms.

Rosalie had taken up position in the kitchen, directing operations for her son's homecoming feast, and Oscar had retreated to his study when Tore's display of unrelenting optimism grew too irritating for him to bear.

'Can I help you?' Anna asked Tore.

'No, thank you,' he said tersely. 'Everything is finished.' Tore knelt on the window seat, his impatient face poking through the rich crimson curtains, waiting for the carriage to arrive.

Anna leant back in the chair and closed her eyes. Her mouth was dry and her hands trembled slightly. When she had received Rosalie's letter telling her of the failed launch and Nils' return, she had wept tears of selfish relief. But now, a week later, there were rumours in the newspaper that Andrée was already planning a second attempt. She prayed it was not true, and, if it was, that Nils would not be joining the next expedition. She knew Erik would do all he could to persuade him not to.

Following the weekend at Mölna Anna had been listless and anxious, counting down the days until her fiancé's return. Whenever she could, she slid between the covers of her bed and slept. Rosalie tried to include her in family events and outings, but she had attended only a few, striving to avoid Erik without seeming rude.

'They're here, they're here!' Tore yelled as he leapt from the window seat and bolted to the front door.

Anna flinched, stood quickly and flattened her skirt. She moved a little closer to the doorway. Turning her head, she could just see the side of the carriage through the crack in the curtains. The carriage door opened slightly and she quickly closed her eyes. Rosalie appeared from the kitchen and fixed her hair in the hallway mirror, poking the errant locks back into place with pins. She stood next to her husband, who had recently reappeared.

'Come here, Anna. Stand by us.'

Anna opened her eyes and walked slowly to the people who would soon be her mother and father. Rosalie gripped

Anna's cold hand. Oscar, the taciturn giant, cleared his throat incessantly. Sven descended the stairs, straightening his coat and tie. He too checked his reflection in the mirror as he passed by and pushed his dark hair from his brow.

'The welcome party is assembled, then,' Sven said as he took his place next to Anna. She looked up into his angular face and smiled. His hands were pushed tightly into his pockets and his usual ease seemed to have evaporated.

Anna realised every person in the house was feeling the same sickening mix of joy, dread and unknowing. All of them longed to support Nils and buoy his spirits, yet all of them wanted to prevent him doing anything so foolish again. They all yearned for and feared the moment when Nils would walk through the door.

'You look exhausted,' Erik said. 'You look as if you haven't slept the entire time you were away.'

Erik had met his brother at the train station alone. The absence of fanfare was noticeable, but it was what Nils preferred. They were sitting opposite each other in the carriage, heading towards Lilla Nygatan.

'It feels like it.' Nils gave a cavernous yawn. He shook his head vigorously. 'Although I think I did get a couple of hours' sleep on the first of August. How is everyone? How's Anna?'

Erik hesitated. 'The family's missed you. Mama has been very withdrawn. Papa has been even more so and Sven has limited himself to a mere three – yes, three – admirers since your departure. Tore has followed the expedition's every move in the newspapers and is currently transforming our family home into something resembling a museum dedicated to you and your achievements.'

'And Anna?' Nils persisted.

'She seems fine. Mama has brought her along to a few concerts and tea parties – you know what Mama's like.' Erik broke off and looked out the window of the carriage for a moment. 'So, is it as the newspapers say: unsuitable winds, storms – unfavourable conditions for a balloon launch?'

'Yes, all that.' Nils sounded weary and his face seemed thin. His eyes were ringed by shadows. He'd only been gone a little over two months but his brother could tell the experience had changed him. 'Once the balloon was inflated and we were ready to embark, the weather went from raging tempest to absolute calm. Neither being conducive to balloon travel.'

'How was Andrée?'

'Absolutely calm.' Nils stifled a yawn. 'Disappointed, of course. But considering the cost and the years of planning, the sheer physical effort alone, he held up splendidly. I never saw any signs of despair or anger.'

Strange, strange little man, Erik thought. He suppressed the urge to speak his mind. 'What about Ekholm?'

'Raging tempest. He and Andrée disagreed over everything. Accusations, reproaches and threats. It was impossible. I had to support Andrée as the leader of the expedition, but many of Ekholm's concerns were well founded. Andrée refused to entertain any of them.'

'I thought they were old friends. What were Ekholm's concerns?'

'The balloon was losing air,' Nils explained. 'Once it was inflated, Ekholm claimed it was losing a little less than seventy kilograms of lift force each day. With that amount of leakage we'd never make it to the North Pole. Ekholm told Andrée that his plans to get to Canada or Russia were a joke. There was no chance the balloon would stay aloft for thirty days.'

Erik wanted to grasp his brother by the shoulders and shake him until he saw sense. He wanted Nils to be angry, frustrated, to swear off a second attempt, seeing Andrée for the fool that he was. Nils' composure disturbed Erik deeply. How could he protect his brother if he wasn't willing to protect himself?

Erik was reminded of an incident when Nils was twelve years old. Their cousins from Gothenburg had come to stay in Stockholm for a week over midsummer. The son of the family, Edvard, who was fourteen at the time, was a devious boy whom the entire Strindberg family disliked, apart from Nils. Erik despised his cousin and attempted to discourage the friendship, pointing out all of Edvard's inadequacies as often as he could. Yet Nils was attracted to his cousin for reasons Erik never understood. Edvard would connive schemes that Nils would be instructed to carry out. Set a basket of old rags alight, tie their dog Gunvor in a tree, steal money from their father's pocketbook – the family still laughed about Edvard's evil influence over Nils during that time. But Erik recalled it as no laughing matter. He had been concerned about his younger brother, seeing a side of Nils he had not been aware of before – easily led, and refusing to listen to reason.

Erik could find no other course of action but to tackle the problem himself, before Edvard and his family returned to Gothenburg the next day. He had been receiving boxing lessons from his father over the summer and invited the smaller child into the garden one evening after dinner. Erik punched him in the face, hard, twice, without saying a word.

The next morning Edvard left Stockholm with a black eye and a split lip. The following year, when his family visited again, Edvard ventured nowhere near Nils and recoiled from Erik like a beaten puppy. Lesson learnt. But Nils had been furious. Although Edvard remained mute about the incident, Nils knew exactly what had happened. He maintained a flinty silence with Erik for days before family life forced him to forgive his brother and carry on as normal. But Erik was no longer thirteen and Andrée's influence could not be overcome with a right cross to the head and a jab to the chin.

Still, this was ridiculous. 'Losing air?' he asked his brother. 'How? It seems a bit late in the day to discover such a massive fly in the ointment.'

'Through the seams. Through the eight million stitching holes along the seams. Lachambre tried to seal them with strips of silk that he glued on with varnish, but the repairs didn't take.' Nils shrugged his shoulders, leant his head against the window and closed his eyes.

Erik looked at his brother's serene face as he dozed, trying to decide what to do. Nils' eyes flicked open again and he looked directly at his brother.

'I want to tell you something about the expedition, but you have to promise not to tell anyone.' Erik agreed. 'Ekholm accused Andrée of rushing preparations. He argued that the balloon should have been inflated sooner, tested in France, before it was transported to Danskøya. He believed Andrée was risking our lives for the sake of his timetable.'

'What do you think?'

'I'm not sure. Ekholm made sense. Everything he argued made perfect sense. But Andrée's resolve is unshakeable. It's extremely persuasive.' Nils shook his head in wonder. 'Then Ekholm accused Andrée of something rather devilish.' Nils cleared his throat. 'Ekholm said that the engineer charged with inflating the balloon told him that Andrée had ordered topping-up of the balloon from time to time in order to throw off Ekholm's measurements.'

Erik frowned. 'It doesn't surprise me. Andrée wanted to launch at all costs. He hopes to be remembered as a hero, and he's willing to risk his life and yours to achieve his ends. The pressure is also mounting.'

'What do you mean?'

'When you left Stockholm and Gothenburg, the crowds cheered, the whole country was behind you. But all the delays have brought criticism from the press and the sponsors. Alfred Nobel, the mad old coot, had his say in the *Aftonbladet*.' Nils' mouth twisted into a sceptical smile. 'Mad he might be,' Erik went on more firmly, 'but the public love him and listen to him. Expectations were high, and they came to nothing. The press, the public, the sponsors, the King - everyone wants results. And it didn't help that Nansen decided to waltz back into Tromsø at exactly the same time as you.'

'Nansen didn't reach the pole.'

Erik leant forward. 'He got bloody close. Your expedition didn't even launch.'

The two brothers were quiet for a few minutes before Nils spoke softly. 'Andrée wants to attempt another launch next year, at the same time.'

'Arrogant bloody arse,' his brother responded. 'And what do you think of that?'

'Ekholm is definitely out. He's made that clear. He doesn't want a bar of Andrée or his expedition. But I'm not sure.'

Erik could not find the words. To even contemplate a second attempt was lunacy. He shook his head and rubbed his forehead lightly with the tips of his fingers. 'It's tempting fate. If you go with him again, it's tempting fate. You've been spared, saved. Don't push your luck.'

'I don't believe in fate or destiny. Have you forgotten that I'm a scientist?'

'What does that mean?'

'Nothing. I haven't decided what I'll do yet, if there's a

second attempt. But Erik, don't mention any of this to Anna or the family.'

Before Erik could respond, the carriage stopped. 'Here we are. Are you ready?'

Nils nodded once before stepping onto the pavement.

TWENTY

STOCKHOLM, SWEDEN
AUGUST 1896

ANNA AND NILS sat next to each other. It was the first time they had been alone since his arrival. After dinner, and following more than an hour of spirited conversation between the men concerning the details of the expedition, Rosalie had pointedly ushered three of her sons and her husband out of the sitting room. Anna and Nils remained, perched awkwardly on the edge of the settee like strangers. The inches between them seemed like miles.

Nils placed his hand on Anna's. Her nervous fingers, plucking at the brocade of the settee, were stilled by her fiancé's warm touch. They looked at each other, taking in and appreciating the other's presence for a few moments before Nils spoke.

'Let's get married now. Tomorrow or the next day.'

Anna was suddenly anxious.

'Why now? We were planning a midsummer wedding.'

'It's August.'

'I know. But it's not midsummer.' Anna knew it was a weak excuse.

Nils removed his hand from Anna's and the distance that had briefly been bridged returned so quickly that her breath caught in her throat. Nils dropped his head between his hands. 'Have you changed your mind?'

'No. It's not that. I'm surprised, that's all. It was your idea to marry in the midsummer. It's when we got engaged – you said it would be romantic. What's changed?'

'I want to be with you now as a husband. I don't want to wait.'

'But you can be with me, you have . . .' Anna faltered, unable to find the appropriate words. She felt herself flush.

'But properly, responsibly, as husband and wife, in our own home and our own bed.' Nils stood and took a seat on the other side of the room, at the piano. 'It's more than that, though. I want our life together to start now, as soon as possible. This very minute, if it can be arranged.'

His urgency panicked her. 'Nobody asked at dinner because nobody wanted to know the answer,' Anna said.

'What are you talking about?'

'According to the newspapers Andrée is already planning a second attempt next summer. Is it true?'

'Yes. He wants to try again. He feels he's disappointed too many people.'

'Are you going?'

'He has asked, or rather assumed, I suppose. I haven't told him anything. Only that I need to spend some time with my family and with you. I'm so tired and I need time to think, to talk about this with you.' He took Anna's hands in his own. 'Shall we forget about this until tomorrow?' he said softly. 'Will you play something for me? I have so missed it.'

'Of course.'

Anna took a seat at the piano. Nils removed his shoes and

lay back on the settee. He smiled contentedly and placed his hand behind his head. When she began, Nils closed his eyes but the smile on his lips remained. She chose Handel. It was the piece Nils had introduced her to during their first meeting at the Larssons'. He had played it by heart, while she on piano and Johanna and Kalle Larsson on violin had struggled with the sheet music, attempting to equal his high-spirited performance.

'Herr Strindberg likes you, Fröken,' Johanna had said later. 'That's how Kalle acts when he likes a girl.'

Anna had told Johanna not to be silly, but she had been quietly flattered and carried herself a little lighter for the rest of the day.

Nils soon fell asleep. Anna began playing more softly until the notes were barely audible. Then she stopped. Nils did not move. She sat on the piano seat and counted to fifty then stood and made her way to the door. As she passed by, she kissed his forehead. Too tired to bid goodbye to any of the family, she hastily donned her coat in the vestibule and left the house. Tore's fastidious decorations had already been removed.

She was only a short distance from the door when she heard it slam. Heavy footsteps followed after her, growing louder in the quiet street as they approached.

'Anna, wait,' Erik called.

She stopped and waited.

'I found my brother asleep and Tore told me you'd left. Tore shouldn't have allowed you to leave alone.' In his haste Erik had failed to put on his coat. His tie and hat had also been forgotten. He looked less formidable, more approachable, without these everyday trappings.

'It's not Tore's fault. I didn't know he saw me leave. I didn't want to be a bother to anyone. I'm quite capable of walking the distance by myself.'

'Nils would never forgive me if I permitted you to go alone. Please allow me? Although I do look a sight. Forgive me.'

Her initial alarm was overcome by Erik's obvious distress, his fumbling words. She found his current state of vulnerability endearing.

Anna nodded and began to walk. Erik followed in her wake, allowing her to lead. It was nearing midnight and the length of Lilla Nygatan was deserted, its naked emptiness made starker by the full moon. Anna felt no uneasiness in Erik's presence. On the contrary, she was comforted by the warmth she sensed from his body and the sound of his breath.

'You must be cold,' she said without looking his way.

'I'm fine.'

She stopped again and turned. His hands were pushed into his trouser pockets.

'You look cold.'

'Perhaps a little.'

Granted unspoken permission, he caught up to her. They slipped into the rhythm of a couple who had taken many such walks together. Occasionally they would look at each other and smile. If she was strolling with Nils, she thought, she would naturally slide her arm though his, nestle in beside him, using him as a barrier against the chill. She clutched her small purse tightly and stared ahead, her eyes fixed on the pavement.

'Nils wants us to get married straight away.'

Erik did not reply, but she noticed a stiffening of his gait. He fell back a little way. Her heart pounded and she wished she could draw the words back into her mouth. Her own foolishness overwhelmed her. But there was no one else in whom she could confide. Gota, her friends, even Rosalie would be excited by the prospect of an upcoming wedding. They would say Nils was a romantic, that he had missed her so much, pined for her while he was away, and that his motives were pure – those of a young man in love. None would understand that his true motives were hopelessness and despair.

When they reached the street entrance to Anna's apartment, Erik finally spoke. His hands still in his pockets, he stared down at his shuffling soles on the pavement. 'What did you say to him?'

'Nothing. I gave him no answer. I think he's agreed to accompany Andrée in a second attempt.'

Erik groaned and looked into the sky. The moonlight shone down on them both.

'Has he talked to you about it?' Anna asked.

'Yes, but he's not sure what he's doing yet.'

'I'm worried.'

'So am I.'

It was not the response Anna had wanted.

They stood face to face for a long time, looking into each other's eyes, searching for an answer. Eventually Anna opened the front door of her building and Erik began the walk home.

'Thank you, Janne. Can you please find Tore and ask him to complete the lessons he was due to complete yesterday for Herr Kall?' The maid nodded to Rosalie Strindberg and left the sitting room.

'With all the excitement of Nils' homecoming, we sent Tore's tutor home. Tore was so distracted. Kall was tearing what's left of his hair out, and the house was in an absolute shambles, so I sent him away. But I did promise him Tore would complete his Latin by this afternoon.'

Anna sipped her tea.

'Your hair looks lovely, Anna. Did you do it yourself?'

'No, it's the handiwork of my sister. She enjoys interfering with my appearance.'

'And your suit – how smart. Gota is very talented. I must call on her soon. She's the best dressmaker in the city, I think.' Anna smiled respectfully. 'Perhaps your sister knows this is a very special day.' She placed her teacup on the table, raising her eyebrows.

Anna wondered what she meant.

'Nils told me of his hopes to marry as soon as possible. I thought perhaps you had come to tell Nils that you agree, that you accept his amended proposal.'

All the warmth seemed to leave the room. Anna picked up her tea and closed her hands around the delicate cup. Then she loosened her grip, realising the pressure might crack the thin china.

'I haven't discussed the proposal with Gota. Not with anybody. I really need more time to think. I'd been looking forward to a midsummer wedding.'

'Well, of course. A wedding during midsummer celebrations would be wonderful. But Nils has missed you terribly and, while it would be a rush to arrange the wedding, I'm sure I can manage it. It would be an honour, my absolute pleasure. I only have sons, my dear, so the bond that has grown between us is very important to me.'

Rosalie's face was hopeful, but Anna saw the undercurrent of fear beneath her optimism. It means more than a marriage to her, Anna thought. In his mother's mind the nuptials between herself and Nils were a contract ensuring he would fulfil his obligations as a husband and stay in

Stockholm. She wanted Anna to be excited. She wanted to plan a wedding with her, choose flowers and table settings, help them decide on their marital home. All this would cement her son's connection to this world.

There was no way Anna could discuss this aspect of it with Rosalie. She would be speaking out of place and she was certain Rosalie herself was unaware of her underlying desperation, so plainly evident to others. Instead she said, 'Yes, I cherish our attachment as well. But I must first discuss everything with Nils and my sister. Who else could I possibly ask to make my wedding gown?'

Her frivolous tone and girlish words seemed to settle Rosalie's anxiety. Anna had often heard other women speak in this lighthearted manner, but for her the charade was not so easy. She sat back in her chair, sipped her tea and, for the next half-hour, until she left the room to visit Nils, the women talked of other matters.

Closing the door behind her, Anna leant against the wall and took several deep breaths. She caught a glimpse of herself in the mirror and checked her hair. As she did so, she heard a door upstairs close and footsteps on the stairs. Her heart began to race.

When he saw her standing in front of the mirror, he stopped. In his waistcoat and tie he looked immaculate. Erik wore his hair slightly longer than fashion dictated and refused to flatten its dark wave with oil. His face seemed to sparkle – he had recently shaved. This was another trend Erik resisted – Anna had often heard him mock his brothers for their carefully waxed moustaches. Hat in hand, he was heading out, Anna thought, probably to work.

He gripped his hat unforgivingly as he stood opposite her

in the hallway, but looked past her, towards the door. She found his refusal to look at her face maddening.

'Are you here to see Nils?' he asked.

'Yes. Your mother caught me when I arrived and insisted on tea . . .'

'He's in his workroom,' Erik said curtly. 'What are you going to tell him?'

'I don't know yet. I need to talk to him first.'

He brushed by her, reaching for the doorhandle. 'I'd just appreciate being spared the humiliation of returning this afternoon to celebrations and toasts to the happy couple's good health,' he said.

There was nothing she could say. A lump rose in her throat and her eyes stung. It took all her will to remain composed. They stood like this for some time, neither of them seeming capable of movement or speech. She willed him to speak, to say something kind. Terrified to look at him, she waited for the door to slam and the sound of his heavy tread as he retreated from the house. She jerked slightly when she felt his hand on her forearm. A knot swelled in her chest but she was still afraid to face him.

'I love you, Anna. I'd do anything to prevent you from being hurt. But this situation is unbearable. I cannot see you so frequently, in this house, with my brother. Each day I wake hoping to see you and when I do my heart breaks. I'll be leaving for America sooner than planned. Goodbye, beautiful girl. You look very lovely today.'

TWENTY-ONE

STOCKHOLM, SWEDEN
AUGUST 1896

Anna approached the door to Nils' workroom. She straightened the waistband of her skirt and ran her fingers blindly over her head, checking her hair. Gota had convinced her sister a different, more cosmopolitan hairstyle was needed this Saturday morning, now that Nils was a national celebrity. She had swept Anna's hair up high and toiled with a hot tongs for an hour perfecting a tuft of tiny ringlets gathered at the crown by a white ribbon. A further feathering of fastidiously crafted curls, much more refined than her own, framed her round face. Anna complained that her hair resembled a bird's nest. Gota argued it was the height of fashion.

Anna did not complain, however, about the outfit Gota had recently sewn for her. She had tailored it from the length of navy-blue linen Anna had received from Rosalie on her birthday. When she stared at her silhouette in the mirror that morning, Anna marvelled at how beautifully it fell over her hips and thighs, coming to rest just above her ankles. A smart, crisp bolero jacket in the same fabric emphasised her neat waist.

When Nils' commitment to Andrée had become known the year before, Nils' father had donated his office, located at the back of the house, to his son so that he might convert it into a workroom. Oscar joked that he was willing to forgo his private sphere for the greater scientific good. Nils and Tore had dedicated the following week to renovating the large, south-facing room. Tore had painted a sign for the door that read 'Do Not Disturb. Explorer at Work'. Part laboratory, dark room and tool shop, the space became Nils' own. It was here that he devoted every spare moment, day and night, to preparations. Anna disliked entering the room. It only served to remind her of what was to come.

Tore's ridiculous sign remained tacked to the door. She tapped lightly. She heard footsteps and the door opened. 'Are you busy? May I come in?'

Nils stood in the doorway. Tore pushed past both of them on his way out.

'Tore! Careful! You nearly knocked Anna over,' Nils called after his stampeding brother.

'Don't worry, I think your mother's looking for him anyway,' Anna said. 'May I come in?'

'Of course. Tore was just helping me develop some film from Danskøya. Some shots are quite good, but as you can see I still have some work to do with the lenses.'

She removed her jacket hurriedly, walked into the room and pretended to take in the photographs – confusing clouds of grey and white. She nodded her head in mock appreciation. This was too soon. She had hoped to enjoy a brief period of ambiguity, a space where she was at liberty to pretend he was not returning to Danskøya.

'Sit down. Can I get you some tea? What time is it?' Nils looked at his watch.

'I had tea upstairs with your mother. She's very happy to have you home.'

'Yes, indeed. Will you have a seat?' Nils motioned to Anna to sit down and she obliged. He sat on the floor in front of her and grasped her hands in his. After a moment or two he rested his head in her lap, sighing as he did so.

Eventually he lifted his head and his gaze met her own. He reached up and allowed his thumb to skirt across her lips. 'Have you thought about what we talked about last night?'

'Yes, I have. Do you intend to go with Andrée next year?'

Nils did not respond for a long time. Her coldness took him by surprise. Anna stared at him, ruthlessly, determined to force him to respond.

'Yes,' he said.

'Then we'll wait until your return to marry.'

'But it could be years. Now we know more about the conditions and what we might face, it will take years. Nansen was gone for three. How can you be so businesslike about this? Are you willing to wait that long?'

'Yes.'

Nils stood. He walked briskly to the window and, as if speaking to the shedding birch outside, said in a low voice, 'Are you punishing me?'

Anna could not find the words immediately. She supposed there was an element of retribution in her decision. She had guessed Nils had already decided on his course of action even before returning to Stockholm. He had given his word to Andrée and that was that.

She believed a more thoughtless girl would indulge him immediately, heed his every wish. But Anna recognised the selfishness in Nils' request and she was unable to accommodate his desires. If he wanted her, it would have to be on her terms.

There was a part of her that refused to believe this scenario was real. Perhaps this was simply another nightmare, she thought. Back in Stockholm less than twenty-four hours, and he was already discussing his departure. From what he had told the family at dinner the night before, the entire experience had been torturous – and the party hadn't even managed to launch. Why would he want to go through it all again? The preparations, the sorrowful departure and the absence of a guarantee. She walked to him and stared out into the garden. The breeze stirred the fallen leaves on the ground outside. Anna followed their movement with her eyes, catalogued their colours: brown, rust, orange, yellow, amber. Tears rose in her eyes, but none fell.

'I'm sorry,' Nils said.

'There are so many colours that I don't know. Perhaps Tore could help me. He's very good with that sort of thing isn't he?'

Nils did not answer.

'This time next year, when the leaves fall, you won't be here. You'll miss this season and the next and probably many. I don't imagine there are distinct seasons in the Arctic.' She looked at him, her face betraying no emotion.

'Anna,' he said. She remained quiet. Not knowing what else to do, he hugged her tight to his chest, crushing the brittle ringlets that skirted her face.

'I'm not punishing you, but I won't marry you now.' She pushed away from him and brushed the hair from her face. 'It would be like admitting that all hope was lost. A resignation to your fate.'

'Nothing's going to happen to me. There's no such thing as fate.'

Anna nodded and turned once again to the window.

'Perhaps,' Nils said, 'it might be easier if I could justify my decision. If you understood more about the expedition.'

She wheeled sharply. Her tone was bitter. 'I have no interest in understanding. Understanding is no cure for the loss I'm already feeling. But I can't ask you to stay if you believe you should go. Your principles and pride are galling to me but they're what I admire about you the most. My sorrow can't be alleviated with rationality. The truth is that I am going to lose you, perhaps forever, and that's all I know at this moment.'

She was breathing hard. Her face had reddened. Nils had never seen her so fierce. From perfect stillness to this. He was lost.

Why was it so complicated, Anna wondered. The situation exhausted her. She knew that some girls, some girls like her sister, loved this kind of melodrama, the theatrics of courtship. But Anna was struggling for air. She wanted to tell him, tell Nils everything. How she had met Erik on midsummer eve last year, that she thought of his brother when she kissed Nils, that she thought of his brother endlessly. Surely that was the only path. But somehow, unwittingly, she had drifted down another path not of her choosing and there seemed to be no turning back. Why were they even talking of marriage? It was totally unfathomable, but to break their engagement now would devastate Nils and his mother. It would tell them she had no confidence in his return. She was trapped. To tell Nils everything was a punishment she was unable to mete out. Incapable of speaking the truth, she scolded him instead.

'And you should not have told your mother about your proposal.' Her voice rose higher. 'She's beside herself with joy at the thought that we will marry soon. I didn't know what to say.'

Nils said nothing, except, 'I'm sorry.'

She walked from the window and sat on the bed. She was powerless. Conquered. Nils lay next to her and rested his head in her lap. She stroked his hair gently, a gesture of compassion. Her fiancé sobbed tears of relief into the folds of her handsome new skirt.

TWENTY-TWO

STOCKHOLM, SWEDEN
AUGUST 1896

THEY SAT opposite each other at the small table in Anna's apartment. Erik held his hat in his hands. His bulk filled the small space. To Anna he looked like an adult sitting at a child's table. Her apartment, positioned at the rear of the building, would once have been the servants' quarters of a much grander home. Measuring a meagre ten feet square, the room had a low roof and Anna guessed Erik would be able to touch the ceiling with the palm of his hand. When he entered, he was forced to stoop under the beams. She looked around the cramped but tidy room and was embarrassed by the magazine cuttings of the current fashions Gota had enthusiastically pinned to the walls.

Two small beds shoved up against one wall, the table they currently occupied, a stove and a narrow wooden bench they used as a kitchen completed the sparse inventory of the women's main living space. The other room was given over to Gota's dressmaking. It also housed their clothes. The bathroom was two flights down, the lavatory a further two flights lower in the small courtyard at the rear of the building. She wondered whether the sight of these lodgings would alter his perception, thrust the reality of her life into full view. In the stillness, she could hear Erik breathing. They were both aware of movement in the adjoining room.

'It smells like hops in here,' Erik said.

'We live next to a brewery.'

'I'll be off now,' Gota chirped as she appeared from the other room. Erik stood, narrowly avoiding a beam. Gota had changed her dress, Anna noticed. 'I'll be back by dinner, Anna,' she said.

Anna nodded at her sister.

'It was very nice to see you again, Herr Strindberg. Do thank your mother and father again for hosting that wonderful weekend in Mölna.' Gota's high-pitched titter made Anna flinch. 'Such a memorable weekend for so many reasons.'

Erik cleared his throat. He stepped towards Gota and stretched out his hand. 'I'll convey your appreciation to my parents. It's been lovely to see you again, Fröken Charlier.' He offered a polite bow.

Gota blushed and, to Anna's relief, moved to the door. 'Goodbye, now. Don't forget to offer your guest a refreshment, Anna,' she called.

Erik raised his hand and shook his head. Anna waited until she heard the street door close before she spoke.

'Thank you for coming so promptly,' she said. 'I apologise for my sister's presence. She was meant to be elsewhere. It would have been inappropriate for me to come to your place of work. And discussing these matters at your house is impossible.'

'Your note seemed urgent so I came immediately. What matters would you like to discuss?' He looked at her directly, without ambiguity, only with kindness. Anna could detect no emotion in his voice, but despite his outward calm his chest heaved vigorously.

'I would like you to reconsider your decision.'

'And what decision are you referring to?' he asked.

'Your decision to leave for Chicago directly.'

'On what grounds are you asking?' A faint smile became evident on his lips. He placed his elbows on the table and leant towards her.

'It's not for myself that I'm asking.' He raised his eyebrows in pantomime interest.

She went on regardless. 'Nils would be shattered if you left before next summer. He confides thoughts in you he can't share with anyone else. And he values your opinion very highly. I believe it would be of great detriment to his cause if you were not here.'

'Your appeal is most altruistic.' Erik made no effort to mask his sarcasm. 'I'll give it some thought. Is that all you wished to discuss?'

He looked at her squarely. The coldness in his eyes was devastating, but there was something else as well. It was the same look she had seen on the palace balcony. A rush of nausea gripped her belly. When she had left the note at his office with the receptionist, Anna had realised that Erik might construe in her brief message more than was written. She wanted to see him, talk to him, ask him to remain in Stockholm for no other reason than as a comfort to her. But her cowardice prohibited her from writing just that in the note. Her own selfishness made her sick. She had contrived artlessly.

The urge to go to him, soften him, was overpowering. She saw herself standing, walking to him and placing herself on his lap. As her arms encircled his neck, she kissed the expanse of his face lightly, burying her face in his warmth and taking in his scent. She could feel his hands on her back, pressing her frame to his, enveloping and constraining. To lose herself in him was her greatest desire at that moment. She sat across the table from him, contemplating her next words.

'Please, Erik, don't be so harsh.'

He stood, too large for the doll's house in which he found himself. He slammed his hat onto the table. 'I, harsh? You know how I feel yet you wish to prolong my torment by asking me to stay. Be honest with yourself, Anna. Is it just that you want to help Nils? Be candid with me, for god's sake. I see the way you look at me. There's passion in your eyes. And your birthday weekend, have you forgotten? I know I'm not mistaken.'

She was afraid to move from her chair, and clenched her hands in an effort to prevent them shaking. In two steps he was standing directly above her. Reaching down, he lifted her chin and looked into her eyes. Then he seemed to melt, and he crouched on his haunches beside her chair.

'Please forgive me. My temper got the better of me. You bring out the best and the worst in me, I'm afraid.'

'I'm not afraid of you. I'm terrified of myself and the damage that my feelings may cause.' She touched his cheek. 'I want you to stay. I need you.'

'Do you love me?'

She wanted to answer yes, respect his plea for honesty. He would be satisfied with that and ask nothing in return. If she told him she loved him, that there was hope for them when Nils departed, then he would stay. But she could not bring herself to utter the words. It would be an admission of her betrayal. 'I don't know. What I feel for you isn't what I feel for Nils, but I'm drawn to you. My request is purely self-ish. Without you here I couldn't endure the next eight months.'

'What are we to do, then?'

Anna moved to the stove and poured two cups of coffee. She placed two teaspoons of sugar in Erik's cup and brought them to the table. They sat quietly sipping their coffee for some time. It was the sound of the brewery workers arriving to begin their shift that prompted Erik to break the silence.

'You two are more similar than I care to admit,' he began. 'You and Nils.'

'How so?'

'You've both committed to a path and neither of you will change course. Damn the consequences. I suppose it shows strength of character.'

Or cowardice, Anna thought.

'I don't want to see you or Nils injured in any way,' Erik said. 'I love you both so very much. So I will stay until he departs.'

'Erik, I can't promise you anything.'

Erik nodded gravely. 'Neither can I promise you that my temperament will lighten, that my manner when I am in your presence will not offend. It will always pain me to see you and not be permitted to touch you, kiss you. But my decision to remain has no bearing on what may lie in the future, Anna. You need me now. That's all I know.'

'Thank you.'

'I must go. I'm sure Gota will be back soon. She'll wonder why I've stayed so long.' He picked up his hat and straightened the brim. 'But please, before I leave, answer one question for me.'

'Of course.'

'Why, if you're drawn to me as you describe, did you choose not to pursue our relationship when I so obviously wanted it?'

Once again Anna was reluctant to answer truthfully. The reasons for her initial rejection of Erik were foolish. She had found his behaviour irritating and condescending that morning, and her pride had been hurt, but chiefly she had been attempting to protect her sister or, more accurately, protect herself from Gota's displeasure if she were to strike up a relationship with Erik Strindberg.

'You must promise to be discreet.'

'Of course.'

'My sister expressed a romantic interest in you that evening. I feared her feelings would be hurt if I were to see you again, if we were to begin a courtship. Then, later that year, I met Nils.'

'I understand. An unfortunate twist of fate. If you believe in fate, that is. Thank you for being frank.'

In the doorway, Anna extended her hand towards Erik. He took it softly and then pressed his lips to her cheek. His mouth lingered by her ear for an instant and then he departed. After a few seconds Anna heard the street door close. With her face pressed close to the window and her breath fogging the glass, she watched Erik pass across the laneway between her building and the brewery and disappear from view.

PART TWO

THE SECOND ATTEMPT

Chicago Herald, Chicago, IL
30 May 1897

ANDREE'S DEATH SURE: DYCHE FEARS FOR THE EXPLORER

ANDREE'S DARING in attempting to reach the Pole in a balloon is almost certain to cost him his life. This is the opinion of Professor Lewis L. Dyche of the Kansas State University, and there are few men in America whose opinions on polar expeditions are of greater value.

'I am afraid Andree will never be seen again if he makes a successful start from Spitsbergen for the North Pole in his balloon,' said Professor Dyche. 'His expedition, as an example of daring, has never been equalled; it is a piece of stupendous courage, but nature in its most terrible aspect is against him, and it is very unlikely that he will come back.

'The theory that the North Pole may be crossed in a balloon is extremely fascinating, but the difficulties in the way are almost, if not quite, insurmountable. Nansen's drift in his boat through the polar currents was completely practicable beside it. Ice and land are tangible things to travel over, but who knows of the currents of the air?

'Andree has already started from Stockholm, Sweden, for the islands of Spitsbergen, half way between Norway and the north pole. The balloon will be filled about June 20, and if the winds are favorable, that is, from the south or southeast, it will be cut loose, and Andree and his party will have started on their perilous, and, I believe, hopeless journey.

'Andree argues that Nansen having failed to reach the North Pole by trusting himself to the currents of the ocean, there is more certainty in currents of air. He relies on the prevailing winds from the south or south-east, carrying him near or across the pole and probably wafting the balloon clear across the Arctic circle to Alaska or Siberia. For a year, circulars from the Russian government have been distributed over Siberia commanding the people to watch for the balloon and to care for its passengers. Similar circulars have been distributed over Alaska and Greenland.'

Difficulties of the Expedition

'It is said that all winds in that country are from the south, because at the north pole it is south in every direction. Winds coming from every direction will produce cross currents that will blow him everywhere and nowhere. There will probably be times when there will be no winds at all, on account of the low temperature, or the winds, taking him to a point he does not desire may abandon him, only to take him up again and bear him out of his course. He may steer a few points in the wind, but he cannot prevail against contrary winds.'

Dangers of Ice Fogs

'The greatest danger he may face is from the ice fogs, so dreadful and penetrating that no clothing is proof against them. They are caused by the south and north winds meeting over the great ice masses. How will he make observations in these impenetrable fogs?

'When he has got to the pole how will he know he has reached it?

The mariner takes his bearings by observations of the sun and moon at midday. There is no midday at the pole. The sun circles around the heavens in gradually narrowing circles until, on June 21, the highest northern point is reached. If he could land and stay awhile he might make such observations as would be valuable. But while he was away from the balloon contrary winds might seize it and bear it away and leave him to die with his discovery. Even should everything be favorable to leaving the balloon and making trips on sledges neither he nor his companions would be in physical condition to stand the work. It takes the work of weeks in the cold atmosphere to accustom one to its hardships.'

Andree May Never Come Back

'As I said before, Andree's expedition is most fascinating in its bare possibilities of success, and eclipses that of Nansen in its reckless daring. But I cannot believe it practicable. I believe the pole will be reached some day overland – or rather by ice – but it will be by a steady, well-planned expedition that will go forward prepared to retrace its steps safely. A dash to or over the pole through the air sounds fine, but I do not believe it is practicable, and I am afraid that Andree's attempt will be disastrous, although I sincerely hope he will get through all right and land in America.

'The fascination for polar exploration is marvellous. It is a challenge that nature throws down to man. "Win the pole," she says, "and great will be your prize." She has awarded prizes for these attempts and the nearer the explorer reaches the pole the greater the prize. Nansen's prize has been worldwide fame and an ample fortune. Should Andree succeed in reaching the pole and returning his name will never die and the world will be at his feet. Many men have considered it a prize well worth the attempt.'

TWENTY-THREE

STOCKHOLM, SWEDEN
MAY 1897

THEY WALKED shoulder to shoulder among the crowds over the recently completed Djurgårdsbron, heading towards Djurgården. Erik, leading the group, stopped suddenly and executed a theatrical jump. 'I hope it holds up,' he said loudly of the new bridge.

While he laughed, his companions, attempting to ignore his buffoonery, continued to make their way across. As they journeyed by foot, buses filled with wide-eyed, finger-pointing festival-goers passed them by.

Anna had dressed lightly for the outing and wore a thin white cotton blouse that she left open at the neck. The cuffs of the wide sleeves sat at her elbow and she had borrowed a friend's hat for the occasion. Despite Gota's dire warnings she had brought no coat with her. Nils had not noticed the new hat. He was inclined to be oblivious to such things. This did not bother Anna, who, firm in the belief she was no great beauty, dressed only to please herself and to be comfortable.

The hat, though, which was poised jauntily on her head, she had admired since Lila purchased it, and she was pleased with the effect it created among her chestnut curls.

Marking their eventual destination was the much derided exhibition hall that had been the talk of Stockholm since the controversial design was placed on public display.

'It's grotesque, an eyesore,' Erik said.

'You're just saying that because your design wasn't chosen,' said Tore. 'I think it's spectacular. You know it's the largest wooden construction ever built. Close to seventeen thousand square metres. I hope it stands forever.'

'That's just what the organisers want idiots like you to believe, so you'll pay your ten kronor entrance.'

'But I'm getting in for free. We all are,' Tore snapped back.

'Thanks to Nils.'

'That's not the point.' Erik cuffed his brother over the head, deciding it was pointless to engage in a debate with a fourteen-year-old.

Anna and Nils followed closely behind Erik and Tore. With her arm linked firmly with her fiancé's and her eyes on Erik's broad back, Anna was enjoying the sensation of being carried along by the throng. The entire city had been whipped into a fever over the World's Fair and Anna was not immune. She could taste the expectation in the air. It was at once salty and sweet. She caught a glimpse of Erik's face as he turned to speak to Tore and she squeezed Nils' arm more tightly.

Nils was leaving for Spitsbergen in five days. For the last eight months Anna had lived in hope that the second attempt would be scuttled. Following the failure of the first launch public favour for the expedition had slumped and previous supporters had turned critic. But Andrée was tenacious and the expedition was going ahead. Gota had advised her to use the eight months wisely, to undermine Nils' resolve as best she could. Her sister also suggested a far more devious scheme to tie Nils to Stockholm and to herself. Anna had been shocked. To bring a child into the world under such pretences was wrong; it was as simple as that.

Banishing her dark thoughts, Anna joined in with Erik and Tore's banter. 'I agree with Tore. It's such a grand statement and the cupola and minarets are breathtaking.'

Both Erik and Tore ignored her comment. Nils said, 'I can recognise that it has merits – architecturally, I mean, although Erik will no doubt disagree. But it really doesn't serve a purpose, does it?'

'My point exactly, brother. What purpose does it serve? Buildings should be functional. This has no purpose whatsoever, apart from ruining quite a pleasant vista,' Erik replied.

Nils seemed unaware that Anna had been slighted. 'The newspapers are already reporting that it will be demolished as soon as the exhibition is completed.'

'Then what an absurd waste of money,' Erik said. 'Thousands of kronor on constructing a disposable building and thousands of kronor more spent disposing of it. Infuriating.'

'You'll never be happy,' Tore interjected. 'You're either bemoaning the sight of it or complaining about the cost of demolishing it. But your misery stems from the fact that your design was not chosen.'

Tore and Nils laughed conspiratorially.

'I have it on very good authority that Boberg and Lilljekvist were owed a favour by the city council. They have lost out on building contracts in the past and they were crying foul, so the council threw them a bone.'

'Ah, are you claiming corruption among the fine upstanding members of the council now?' Nils said.

'Not at all, not at all,' Erik said. '*If* the members of the council were fine and upstanding.' The brothers smiled at one another.

'But your firm has designed quite a few buildings for the Great Exhibition. Isn't that so?' Anna enquired, although she knew exactly which projects Erik had been responsible for.

'Yes.'

Anna said no more to either Erik or Tore. She did not want Nils' attention drawn to their obvious snubs. She understood why Erik was treating her with such disdain. He had warned her of this. It had been eight months now, but at every encounter, each time they crossed paths, his pain was obvious. In Anna's presence his moods ranged from churlish to rude to sullen. Yet, strangely, she was glad he had agreed to her request and stayed in Stockholm. Even at his most disagreeable he was a comfort to her. Nevertheless, when she was in the company of her fiancé and Erik she found herself play acting. From her arm looped through Nils' to her breezy attempt at conversation – it was all pretend. She was puzzled, however, as to why Tore was so aloof, and had been for a considerable length of time. She eventually reasoned that he was fourteen, and young men of that age could be extremely difficult to get along with.

The four walked on for a while then stopped while Erik and Nils removed their coats and slung them over their arms. Leaning over the railing, Anna squinted to catch a glimpse of the boats below ferrying even more people to the dock at Djurgården. But the sun, glinting powerfully off the lake, was blinding and she turned her head away quickly.

'What time are we meeting Andrée?' Anna asked.

Nils detected a loud 'tsk' from Erik's direction.

'Midday, by Erik's favourite building.' He looked down at his watch.

'What time is it now?'

'A quarter to.'

The route across the bridge was slow. The brothers discussed their plans for the day. All were eager to walk through Skansen, the country's first open-air museum and zoo. Tore was excited at the prospect of hearing the explorer Sven Hedin speak and also listening to King Oscar's opening address. Erik tormented his younger brother, joking that he would be a perfect exhibit for the first zoo in Sweden. Nils hoped to view a film made by the Lumière brothers from France. The men chatted contentedly while Anna took in her surroundings.

When the group eventually came to the end of the bridge, the crowds quickly dissipated and they released a collective sigh of relief. The impressive expanse of Djurgården, peppered with new building works, museums and stalls, all decorated in the Swedish colours, lay waiting.

'Ah, perfect timing. Have you just arrived?' Sven appeared from nowhere, an attractive young woman dressed in pristine white linen on his arm.

'We came from the city. Walked over the bridge. It was very slow. Which way did you come?' Nils asked.

'By ferry. I thought we'd be late. There was quite a lot of pushing and shoving to get aboard.'

Looking as dapper as usual and showing no sign of the heat or the ordeal on the ferry, Sven straightened his tie and brushed his black hair from his forehead. 'I'd like to introduce Fröken Lotta Dahl. Lotta, this is my family.'

The group exchanged pleasantries before Nils drew Anna's wrist to his face and checked her timepiece. 'We still have some time before we're due to meet Andrée. I'll get us some lemonade.' He strode off towards a small kiosk. Tore charged behind him, and Sven and his companion followed as well.

Left alone with Erik, Anna shot an anxious glance towards Nils. The queue at the kiosk was long. She could just make out her fiancé, standing, hands in pockets, at the end of the line. She smiled weakly at Erik then bent her head and stared at her feet.

'I like your hat,' he said.

'Thank you.' Anna met his gaze. 'It's not mine. I borrowed it from my friend Lila.'

'It's very pretty nonetheless and suits you perfectly. The cornflowers embroidered on the band set off the colour of your eyes beautifully.'

'Sven's new friend is very lovely,' Anna said, embarrassed.

'Not a dash on you,' Erik replied, before stepping a safe distance away.

TWENTY-FOUR

STOCKHOLM, SWEDEN
SEPTEMBER 1930

STUBBENDORFF WANDERED around the sculpture hall of the Liljevalchs konsthall on Djurgården waiting for Sven Strindberg to appear. There were many visitors strolling the hall, weaving in and out of its magnificent arches, but from what Stubbendorff knew of the gallery director, man-about-town and art devotee, he would be difficult to miss. He had arranged to meet Strindberg through his secretary two days before. The secretary had instructed him to be in the main hall at eleven o'clock. Strindberg did not work from an office.

Stubbendorff had only been in this gallery once before, many years ago, and had failed then to notice its grandeur. Sunshine streamed in from the skylights that surrounded the mezzanine. He raised his head and turned slowly around, this time properly taking in his surroundings. People stood on the mezzanine chatting, leaning on the railing. A number of smaller exhibition rooms led off the main hall. The sunlight and the sculptures, the footsteps and soft murmurs, warmed what Stubbendorff imagined might otherwise be a cold, hostile space.

Strindberg had been the gallery's director since it opened in 1916. He had worked tirelessly to make the first contemporary public gallery in Sweden one of the foremost art spaces in Europe. Family connections and the strength of his personality had ensured this. As he waited, Stubbendorff took in the sculptures and the names of the artists. He was especially interested in the work of Tore Strindberg. Since meeting the sculptor a week ago, Stubbendorff had thought a great deal about art, sculpture and the Strindberg family. Four startlingly gifted men born from the same parents. Stubbendorff thought the odds of this were extremely long. What magic had Oscar and Rosalie worked to mould such characters?

Leaning in, examining a work, Stubbendorff noticed from the corner of his eye heads turning. The low hum of conversation had suddenly become a cacophony of frantic whispers. Looking up, Stubbendorff saw immediately what had sparked this unexpected change.

A statuesque, self-assured, colourfully clad crane of a man suddenly filled the imposing space. Poised like one of the sculptures he stood among, he drew everybody's gaze. Stubbendorff's journalistic eye told him this was a showman – a far more sophisticated showman than a character like Bergman, but a performer nonetheless. This was one reason, Stubbendorff thought, why the Liljevalchs konsthall was so well patronised. There was an extremely good chance one might catch a glimpse of its renowned director. He was his gallery's greatest exhibit.

When the spell had broken and activity resumed, people crowded around Sven, shook his hand and complimented him on the gallery. Stubbendorff looked on amused.

Once the excitement was over and the admirers had drifted away, Stubbendorff approached him.

'Herr Strindberg. I'm Knut Stubbendorff.' He offered his hand. 'I'm the writer you arranged to meet.'

'Yes, of course. How good to see you. I spoke with my brother about your visit. He was quite taken with you.' Strindberg shook his hand warmly. 'He said you helped him escape the mire of his work. I believe that's how he phrased it.'

'Oh, that's extremely nice of him to say. I really don't think I did that much.'

'Not at all, not at all. He ordered that I should be as much help to you as possible.' Strindberg's smile commandeered his entire face. The openness and amiability of the brothers amazed Stubbendorff. Tore and Sven Strindberg were the first individuals he'd met who were entirely without agenda, who only aimed to be of assistance. Even more extraordinarily, they were genuinely supportive of a stranger investigating their family's history.

'But before we discuss Nils, Herr Stubbendorff, I would like to show you around this gallery.'

The cynic in Stubbendorff whispered that this was nothing more than a public-relations exercise. But as Strindberg grinned and placed his hand in the middle of Stubbendorff's back, directing him out of the main hall, Stubbendorff's reservations suddenly vanished.

Strindberg's unexpected appearance in each room of the gallery garnered a similar response to the welcome he had received in the sculpture hall. As he chatted to visitors, Stubbendorff stood back and studied this work of art.

Sven's thick hair was swept back from his triangular face in a brilliant white coif. His moustache, of an identical hue, was waxed into two slender sickles that curled upwards, leading the eye to his elegant nose. Strindberg's nostrils were the longest Stubbendorff had ever seen. The man stood over six feet three inches, Stubbendorff guessed. He was fifty-six years old but his blue eyes were those of a boy and they sparkled incessantly as he spoke.

Stubbendorff noticed that Strindberg talked very quickly, but he moved deliberately, gracefully. He reminded the reporter of a beautiful insect – a praying mantis in a green and violet plaid suit. While Strindberg performed for the crowd, the younger man admired his skill, the ease with which he leapt from topic to topic, the genuine courtesy and gratitude with which he greeted patrons and the knowledge with which he spoke about the artworks.

'Ah, here is one of my favourites, Herr Stubbendorff. It is by a Spanish painter, Salvador Dalí. Have you heard of him?'

'No, I haven't.'

'I have been following his career for more than a decade and I finally got my hands on this.' He turned to the large canvas on the wall. 'I found it at the Dalmau Gallery in Barcelona. I met the artist at the time, a remarkable fellow. Rather flamboyant.'

Stubbendorff moved closer to the painting to conceal his amusement at his host's lack of personal insight. He read the title: *Figure at a Window*.

'It is a portrait of his sister, Ana María. Throughout his career she has been his only model.'

The portrait, painted predominantly in light blues and lavenders, showed only the back of a woman leaning on a windowsill looking out to sea. Her dress fell in soft waves over her torso and buttocks. The only object in her view was a small sailing boat in the distance.

'This is not typical of Dalí's style. But of all his works this one touched me for some reason. It's quiet, peaceful, and the woman seems a little lost,' Strindberg said. 'I thought I should give her a home here.'

'It's beautiful. I'm sure Ana María will be very happy here. You have an extraordinary gallery, Herr Strindberg.'

'Thank you very much. That's always wonderful to hear. Now how can I help you? Tore told me you have Nils' journal, and that you want to find out about our lives back then, that you're trying to find Anna.'

As they strolled, the reporter deftly outlined his mission.

'To be honest with you, I was never very present in those days. Much of the time I was in my own world. I was studying at university and drifted in and out as the mood struck me.'

They walked on through the gallery's numerous rooms. 'But of course I do remember Anna. She stirred up quite a lot of emotion in the Strindberg home.'

'How do you mean?'

'I was never sure, of course, but I always suspected Erik of having feelings towards her. Whenever she was around, he was particularly boorish, yet when he looked at her I saw only tenderness. I found it rather amusing. I was entertained by Erik's churlishness whenever she visited.'

Stubbendorff was shocked. 'Do you think she shared his feelings?'

'I think she was aware of them. Her discomfort whenever she was in Erik's presence was palpable. I regret to say that I rather enjoyed witnessing that also. But she was devoted to Nils. That was obvious.'

'But your brother's journal gives no indication of this. He writes of Erik only with the highest regard and he loved Anna dearly.'

'Oh no, no, no. Nils wouldn't have noticed a thing.' Strindberg placed his large hand on Stubbendorff's shoulder. 'Nils was a fiercely intelligent man, but not what I would call worldly. The subtleties of love confounded him. I doubt if Erik would ever have acted on his affections. He and Nils were best friends. Whatever his feelings towards Anna, he attempted to hide them, however badly. On the other hand Nils was naive. It would not have entered his mind that his brother might have a romantic interest in his fiancée. Erik could have swept Anna into his arms and had his way with her in the coat closet and Nils wouldn't have noticed a thing. Their similarities I could count on one hand, Herr Stubbendorff, but they were very close. I can't imagine Erik would have pursued Anna.'

Stubbendorff nodded slowly, absorbing the information.

'I felt for Anna, though, after Nils was lost,' Sven told him. 'She simply disappeared. For a number of years she was one of our family. We shared many happy times together. Then she was lost to us. I know my mother, having no daughters, was particularly distraught at losing her so soon after Nils.'

'Do you have any idea where she might be living, whether she is even in Stockholm?'

'I haven't a clue. Mama may be of more help.'

'Do you think she would mind discussing this matter?' Strindberg shook his head.

'How would I go about contacting her?'

'She lives with me, Herr Stubbendorff. She moved from Lilla Nygatan a few years ago. Tore and his models and wives and children, not to mention the art he's hoarded over the years, essentially shoved her out of the house. He's a wonderful artist and a loving brother and son, but the house is chaos. My mother couldn't bear it any longer.

'She enjoys discussing those days, when she had her four boys under the one roof with a world of opportunity awaiting them outside. I'm certain Mama will be more help regarding Anna as well – they were extremely close. Why don't you pop around? Let's see . . .' Strindberg closed his eyes and thought for a few seconds. 'She's usually home in the afternoons. My secretary will give you the address. Come around tomorrow afternoon, at about four. If there's any change, my secretary will telephone you.'

'I'm very grateful. One more thing, if you have time: is Erik still living in America?'

'Yes, but he'll be arriving in Stockholm next week. As soon as the camp was discovered, he sought immediate passage. He wants to be here for the funeral.'

Stubbendorff had no idea how long he had spent with Sven Strindberg but the sun was high in the sky when he left the gallery and his stomach grumbled. Despite his hunger he decided to walk back from Djurgården over Djurgårdsbron. He needed air and he needed to think. He leant on the railing and looked into the water. In his mind his task had been simple – deliver Nils Strindberg's journal to his fiancée. But after meeting with Sven, he realised he could possibly be unearthing family secrets that might best remain hidden.

His good sense told him to leave off, politely cancel tomorrow's meeting with Rosalie Strindberg and post the journal to either one of the brothers along with a courteous note explaining he was too busy to go on with the search. He closed his eyes in an attempt to find his way. When he reopened them, the sun glanced fleetingly off the water into his eyes and he turned away quickly.

This journey had begun with the purest of motives – to honour the dead and deliver the journal to its rightful owner. But Stubbendorff had now been drawn into the intrigue. He took out his notebook, unfolded Palmgren's letter and walked in the direction of Munkbroleden.

Stubbendorff paced the length of his small living space. He stared out the window onto the empty street below, picturing the people of Stockholm asleep in their beds. He lit a cigarette and sat down at the table, feverishly flicking through the pages of Strindberg's journal, hoping he had missed something, but knowing he hadn't.

Stubbendorff had been unable to locate Gota Neve that afternoon. The current residents of Munkbroleden 32 had never heard of Gota Neve, or of Gota Charlier. He leant back in his chair, exhausted and frustrated, and caught sight of a toy sail boat that had run aground on the top of his book shelf. He salvaged it from its resting place and resumed his seat. He fingered the sail and the rudder delicately.

When he was eight, his father had helped him build the boat. Together they had expertly painted the small, wooden vessel in the Swedish colours. One summer's afternoon they took it to the lake – his father had told him that every ship needed a proper launch. After making a few adjustments to the rudder, he had gently pushed it out to the middle of the lake. Father and son had been enormously pleased with the results. He recalled his father saying, proudly, 'Not bad for a bank clerk.'

Then his father had been interrupted. A colleague from work, or perhaps a neighbour, had spotted him and called out.

'Wait there, Knut. Hold tight to the string. I'll be back in a minute,' his father had said before running up the bank to greet his friend.

Stubbendorff had turned to check his father was in sight and accidentally dropped the string. Before he could recover it, the wind had caught the boat's sail and the craft had taken route to the far side of the pond and had become snagged on a cluster of tangled twigs.

Concerned his father would be angry that he had not

followed instructions and worried that his boat would be lost forever, Knut rolled up his trousers and waded into the water.

A chill immediately shot through his warm body as the mud from the lake floor squelched between his toes. He turned and looked to his father, who was still occupied with his friend. As he took hesitant steps towards the craft, each time his feet sank into the mud he was reminded of his own recklessness and he was thrilled.

The water now reached his knees and the boat was close, just a few steps away.

'Knut, get back here!' he heard his father call from the bank. 'What on earth are you playing at?'

'I've nearly got it, Papa. I'm nearly there.'

Then he fell.

The floor of the lake dropped away. Splashing gracelessly in the water, he pedalled his legs fearfully beneath him. Panic gripped his throat and, as he opened his mouth to shout out to his father, the lake flooded into his lungs.

Then he felt a hand on the back of his shirt. He was hauled out of the water and into his father's arms.

Stubbendorff looked down at the cigarette between his fingers. It had burnt down. He placed it in the ashtray and lit another.

He was still floundering, he thought. He had waded into this mystery and now there was no one to show him the way out. He carefully placed the boat to one side, opened his notebook and began to read.

TWENTY-FIVE

TORQUAY, ENGLAND
SEPTEMBER 1930

ANNA'S HEAD THROBBED. With her cheek resting in her hand, she sat at the table and sipped her tea. Her view of Gil was obscured by the *Daily Express* he held aloft. Occasionally one side of the newspaper would fold onto itself – an indication her husband was taking a bite of his toast or a sip of his tea.

'The funeral is late next week. Your lot are pulling out all the stops, it seems. Sounds like it's going to be a grand affair. Military honours, brass band, mausoleum carved in marble. One of their brothers, ahhhh' – Gil pulled the newspaper closer to him – 'Tore, Tore Strindberg, is building a memorial. You ever heard of him?'

'Yes.'

'So he's famous, then?'

'Yes. Quite. In Sweden and abroad.'

Gil folded his newspaper carefully and placed it beside him. He leant across the table and touched Anna's fingertips with his own. 'What's wrong, my sweet? You haven't been yourself in days.'

'I've got a terrible headache and I'm very tired, that's all.'

'You didn't have to get up and make me breakfast. I can toast a couple of slices of bread and brew a pot of tea.'

Anna smiled and nodded wanly.

'You haven't been sleeping very well. I can feel you tossing and turning all night. Why don't you go and see the doctor today?'

'Yes, I will. That's a very good idea.'

Anna wanted him to leave. She lived in fear of her husband's daily updates. He had become fixated on the expedition, the men, their lives and families. She presumed his naval past had left him with a certain fascination for stories of adventure and exploration. But combined with the nightmares and her lack of sleep, Gil's interest in the topic was making her life unbearable. Besides, it was only a matter of time before her name appeared in the newspapers as well.

Sitting in her English kitchen opposite her English husband, she found herself, once again, trapped.

Gil stood up and moved behind Anna's chair. He massaged her temples lightly with his thick fingers. She closed her eyes, enjoying his touch.

'What would you have been at the time? Twenty-five or twenty-six?'

Anna's eyes opened. 'Yes, about that.' She shifted in her seat, pulling her head from Gil's hands. 'You'd better go. It's getting late.'

'Right you are. Drop in for a visit if you're seeing the doctor. You don't do that very often anymore.'

'If I have time.'

'Goodbye, now. I love you.' Gil bent to her and pulled her face to his. He kissed her on the mouth. Then, holding her cheeks in his bulky hands, he studied her pale face intensely.

After a few seconds she broke the gaze, made anxious by its possible meanings.

'I love you too. Have a good day.'

Once she heard the click of the front gate, Anna unfolded the newspaper and quickly scanned its contents until she found the article about Andrée and the expedition. She put it down and stared at the wall in front of her briefly before renewing her search. None of the information was new, merely a rehash of what had been reported previously about plans for the funeral and details of the expedition. Most of the coverage tended to focus on Andrée. Anna assumed it was because he was the most colourful of the three men, the oldest and the leader. The article included superficial insights into his character from past associates and acquaintances. All his immediate family members were deceased and, in Anna's mind, it didn't seem those living who knew him actually knew him very well. Each day, the portrait of Andrée the English press was painting was increasingly becoming that of a madman – a fanatic intent on reaching the North Pole at any cost. That had been Erik's opinion, she recalled, but Anna had never believed it to be the case.

There was nothing in the articles indicating that any of the Strindbergs had spoken to the press. Knowing them well, Anna was not surprised. They would strive to protect Nils' privacy at all costs.

In a shorter article, beneath the main story, there were statements from a man named Hallen, captain of the boat chartered to take a newspaper man to Kvitøya. The story also included an interview with a representative from the Scientific Commission in Stockholm, discussing the items found on the island. Her headache forgotten, she sat up straight and her breathing grew fierce. Her eyes dashed from left to right frantically, eager to fix on any mention of something belonging to Nils.

There it was. Photographs. Numerous rolls of photographic film had been discovered, mostly exposed, the article reported. Now in the hands of the Royal Institute of Technology in Stockholm, the images might well be salvageable. The institute had been Nils' place of work. A faint smile crossed Anna's lips. She wondered whether there might be someone still employed there who had worked with him or even remembered him. She refolded the newspaper carefully and went upstairs to the bedroom.

Anna found the wooden box. Still in her dressing-gown, she sat on the bed and laid the items out on the floral bedspread her sister-in-law had made for her wedding. She picked up a small photograph Nils had taken of her. It had been winter, a spectacularly cold day, and Nils, in his enthusiasm, had forced her into a park to test his latest lens, arguing that the light and conditions were perfect and most likely to resemble the conditions he would face during the expedition.

Anna studied the photograph for some time. Scrutinising every detail, she pictured Nils standing opposite her, behind the camera. In the snow, in the park, she remembered him taking what had seemed liked hundreds of photographs while experimenting with various lenses, apertures and shutter speeds.

As he explained his methods and reasoning, he scribbled furiously in his notebook and she stamped her frozen feet.

'I'm sorry,' Nils said, hugging her to him. 'You're frozen through. Let's go home. Janne will make us some hot chocolate.'

'Please don't be concerned. My frostbite will be in the name of science.'

They held each other tighter, stamping their feet as they did so. Nils gave Anna a quick kiss on the cheek then hastily returned his equipment to its case.

The next day he ushered her into his room. She was greeted by photographs of herself strung on lines running the length of the space, banners decorated with only her. The sight of her image replicated so many times was startling and made her laugh nervously. Each likeness was slightly different, but her pose and expression remained similar. Positioned next to the trunk of a tall spruce, she stood arms akimbo, face-on to the camera. A glimmer of a smile was apparent.

'I'm rather happy with how they turned out, but I'd like to try something a little different next time.'

'Next time you can ask Tore to be your research partner.'

'These ones are quite lovely, I think,' Nils said as he directed her to a corner of the room. Anna noticed a bed had been placed there. She hoped he was getting enough sleep.

'Here they are.'

She hadn't realised at the time, but Nils had taken a number of close-up photographs of her face. Unlike the others these were more candid, her mouth wide in speech, eyes lively in conversation as she stared into the lens unaware the photographer was at work. Wayward curls escaped onto her face from beneath a thick woollen hat she had knitted when she was a girl. Her nose showed a number of small crinkles.

'They're not very flattering. I prefer the ones taken from a distance.'

'You look lovely. Here, take one.' Nils unpegged one and gave it to her.

'Thank you. But I have no idea what I'm going to do with it.'

'Give it to your sweetheart.' He laughed and sat down on his bed, drawing her to him in the same motion. Before she could smile, he kissed her on the lips and his hand lightly caressed her thigh.

She realised there was something different in his kiss and embrace. Both seemed more intense, as if his life depended on being with her at that moment. He broke from her then began gently brushing his lips across her throat and neck. His hand lightly cupped her breast. Anna pulled him to her and stared for a moment into his crisp blue eyes. There was a longing there she had never seen before. Anna brought Nils' mouth to her own and kissed him deeply. She lay down on the pillow and opened herself to him for the first time.

Anna replaced the photograph in the box and shut the lid. She lay down on her side, pulled her legs close to her chest and closed her eyes. When the fate of the expedition became obvious, Anna could no longer leave her home without becoming the recipient of well-meaning condolences. Every word felt like an accusation. Every street she strolled down served as a reminder. She could no longer visit the home of the Larssons. In her mind every opening door and footstep on a staircase heralded Nils' entrance into the room. It was difficult to breathe. Sleeping became impossible. Life was impossible. There was only one person to whom she could turn. Anna decided to leave Sweden. She had never returned.

Dear Gil,

I have enclosed a photograph taken on the day of my engagement to Nils Strindberg. There is too much to try to explain in a letter, the entanglements of the last thirty years have overwhelmed me. How do I write everything down on paper when it is still such a mess for me?

There is so much you don't know about my life and I am going

to tell you, but I must return to Stockholm first. I have to go to Nils'
funeral.

Please don't come after me. Just trust that I will come back, if
you will have me. Know that I love you and cherish our life
together.

Anna

Gil sat on the bed holding the letter that had been left for
him. After arriving home from work and searching the house
for his wife, he had discovered it resting against a pillow. His
name, written on the envelope, was in her flowing script. He
read the single page a number of times in the hope that he
had misunderstood its contents and that, after a further
reading, Anna's actions would become clear.

He examined the photograph she had placed in the envelope along with the letter. Had she thought he needed proof
of her past? Gil wondered why she had never told him of this
engagement. Had she thought he would be jealous? It was
more than thirty years ago. She was well into her thirties
when they had met and married. He was under no illusions.
He knew there had been men before him. But Anna had
never wanted to discuss her past in any detail. He understood this reluctance better than most and didn't press her,
hoping she would tell him about her background when she
was ready, but she never did.

Although she pleaded against it in the letter, Gil's first
instincts had been to follow and find her and drag her home.
But he wasn't that sort of man. Anna knew him too well.

He stared hard at the girl in the photograph. This young
woman was not his wife. She wrote that she would come
home again, but what then? Anger welled in his chest. In a
sense he had been cuckolded for the past two decades. Years
of private desires and fears that she had never shared with
him. He had carried on cheerfully and foolishly, living with a
woman he didn't know. She'd been a shell of a woman

whom, he suddenly realised, he had never been able to make complete.

They were to celebrate their twentieth anniversary the following week. Gil had booked a trip for the two of them to London. A room at Claridge's for the weekend and a show, *Private Lives*. Anna had seen the reviews and had mentioned to Gil in passing that it sounded very clever. It had taken all of his resolve not to tell her about the surprise. Gil stood and stormed to the window. Flinging it wide, he gulped the cool evening air and began to cry.

TWENTY-SIX

TORQUAY, ENGLAND
SEPTEMBER 1930

THROUGH THE WINDOW a streetlight illuminated the peaceful scene. She was fascinated by the baby's downy face. Wrapped snug in a blanket that was barely blue, the child occasionally flinched. Her lips opened and closed. A small pink tongue emerged as if wanting to taste the unknown outside her slumbering body. Her eyelids flickered. Sometimes a tiny hand made its way through the tightly folded swaddling and pushed out into the cool air. Her mother gently manoeuvred the fugitive limb back into captivity. The only sound was the contented gurgle of the baby's belly.

When she was satisfied sleep had finally taken the infant, the woman began to stand. With her eyes on the resting child, she inched little by little to her feet, barely breathing. Once upright she walked with a light and deliberate tread to the cradle positioned next to her own bed and lowered the bundle onto the mattress. She removed her robe and slid between the bedclothes.

In the quiet, patiently waiting for sleep to arrive, the woman became aware of the hoarse breathing of the figure lying beside her. She laid her hand on the man's broad back, attempting to quieten him, and struggled to listen only to the breathing of her own child in the cradle. Closing her eyes tightly, she could just distinguish the child's short, irregular breaths and was soothed. She relaxed, slept.

Anna woke with a start. The room was dark except for the streetlight's intrusive glare. She rolled onto her side and nestled her head into the pillow. Her hands, positioned as if in prayer, were resting under her cheek. Closing her eyes and sweeping her mind of all thoughts, she endeavoured to recognise the sound of her child's breath, the sound of life from the cradle. Straining to hear the familiar, eyes closed tight, she propped her body up on one elbow. Her heart pounding, she moved slowly to her feet and stood over the cradle.

The baby was just as she had left her. But as Anna reached into the cradle to touch the child's velvety cheek, she knew her daughter was dead. She noticed one hand poking from the shroud, pressing against the baby's chin. Anna held her own hand to her baby's mouth and felt no air, then wrapped her fingers tightly around those of the baby. She could still feel her daughter's warmth as she brought the baby to her chest.

Anna's eyes shot open suddenly. Her breathing was heavy. Her hands gripped the arms of the seat and her knuckles were white. Without moving her head, she cast her eyes around the carriage, not certain where she was.

'Are you all right, love?' An elderly woman sitting beside

her touched Anna's forearm lightly. 'You were dreaming, I think.'

'I'm fine, thank you.' She took a few deep breaths and tried to relax. 'How long until we arrive?'

'About an hour.'

Anna smiled in thanks and the woman went back to her knitting.

She looked out the window at the passing scenery. The woman's busy fingers were reflected in the glass. Anna yawned widely. She felt exhausted but full of purpose. Her decision to leave Torquay had been sudden. She had hastily written the note to Gil, telling him about her engagement to Nils. Erik would have to come later, if ever. She had packed a small case then walked from her home. She was not certain for how long she would be away. Neither was she certain that Gil would understand.

Anna sank lower in her seat and turned her head towards her neighbour. The woman's hands were knotted and the skin covering them resembled paper, but they were beautiful and mesmerising as they deftly controlled and guided the needles through the pale blue wool. 'What are you making?'

'A jacket for my grandson. He was born on the third. I'm going to visit him.'

'Does your family live in Ramsgate?'

'Yes, my daughter and her husband and children. They've asked me to move, to be closer to them. But I could never leave London. Home is where the heart is, as they say.'

Anna nodded in agreement.

It was thirty years since she had left Stockholm and Gota and the Strindbergs. Erik had promptly seen to all her arrangements. He had found her a position as a governess and organised her passage. She had left Stockholm quickly and without deliberation, allowing Erik to see to her future.

Her flight from Stockholm had been planned without

Gota's knowledge. On the morning of Anna's departure Gota had handed Anna a list of errands and chores to do that day. Once her sister had left for work, Anna had gone through the list methodically, drawing a line through each task once it was done. Then, turning the note over, she wrote a short letter of explanation and propped it up on the table in the small apartment the sisters had shared for eight years. She had not seen or spoken to Gota since.

'You're very talented,' she told the woman. 'The jacket is beautiful – so detailed. He'll be a very well-dressed young man.'

'My mother taught me when I was a girl. You don't knit?'

'No, not really. My sister was very good. She was a dressmaker and was gifted at all those things – sewing, knitting, embroidery. But whenever I tried anything like that, it was like I had six fingers on each hand.' They both laughed. 'An old friend said I was useless at the finer arts because my hands were so big, but they were the perfect size for playing the piano.' Anna held her hands up for closer inspection.

'Ah, you play the piano. Now that's a wonderful gift.'

Anna smiled and closed her eyes. She did not want to keep talking to this woman. She didn't want to explain her reason for going to Stockholm. She had no intention of meeting Gota or any of the Strindbergs. Too much time had passed; there was too much to explain. She did not want to lie to people she still held precious. Seeing Nils' coffin, paying her respects – she hoped it would bring her nearer to an ending. Her treatment of Nils had been abominable; her treatment of Erik, similarly so. But there was nothing she could do now to set things right. What she longed for was simply a conclusion to that chapter of her life so she might truly begin another with Gil. Anna was determined not to squander his love as well. The endless twilight of the past had shaded their relationship for too long. And of course there was the child. To glimpse the woman the infant had grown into was important to Anna. It would be another ending of sorts, she hoped.

Once so desperate to leave and now so desperate to return. No one would ever understand her. Erik had tried, but even he had failed.

She kept her eyes shut tight as the conductor walked through the cabin. She felt the rush of air as he passed her seat. It was fifteen minutes until the train arrived in Ramsgate

Arthur Lynch

Black and White: A Weekly Illustrated Record and Review

7 August 1897

THE ANDRÉE BALLOON EXPEDITION TO THE POLE

The account which follows of the departure of the balloon
Örner, with its three intrepid passengers, Messrs. Andrée,
Strindberg, and Frænkel, is taken in great part from the
journal of M. Alexis Machuron, the balloon expert, who
represented at Spitsbergen his uncle, M. Lachambre, the
constructor of the balloon. The details contained in the
journal have, however, been eked out with information I
gathered from M. Machuron during a long conversation the
day of his return to Paris.

From the beginning of July all the members of the expedition were becoming impatient to start, as every day gained
meant a day longer of summer and daylight for the chance of
completing their task. M. Andrée was especially determined
that there should be no hitch this time. 'I will start for the
pole,' he said, 'on this occasion, cost what it may, and in spite
of the difficulties that may arise.' On 11 July he was exceed-
ingly silent during the morning, and apparently locked up in
his own thoughts. At about ten o'clock he went to take note
of the various meteorological instruments – anemometer,
thermometer, barometer & c. – which he had brought with
him. The wind was then south-south-west.

About an hour afterwards Andrée suddenly announced
that he was prepared to depart that day. He called together
the other members of the expedition, as well as the captain of
the *Svensksund* and M. Machuron, and asked their advice,

beginning with Machuron. All responded affirmatively, and at eleven o'clock the work of preparation began. The carpenters, aided by all the sailors of the *Svensksund*, began to demolish the northern side of the shed, while at the same time the southern side was made higher in order to protect the balloon against the wind, which was becoming stronger. The great difficulty was to allow the balloon to ascend without danger of tearing its tissue against the walls or posts of the shed, and these walls and posts were padded in their prominent parts with felt. As the shed was being demolished the balloon, with its great height and circumference and distended surface, looked more like a building than an object lighter than the air. It began to roll a little, however, and large bands were passed around its circumference and tied to the uprights of the shed. The whole surface was carefully gone over to detect any leakage, and weak spots were patched up.

All the work was carried out with the greatest rapidity. All the members of the expedition helped, and the herculean strength of M. Frænkel was especially noticeable in the way in which he handled with ease enormous beams and weights that an ordinary man could hardly move. The last thing to be done to make the balloon ready was to attach the car. This was accomplished at about two o'clock, the car being attached to the ring, which in turn was held by three stout ropes fixed to large pegs driven into the ground.

Everything was now ready, and the solemn moment of departure had arrived. The leave-takings were very touching, although hardly a word was uttered by anyone present, and there was no kind of ceremony. Indeed the rapidity and businesslike nature of the proceedings left no room for anything superfluous. The members of the expedition shook hands warmly with those who were to remain, and a feeling of suppressed anxiety and emotion seemed to reign among all present. The three explorers were remarkably calm. M. Andrée appeared to be as cool and collected as on any other day, and his air of quiet confidence completely reassured the others. Frænkel was vigorous and hearty, while Strindberg, though equally brave and resolute, could not repress a slight trembling of his hands.

Andrée mounted the car, looked all round to assure himself that everything was in order, and then in a tone of command called out, 'Strindberg!' Strindberg mounted. 'Frænkel!' Frænkel mounted. 'Come!' said Andrée cheerfully, and no other word was uttered.

The captain of the *Svensksund* was in charge of the sailors appointed to cut the cords. First the bands that held the balloon round the centre were released, and the balloon began to roll again. It was necessary to look out for a moment of comparative equilibrium. Both the captain of the *Svensksund* and M. Andrée watched attentively. Suddenly Andrée cried out, 'Cut!'

The sailors plied their knives at once, and in a moment the balloon, released, bounded 300 feet into the air.

Wild cries of 'Hurrah!' and 'Bon voyage!' were raised by the spectators on shore – hardly answered, however, by the occupants of the balloon, for they were wholly intent on watching the course of their aerial ship. Almost immediately after mounting, the balloon fell rapidly again, and skimmed the surface of the waves. The wind was now blowing violently, and the balloon was carried swiftly away. It rose, and then pursued its way at an even height from the surface of the water, moving very rapidly. The three navigators waved their handkerchiefs at those on shore, and this they continued to do until the balloon had passed out of sight away on the horizon. It did not remain in view more than half an hour, but those who were watching it remained mutely gazing over towards the horizon long after the faint speck had vanished. They had witnessed the start of one of the greatest feats of adventure the world has ever known.

TWENTY-SEVEN

STOCKHOLM, SWEDEN
MAY 1897

THE ATMOSPHERE STRUCK Anna the moment she entered the house. Rosalie greeted her with a strained smile and Anna followed her into the sitting room. Nils jumped to his feet and hugged his fiancée tightly, skittishly. Sven and Tore were engaged in a game of chess. As they deliberately moved their pieces around the board, it occurred to Anna that she had never seen the brothers play in this way before – silently. Erik, leaning on the mantle, strummed his fingers along the oak. He nodded a cursory welcome. Oscar sat rigid on the settee alongside a grinning young man Anna had never seen before.

'Anna, I would like you to meet Knut Frænkel,' Nils said. Frænkel stood and shook her hand.

'I'm sorry to be late. I was delayed at the Larssons',' Anna explained to her hosts.

'That's quite all right, my dear,' Rosalie said. 'We are still waiting on Professor Andrée.'

'Can anyone actually confirm that Andrée is a professor? He has been given this title, but all he holds is a degree in mechanical engineering from the Institute of Technology,' Erik said. Nils directed a brief grin towards Anna.

'Not tonight, Erik, my darling,' Rosalie cut in. 'Nils leaves the day after tomorrow. Can we all please try to make this evening as pleasant as possible?'

Erik cleared his throat. His eyes twinkled with mischief.

'With all due respect, Herr Strindberg' – Frænkel's sudden boldness took Erik by surprise – 'I believe he has earned the title of professor. He is a professor of physics, I believe.'

'Forgive me, Herr Frænkel, for my ignorance. But I had no idea he was a physicist as well as an engineer. Such an accomplished gentleman. Nils, as a physicist yourself, were you aware your learned leader was a professor of physics?'

Nils was diplomatic. 'It's more of an honorary title, I believe. One he was given for his work in the field of aero-nautics.'

'And who gave it to him? Was it bestowed on him by himself?' Erik queried innocently.

Nils smiled, but his shoulders drooped. His father came to his rescue.

'Erik, enough about Andrée, whatever and wherever he may be.' Oscar looked seriously at Nils. 'Tell us about your trip.'

The doorbell rang. Sven and Tore ceased their chess game and stood, straightening their ties. Oscar stubbed out his cigarette and Rosalie fixed her hair quickly in the mirror above the mantel. Nils edged a little closer to the door, ready to greet the man, professor or not.

Janne entered alone. She handed Nils a note. He read it quickly and then faced the group. 'Andrée is unable to attend this evening. His mother took ill yesterday and she died early this morning. He's in Gränna presently, expected to return to Stockholm tomorrow.'

The room was quiet for some time. Anna glanced around at those assembled. She could see Nils' mind at work, mapping the possible consequences of this unforeseen event. Frænkel's confusion was evident. Rosalie and Oscar were clearly overjoyed. Tore's brow was furrowed in indignation and Sven looked at Nils with concern. Erik was staring directly at Anna. She couldn't read his expression – hope, joy, disappointment? Anna turned again to her fiancé. It was up to him to speak, to break the silence, but she could see he was disoriented, his eyes fixed on the telegram in his hand.

'You'll still be going, won't you?' Tore's distress was plain in every syllable.

'I don't know,' Nils replied. 'The launch cannot be postponed. Favourable conditions – we have such a small window.' He spoke haltingly then sat on the sofa heavily. No one was certain whether he was saddened or relieved. Rosalie went to him and took her son's hand.

'Perhaps it's a sign. Perhaps this expedition just wasn't meant to be,' she said.

'Your mother is right.' Oscar took up his wife's lead. 'I mean, your failure to launch last year and now this. I think someone is trying to tell you something.'

'Why don't you wire Andrée back immediately?' Rosalie said. 'Say that you see this unexpected tragedy as a sign, a portent, that the expedition should be cancelled. You're thinking of his wellbeing, of course. It's fate's way of preventing another such tragedy. What do you think?'

'I don't believe in fate, Mama. Neither does Andrée,' Nils said, still clutching the telegram.

Erik went to his brother and took the note. He read it himself and stuffed it in his pocket.

'I think, Mama, this conversation might be better left

until we receive further news. There's a very good chance the expedition will be cancelled. Andrée was quite devoted to his mother, I've heard. It would take a man of unique character to leave on an Arctic expedition just two days after his mother's death. We should probably leave it at that.' Erik spoke gently, wary of trying to strongarm his brother down a particular route.

Rosalie nodded in agreement, realising her misstep.

Then, taking Nils by the shoulders and raising him to his feet, Erik said, 'All you can do is wait for further direction from Andrée. A professor is bound to know what the most appropriate course of action should be.' They all looked to him for a moment, stunned, and then burst into laughter. The shadow temporarily lifted.

'You're a terrible child, Erik Strindberg,' Rosalie said, wiping her eyes. 'I think it's time we began this dinner.' She led the way from the sitting room.

Following the meal, when Frænkel had gone home and Anna was playing for the rest of the family, Nils discreetly tugged at Erik's coat sleeve and left the room. Erik stood and followed him. All except Anna were ignorant of their departure. Her finger struck a wrong key and she smiled awkwardly in apology.

Once the brothers entered Nils' workroom, the younger looked to the elder as he had done thousands of times in the past. His eyes were expressive, hopeful. 'Do you think it will go ahead?'

Erik shrugged his shoulders. 'On the one hand the man's mother, a woman he idolised, has just died. On the other he's a fanatical self-promoter who suffers extreme narrow-mindedness. What do you want to happen?'

Nils shook his head. 'I hope the expedition is cancelled. Too much of my life's been devoted to this blasted launch.'

Erik sat on the bed and looked at his brother, bewildered. He rubbed his forehead. He recognised the opportunity, the only opportunity that had arisen in the past eighteen months. He stood and moved towards Nils. 'It's not too late. If Andrée does go ahead, it's not too late to withdraw.'

'That would be impossible. The family name and my position at the university only count for so much. Reputation is everything in Stockholm,' Nils responded bleakly. 'You're aware of that. If I backed out now, at the eleventh hour, it would ruin me. I am a man of my word, Erik. Placed in the same predicament, under the same circumstances, what would be your decision?'

Erik thought some time before answering. To answer truthfully would be to relinquish the advantage he had only minutes ago gained. But it was Nils. He couldn't lie. 'I'd go,' he answered quietly.

Nils nodded wearily. 'I have no faith the air balloon will get us to the pole. Ekholm's concerns last year were valid. Andrée has made no significant changes to the balloon.'

Erik pressed forward. 'If you feel your life is at stake, withdraw. I'll support you in your decision. I'll speak to the press on your behalf. I'll punch any man who dares call you a coward.' He took care to keep the desperation he was feeling out of his voice. 'After that you and Anna can come to America. I'm certain they need physicists in Chicago as well. Start again in another country.'

Nils ignored his suggestion. Erik doubted whether he had even heard it. 'I believe it'll come down to sledges, travelling as far as possible in the balloon and walking the rest of the way, pulling our supplies on sledges. Andrée chose Frænkel mainly because he's fit, and I'm strong and healthy. I think by foot we'd have a greater chance of reaching the pole anyway.'

He hesitated. 'If Andrée decides to launch on Sunday and it all goes wrong, will you see to Anna?'

Erik had been certain Nils knew nothing of his feelings for Anna. Did he suspect? 'What do you mean?'

'Take care of her, support her, love her, if that's possible. There's something in her . . . a sadness I see sometimes. Perhaps I'm imagining it.'

'I'll do everything in my power to ensure her happiness,' Erik responded flatly. The brothers left the workroom and rejoined the others.

NILS STRINDBERG'S JOURNAL, 23RD JUNE 1897

I sit alone in the balloon house with the somewhat more than half-filled balloon beside me. Hard winds from the NE whistle through the upper parts of the balloon house and in the mountain above. I hold watch beside the hydrogen apparatus, but now I am free from duties as the filling is going well. It is strange to sit here now, once more, and to think that I am engaged to the best girl in the world, my sincerely beloved Anna. Yes, I may shed a tear when I think of the happiness that has passed and that may never again be returned to me. But what would this matter to me if I merely knew that she would be happy. But I know that she loves me, which makes me proud, and that she would be deeply affected by my departure. Therefore I cannot neglect in my sadness to think of her and the happy times we spent together this winter, and in particular this spring. But allow me to hope. The balloon is now varnished and much tighter than last year; we have the summer before us with its favourable winds and sunlight. Why wouldn't our mission succeed. This I fully believe.

TWENTY-EIGHT

STOCKHOLM, SWEDEN
JULY 1897

Anna sat opposite her sister, sipping her coffee slowly. Gota had never read the newspaper until the past week. Since the launch, she had followed any update regarding the expedition and the flight of the *Örnen*. Anna was not certain where this curiosity had sprung from, but Gota delighted in her new pastime.

Nils had left Stockholm in May. Anna had not seen him in almost two months. His farewell had not been as she had expected. It was rushed and uncomfortable. Erik was present, as was the rest of the family, as Nils boarded the train for Gothenburg. He had only learnt that morning that the expedition was going ahead. Everyone was disappointed, even Tore. Sven had told Anna when he arrived at her apartment in the early morning that a telegram from Andrée had been received only an hour earlier, informing Nils that he had no intention of cancelling or postponing.

'Mama is devastated; so is Erik,' Sven had said. 'I guess we all thought there was a chance, a bloody good chance, that it might be off.'

'What about Nils?'

'He's determined to make the best of it, I suppose. Maybe he's just putting on a brave face for Mama. Erik's working hard to stop him leaving, but I think it's too late.'

At the station, newspaper reporters and crowds had surrounded Nils as he walked towards his carriage. Anna and his family stood back, waiting for the throngs to disperse, but they did not. Nils was distracted and distant, and he barely looked at his fiancée. A peck on the cheek and he was gone, bustled onto the train by wellwishers. As the train pulled away from the platform, she noticed tears running down Tore's cheeks. She placed an arm around his shoulder, but he recoiled at her touch and drew away, going to stand next to his mother. Anna stood alone, hurt and confused by Tore's rebuff.

'Don't worry about Tore. He's upset, that's all,' Erik said. 'May I walk you home?'

Anna shook her head. 'I don't think so. You should be with your family.'

'You're part of the family. Why don't you come back to the house?'

Anna had declined. Her own company was all she desired that afternoon. She walked straight home and climbed into her bed. It was only two o'clock in the afternoon but she slept until the next morning.

'So, dear sister, we should be on the lookout for a pigeon.' Gota giggled and shook her head. 'How silly.'

'Pigeon? What are you talking about?'

'Well, it says here.' Gota pointed her pudgy finger at an article on the front page of the *Aftonbladet*. 'It says here that Nils sent a love message to you via carrier pigeon.' She giggled again.

Anna wondered whether he had done this or it was a tale invented by a whimsical journalist.

'I can't see Nils doing that, can you?' Gota said.

Anna shook her head. 'I'm not sure.'

'Will you be seeing Erik, do you think?' Gota asked, all traces of playfulness gone from her voice.

'I shouldn't think so.' Anna stood without a word. She heard a muffled snort of derision as she left the room.

The World, New York
July 1897

DID THEY ESCAPE FROM ANDRÉE?

Manchester, England, 12 July – The steamship *Ragnhild* has arrived here, bringing four carrier pigeons labelled 'North Pole Expedition'.

Two of the birds are numbered 05 and 106.

No message was attached to either. The captain reports that they alighted on the steamship when she was in the North Sea, and seemed exhausted.

Carrier pigeons labelled 'North Pole Expedition' flying homeward without messages indicate either that they escaped through somebody's carelessness or that the expedition to which they belonged met with disaster.

These stray pigeons may have been taken by Prof. Andrée in his balloon when he soared away from Dane's Island on 1 July, as is supposed, to get a bird's-eye view of the North Pole. If they were his messengers he undoubtedly took them from his home in Stockholm. Then, in their instinctive flight from regions north of Dane's Island towards their home in Sweden, they naturally would fly over the North Sea, and after a journey of 1500 to 1600 miles must be exhausted.

TWENTY-NINE

BJØRNØYA, NORWAY

15 JULY 1897

THE YOUNG MAN was awoken by squawking gulls. Two of them. They circled the masthead a number of times as Ottosen stood and bent his neck backward to gain a better view of them. He saw the source of the gulls' rancour. A third bird, of a kind he did not recognise from that distance, had settled on the masthead.

I should wake the captain, he thought. If the din went on, the entire crew would be roused. It was his first night onboard the *Alken* and the fifteen-year-old had been assigned to stand the night watch. He thought it odd that the term 'night watch' should be used when, in July, the sun did not set. But from what his crew mates had told him of the captain, he believed it would be unwise to point this out to Ole Hansen.

Ottosen made his way below deck and knocked softly on the captain's door. When he placed his ear against the wood,

Hansen's throaty snore was audible. Ottosen knocked harder.

Hansen came to the door. His eyes were still shut. 'What time is it?'

'Two o'clock, captain.'

'My god, this better be good.'

'A peculiar bird, a ptarmigan, I think, is sitting on the masthead.

It was chased there by two seagulls.'

'And?'

'And the gulls are making a lot of noise.'

'Come here, boy,' Hansen ordered as he sat on his bed. 'Put on my boots for me.'

Ottosen did as he was told. The captain then stood sleepily and reached for his gun. Ottosen followed the captain up to the deck.

Once in the open air Hansen's eyes opened fully and he became aware of the gulls taunting the resting bird.

'It's not a ptarmigan. It's a pigeon. It must be hurt.'

As the boy looked up, Hansen fired three shots off in quick succession. Ottosen flinched violently and his ears rang. Before he had time to compose himself, Hansen was back below deck. Ottosen ran to the side of the ship and looked into the water. The bodies of three birds floated lifeless in the sea.

It was not unusual for the *Alken* to run into another sealer during the summer. Most captains took advantage of the warm weather and clear conditions to fill their coffers, hopefully ensuring a relaxed and restful winter. Hansen was glad when they came across the *Fjert* a short distance from Bjørnøya.

'Hello there. Come aboard, Fosse. Come and have a drink with me.'

Hansen and Fosse both came from Torvig and had known each other as boys. The men shared similar career paths and demeanours. 'Thank you, thank you,' Fosse called from the bow of the *Fjert*. 'I'll be right there.'

Once the men were settled in Hansen's cabin with a bottle of vodka, they began to discuss their families, mutual acquaintances and the highs and lows of the season. One of those lows for Hansen was his early-morning awakening by his young deck hand. Hansen related the story to his friend in great detail. In hindsight he found the incident quite amusing. More so from the perspective of frightening the inexperienced seaman within an inch of his life than from being roused at two in the morning.

'Perhaps it was one of Andrée's pigeons you shot,' Fosse laughed.

'Ay? What do you mean?'

'You know. Andrée. That daft explorer in the balloon. He took a flock of carrier pigeons along for the ride. Apparently he plans to send messages back to Stockholm with them. Fool.' Fosse shook his head at the stupidity of the idea and finished another glass.

Hansen did likewise. 'When did he leave?'

Fosse looked at his friend in enquiry.

'The balloon chap. When did he leave?'

'Two or three days ago, I think.'

'You know, this pigeon, the one I shot. I thought it was poorly. It might have been tired.'

Fosse nodded in agreement as he raised a glass to his cracked lips.

As the afternoon wore on and the bottle emptied, the two seamen became convinced the pigeon had belonged to Andrée.

Overcome with drunk regret, Hansen ordered the *Alken*'s about-face and the vessel returned to Bjørnøya.

The slain pigeon was recovered. As he examined the sodden bird on deck, Hansen discovered a small cylinder, coated with paraffin, wired to its leg. Inside was a note on parchment, written in Andrée's exacting hand, detailing the position and speed of the balloon on 13 July at twelve-thirty in the afternoon.

We have just stopped for the day after drudging and pulling the sledges for ten hours. I am really rather tired but must first chat a little. First and foremost I must congratulate you, for this is your birthday. Oh, how I wish I could tell you now that I am in excellent health and that you need not fear for us at all. We are sure to come home by and by. Yes, how very much all this occupies my thoughts during the day, for I have plenty of time to think and it is so good to have such happy prospects for the future as I have, to think about.

Now we have camped for the night and had coffee and biscuits and syrup. Just now we are putting up the tent and Frænkel is taking the meteorological observations. Now we are enjoying a caramel, it is a real luxury. You can fancy we are not over-delicate here. Yesterday evening I gave them (for it is I who attend to the housekeeping) a soup which was really not good, for that Rousseau meat-powder has a bad taste and one soon becomes tired of it. But we managed to eat it in any case.

Well, we have stopped for the night on an open place, round about there is ice, ice in every direction. You saw from Nansen's pictures how such ice looks. Hummocks, walls and fissures in the sea alternating with melted ice, everlasting the same. For the moment it is snowing a little but it is calm at least and not especially cold (-0.8°). At home I think you have nicer summer weather.

Yes, it is strange to think that not even for your next birthday will it be possible for us to be at home. And perhaps we shall have to winter here for another year or more. We do not know yet. We are now moving onwards so slowly that perhaps we shall not reach Cape Flora this winter, but like Nansen, will have to pass the winter in an earth-cellar. Poor little Anna, in what despair you will be if we should not come home next autumn. And you can imagine how I am tortured by the thought of it, too, not for my own sake, for now I do not mind if I have hardships as long as I can come home at last.

– Nils Strindberg's journal, 25 July 1897

THIRTY

STOCKHOLM, SWEDEN

JULY 1897

HE WAS STANDING by the front door when she left the Larssons' apartment.

'Happy birthday, Anna. Many happy returns of the day.' Erik presented her with an extravagant bouquet of gerberas and larkspur. Anna avoided his eyes, directing her gaze instead to the flowers.

'Please accept them. It must be difficult for you today. My motives are genuine. No strings attached, as they say.' A nervous chuckle escaped him.

She looked into his face and saw only decency. She was also touched that he remembered the date. 'Thank you. It's been quite trying today.' Anna held her arms out and Erik laid his gift across them. 'They're lovely. Heavy, but lovely,' she said. The blush of embarrassment that appeared on Erik's ruddy cheeks was only the second she had ever seen.

'May I walk with you a little way?' he asked.

'Yes. That would be nice.'

'May I take the flowers from you? I fear you won't be able to see where you're going.'

'I'd be most grateful.'

They strolled along Prästgatan, comfortably silent until they reached the harbour. The evening air was warm and she could smell the sea. Before they went their separate ways, Erik invited her to sit.

'Are you still enjoying working at the Larssons'?'

'Yes, quite. Although I've been distracted lately. I'm hoping that will soon pass.'

'Yes, yes, of course. Did you read the notice in the *Aftonbladet* yesterday evening about the carrier pigeon? It bodes well.'

'I saw it.'

'Quite a tale,' he added. 'You shouldn't be a stranger at the house. You're still part of the family . . . Mother misses you terribly, you know.'

He looked towards the boats in the harbour. 'If my presence when you visit is undesirable . . .'

'Not at all. I'll try to call next week.' Fearing she would be coaxed into giving an exact time, she said hastily, 'But I must go now. Thank you for the flowers.'

They stood and, as Erik passed over the bundle, he touched her fingertips softly. At that moment Anna wanted to fall into his arms, promise him anything, in return for a minute of calm. It took everything she possessed to stop herself from doing so. Ignoring every instinct, she turned away and faced the sea.

'Remember, Anna, if there's anything you need it would be my pleasure to help.'

'I'm sure I'll be fine.'

She could tell there was more Erik wanted to say. Finally, he began. 'I'm leaving tomorrow for America. My train leaves at two o'clock.' He hesitated and took her hand. 'If you'd like to come to the station to say goodbye . . . My father alone is escorting me. There have been too many goodbyes in our family recently. I don't think Mama could endure another. Your presence at the station would mean . . . I can't describe what it would mean. I'll be sitting in the first-class carriage.' He released her hand when three people waiting for the ferry stood close to them.

By the time Anna responded, the ferry had arrived at the dock. 'I'm sure I'll be able to be there. It's my half-day tomorrow.' She sensed Erik's gaze on her departing figure. She refused to look back.

Here one day passes like another. Pulling and drudging at the sledges, eating and sleeping. The most delightful hour of the day is when one has gone to bed and allows one's thoughts to fly back to better and happier times. But the immediate goal now is our wintering-place. We hope to find things better in the future. Now the others are coming back and we shall continue the drudgery with the sledges. Au revoir.

– Nils Strindberg's journal, 26 July 1897

She took a seat by the window of the cafe. The platform was in clear sight and the train to Gothenburg was waiting. Anna sipped her coffee slowly. She hoped she had not missed him. She had arrived early to ensure that would not be the case. She did not actually feel like anything to drink, but the cafe was the least conspicuous place from which to view the platform and the proprietor was surly. She had thought she'd better order something.

At a quarter to the hour Erik and his father made their

way along the length of the train. They stopped outside the first-class carriage and placed the luggage on the platform. It was quickly attended to by a porter. The two men looked at each other before embracing. They hugged tightly. Anna believed she witnessed Erik's feet leave the ground for an instant. She could tell Oscar was saying something into his son's ear. When they broke apart, Oscar wiped his eyes on a handkerchief and blew his nose. They shook hands. A brief conversation took place. She could see Erik's head nodding soberly.

Anna understood from Erik's gestures and expressions that he was advising his father to leave. Oscar patted his son on the back and then nodded. Father and son shook hands once again. Before departing, Oscar placed his hand firmly on his son's cheek, there was a brief interchange and father and son laughed heartily before Oscar Strindberg retraced his steps to the end of the platform. Erik watched him go and looked at his watch. He then glanced at the clock on the platform. Anna checked the time as well. It was five minutes to the hour.

Erik pushed his hands into his pockets and looked up and down the length of the train, from front to back. His gaze returned to his watch for an instant. Anna saw his chest rise and then descend. The whistle blew and Erik turned to the train. She wondered how long he would stand there, waiting. As he checked the time again, a porter emerged from the train and spoke to him on his way to the next carriage. Erik nodded. He craned his neck and peered along the platform once more before finally ascending the steps to his carriage. Watching him board the train was agonising. The urge to go to him was overwhelming. She imagined she could see his face pressed to the window as the train pulled out of the station.

THIRTY-ONE

This buoy is thrown out from Andrée's balloon at 10.55 G.M.T. on
11 July 1897, in about 82° latitude and 25° long. E.fr.Gr. We are
floating at a height of 600 metres [1950 feet].
All well
Andrée Strindberg Frænkel

KOLLAFJORD, ICELAND

14 MAY 1899

THE SUN HAD JUST BEGUN to lose its heat when Fjalar Jónsson
decided to carry his strange discovery home from the beach.
Although it was not large, it was oddly shaped and difficult
to manage. The wire that encased the bulky teardrop was
rusty and sharp. The twelve-year-old removed his coat,
threaded an arm of the woollen jacket through the wire and
flung the object over his shoulder. Satisfied, he marched up
the grassy hill towards Hlit Farm.

'What have you found? What is it? Let me see.' Katrin met him at the door.

'Be quiet. It's none of your concern. Is Papa in yet?' Katrin, Fjalar's ten-year-old sister, was shut down abruptly. After his long trek from the seaside the boy was in no mood to humour the bane of his brief existence.

'You're late, anyway.' Katrin disappeared sulkily into another room, no doubt to complain of her brother's behaviour.

Fjalar placed the object on the table in the kitchen and sat looking at it quietly. He had no clue as to its purpose. It certainly was not anything you'd find on a farm. Perhaps it belonged to a fisherman, he thought, or maybe it had fallen off a warship. The boy stood and, gripping the large cork that sealed its only opening with dirty fingers, pulled hard. The cork crumbled about its edges and left a dusty residue on the spotless table but it remained firmly wedged. He was certain his father would know what this unusual object was. He hoped he would be allowed to keep it.

'What have you brought home now? Get that off my kitchen table,' Fjalar's mother screeched as she entered the kitchen. She grabbed his broad shoulders in her large hands and turned the boy towards her. They stood eye to eye. She shook his frame in time with her words, a comical habit that always amused her husband. 'That table needs to be set for supper. Your father will be home any minute and he'll want his supper waiting for him. Now get that thing outside.'

Knowing better than to argue with his mother, the boy was lifting the object from the table when his father opened the door. His frame filled the doorway and his entry into the house brought with it the familiar smell of sheep.

'I can hear you screaming from the barn, woman,' his father boomed. Then, noticing his son's find, his tone suddenly changed. 'What have we got here?'

Jón Stefánsson's wide, blue eyes twinkled. He knelt by the side of the table to get a closer look. Sand fell from the object as Stefánsson rolled it back and forth across the table examining it.

'I'm not sure, Papa. I found it on the beach this afternoon. I thought perhaps it might be a mine from a warship.'

'Sorry to disappoint you, son, but it looks to me like a buoy. See, it's made of cork. Although it does seem much heavier than cork. It's more likely to belong to a fisherman than the Royal Navy.'

'But look.' Fjalar pointed to the sealed opening. 'It might have something inside it.'

'Ah, that is interesting. Shall we take a look?'

Stefánsson's wife and daughter stood back nervously while Fjalar and his father prised the cork free with the aid of a small knife.

Hidden inside the buoy was a small glass cylinder, wrapped in a woollen sock and sealed with a smaller cork.The cylinder had been thoroughly covered with what Stefánsson assumed was beeswax.

'See inside, it's steel.'

The boy poked as much as he could of his face into the opening, then felt inside with his hand, following his father's direction.

'It must have been covered in cork so it would float.'

Removing the cork from the small cylinder, they discovered a note.

'It's in Swedish or Norwegian, I think,' Stefánsson said.

'What should we do?' Fjalar enquired.

After a few moments of thought the farmer stood and slotted the note into the cylinder and the cylinder into the buoy, just as the boy had discovered it.

'I'm going into Flateyri. Grímur will know what to do. He can speak Swedish.'

'What about supper?' his wife said testily.

'I won't be long. You go ahead. Fjalar, you coming?'

'It could just be a child's silly trick. You're wasting your time,' his wife harped as Stefánsson packed up the contents of the buoy.

'Don't start drinking with that blowhard or you'll never get home,' she hissed.

His joyful son fumbled into his coat and ran out the door, following in his father's wake.

It turned out that Stefánsson's friend Grímur did not speak Swedish or Norwegian or Danish. He spoke no language except Icelandic. Over a half-bottle of schnapps, the farmer and the blacksmith discussed what should be done. Fjalar sat between them, listening intently. At ten o'clock it was decided that Grímur would post the buoy to the Governor in Reykjavik in the morning.

From Reykjavik the buoy was dispatched to an old family friend of the Governor's, the Minister for Iceland in Copenhagen. He then forwarded it to Stockholm.

By the time Anna discovered the communication buried in the depths of the *Aftonbladet*, Gota had given up reading the newspaper. Anna was relieved her sister had not seen the eighty-two-word article on page fourteen as she would have complained tirelessly in regard to its brevity.

ANDRÉE'S JOURNAL, 4
SEPTEMBER 1897

September 4. Strindberg's birthday. Festal day. I awakened him giving him letters from his sweetheart and relations. It was a real pleasure to see how glad he was. Today we have had some extra food in honour of the occasion. The breakfast consists of bear's meat with bread and Stauffer's pea soup with bear's meat and bear's fat. At dinner, fried bear's meat, bread and pâté de foie gras, Stauffer-cake with syrup sauce, syrup and water, speech for Nils, Lactoserin chocolate. Strindberg celebrated his birthday by falling very thoroughly, sledge and all, into the 'soup'. We had to pitch our tent after three hours' march, and then had a very troublesome and time-wasting business to dry him and his things. Much of the bread and biscuits and all the sugar damaged, but we had to keep it in any case, and this was done by drying part of the bread slowly and using it as before. The remainder was fried along with the bear's meat and the sauce. The sugar is poured into the chocolate and coffee in its liquid form. The biscuit-mud is mixed with cold water and then boiled together with the chocolate. It was a pretty grave misfortune, but the worst of it is that it makes life more uncomfortable for us. The accident to Strindberg's sledge did not lessen our festal mood – we were jolly and friendly as usual. The altazimuth became wet through with salt water, but was washed out with fresh water and dried, and did not seem to suffer any damage. Strindberg's chronometer also seems to have escaped. Ivory gulls swarm around us and keep up an awful row.

THIRTY-TWO

ÅBY, SKÅNE COUNTY, SWEDEN

SEPTEMBER 1899

ANNA PUSHED herself up on her hands and gasped. When she opened her eyes, it was dark. She wondered whether this was death. Then, remembering her reality, she allowed her arms to relax and lay back down, dejected. As she stared at the ceiling, thinking of the dream, she was aware of the breathing of others in the room. She closed her eyes and attempted to recall the details of the dream she had believed to be real, trying also to recall the feeling of contentment she had experienced. It was too difficult to achieve in this room, in the presence of others. Anna rolled onto her side in her small bed, disappointed.

Instead she looked at the silhouettes of the children in the surrounding beds and turned her attention to their lessons for the morning. She would begin with dictation, she decided, then they would revise a multiplication table – four, that always gave them trouble. This would be followed by refreshments and a walk outdoors. As much as she strived to focus on her life now, in the present, in Åby, her mind kept drifting back to the sweet awareness of oblivion she experienced in the dream. In the lake, in the dark, with only a thin shaft of moonlight brightening the scene. Deeper and deeper until nothingness.

As the months passed and the possibility of Nils' return seemed increasingly unlikely, Anna had grown desolate. She was aware she was crumbling but was powerless to stop the collapse. It troubled her greatly when she realised one day that it was not grief she was feeling but culpability. Gota could not help her. She wouldn't have understood her sister's collusion in Nils' death, her belief that her love for Erik was to blame. There was no way to explain it; Anna couldn't really comprehend it herself. Exhausted from the self- scrutiny, Anna slept. Endlessly. There were days when she did not leave the apartment and ventured rarely from the safety of her bed.

At times Anna recognised her irrationality. Quite suddenly and without explanation it would all become clear. In her mind she waged a war against self-judgement and fought to keep her thoughts lucid. But these occasions were rare and Anna was always overpowered by guilt in the end.

When she was asked to resign her position at the Larssons', she handled the situation calmly. Margrit Larsson was apologetic, but the frequent absences were interfering with Kalle and Johanna's education. She told Anna that she had lost her shine. Anna supposed that she had.

Gota's remedy for her sister's malaise was to keep her busy. But she could not fathom the depths of Anna's despair. She often repeated the phrase 'Time heals all wounds', but the sorrow in Anna was too acutely embedded to be so easily dislodged.

At her wit's end, Gota eventually arranged for Anna to

stay with their cousin Ida in Åby. Neither Anna nor Gota had seen Ida since they left Skåne County years before. Ida had seven children and Anna would help with their lessons. Gota hoped the quiet and the country air would soothe Anna's temperament. Shunted to Åby and living among strangers, it soon dawned on Anna that her life had become unliveable.

Anna heard the rooster crow. She quietly slunk from her bed and lit a candle. She sat at the small writing desk in the corner of the crowded attic room and wrote a brief note. After folding the paper twice, she placed it under her pillow and then made her bed. In her nightgown Anna left the house and stood still for a time to allow her eyes to grow accustomed to the dark. When she was able to make out the surrounding fields, she quickly scanned their borders for Karl, her cousin's husband, who she knew would already be at work. She hastily collected stones from the border of a garden bed Ida had built under the window and carried them in the shirt of her nightdress. The morning air was biting. On her way upstairs she retrieved her cousin's sewing box and an apron from the kitchen bureau. Under the dim glow of a lamp she set about sewing the stones into the large pocket of the apron. She had finished by the time she had to help Ida prepare breakfast for the household.

When the group came to the lake, the four boys immediately began throwing rocks and sticks into the water. The girls screamed and ran from the bank for fear of being splashed. Anna held tight to Frida's hand, as she was only five years old. The weather was still quite warm for September and Anna led the child to the water. They knelt on the bank and placed their hands on the surface. Frida laughed merrily. The water was cold.

The older children began to play tag and Frida soon left Anna's side and joined the game. Anna sat by herself on the bank, distractedly pulling at the grass as she tried to recall her dream. Her meditation was interrupted by the eldest boy, Krister. 'When do we have to go home, Anna? How long do we have?'

'It's getting late. You may play for another ten minutes. Your father needs your help this afternoon.'

The boy ran off to rejoin the game. Anna stared into the lake, her brow creased, and wondered what lay beneath its still surface. After a few minutes she stood, brushing off her skirt. She called to the children to return home. She would follow in a few minutes. The children groaned but began to walk back towards the house.

When they were out of sight, Anna carefully undid the laces of her shoes. Once removed, she placed them side by side on the bank. Noticing they sat oddly, she reversed their position. Then she removed her watch and placed it in the left shoe. She took off her jacket and lay it next to the shoes. It was the handsome blue bolero made by Gota. It had faded in the years since it was made but still fitted extremely well. Anna didn't want it ruined. From her bag she removed the apron and tied it around her waist in a double knot. Then she walked into the lake, purposefully and without trepidation despite the chill of the water. When the water reached her waist, she stood for a few minutes enjoying the mud's controlled ooze beneath her feet and between her toes. Then she lay face down in the water.

It was Josef who discovered her only two or three minutes later. He had forgotten his hat and had returned to the lake to retrieve it. As it was not the time of year to swim, he thought Anna must have lost her footing on the bank, though he did think it strange his cousin had removed her shoes. The boy waded into the cold water and grabbed her ankles. He thought he would be able to flip her over onto her back, but it was impossible. When he tried, she sank deeper. He walked a little further and grabbed his cousin around the waist. Her head jolted out of the water violently, her mouth opened wide and she inhaled and splashed desperately. Josef pulled her to the bank and sat next to her while she lay on the grass coughing. The amount of water expelled from Anna's mouth with each cough amazed the twelve-year-old.

'I'll get your shoes, Anna, then we should go back or you'll catch your death.' Josef stood and fetched her belongings.

'Thank you, Josef,' Anna said as the boy handed her the shoes. He set about helping her untie the sodden apron strings.

As Josef escorted Anna back to the house, he fought the urge to ask her how she had fallen into the lake. He knew something was not as it seemed. When they entered the front door, Anna was still dripping. Ida dried her off and made her drink a glass of vodka. Josef was sent to fetch the doctor. Severe melancholia was his diagnosis. He recommended the familiar. After only five days in Åby, Anna was returned to the train station by her cousin's husband and shunted back to Stockholm. No one had found the note she had left. She had thrown it into the fire that afternoon and taken out another piece of paper from the writing desk. That was when she had decided to write to Erik.

ANDRÉE'S JOURNAL, 1 OCTOBER
1897

October 1, 1897, New Iceland (Kvitøya). The evening was as divinely beautiful as one could wish. The water was alive with small animals, and a bevy of seven black-and-white guillemot youngsters were swimming there. A couple of seals appeared too. The work with the hut went on well, and we thought we should have the outside ready by the second. But then something else happened. At five-thirty o'clock in the morning we heard a thunderous crash and water streamed into the hut. And when we rushed out we found that our large, beautiful floe had been splintered into a number of little floes, and that one fissure had divided the floe just outside the wall of the hut. The floe that remained to us had a diameter of only 80 feet, and one wall of the hut might be said rather to hang from the roof than support it. This was a great reversal in our position and our prospects. The hut and the floe could not give us shelter, and still we were obliged to stay there for the present at least. We were frivolous enough to sleep in the hut the following night too. Perhaps it was because the day was rather tiring. Our gatherings were scattered among several blocks and these were drifting here and there, so that we had to hurry. Two bear carcases, representing provisions for two or three months, were lying on a separate floe, and so on. Luckily the weather was beautiful, so that we could work in haste. No one had lost courage; with such comrades, one should be able to manage under, I may say, any circumstances.

THIRTY-THREE

AND SO ONE has to go on and hope for a year at least; and even after that don't draw too unfavourable a conclusion, for they may have long distances to walk before they reach inhabited places.

At present I read Nansen's book with great interest, and in my thoughts I place 'the three' in the same or similar situations. Since they have rifles and sufficient ammunition and the necessaries for a journey over the ice and a stay over the winter, I suppose they can do it, although with difficulties to overcome.

Andrée and Nils, whom I know best, are such characters that if possible, they make the impossible possible; and they have surely intelligence enough to figure out the best way of getting out of their emergencies. Andrée's ideas and Nils's Anna are two mighty levers and self-protections, and the love of life will help along too.

– Letter from Oscar Strindberg to Erik, June 1898

CHICAGO, ILLINOIS, UNITED STATES

JANUARY 1900

'Hallå, Fröken Charlier.' It was the first Swedish Anna had heard since arriving in Chicago but she recognised the confident baritone immediately. Before she had time to turn in her seat, Erik moved in swiftly, took her hand and held it to his lips. He sat down in the seat opposite her at the tearoom. His handsome face beamed. 'It's lovely to see you again. I'm so glad.'

Anna nodded. Her hands were clenched in her lap under the table. 'I'd like to thank you for everything you've done, helping me to get here, and for securing a position for me. I only moved in with the Gilchrists yesterday, but I'm already quite settled. Mr and Mrs Gilchrist have been exceptionally helpful and welcoming and the children are delightful. I believe I'll be tutoring them in—'

Erik halted her monologue. 'Why so formal, Anna? We're old friends. I'll always come to your aid.'

'To my rescue, you mean.'

Compassion softened his tone. 'I've written to you so many times since I left Stockholm. I've been so worried ... I wrote to my mother. Her reply gave me no joy. I should have done more. I shouldn't have allowed the situation to become as serious as it did.'

'I received your letters. I should have written back. It's not your responsibility to safeguard my happiness.'

He looked down thoughtfully to the teaspoon he was tapping on the table. When his eyes returned to hers, he spoke more lightheartedly. 'I was thrilled when I saw the envelope, my name written in your handwriting. But it was painfully obvious from your letter you were despairing. There was nothing else I could do. I'm happy to help you in any way I can and . . .' he stopped and said more reticently, 'I don't expect anything in return.'

'Well, thank you,' she said, more tenderly this time.

Erik ordered afternoon tea. While they were waiting for

it to arrive, Erik and Anna made uncomfortable small talk about the weather, news from Stockholm and the turn of the century.

'You're looking very well. A little thinner, perhaps, but as pretty as ever.'

'I think the turbulent seas of the Atlantic are responsible for my weight loss. I'm sure I'll plump up soon,' Anna joked, indicating the tiered stand covered with sweets that the waitress had placed on the table between them.

As the afternoon wore on, Anna relaxed into Erik's presence. It had been almost three years since she had seen him, but she soon discovered that none of her feelings had dampened over time. She frequently revisited that afternoon at the railway station, he courageously waiting for her, she too craven to face him. Anna often imagined herself stepping onto the train with him, leaving Sweden for America, and wondered what course her life would have taken. Now she wondered if he ever had similar thoughts. Anna hastily pushed these notions from her mind.

As Erik chatted about his work and friends and life in Chicago, she kept her eyes on his face. Occasionally an acquaintance would pass by the table and exchange pleasantries with him. It seemed Nils' prediction was correct: Erik was doing extremely well in America. He was a partner at a leading architecture firm that had risen to prominence following the building boom brought on by the great fire thirty years before. He spoke fervently about the structures of the future that he termed 'skyscrapers'. He was articulate and passionate and Anna was captivated.

'I could show you what I'm talking about. I'd enjoy giving you a guided tour of the city. You could see some of the buildings I've designed,' Erik suggested.

Anna did not answer.

'You know Chicago is deemed "the second city" to New York. What a very, very inaccurate description.'

'You seem to have made this your home,' said Anna. 'I hope I can do the same. But don't you miss Stockholm? After all the work you did for the World's Fair, you became so much a part of the city.'

'Someone complained to me once that they no longer enjoyed strolling around Stockholm because they were faced with my shoddy handiwork around every corner.'

A recollection flickered faintly across their faces.

'No, I don't miss it,' Erik said. 'I'm ashamed to admit that I haven't been home in all this time. But various members of my family have visited me. I do sometimes pine for them. Moving your life to a new country can be very lonely, but necessary.'

Anna found herself drawn into his orbit. Everything he spoke of she found interesting and he hung on her every word. It seemed an eternity since she had been lost in a moment like this, enraptured. He was genuinely concerned with her welfare and, she had to admit, he was likely the only person who might understand her dilemma. Surely he must feel a similar kind of remorse. It stood to reason.

Nils was not spoken of. Anna's illness was not spoken of. She was grateful the past was not mentioned at all. In Stockholm, Anna believed, Erik had strived diligently to maintain a persona. He took control when others were unable. He had removed himself from Stockholm because he found himself in a predicament over which he had no control. At times she found this smokescreen choking. But Anna had seen the facade crumble. Perhaps she was the only person who ever had been permitted a glimpse of his true self. Now he was relaxed and unguarded. For him, it seemed to Anna, the shadow of Nils had lifted.

The crowded tearoom was emptying as the sky outside

grew dark. Waitresses shot irritated glances at the stragglers. Erik asked for the bill, paid and then walked with Anna out to the sidewalk. After a few moments adjusting their coats, hats and gloves, an uneasy smile between them prompted Erik to say, 'I shall escort you back to the Gilchrists'?'

They both knew there was a greater meaning to that question than it at first conveyed. Looking up at his alert face, Anna could easily read expectancy, hope in his eyes. It was a kind of optimism that was contagious. After three years of despair Anna discovered herself craving what she saw in Erik's eyes. She realised the weight that rested on her next words, her next actions. She took Erik's arm and the snow crunched under their feet as they walked away from the tearoom.

THIRTY-FOUR

CHICAGO, ILLINOIS, UNITED STATES

AUGUST 1907

AT CONSTANT INTERVALS Erik would open the bedroom door to see if she had woken. She kept her eyes closed lightly, willing him to cease this frequent irritation. Anna had no idea of the time. She feared looking at the clock on the bedside table next to her in case he was to enter at that moment. But she guessed it was quite late. The room was growing musty and her body was hot beneath the bedclothes. Anna heard the door open softly, then footsteps moving towards the bed. The curtains were drawn open and she could sense daylight on the other side of her eyelids.

'My darling, wake up, beautiful girl. I want you to see something.' Anna did not stir. She could feel his breath on her ear.

Erik shook her shoulder gently until she gave in. She rolled onto her back and squinted into his sunny face. 'Something has arrived for you. It's in the parlour. Please, will you come out and see it?'

'What is it?'

'A gift.' Erik kissed her lightly on the lips.

She smelt powder on his open collar. He was dressed only in his shirt and suspenders. He must not be going to work, she thought. She could not remember if he had gone back to work since the birth. She had grown oblivious to time. Anna stood and allowed him to help her into her robe. It was cool on her warm body. He led her down the hall, his vast hand covering her eyes. The smell of soap lingered on his hand, but when she inhaled more deeply she could smell a trace of something else. She breathed in: it was the milky scent of the baby. He has probably been playing with her or holding her, she thought, while he waited for his daughter's mother to wake. Even in her sorrow Anna could easily admit that her baby was fortunate to have Erik as a father. Since Albertina's birth he had, without complaint, assumed many of the duties belonging to a mother. Erik's care for her and devotion to the child impressed Anna immensely. His generosity, love, she supposed, was infinite. But it was not enough to wrench Anna from her bed.

Each day, as she lay in her bedroom or in the sitting room, she could hear him happily engaged in baby talk with the infant. The pleasant sound of his laughter filled the hallway from the nursery. Although she wanted to, needed to, the effort to lift her body out of the bed was insurmountable.

They came to a stop. From the smell of the flowers she knew they were in the parlour. 'Keep your eyes shut.' Erik removed his hand, grabbed her upper arms and twisted her body into a suitable position.

'Are you ready?' Anna nodded. 'Open your eyes.'

'Oh my.' Anna could say nothing more. The room had

been rearranged to accommodate the large instrument. She wondered how Erik had arranged its arrival into the home. How had she been so unaware? This knowledge added to her shame. Anna heard a noise from the doorway. She turned. The nurse, Suzanne, stood rocking the baby in her arms. Anna looked at the grinning woman, who had not wanted to miss the marvellous spectacle.

Erik led her over to the piano excitedly and pulled the stool out. He pressed her to sit and she did so. His face was aglow. Anna smiled and lifted the shining fall board. It did not have a smudge on it. She imagined Erik giving it a final polish with his sleeve before he brought her out. She placed her fingers lightly on the keys. The touch was alien.

He stood next to her, looking down, waiting for her to gush. She mustered her energy. 'It's beautiful. Thank you. But it's so unnecessary. It must have cost a fortune.'

'But do you love it?'

'Yes, I love it. I'm shocked, that's all.' She sat at the piano, unable to move.

Erik took a seat next to her. He fingered the gold cursive above the keyboard. 'It's a Steinway & Sons parlour grand, manufactured using East Indian rosewood. I thought that sounded extremely impressive. I wish you could have assisted me in the choice, made the choice, but I wanted it to be a surprise. I hope I've chosen correctly. Try it out. Does it work?' Erik chuckled and placed his hands in his lap.

Anna's fingers were still frozen in position. She was surprised by her nervousness and the strength of her feelings. She hadn't realised until that moment how much she missed playing. What used to be a daily practice had been absent from her life since her employment had ceased at the Larssons' years ago.

'Go on,' Erik insisted. 'I've been looking forward to this

moment since I made the purchase.' Then, looking to Suzanne, 'Do we have time? Before the baby's next feed?'

'Of course. We have about an hour.'

'Thank you, Suzanne. Mrs Strindberg will meet you in the nursery in an hour.' The nurse departed with Albertina.

Anna closed her eyes and waited for a piece to come to mind. She could sense Erik's anticipation, his hushed urging. If she could give him nothing more, she needed to give him this. Play the music vibrantly, lovingly, to repay him for his compassion. Anna began slowly, her fingers tentative on the keys. She searched the depths of her memory to recall the piece. Gradually the music began to flow more naturally, the keys now an extension of her fingertips. Transported from her surroundings and from the man perched beside her, she gave her body liberty, the full thrust of her passion driving the performance. Unaware of her movements or the progression of the piece, she permitted her sorrow to give way to the intensity of her playing and the power of memory.

At the conclusion of the piece her chest heaved, shimmering with beads of sweat. Her fingers rested on the keys. The strength of her feeling was terrifying and she remained still. Erik was motionless as well. This surge reminded them both of what had been absent since the birth. The hollowness and the numbness that had been so foreign to her at first had steadily become her accepted state of being. Erik had filled Anna's shoes for much of the baby's existence and his role of caretaker, whether it was desired or not, fit him very well. Anna had let her unhappiness consume her and she allowed Erik to take her place. But this performance reminded them both of her capabilities. It would be difficult now for her to shrink back into her misery.

'That was wonderful. I'd forgotten how beautifully you played. What was it? I can recall hearing it before, but I can't place it.'

'It's Handel.'

He nodded thoughtfully. The movement of Anna's hands leaving the keys and folding in her lap prompted him to kiss her on the cheek.

It was rather formal, Anna thought. Was it a thank you? She turned to him, hoping he would be able to read what was in her eyes. He bent lower and burrowed his face into her neck, forcing her head back. Small kisses made their way from her chin to her chest. One large hand supported her head, the other tenderly cupped her breast as his index finger gently orbited her enlarged nipple. Her robe fell from her shoulder. Anna permitted herself the pleasure of this sensation and let her eyes close and her head fall more heavily into Erik's hand. Her hands, which had gripped the edge of the stool, now moved to his shoulders and slid under his suspenders, angling them off his square frame. He released a soft groan, before standing, taking her hand and leading her into the bedroom.

Anna gave herself over to him completely for the first time since the birth. Even though his craving was evident, he was a generous, restrained and watchful lover. After gently removing her robe and nightdress, he laid her on the bed. When she attempted to cover her nakedness, her chafed nipples and her soft belly, with a sheet, he held her arms to her sides softly and flung the bedclothes to the floor. He kissed the entire length of her body meticulously, as if reacquainting himself with its secret recesses, allowing his tongue the freedom to explore her desire. Aware of the presence of the nurse across the hallway, Anna turned her face into the pillow, muffling her delight. Erik was never an inhibited lover – quite the opposite – but this time was different. It was as though he was in awe of her, revering her. When she attempted to guide the lovemaking, he firmly but gently rebutted her advances. She heard him whisper, 'I do so wish I'd seen the birth of Albertina. You're a remarkable woman, Anna. How I love you.' He took care to position her just so, to ensure her swollen breasts were not crushed under his weight. When he finally entered her, he did so cautiously, checking her reaction so as not to cause pain.

'It doesn't hurt,' she whispered. 'It feels perfect.' Their love-making was not hurried. When they both eventually climaxed, it was with a comfortable and loving ease.

Her lovemaking with Nils had always been marred by a sense of urgency. They had never lingered over each other's bodies. This may have had more to do with their circum-stances at the time and Nils' state of mind than with his prowess. As Erik embraced her and kissed her lovingly on the back of her neck, she recalled their first time together. She had been in Chicago for eight months when Erik insisted on taking her to New York with him for the Labor Day weekend. He had been invited by one of his firm's clients. They travelled in the first-class carriage on the train. Once they were seated, Erik produced a small, black box from his pocket. Anna knew immediately what it held.

'Am I permitted to place it around your neck?' Erik asked.

'Yes. Thank you. I've often wondered what became of it. Whether you returned it to the store or gave it to another woman...'

'You amaze me. After all this time you still refuse to accept just how much I love you. There has never been another woman and, as for the store, I had the pendant custom made. There's not another like it.'

When they arrived at the stately home in Washington Square, Erik introduced her as his cousin from Stockholm. He had furnished her with a grand new wardrobe for the excursion and, that night after dinner, when they made their way to their separate rooms, he had whispered in her ear, 'You take my breath away.'

Lying on the bed in her silk nightdress, a further gift, she had struggled to find sleep. Eventually and without excessive deliberation she padded softly down the corridor in bare feet and tapped on Erik's door. It was past midnight and he was still clothed, although his shirt was unbuttoned and his suspenders hung by his sides. The bedside lamp was on and a book lay open on the bed. Caught in the momentum of the moment, Anna entered the room and kissed him hungrily on the mouth. When they drew apart, he pulled her back in and enveloped her in his arms.

Assuming she was a virgin, he had made love to her that morning with a concentrated cautiousness. As he looked into her face for any sign of discomfort, a sudden glint of recognition shot across his eyes. Anna thought he would stop, pull back, throw her out. She held her breath, then he continued, but more passionately, more naturally. Neither of them ever spoke of that moment. At first light, when a fine strand of sunlight pushed eagerly through a crack in the curtains, Erik escorted her barefoot back to her own bedroom.

Anna lay in the crook of his arm recalling that night. If there was just this and nothing else, she would be happy. She angled her face in order to see his. His eyes were closed but she knew he was not asleep. 'How did you know to be gentle like that? You were so considerate,' she said.

'I did some reading,' he said matter-of-factly and hugged her tighter. 'It stands to reason, doesn't it? Only a fool would rush the gates, so to speak.'

'What did you read?'

'I borrowed a few obstetric and medical texts.' He spoke nonchalantly, as if this was part of his daily routine. He was a constant source of surprise.

'I read up on the effects of pregnancy and childbirth on a woman's body. I wanted to know what was in store for you before and after the birth. It was extremely fascinating. It's simply blind ignorance that men choose to stay in the dark about these matters.'

'I appreciate your diligence.'

They giggled like children. He rolled onto his side and rested on his elbow. He brushed the flat of his hand lightly over the length of her body like a magician performing a conjuring trick. Then he bent his head and kissed the tip of one nipple. 'I think it's time to feed Albertina, my love.'

Annoyed that he would ruin this beautiful respite, she turned away from him. Her breasts throbbed.

'You promised, Anna.' He touched her shoulder. 'I'll help you through anything, but you promised to feed the baby. It's best for her. It will help you love her. We agreed.'

'I do love her . . .'

'Feel close to her, connected. The doctor explained that nursing Albertina yourself was fundamental to your recovery.'

She knew that he struggled to understand her, to reconcile her weaknesses. His rationality proved a barrier he could not conquer. She found her nightdress and robe on the floor and walked from the room.

He entered the nursery while she was feeding. Anna, sitting in a rocking chair, stared hard at the steady rhythm of the baby's mouth. She had found fixing her concentration on one aspect of the process gave her the ability to remove herself from the moment. He leant against the door frame and smiled at the maternal scene. 'Suzanne, will you leave us, please?'

Once the nurse had departed, Erik closed the door and took a seat on the floor in front of the rocker. He massaged Anna's bare feet. 'I want to get married,' he said plainly.

Anna stared at her daughter's face. 'It's not the right time. When I am well. I can't think of it at present.'

'When will there be a right time, Anna?' She did not look at him. 'I proposed to you in New York and you said it was too soon. I proposed again when we discovered you were pregnant, and you said after the birth. Here I am again.' He stood and paced the length of the nursery.

'We are, for all intents and purposes, married,' she said. 'Everyone believes it to be so. I don't understand what a ceremony will prove.'

'It will prove to me that you love me. We are living a secret, a scandalous secret that if discovered by any one of my colleagues or associates would mean expulsion from my position, from society. You are my mistress, a kept woman. I want you to be my wife.'

She stood and gently manoeuvred the baby to her shoulder, patting her daughter softly on her back. She could hear her tiny belly gurgling.

Erik took her seat and rocked violently back and forth.

Anna changed Albertina's diaper, wrapped her tightly in a light-blue shawl and placed her in her cradle. 'Shhh. You'll wake her.'

Erik ceased and placed his head in his hands, then spoke in a strained whisper. 'For the past seven years I've lived like this. I've never asked you for anything. You've never even told me you love me. I've learnt not to expect it and I can live without it. Since you arrived in Chicago, I've treated you with kid gloves and indulged your sensitivities for fear you'd harm yourself again. But now that we have a child, I want to be a family. My daughter is not going to be raised amidst this deception.' She could see he was attempting to control his temper. 'For god's sake! I want my family to know I have a daughter.' Albertina's eyelids flickered but she didn't wake.

It was true, they were living a deception. His business

colleagues and friends assumed they were married. She remembered Erik once invented an entertaining story for them, culminating in an elopement in Niagara Falls. He had even purchased a thin silver band, which she wore on her left hand. But his family knew nothing about her presence in this house or the birth of Albertina. Anna could see the burden of this duplicity weighed heavily on Erik. He had been holding his breath for seven years. But even the knowledge of this and the real possibility of losing Erik could not overcome the enormity of her guilt and allow her to commit entirely to a new path.

'I'm sorry. I don't know why, but I can't.'

'Of course you know why. Do you think I'm stupid? He's not coming back. Nils is dead. He has been for a decade and for a decade our lives have been suspended. The power of your denial terrifies me, Anna.'

Anna was in no denial. She'd begun to grieve for Nils the day he stepped onto the train for Gothenburg. As much as he struggled to understand, Erik still believed she harboured hope of Nils' return. How wrong he was. She searched her mind for a way of telling him the truth. That he had unwittingly become a co-conspirator in her crime. That her love for him only made the situation all the more untenable. How could she explain without fuelling his anger towards her further, without triggering a rift within the Strindberg family?

He stood and went to her at the cradle. The couple looked at their sleeping child for some time before Erik began again, softly. 'Before Nils left, on the evening of his farewell dinner, do you remember? Frænkel was there. Nils received the note from Andrée about his mother's death.'

She nodded. Anna recalled the evening vividly. That evening a glimmer of a chance had hung in the air. After the news Andrée's message relayed, the group's mood had lifted.

She also remembered Erik and Nils slipping from the sitting room after dinner and their return, their faces weary with contemplation.

'Nils asked me that evening to take care of you. He asked me to love you if he were to die.' He looked to her imploringly. 'Why won't you allow me to honour my brother's request?'

Erik did not divulge this secret lightly. He wanted to be loved for himself, not because his brother had given permission. It was a final, despairing attempt to induce her to reason. Her refusal to respond pushed him into an involuntary rage. He raised his voice and the baby began to cry.

'I fear that if Nils walked through the door now you'd give up everything – our life here, me, Albertina. I curse the moment I fell in love with you.' He turned away from her and sat down heavily in the rocker.

What the situation called for now was honesty, brutal and open honesty. She needed to tell him everything. That they had been discovered. That Nils knew all and went to his death in the knowledge that his fiancée and his brother had betrayed him. She wanted to tell Erik how much she loved him, but how that love was a permanent reminder of her infidelity. Anna had to tell him everything, then he would finally understand. For all these years he had been attempting to piece together the puzzle of her actions without all of the fragments. A lump was rising in her throat, the words were coming. She walked to him and sat across his lap. She placed her arms around his neck and said softly in his ear, 'You're absolutely right. Now that we have Albertina, we should be wed. Of course I'll marry you. Whenever it pleases.'

Erik sat alone in the darkened sitting room. The full moon shot a scornful pillar of light across the Steinway & Sons parlour grand and he clutched Anna's brief note in his hand. He took a handkerchief from his pocket and rubbed both his eyes vigorously. When he had composed himself, he walked to the door.

'Suzanne. Would you mind coming here?' he called from the doorway.

The nurse entered holding Albertina to her shoulder. She rubbed the child's back gently.

'Sit down, please,' he instructed as he relieved Suzanne of his daughter. 'Tell me everything that happened today. Everything. One event at a time.'

Erik paced the room with Albertina in his arms as Suzanne sifted through the events of the day. 'After you left for work, Mrs Strindberg took the baby for a walk. They were gone about an hour. When they came home, she fed Albertina and then requested that I take her out again.' Erik nodded. 'I thought it was odd to take the baby out again, and I said so. All that fresh air would make her overtired. Too much of a good thing . . . But she insisted, saying that her doctor was arriving shortly for a consultation and she wanted the baby out of the house for at least an hour.'

'Did you see the doctor arrive?' Erik kissed his dozing daughter's forehead softly.

'Yes. At about eleven. It was that one with the beard and the spectacles. The gruff German one.'

'Dr Brüner. He's Austrian. Go on.' Erik had not arranged the doctor's appointment for Anna.

'When he arrived, Albertina and I left. When we came home, there was no sign of Mrs Strindberg or the doctor. I waited until three o'clock. That's when I telephoned your office, thinking something was wrong. It's unlike Mrs

Strindberg to go out for a long time . . . by herself.' Suzanne shifted awkwardly in her chair.

Erik nodded thoughtfully. 'And that's all? Did you read the note Mrs Strindberg left?' He pointed to the mantel on the opposite side of the room.

'Of course not. It had your name on the envelope.'

Suzanne had opened and read Anna's note at two-thirty that afternoon after discovering the envelope propped up on the mantel next to the silver heart-shaped pendant. She had thought it over for half an hour before deciding it warranted a telephone call requesting her employer leave work immediately and come home.

After Erik had read the letter, he telephoned the police and then Dr Brüner. The police requested a photograph of Anna to help them in their search. When Dr Brüner was informed, he was shocked by Anna's abrupt departure. He told Erik their conversation that morning had been a constructive one.

'Can you tell me, doctor, when did Anna make the appointment with you?' Erik asked.

'About a week ago, if I recall. I was surprised when she came to my office at the university. You've arranged all my visits in the past.'

'What did you discuss?'

'Mr Strindberg, you know I'm not at liberty to say.'

'Can you tell me anything? Was there any indication she might leave or . . . harm herself again?'

'Don't fear the worst,' Dr Brüner reassured. 'Anna probably just requires a short time alone to gather her thoughts. The strain placed upon a new mother is quite overwhelming for some women.'

When the doctor left, Erik hugged his daughter firmly to his chest. Based on Anna's history, he did fear the worst. Anna's note gave nothing away and he was uncertain of its meaning and her intentions. However, he was certain her departure had been planned some time in advance. The realisation that she had never meant to marry him, that her acceptance of his proposal was merely a ruse, hurt him greatly. The clandestine visit by the doctor was perhaps a final attempt to seek help. When that had failed, she had fled immediately.

He looked at the clock – it was two in the morning, and he still held Albertina in his arms. His daughter was asleep and her father was exhausted. He took the infant into bed with him and lay down with her nestled tight into the crook of his arm. He resolved to contact a private detective first thing in the morning.

THIRTY-FIVE

STOCKHOLM, SWEDEN

OCTOBER 1930

STUBBENDORFF GLANCED at the clock on the Southern Bank
Building. He was a few minutes early for his meeting with
Rosalie Strindberg. He wandered, hands in pockets, to the
water and looked back at the house. He should have known
the house would reflect the man. Prominently located on
Skeppsbron, the four-storey residence overlooked the busy
harbour of the same name. Sven Strindberg's home was
colourful and grand. The ornate facade of the building was
painted in a daring combination of turquoise and yellow.
Stubbendorff imagined Strindberg stepping out of his front
door each morning, wearing a similarly striking combination
of hues, a living representation of the building. He regularly
passed along Skeppsbron and had noticed this house many
times. It was the least modest on the extensive promenade.

At four o'clock promptly Stubbendorff lifted the heavy
door knocker and banged it three times. As he waited, he

stared at the angry lion's head and wondered where Strindberg might have unearthed it. Florence perhaps, Stubbendorff thought. He had seen similar designs in books. A maid showed him into a large south-facing room. Although the afternoon breeze was cool, no fire was lit in the hearth. It was not needed. Sunlight surged in through the fully drawn curtains. Stubbendorff realised that self-aggrandisement was not the only reason Strindberg lived in this house. The wide windows perfectly framed the harbour, creating a living work of art. People crossed the forefront of the picture while, in the background, fishermen and seamen on board their boats or on the docks went about their daily business.

Lost in the scene, he was startled by a voice from the doorway. 'Good afternoon, Herr Stubbendorff. I am Rosalie Strindberg.' He turned and greeted her. Stubbendorff knew that Fru Strindberg was seventy-nine, but this woman appeared much younger. Her white hair was swept back in flowing waves from her face and knotted at the base of her neck. As she walked forward, Stubbendorff noticed her height. She stood at least five inches taller than him. Her stature was made more noticeable by her slender, elegant figure.

'It's extremely generous of you to meet with me, Fru Strindberg. I trust you are well. This is such a lovely home and a beautiful room.'

Rosalie Strindberg cast her eyes about the room and nodded. Stubbendorff cleared his throat. 'I have met with both Tore and Sven – they are remarkable men. You must be extremely proud.'

'Yes, I am.'

'I'm not sure if your sons have told you anything about me . . .'

'Tore and Sven have touched on it. They told me you

were with the party that discovered my son's remains.' She made her way further into the room.

Her directness shocked the writer. He abandoned his previous course and decided to follow her lead. 'I didn't discover the camp. I came afterwards. But yes, I did find many human bones. Remains, as you say.'

'You must understand, Herr Stubbendorff, that the discovery on Kvitøya has resulted in a great upheaval to the family. We laid Nils to rest thirty-three years ago, grieved for him, paid tribute to him and then went on with our lives. I can understand the morbid fascination with which the rest of the world views this find. But I accepted Nils' death many years ago. The state funeral I cannot do anything about, but I see no good in writing about Nils' life in the newspaper.'

Then Stubbendorff saw the element of Rosalie Strindberg that defied her youthful appearance and professed her age, experience and tragedy. Like her sons she had intelligent blue eyes. Their colour was vivid and they dominated her thin, sculpted face. They regarded Stubbendorff with confidence and consideration. But they were without soul, without intensity. They made her appear a woman who had lived too long.

'I understand. But I'm not here as a journalist. When I travelled to Kvitøya, it was on assignment for the *Aftonbladet*. But I resigned my position when I came home.'

Rosalie sat and leant back in the armchair. She crossed her long legs and folded her hands in her lap. Stubbendorff understood her gesture as consent to continue.

'I found Nils' personal diary on Kvitøya. In it were reflections of his family and friends. It also contained a series of letters, love letters if you like, to Anna Charlier. His fiancée, I believe.'

Rosalie nodded gravely.

'I would like Anna Charlier to read the letters.'

'Why?'

Her question startled him. Stubbendorff believed the answer was obvious. 'The letters are beautiful, written purely from the heart. I don't know what her situation is at present. But I'd like to find her and give her the opportunity to read them. If their relationship was as your son describes in his journal, then they may grant her a resolution to what was surely a tragic episode in her life.'

Stubbendorff found himself arguing Anna's case, pleading for this flint-faced woman to bestow mercy. He wondered why he had to plead. His interviews with Sven and Tore Strindberg and the diary itself all led him to believe Anna Charlier was a de facto member of the family, that her place within the Strindberg household was firmly rooted. Stubbendorff believed that her relationship with Rosalie, the head of the family, had been the linchpin to that status.

'I see. May I read the journal, please?'

He had not been asked this question by her sons. The prospect moved Tore to tears and Sven did not mention it. Still standing, he lifted the pages from his satchel and handed them to the woman.

'Please leave me now. Come back in an hour.'

Stubbendorff strolled along the waterfront, perplexed. This was not the woman Sven had described nor was it the care-free mother Nils had written about in his journal. She had no interest in talking about the past, especially of Anna Charlier. Stubbendorff disliked her. Her sons had displayed an unex-pected warmth and generosity, but their mother had made him feel like a schoolboy. It was an abrupt assault from which Stubbendorff was still smarting. Were all mothers like this, he wondered. Could he have conducted the meeting any differently? There was no question that she viewed Stubbendorff as a threat. Was it fear of a scandal that plagued her, or something more? He imbibed the sea air in an effort to clear his head. The sun was fast becoming low in the sky and the wind was freshening.

He reached Carl Milles' *Sjöguden*. The great red granite monster laughing at the sea had always been a favourite of his. He remembered when Milles finished the work. He was only about seven. His father had shown him a picture of it in the newspaper. Stubbendorff remembered being fascinated by the glorious bulk of the sea beast and the timidly resigned, bare-breasted mermaid he had pressed like a limpet to his bulging flesh. Father and son had examined the photograph, discussing every glorious curve of the beast and of his captive. The photograph had prompted a disagreement between his devout mother and his far more liberal father. They had argued vigorously, his mother adamant that a child should not have been shown such an indecent image. She went on to chastise her husband for viewing the picture as well. His father had folded the newspaper, placed it under his arm and retreated into the bedroom without saying another word to his scolding wife.

Stubbendorff hadn't understood the fuss. He was far more engrossed by the series of chins leading down the god's neck to his ample belly than the sight of a mermaid's breasts. Furthermore, Stubbendorff was too young to be quizzical about the creature's intentions. Of course, he could not speak for his father on these matters.

About an hour later his father had emerged, coat, tie and jacket donned.

'Get your coat and cap, Knut,' he instructed.

'Where do you think you're going?' his wife snapped in a tone of urgency her son had never heard before.

'Ready?' he asked once Stubbendorff was suitably attired.

The boy nodded meekly and his father led him out the door.

They walked for what seemed like hours, but they eventually found themselves on Skeppsbron, overlooking the harbour. His father had bought them both a fruit ice from a vendor, and they had sat by the waterfront cross-legged, to eat them. The boy was amazed by his father's concentration while eating the ice. He seemed to be relishing the treat more than his son. It was the first time he had witnessed his father sit in this manner, partaking in an experience his mother would deem frivolous. Stubbendorff recalled that on the walk home he had removed his coat in loving imitation of his father, who had offhandedly thrown his over his shoulder. They arrived home flushed and excited as the sun was setting. Before they took the stairs, his father brought out from his pocket the page from the newspaper that had caused the disruption. He placed it carefully into the inside pocket of his son's coat and winked.

Greeted at the door by Stubbendorff's mother, the pair were scolded harshly. It was unseemly for a boy to remove his coat in public. The son was sent to bathe before supper. The father retreated to the bedroom with a book and closed the door. Stubbendorff had placed the page from the newspaper in his toy chest, concealed in the centre of one of his most treasured books.

Stubbendorff took one more turn around the statue's girth then slowly made his way back to the house in which Rosalie Strindberg was waiting.

She opened the door before Stubbendorff had a chance to use the lion-headed door knocker.

'That thing is grotesque.' Rosalie's brow furrowed in

disgust as she pointed to the elaborate piece of door furniture. 'It makes me shudder every time I hear it pound and I've been hearing it for many years.'

She ushered her guest into the room they had been in earlier. The pages of her son's diary were in her hand. 'I saw you walking back from the quay.'

Her mood had altered markedly. Once again Stubbendorff found himself on the back foot. This time he was ready for battle but the enemy seemed to have surrendered.

'I was looking at *Sjöguden*. The sculpture sparked quite an argument between my father and mother when it was created,' he told her.

'It was finished in 1913, I believe. You must have been very young.'

Stubbendorff nodded and was offered a seat by the window. Rosalie sat opposite him. There was a tea tray placed on the table.

'You know, Milles had a grand design to create a series of sculptures based on myths along the entire promenade,' she explained. 'But his plans never came to fruition. Thwarted by an unadventurous and conservative city council, I'm afraid. We were thrilled when they finally agreed to place it here, by the harbour.'

'Did you know the man?'

'Yes, he and Sven were very close. They went to college together. He was a frequent visitor at the house, until he went to Paris, that is. That was the year Nils disappeared. Sven, no doubt, had been instrumental in persuading the city council to erect the sculpture outside his front door.'

'It's magnificent, and so unusual, so unlike the other public sculptures in Stockholm. It's one that I've admired since I first saw it.'

'A sentimental attachment, perhaps?'

'As I said,' Stubbendorff began sombrely. 'It caused a

commotion in my house, but led to a rather unique afternoon with my father. He died shortly afterwards. So yes, I suppose I do have a sentimental attachment to the work.'

Rosalie began to pour the tea. 'I apologise for my behaviour earlier. I was extremely rude. Over the last thirty-three years I've managed to bury much of the past. But after reading Nils' journal – I didn't get very far as I suddenly felt I was invading his privacy – I remembered just how very much I cared for Anna. That's partly what I've tried to forget.'

The two were quiet for a moment.

'May I ask,' she went on quietly, 'why you kept the journal?'

Stubbendorff sensed he was sailing on uncharted waters. He was a twenty-five-year-old journalist who, until this point, had successfully navigated through life and career on the congenial breeze of his personality and an astonishing ability to veer away from uncomfortable situations. He was ill-equipped to pilot the rough seas he saw coming. Instinct told him to stand and run from this house. Hurl the diary in the harbour and beg forgiveness from Bergman.

'Primarily so Anna Charlier could read her correspondence, as trivial as that seems.' Stubbendorff did not wish to elaborate any further. He was embarrassed to admit to the attachment he felt to the Strindbergs, how he had been drawn into their world through the words of Rosalie's son. He feared it would make him seem pathetic and desperate.

'That's a noble motive, Herr Stubbendorff.' Rosalie smiled at him, appreciatively, he thought. 'Anna Charlier disappeared with the expedition. After July 1897 she gradually faded from our lives. I said goodbye to Nils and then Erik and within two or three years Anna had vanished completely. It happened gradually, very gradually. I wish I could have drawn her closer to us, but all my efforts only seemed to drive her further away. It still baffles me. She gave up on Nils faster than anybody else. Perhaps *she* had merely wanted to forget.'

'It must have been very difficult for you. You were very close, I understand?'

'We developed a very special attachment. I was without daughters and her presence in the house satisfied a part of me that, until her entrance into our lives, I'd never felt lacking. But as soon as she was gone, a hole was gaping. Of course, once Nils' disappearance was certain, I didn't suppose she should grieve forever or be held back from life. She was a young woman. It was natural she would one day marry and have children. But I had hoped to be a part of her healing and acceptance and, ultimately, her future. My bitterness towards Anna has hardened over the years. But, as foolish as this may seem, I think its root cause is my sorrow over losing a daughter.'

'So she simply disappeared without trace?'

'Yes. And I have no inkling where she went or where she might be at present. I knew she was having difficulties coping. I believe she gave up her position as governess and I think she went to live in the country for a short time with relatives.'

'Do you know where?'

'Skåne County, I believe, where she was born. You see, her sister was my seamstress.'

'Gota?'

Rosalie's eyebrows rose in surprise at Stubbendorff's knowledge.

'Tore remembered her name.'

'That's correct. She came to the house one evening in December 1899, distraught, completely overcome. Anna had gone. All she had left was a short note pleading with her sister to accept the situation. There were no hints as to her destination. The note was brief and cold. Unapologetic, actually. It was written on an old scrap of paper. Gota pleaded with me to help find her sister but I refused. Anna's tone was adamant. She did not want to be found. I had to respect her wishes.'

'And that was all the note said?'

'Yes. Three or four lines. That was all.'

'Do you know how I might find Gota? Are you still in contact? I believe she married a man called Neve?'

'That's correct. She married quite late in life. I know this only from acquaintances who still use her services. Gota was a wonderful dressmaker, but she was a gossip and a mischief maker. So different from her sister. I saw Gota's true nature that evening.'

'How so?'

Rosalie crossed her legs. The topic made her visibly uncomfortable. 'She insinuated Anna had fled to America to be with Erik. Well, she more than insinuated. She was really quite vulgar. She demanded that I become involved. I refused. I didn't believe a word of it. Gota was a rumour monger, pure and simple. I thought the best way to manage the situation was to sever the relationship.'

'Do you think there may have been some truth behind her accusations?'

'Not at all. Erik and Nils were very close. Erik delayed his leaving for America to be with Nils in the months before the launch. But they were odd companions. They were so very attached but they were often at war. From the time they were infants, they were always disagreeing about something or other. Erik tasked himself with being the protector to his younger brothers. It was a role Nils detested,' Rosalie explained further. 'Erik was, still is, larger than life. He unintentionally overshadowed Nils and I believe Nils spent a great deal of his life attempting to be his own man and not merely Erik Strindberg's younger brother. But, having said that, they were loyal friends and nobody knew Nils better than Erik.'

'But I assume that Erik and Nils' attachment would have made for a close connection between Erik and Anna also.'

Rosalie thought for a moment. 'On the contrary, Herr Stubbendorff, as strange as that may seem. There was a constant tension between the two. I cannot speak to the source of their animosity, but I imagined both Erik and Anna felt they had ownership over Nils. Neither of them could reconcile with the other's role in his life. He needed both of them. Neither of them could satisfy everything that he needed.'

'Jealous of the other's relationship?'

She nodded. 'It was a pity. Nils loved them both so dearly, although I don't believe he was aware of their feelings. Erik and Anna remained entirely civil towards each other. Nils was far more concerned with the nuances of science than with those of human relationships.' Then she laughed abruptly, as if an amusing, long-forgotten memory had just popped back into her mind.

'Tore, on the other hand, did not keep his feelings hidden. My goodness! He felt immensely threatened by Anna. He loved his older brother very much, worshipped him, and he did not take kindly to Anna becoming the focus of his attention. He treated her like she didn't exist. The tactics of a thirteen-year-old boy are not subtle.' She shook her head.

Stubbendorff laughed quietly before asking, 'Do you have any idea where Gota is living now? I've checked her last known address and it was a dead end.'

'The last I heard of Gota was at least two or three years ago. At that time she was living in Kindstugatan. It might be a good place to begin if you wish to find her. Beware, though, Herr Stubbendorff, she can be quite a tricky customer.'

'Thank you, I will.' Stubbendorff jotted the street name

down in his tattered notebook. 'I believe your son Erik will be returning to Stockholm shortly?'

Rosalie placed her teacup on the table and straightened her back. She resembled a child being offered their favourite dessert. 'Yes. I'm very excited, despite the circumstances. It will be the first time I've seen them in five or six years.'

'Erik and his wife?'

'No, Erik is a widower. His daughter, my beautiful American granddaughter, is accompanying him.'

'How old is she?'

'She turned twenty-three this year.' Rosalie's eyes brightened and Stubbendorff was suddenly aware of the likeness to her sons.

'She has been a blessing, a godsend. Her mother, Erik's wife, died shortly after her birth. As you can imagine, he was distraught, but he devoted himself to that child. She gave him a purpose. They're inseparable. Erik has never remarried, although, from what I understand from my granddaughter's letters, many women have tried to lead my son to the altar.'

'How tragic. Was his wife Swedish?'

'No, she was an American. I never had the opportunity to meet her. They were together for such a short time before she passed. A whirlwind romance followed by an unpretentious wedding, my son led me to believe at the time. It took Erik many years to reconcile with his loss, but he had his little daughter as a living memory, I suppose.' She smiled and her gaze drifted to the window.

'I have other grandchildren, of course, and they are all delightful. But there is something unique about my wonderful, darling American.'

Rosalie walked to the mantel and retrieved a framed photograph of a lovely young woman, smiling broadly and without restraint. Her curls were held back from her face by a ribbon. The journalist examined it earnestly.

'She has the forthright nature and boisterousness of her father, but she also possesses a profound gentleness that must be the inheritance of her mother. And she plays the piano beautifully. She's exceptionally accomplished in this regard. Erik ensured she had the best education money could buy. But he refused to send her away to boarding school, even though many he knew argued for it.'

Erik Strindberg knows his own mind, Stubbendorff thought.

'My granddaughter and I have a special bond, even though I sadly do not see her as frequently as I would hope,' Rosalie went on. 'But they're due to arrive early next week and Sven has arranged for them both to stay here during their visit.'

Rosalie fell quiet and set her eyes on the window. They flickered with animation. Stubbendorff gazed at her, contemplating how he should word his next question. At that moment she was unaware of the room in which she was seated and her guest's presence. She was oblivious to the incessant scratch of the writer's pencil as he scribbled copiously in his notebook. Then her smile slowly faded and she was released from her imagination.

'Thank you for your kindness, Fru Strindberg. You've been a great help. But I must go now.' Stubbendorff stood and slid his notebook into his bag. 'I hope the homecoming of Erik and your granddaughter goes well.' He handed Rosalie the photograph. 'She's very striking. What's her name? I don't think you told me.'

'Albertina. Albertina Rosalie Elin Strindberg. We call her Tina. A lovely name, no?

'A very lovely name.' Stubbendorff's mind hurriedly flicked through the immense catalogue of details it had acquired over the weeks since Kvitøya, attempting to recall where he had seen that combination of names before. They were all so familiar. Then it came to him. Palmgren's note, which revealed Albertina as Anna's middle name and Elin as Gota's, appeared in his mind's eye. He hoped his surprise was not apparent.

'Goodbye, Herr Stubbendorff. I'm sorry I couldn't provide you with more information.' She retrieved the journal from the writing desk and placed it in her guest's hand.

'And thank you for allowing an old lady to ramble about a past in which you have no interest.'

They shook hands. Stubbendorff was eager to find a quiet place to sit.

This could be no coincidence, Stubbendorff concluded. He turned the pages in his notebook, swiftly checking dates. Albertina was the daughter of Erik and Anna. It had to be. Erik and Anna were not at war over Nils as Rosalie imagined – they were in love. Sven had been correct in this, but he had no idea how deep the feelings ran. Nils had no knowledge of this, it was clear from his journal, so where was he placed in this situation? Could Anna have been in love with both brothers? When she had disappeared from Stockholm, she must have gone to America to find Erik. They'd had a child and then Anna had died. Their relationship had been kept a secret from his family because of its sensitive nature. For the past three weeks Stubbendorff had been looking for a dead woman. Stubbendorff realised he was perspiring. He removed his coat and threw it across the seat next to him.

He told himself that he should be excited that the mystery had been solved. If he wished, he could sell this story to Bergman for one hundred and fifty kronor, at least. Bergman would be mad for it – a love triangle, a doomed expedition, a secret child, a tragic untimely death. But none of this was important in the face of Stubbendorff's overriding sense of utter disappointment. His reward was meant to arrive at the moment he met Anna Charlier and delivered Nils Strindberg's diary. He could not understand the complexities of the relationships Anna had with either Erik or Nils, and now he probably never would. He removed the journal from his satchel, ordered another cup of coffee and reread its contents once again, searching for a satisfactory conclusion for himself.

The same afternoon Anna arrived at the Berns Hotel on Västerlånggatan. She placed her bag on the bed and walked to the window. She pulled back the curtains and looked at the street. 'It's a lovely view, a lovely room. Everything is fine.' She unlocked the heavy window and opened it wide.

'No one has ever called it a lovely view before, madam. It's just a street.'

'Of course, but it's a Stockholm street. I'm happy to be here.'

'The bathroom is down the hall to your left and breakfast is served between seven and nine in the downstairs parlour. Is there anything else I can help you with, Fru Hawtrey?'

'No, thank you.'

The young maid departed and Anna stretched her body far out through the open window. It was five o'clock and the street was busy with a mix of stern-faced, suited men leaving work and others making their way along the popular thoroughfare preparing for an evening's entertainment. The jumble of their laughter and chatter was barely audible. I will walk along there tomorrow, after breakfast, she thought, and see how it has changed. Anna recalled walking its length many times with Nils, and once with Erik. She yawned. Five days of travel had taken their toll. When she arrived at the train station in Stockholm, it had been with a sense of relief.

Now, in this room, overlooking Västerlånggatan, she was filled with a sense of exhilaration. She wanted to join the pedestrians, to run downstairs and walk among the narrow streets whose stones she had not trod for three decades. She wondered how the city had changed in her absence. Did the brewery still exist in Stensbastugränd? Was the Larssons' home still painted in that welcoming shade of yellow? Did the snarling head of a lion still greet guests at the Strindbergs' door? She closed her eyes tight and turned from the window. When she opened them, the bed appeared to invite her warmly. She slipped out of her shoes and slid in between the sheets fully clothed.

THIRTY-SIX

CHICAGO, ILLINOIS, UNITED STATES

DECEMBER 1916

WHEN TINA CAME to her father's bedroom, the door was ajar and the light was on. The child could not get back to sleep following a bad dream. Whenever this happened, it was her practice to leave her own bed and slip into her father's. The bed was so large and she was so small that he usually did not notice her sliding stealthily under the covers. In the morning he would always complain she had kept him awake with her snoring, but she knew he actually enjoyed the sensation of waking with his daughter snuggled against his broad back.

She listened at the doorway. She could hear him in the bathroom, taking a bath, she guessed. The nine-year-old reasoned that if she was able to fall asleep before he came to bed he would not disturb her rest by insisting she return to her own bed. She ran lightly, quickly on her toes across the room and leapt onto the bed. She was cold and she nestled under the comforter. Just her tiny face was visible among the billowy expanse of the bed. Her father's bed was so much more comfortable than her own, she thought. She pressed her face contentedly into the pillow and sighed.

Then she noticed her father's pocketbook on his side table. She listened again. She could hear the sounds of water lapping against his body. He was washing himself. Tina pushed the comforter away and crawled across the bed to the table. Like an expert thief, she noiselessly opened the wallet. Her father carried several photographs with him. There was a photograph of herself taken on her fifth birthday, a family photograph of her grandparents and uncles that was also in a frame on the mantel above the fireplace, and one of her father and Uncle Nils when they were boys. Then there was one more, an image of a woman she did not know but assumed was her mother. This was the photograph in which she was most interested.

Even at this age Tina could see the resemblance between herself and this woman. The curly hair and the brown eyes were the most obvious similarities, but there was also the way the woman's nose crinkled in the photograph. The child had seen the same feature in the mirror, and her father never failed to point it out.

Using the fingernails of her thumb and middle finger, she drew the photograph from its place in the leather sleeve. She sat on the bed cross-legged, examining the face in the photograph as she had many times before. As her father had never volunteered this photograph for her inspection, she was always wary of asking to see it. Some time ago Tina had discovered the woman quite by accident when, in a moment of boredom, she had removed the contents of the wallet and laid them out on the floor. Her father had never forbidden her to touch his belongings, but there was an element of risk attached to the endeavour, one she enjoyed. She wondered at the time why he had never shown her this woman. She thought it would make him sad to do so. Tina had taken to frequently removing the photograph and staring into the woman's face.

This evening, gazing as usual at the image, she tried to imagine how the lady would speak. The white background suggested snow. Although it snowed a great deal in Chicago, Tina believed this photograph had been taken in Sweden. A tree, partially obscured by the woman's head, did not resemble any she had seen in Chicago. But her father had told her that her mother was American and her name was Constance, that she had died shortly after giving birth to her. Constance's final words, according to her father, were, 'When she is old enough to understand, tell our princess how much I love her and that I will always be with her.'

Tina did not care very much for her mother's name, but the tales of her death captivated the child. Apart from her dying words, the only possession her mother had bequeathed was a heart-shaped pendant that Tina was still not old enough to wear. When she asked to see it, her father, who was keeping it safe until her sixteenth birthday, would remove it from a locked drawer in the bureau in his study, open the box and place it on his desk for her perusal. It was a ritual the child enjoyed immensely. Her father's movements were precise and graceful. He prolonged each stage in the ritual, aware of his daughter's proclivity for suspense. Although she knew what the small velvet box contained, she found the anticipation thrilling. He had only placed it around her neck once. She remembered it was cold and heavy. The knowledge it had once touched her mother's skin brought them closer in the child's mind.

Tina heard her father rise from the water, the sound of the towel being pulled back and forth across his body and the heavy tread of his foot stepping from the bath. She hastily replaced the photograph in its correct position between its neighbours, closed the pocketbook and placed it back on the exact spot on the table on which she had found it. She repositioned herself in the bed and shut her eyes tight.

When Erik walked into the bedroom and saw his daughter's eyes squeezed tight, he released a loud 'humph' and smiled. He climbed into bed beside her. Tina wriggled across the bed and wedged her head in the crook of his arm.

PART THREE

THE AFTERMATH

THIRTY-SEVEN

STOCKHOLM, SWEDEN

OCTOBER 1930

'Thank you very much for meeting with me, Fru Neve. I hope my visit is not an imposition.'

'No, not at all, Herr Stubbendorff. I find it exceptionally enjoyable to receive visitors these days.' Gota showed the writer into her apartment. She was wearing a tightly fitted dress. Her red lipstick dominated her round face.

'Tell me, will the photographer be here shortly?'

'I'm afraid there is no one else coming today, Fru Neve.'

'But you're a journalist.' Her disappointment quickly turned to annoyance. 'You told me on the telephone you were a journalist wanting to discuss Anna.'

'Yes, that's true. But I am not here on behalf of a newspaper.' It had not been his intention to hoodwink Gota. He thought he had been particularly direct when they spoke. He repeated what he had explained on the telephone. 'I was the journalist who visited the Andrée camp on Kvitøya. I apologise if you were misled, Fru Neve.' Stubbendorff's deference calmed her. As a reporter he had witnessed this phenomenon many times. Gota Neve hoped that a modicum of fame would land on her through her tenuous connection to the Andrée expedition. She had wanted to be misled.

'Why do you wish to discuss my sister, then?'

'I discovered a number of items at the camp that once belonged to Nils Strindberg, your sister's fiancé.' Gota nodded. 'I believe there's one item that your sister may have appreciated reading.'

'Well, I don't know where she is,' she informed him curtly. 'She disappeared in 1899 and I haven't seen her since. Thirty years she's been gone and I wouldn't know where to find her.' She sat down heavily in a plump armchair. Her bosom came close to overwhelming the bodice of her dress. 'Would you like a refreshment, Herr Stubbendorff?' she asked.

Stubbendorff politely declined. He did not want to prolong this visit if he could help it. 'You were living with your sister at the time?'

'Until she ran away, we'd always lived together. We were inseparable,' she said defiantly as if some might dispute her statement. She smoothed her skirt over her thick legs.

Stubbendorff was disheartened. He had hoped Rosalie Strindberg had been mistaken in her portrait of Gota. 'There was never any word from Anna in all those years? You have no clue where she might have gone?'

'I had my suspicions,' she said cagily, without elaboration. 'It was quite a blow, as you'd imagine, when she ran away. But I got over it. Time heals all wounds, as they say.' She grinned smugly.

Stubbendorff nodded but found himself unnerved. He didn't believe the disappearance of one's inseparable sibling was ever something to be got over. Tore Strindberg still carried his brother's disappearance with him every day.

'I have reason to believe your sister may have died, some years ago, in 1907 or thereabouts.' He aimed to unsettle. His ill feeling towards Gota was growing. She shifted in her seat and carefully smoothed her hair.

'That may very well be. I've received no news regarding her death.' She made no attempt to feign sadness. 'Herr Stubbendorff,' she said bluntly. 'I've considered my sister dead since 1899, when she left.'

Stubbendorff pretended to write in his notebook while he considered the woman opposite him and the direction he should take. He had already dismissed his original purpose in coming to see her. The idea of handing over Nils Strindberg's journal to this woman made him sick. She was cold and insensitive. Base. But he wondered if there were not some other issue she might be able to shed light on. Gota was keen to talk. She wore her self-importance like a badge of honour and she considered the knowledge she held valuable. All Stubbendorff had to do was guide the conversation in the direction he wanted it to head.

'Fru Neve, can you enlighten me as to Anna's relationship with Erik Strindberg?'

Her face brightened and she shifted in her chair. 'I can tell you quite a lot about that. Are you sure you wouldn't like some coffee? A little schnapps, perhaps?'

Stubbendorff shook his head.

'Erik Strindberg was in love with her. That was obvious. Anna, on the other hand, didn't know what, or who, she wanted. She should have wanted Erik Strindberg. Any woman in her right mind wanted Erik Strindberg. But she passed him over for his brother. Nils was handsome as well, but a little vague – scatty, I'd call him. Erik was the real catch.'

'Did your sister form an attachment to Erik, that you know of?'

'Not a formal attachment, if that's what you mean. But there was some fooling around going on.' She winked knowingly. 'I caught them once and he came to our apartment to visit her a few times. Your guess is as good as mine as to what went on.'

Stubbendorff maintained his air of objectivity. 'To your knowledge, Nils never discovered the affair?'

'No. No idea. But it all ended in 1897 when Erik left for America.' She folded her hands on her lap. 'I urged Anna to go with him. Any fool knew the chances were slim of Nils ever returning. But she refused, stayed in Stockholm and wallowed.'

'Wallowed?'

'In her misery, Herr Stubbendorff.' Her face was hard for an instant before she checked her manner. 'She slept all day, lost her job as a governess, wasn't fit to be seen. When it came to the point where I could no longer bear it, I sent her to the country to live with our cousin in Åby. I thought fresh air might do the trick, perk her up. Then, stupid girl, she tried to kill herself. Walked into a lake, apparently, and set about drowning herself. Have you ever heard anything like it? Neither had I. Anyway, she returned to Stockholm and within six months had run away.'

'Why do you think Anna ran away, Fru Neve?'

'That's a very interesting question, Herr Stubbendorff.' Gota pondered this for a time. 'She was embarrassed. Anna made a mess of her life in Stockholm and hoped to put the disaster behind her.'

'Is this what she wrote in the note she left before departing?'

'That note said nothing, Herr Stubbendorff. A total waste of time writing it.' Then her gaze became more intense. 'How did you know about the note?'

'I've spoken to Rosalie Strindberg. She told me you came

to see her on the evening you discovered your sister missing. She spoke very highly of your tailoring skills, Fru Neve.'

Gota smirked. 'Rosalie was of no help. She had, still has I imagine, connections.' She said the final word deliberately. 'But she wouldn't lift a finger to help me find Anna and she wouldn't even entertain the idea that she'd fled to America to be with Erik. She had the power to find my sister and the only effort it would have taken was a telegram to her son or someone else that she knew in Chicago or . . .' Gota stopped and waved her hand above her head hoping to locate the end of her indictment. 'Anyway, she read the note and said matter-of-factly that it seemed to her that Anna did not want to be found. She would probably return when she was ready. Give her time, she said. Well, Herr Stubbendorff, is thirty years long enough?'

Stubbendorff nodded and scribbled needlessly in his notebook. He wanted to leave quickly. The sadness, utter sorrow, Anna was experiencing, and her only family was oblivious. Stubbendorff could not explain why Anna had left Stockholm and he was certain Gota Neve, despite her slap-dash certainty, did not know either.

Stubbendorff had grown protective of Strindberg's journal. Far more than a historical artefact, the journal was a door to another world. The characters Strindberg portrayed in his writing had come to life for Stubbendorff; he had become invested in their lives and their dreams. He was not certain whether it was possible or too late, but he longed to give those involved in this extraordinary narrative peace. He would rather see the diary in the hands of the Scientific Commission than in the pudgy paws of Gota Neve.

'Thank you for your time, Fru Neve. I must be going. I'm very sorry for the loss of your sister.'

'Are you certain you would not like a refreshment before you leave?'

'No, thank you, Fru Neve. You have given me quite enough this afternoon.' Stubbendorff descended the stairs to the street two at a time.

Stubbendorff had taken to walking the darkened streets of Staden mellan broarna, the old town, when it was impossible to sleep. It was pointless to try to force it. So he got up from his bed, dressed and headed out, walking and smoking until sunrise. This was the time when his head was clearest, when he was most able to separate himself from events and contemplate facts. He hoped walking the same streets that Anna, Erik and Nils had once walked would allow him to view events from their perspective. Over Djurgårdsbron to Djurgården then back to Lilla Nygatan and past the home of Tore Strindberg. Sometimes he would stop on the opposite side of the street and down a little way, lean against a wall and contemplate the house. On other mornings he would wind up on Skeppsbron, sitting by Sven Strindberg's house, *Sjöguden* in clear sight.

He was uncertain how this routine helped him, but he discovered accepting his sleeplessness, rather than fighting it, unlocked his vision and, somehow, cemented his commitment. Still reeling from his interview with Gota Neve, Stubbendorff was unsure what his next step should be. The funeral was just two days away. Erik Strindberg and his daughter were currently asleep in a house that stood nearby and the knowledge that Anna was dead was whittling away at his resolve.

Sitting in the cold, cupping his hands around another cigarette in an attempt to light it, Stubbendorff decided he must meet with Erik Strindberg. The thought filled him with dread. But Erik held the power to unravel the mystery. When he eventually did talk to him, he wanted to be in possession of all the specifics. Was it grief over Nils' disappearance or her love for Erik that drove Anna from Stockholm? If she was in love with Erik, why attempt suicide? There was a layer of this tragedy he was yet to uncover. He stamped out his cigarette, maddened by the knowledge that it was Anna with whom he needed to talk.

Studying Nils' journal and his own notes again that morning, he discovered that the only ill-fitting piece to the puzzle was Tore. Rosalie mentioned his dislike of Anna, and Tore himself referred to an incident when he lashed out against his brother's fiancée. It might be as Rosalie suggested, a jealous schoolboy angered that his devoted older brother was distracted by a woman, but he needed to know. He would speak with Tore.

THIRTY-EIGHT

STOCKHOLM, SWEDEN

OCTOBER 1930

BY TEN O'CLOCK Stubbendorff was retracing his steps to Lilla Nygatan. He had telephoned at nine and Tore Strindberg had said he would be happy to meet the journalist at half past ten. When he returned to his apartment, it was light and the cafe was only recently open. Skarsgård was curious about his 'nocturnal wanderings', as he called them, and questioned Stubbendorff relentlessly. He was confident his lodger was frittering away his windfall in bars or brothels. Stubbendorff remained as annoyingly uncommunicative as ever. He had eaten some bread with jam and drunk two cups of strong, sweet coffee in the cafe. Following a bath and a shave he was on his way again.

Despite his lack of sleep Stubbendorff's eyes were bright and his gait energetic. His cheeks were flushed and, to an impartial observer, he might have resembled a young man on his wedding day. He exuded passion and purpose.

Halfway to his destination he stopped a man and asked the time. When he continued, it was at a greater pace. When he rounded the corner of Lilla Nygatan, he was at a run. By the time he reached the front door, he was panting hard. He allowed himself a minute or two to recover then rang the doorbell. A conservatively dressed Agneta answered.

'It's lovely to see you again, Herr Stubbendorff.' The left-hand side of her mouth transformed into an attractive, if wry, curl.

'Likewise.' Stubbendorff looked downwards and fixed his eyes on his shoes. He was aware of the colour rising in his face. 'I hope my phone call and request were not an intrusion.'

'Not at all.'

She led him along the cluttered hallway to the artist's studio, tapped lightly on the door and pushed it open. 'Herr Stubbendorff has arrived. Shall I show him in?' The door opened to its full extent. Tore Strindberg took his hand eagerly and shook it vigorously.

'Thank you, Agneta. Some coffee, please.' She departed and Strindberg, still clasping Stubbendorff's hand, pulled him across the studio as an excited child would his mother. He halted in front of three easels positioned in a semicircle. On each was a sheet of paper depicting a sail-shaped structure, each from a different vantage point.

'Is this the memorial?' Stubbendorff asked.

'My design for the memorial, yes. What do you think? I was delighted you telephoned. I've been meaning to track you down. You were my inspiration for the piece.'

'You give me too much credit, Herr Strindberg.' As Stubbendorff studied the sketches, a lump rose in his throat. To the writer the design resembled the prow of a ship cutting through water. Engraved on the sail was what he assumed was the route the explorers took in the balloon and on foot, over ice, through the Arctic.

'I telephoned the commission. They were able to tell me the exact route of the expedition, based on the evidence in Andrée's diary. He tracked their course meticulously. It will be stone, and stand roughly six metres high,' Strindberg said.

Stubbendorff moved in to examine the carefully drawn trail. 'My goodness, what a journey. I read Andrée's logbook, but until you see it traced like this the magnitude is difficult to comprehend.'

Tears welled in Stubbendorff's light-blue eyes. He felt a hand on his back.

'Don't worry. That's exactly the reaction I want. I've shed a number of tears myself in the process.'

Stubbendorff smiled.

'You're speechless. That's always a good thing.' Strindberg laughed. 'Coffee?'

Stubbendorff nodded. 'It's wonderful, a credit to you and your brother.'

'Thank you for your advice. It would have remained a blank page in a sketchbook if not for you.'

The men sipped their coffee in silence. Stubbendorff took his cup and strolled meditatively around the studio, examining Strindberg's sculptures, engravings and sketches. He was struck by a sense of privilege. How fortunate he was to be casually taking in Tore Strindberg's work, to have had the first glimpse of what might be his most significant piece. He turned to Strindberg. 'I hope you don't mind me . . .'

Strindberg lay back on the settee, a shadow of a grin apparent on his lips. He waved his hand, instructing the young man to go on. 'Are you an art lover, Herr Stubbendorff?'

'Yes, very much. I've just never really made the effort to go to galleries and exhibitions. I'm afraid I've wasted a good deal of time on other less noble pursuits. Visiting your brother's gallery was an experience. He's an extremely talented director.'

'He's terrifyingly good at what he does, and quite a character.' Strindberg smiled more openly. 'So, Herr Stubbendorff, what brings you here today? What is the sensitive matter you need to discuss?'

Stubbendorff placed his cup on the table and sat opposite the reclining artist. He had scripted his conversation with Tore Strindberg but now, in the studio, drinking coffee with him as he relaxed on the settee, his planned approach seemed too formal. He decided to speak to Strindberg as he would a friend.

'I met with your mother last week.' Strindberg nodded. 'She was extremely helpful regarding seeking out Anna Charlier. But she did mention something that bothered me.'

Strindberg raised his eyebrows.

'She described your relationship with Anna at the time. Your treatment of her was hostile?'

The small man sat up and placed his cup on the table. He joined his hands and leant his elbows on his knees. 'I'm afraid so.'

'When I visited here, you told me that you'd lashed out at Anna and that you'd like the opportunity to apologise.'

Strindberg placed his head between his hands. Plaster was encrusted around the rims of his fingernails, giving the snowy tips of his fingers the look of sculpted appendages.

'I was hoping you might be able to shed light on your relationship with Anna.'

Stubbendorff was nervous. It was entirely possible Tore would raise his head and throw him out of his studio, claim ownership of the journal and warn his family about the meddlesome reporter.

After a short time the artist pushed his fingers through

his dark hair and raised his head. 'I would like to pre-empt my confession with a statement.'

Stubbendorff nodded in encouragement.

'I was a boy. Fourteen at the time. And I was an idiot. Please don't hold my past actions against me.'

Stubbendorff realised it was not he who should be nervous. Tore was on the verge of an admission that, he guessed, had probably plagued him for thirty years.

'Of course not.'

'It will do me good to unburden myself. Get it off my chest, as they say.' He smiled slightly. Clearing his throat, he looked at his interviewer directly.

'When Anna entered our family, I loved her. She was amusing and warm and never seemed to mind me chasing after Nils and monopolising his time. She was full of fun and she could be as boisterous as I was. Apart from my mother there were no women in my life. I embraced her as a sister.

'Then, on the evening Nils told us he was going to accompany Andrée, I saw something that I didn't understand at the time.' Strindberg stood and walked to the window. 'Unlike everybody else I was excited, thrilled my brother was going to become a national hero. Mama sent me off to bed. She was annoyed I'd sided with Nils. I couldn't sleep. Such news!'

Stubbendorff nodded.

'After a while I heard a sound from the courtyard below my bedroom. It was a stifling night and my window was open. Anna was sitting there, humming to herself, very softly, a mournful kind of a tune. I remember thinking it wasn't like Anna to be morose. Then Erik joined her and they kissed quite fervently. I was furious, outraged. Erik announced his undying love and they had an argument. I couldn't hear all the details. But I can still see Anna sitting next to Erik and taking his hand. The look on her face was unmistakeable. She loved him too. Even to a boy – a child – it was obvious.'

'And you told Nils of this?'

'No, never. From that point I treated Anna with complete and utter disdain.' He shook his head in disbelief. 'I hated her. I truly hated her. I believed she was betraying my brother, Sweden's pride and joy.'

'Did you direct any of your rage at Erik?'

Strindberg laughed abruptly. 'Of course not. He was my brother. He could do no wrong. Nils was my closest friend but Erik was my hero. We weren't as close but Erik was everything I wanted to be – confident, strong, handsome, successful, amusing . . . In my eyes he was perfect.' Strindberg sighed. 'This is becoming easier, Herr Stubbendorff. It's remarkably pleasant to relieve oneself of guilt.'

'But why do you feel guilty? Just because you treated Anna a little shabbily . . .'

Strindberg held up his hand. 'I haven't finished.' He sat down next to his guest. 'Two months after Nils left for the second time, everyone knew he wasn't returning. The updates of progress never came. It was a terrible time for the family. I was the last person to give up hope and when I did it was shattering. I felt as though I'd killed Nils myself.'

Strindberg took a deep breath before going on. 'At about this time, or maybe shortly after, Anna came to the house one day. I was in this room, Nils' workroom. It comforted me to be in here with his equipment and photographs. I'd often lie on his bed and press my face into his pillow. I lived in fear of the day it would lose all trace of his scent. Anna walked through that door one day when I was in here. I dare say she had similar intentions.'

Stubbendorff imagined Anna Charlier burying her face in her dead fiancé's pillow.

'I was beastly. I shouted at her, told her I'd told Nils about her love affair with Erik. That he died knowing she didn't love him. She tried to explain, but I wouldn't listen. To me it was black and white. She ran from the room and I never saw her again. Of course, I'd told my brother nothing. Yelling at Anna was just a way to purge my grief.' Strindberg wiped his eyes with a paint-stained handkerchief.

Anna's subsequent actions suddenly made sense, Stubbendorff realised. Believing her fiancé had gone to his lonely and premature death with the knowledge that she was in love with his brother would have been devastating. Her own guilt and shame were surely overwhelming. It explained her suicide attempt and her flight from Stockholm.

Stubbendorff laid his hand sympathetically on Strindberg's shoulder. 'You were a child buried in sorrow after the loss of your dearest brother. You can't be held responsible for your actions.'

He didn't possess the strength to inform Strindberg of Anna's death.

'In hindsight, now I have a little more experience of the complications and agonies of love, I wish I'd been kinder.'

'You've never spoken to Erik of this?'

Strindberg shook his head. 'When the incident occurred, he'd already left for America. By the time I saw him again, it seemed inappropriate to stir up the past. The family had finally come to accept Nils' death. I was a boy. How was I going to broach the subject with him, delicately, sensitively?'

'I understand. Thank you for telling me this. It helps in my understanding of Anna Charlier and her actions.'

Strindberg took a moment to gather himself, folding his handkerchief carefully before placing it in his pocket.

'I'm glad I told you, Herr Stubbendorff. I knew you'd under- stand. You have an artist's soul, I'm positive of it. There are always shades of grey, aren't there?'

Stubbendorff nodded slowly.

'Have you had any luck tracing Anna?'

'No, not as yet. The search goes on. But if and when I do, I'll certainly tell her that you'd like to speak with her.' Stubbendorff did not have the courage to tell the artist the truth.

'Excellent. I can't take back the past, but I'd like to ask her forgiveness, and explain how I regretted my words. I hope she managed to find happiness.'

'The more I learn about Anna Charlier, the more complex and nuanced she seems. More so, I believe, than anybody understood.'

The men were silent for a moment, each considering the mystery of Anna Charlier. Finally, Strindberg broke the silence.

'Will you be attending the funeral or memorial ceremony, or whatever they're calling it?'

'I think I'll brave the crowds and go along. I've become strangely entangled in the life of Anna and your brother.' Stubbendorff would have liked to include the rest of the Strindberg family, but he feared it would make him appear overfamiliar or grasping.

'It's not strange at all, Herr Stubbendorff. You've invested a great deal of time and effort in finding Anna. When you think about it, it's quite an extraordinary situation Anna found herself in. Novelists would call it a love triangle, would they not? I can see it has captured your imagination.'

Strindberg embraced his guest firmly. It was odd but not uncomfortable to be hugged by a man, and Stubbendorff gave in to Tore's muscled arms. When they had released him, Stubbendorff said, 'Thank you again for all your help. I'm greatly honoured to have helped you in your task as well.'

'When the memorial's erected in Norra kyrkogården next year, I want you to be standing by my side, Herr Stubbendorff.'

Stubbendorff was overcome. He showed himself hastily out to the street and inhaled deeply. The lump had returned to his throat and his chest was swollen with possibility. He had uncovered a significant piece in the puzzle that was Anna Charlier. Yet he craved more. After stealing the journal and embarking on the search, he felt duty bound to seek out the person to whom the diary could be surrendered. Perhaps this person was Erik Strindberg.

Anna found herself outside the Strindberg home on Lilla Nygatan. She stood on the opposite side of the street for almost half an hour. It looked exactly the same, she marvelled. The curtains in the sitting room window were a different colour and that ghastly knocker had been removed but in the main the house was just as she remembered. She wondered if the home still belonged to a member of the family.

The door opened and a man exited. He stopped outside for a moment as if taking in his surroundings. Then he leant against the wall and hung his head until his chin touched his chest. When he raised his head, there was a greater certainty to his manner. Anna checked his appearance, searching for a family resemblance. He was far shorter than any of the family and his hair was almost white. Likewise, his complexion was pale, so pale it was striking. 'Lily-white' Gota would have once described it. His face was eager and alert and there was something else. He had a talent for making mischief, Anna recognised. There was a puckish air about him. He pushed his hair from his brow, placed his satchel on his shoulder and went on his way. Anna had never actually seen anyone walking with a spring in their step before. She doubted whether he could be the son of any one of the brothers. Although she had not seen the man Tore had grown into, he was raven-haired as a boy, like Sven and his mother, and quite athletic. Anna scrutinised the stranger as he entered a cafe further along the street.

She kept watch for another half-hour, hoping to catch a glimpse of someone she might have known once. When she departed, she passed by the cafe and stopped at the window, measuring her appetite for a moment. Before she went on, she looked in the window. The young man was sitting at a table writing furiously in a notebook. A cup of coffee sat untouched before him. He looked up from his work and smiled at the pretty woman standing on the other side of the glass. He liked the way her hair was piled messily on her head, certainly not the fashion but so becoming. Stubbendorff had never seen eyes so dark. He could barely distinguish the pupil. They seemed to study him in his entirety in a mere instant. She returned the smile and then strolled on to Stensbastugränd.

THIRTY-NINE

STOCKHOLM, SWEDEN

OCTOBER 1930

STUBBENDORFF APPROACHED the house on Skeppsbron for a third time. The lion's head now bore a jaded expression of familiarity. He knocked its hammer hard on the door three times.

'Good morning, Herr Stubbendorff.' The maid opened the door and led the way to the sitting room. Even on this visit, the outlook from the large window managed to impress him. 'I will inform Herr Strindberg that you have arrived.'

He walked to the mantel and stared at the picture of Albertina - Tina as her family call her. He had never seen a picture of Anna. The only image Stubbendorff had of her was one painted by Nils' words in his journal. He wondered if the resemblance that now seemed so remarkably striking had been created solely from the knowledge that she was Anna's daughter, or whether the likeness really did exist.

Chestnut curls and brown eyes. Nils mentioned these elements frequently.

'Good morning, Herr Stubbendorff. I'm Erik Strindberg.'

Stubbendorff turned and faced a silver-haired leviathan who filled the doorway.

'My brothers and mother have praised you endlessly. It's delightful to meet you.'

He walked towards Stubbendorff and shook his hand. His grip was strong and his voice similarly so. The younger man steeled himself.

'It's extremely generous of you to see me, especially since you've only recently arrived in Stockholm. How are you finding the city after thirty years' absence?'

The two men spoke at length about the changes that had occurred in Stockholm over the previous three decades. As a short man, Stubbendorff was irrationally intimidated by men and women significantly larger than himself. Regardless of who they were, he felt foolish in their presence. But Erik was affable and aware. He invited his guest to sit and positioned himself opposite Stubbendorff to talk. Stubbendorff assumed that a man of Erik's stature might feel just as foolish standing next to a short person.

Their easy conversation was interrupted by the maid returning with a tray of coffee. Strindberg leant back in the armchair by the window and looked at the harbour. His fingers strummed absently on its arms.

'I've come home on several occasions during that time but it does seem markedly changed on this visit. Perhaps that's due to the reason for my return.'

Stubbendorff nodded thoughtfully.

'My family inform me you discovered Nils' journal on Kvitøya?'

'That's correct.'

'And you wish to convey the journal to Anna Charlier?' Erik asked as he poured the coffee.

'That was my original undertaking.' Stubbendorff replied. 'But I've since learnt of Anna Charlier's death.'

The coffee pot returned to the tray with a loud clatter. Coffee spilt from the cups as Erik stood. 'What? Dead? From whom or where did you get this information?'

Erik loomed over Stubbendorff's chair, his eyes demanding an immediate answer. He was not angered, that was apparent. He was wounded, stunned, Stubbendorff thought. The news of Anna's death had been a genuine shock. Could he have got it all wrong?

'Please, have a seat,' Stubbendorff said. 'I should explain. However, I must speak frankly, Herr Strindberg.'

Erik sat. Leaning forward, he said quietly, 'I have discovered over the years, Herr Stubbendorff, that is the only way one should speak.'

'In my determination to track down Anna Charlier, a great deal of sensitive, private information has come into my possession, mostly pertaining to the relationship between yourself and Anna.'

Erik raised his head. No unfriendliness was present in his alert, blue eyes.

'It began with Sven. He said he always believed you harboured feelings for Anna. But when I met with your mother, she said that you and Anna had shared a strained relationship. She put the conflict down to jealousy over Nils.'

Erik merely stared gravely at his guest, so Stubbendorff went on. 'But the most useful piece of information your mother offered was your daughter's name, Albertina – Albertina and Elin are Charlier family names. I didn't believe it was a coincidence.'

'It's no coincidence, Herr Stubbendorff.'

'When your mother then informed me of your wife's

death, I naturally assumed . . .'

'Of course, it's a logical leap.' Erik exhaled and leant back in his chair.

'Why hasn't anyone else made the connection? Your mother . . .'

'In regard to Nils and Anna, Mama only sees what she wants to see.'

Stubbendorff nodded before Erik continued.

'Anna didn't talk much about her background. She was from farming stock and I think she was concerned about being patronised. She needn't have worried.' Erik looked rueful for a moment. 'But as far as I know, Anna is still alive.'

'But you don't know her whereabouts?'

'I've not heard from her or seen her since the day she left Tina and me in Chicago. That was September, 1907.' He turned sharply towards Stubbendorff. Bitterness soured his rich voice. 'But if she's anywhere at this precise moment, it will be Stockholm. She'd never miss the funeral.'

Despite the tension in the room Stubbendorff was immediately lifted by this information. There was a strong chance Anna was alive – she would be fifty-nine. There was also a chance that she was in Stockholm.

'Forgive me, Herr Strindberg, but I'd like to know more about your relationship with Anna. Now that I know she's most likely alive and in Stockholm, I'd appreciate your help in locating her. I believe the only way I can do that is to learn the true story and I feel you're a forthright man.'

Erik sighed deeply and took a seat. 'Who else have you spoken to?'

'Your brothers, your mother and Anna's sister, Gota.'

A smile took possession of Erik's face and unexpectedly lightened the atmosphere. 'She was a piece of work. She was desperate for a wealthy husband, any husband. I think it motivated every thought she ever had. Nils and I, for the life of us, couldn't understand how she and Anna were sisters. They were so dissimilar. Anna was so—' He broke off for an instant. 'Gracious.' He shook his head in disbelief. 'You know, Gota was the reason Anna initially rejected me.'

'Really?'

'It was midsummer 1894. Anna caught my eye, and I fell for her immediately. But she rebuffed my advances. I learnt later she wanted to spare Gota's feelings. Nils and I made fun of Gota constantly. Not in front of Anna, of course. Even in those early years I sensed she was not on Anna's side.'

Stubbendorff raised his eyebrows.

'There was a time in Anna's life when she needed her sister's help.'

'When your brother disappeared?'

Erik nodded. 'I don't mean to overdramatise, but it was life and death. Gota couldn't understand the grimness of her sister's predicament.'

'She did appear a rather shallow sort.'

'You're too generous, Herr Stubbendorff. But no more of her. Tell me, what prompted this search for Anna? I'm interested.'

'When I discovered your brother's journal and the letters to Anna, I was moved. His writing moved me,' Stubbendorff explained. 'I don't believe they were written with any thought that she'd one day read them. Quite the opposite. I believe your brother knew his situation was hopeless. That's what's so remarkable about the letters – the hope they convey in the face of immense despair. The memory of Anna was life-sustaining for your brother. If anyone valued me that much, I'd want to know. I simply thought Anna should read them as well.'

Erik stood and walked to the door. He called for the maid to bring more coffee. Then he took his seat again. He lay his head back and closed his eyes. His large hands gripped the arms of the chair. As Stubbendorff waited for the man to speak, he studied his face and his cadenced breathing. Erik Strindberg was the antithesis of himself, he thought. In his early sixties he was still handsome and, like his brother Sven, his white hair only added to his arresting appearance. He was forthright and open and extremely successful in his profession. Yet he had remained unmarried. Stubbendorff wondered whether the memory of Anna Charlier had been life-sustaining for Erik also.

With the arrival of the coffee Erik opened his eyes and straightened in his seat. 'It's difficult to know where to begin, Herr Stubbendorff. You must realise that I've never shared these memories with anyone, not even my daughter. She knows nothing about her mother. I invented a tale when she became curious about her. She believes her mother died when she was a baby.'

As he poured more coffee for the two of them, he said, 'I'd like you to guarantee that Tina won't discover her mother's identity. To learn your mother abandoned you, regardless of the reason, would be devastating, even at her age.'

When Stubbendorff had pledged his silence, Strindberg said, 'I shall begin at the beginning.'

Starting with their initial meeting on midsummer eve thirty-six years before, Erik spoke in great detail about his relationship with Anna Charlier. Their first flirtations, their deepening bond, her letter to Chicago seeking his assistance, the birth of Tina and, finally, her disappearance. Often his expression would become quizzical. Occasionally he would remove his handkerchief from his coat pocket and casually dry his eyes. At other times he laughed heartily as he related a fond memory of their brief life together. But most often he spoke unemotionally about his life with Anna Charlier.

Overwhelmed by the torrent of information, Stubbendorff slid his notebook into the satchel early on, deciding instead to appreciate Strindberg's story. 'It's remarkable your brother was never aware.'

'You wouldn't think it remarkable if you knew Nils.' Erik smiled. 'He was so intensely involved in his work, he rarely noticed anything outside of his laboratory.' He was silent for a moment and laughed.

'There was just one occasion when I thought he might have an inkling of my feelings but I'll never know for sure. I suggested to Anna once that we come clean and tell Nils everything. She refused. But you know what the funny thing is?' He leant forward in his chair. 'He would have understood. He would have been happy for us. Sometimes I imagine how my life might have been different if I'd told him, despite Anna's objections. It was a strange feeling, Herr Stubbendorff, to be so in love with a woman but to have that love tainted by the burden of betrayal.'

'Did you try to find her?'

'Of course. I informed the police immediately and hired a private detective when they couldn't find her. The police did seem confident that she was still alive. The detective found a trace of her, however. A booking clerk with Cunard said he recognised her photograph as a woman who might have purchased passage to England.'

'Did you try to find her there?'

'I thought about going there, searching for her. But I suppose I realised if she went to England she didn't want to be found by me.'

'She hurt you greatly, didn't she?'

Erik didn't respond, but the answer was plain. After a moment he said, 'Her doctor, who had greater insights into Anna's mental state than I, believed she'd return one day. I merely wanted to know that she hadn't tried to harm herself again. I was hopeful she was safe and that she'd come home, if not for me, then for Tina. Even after twenty-three years I often ask myself whether, if Anna walked through the door now, I'd take her back.' Strindberg laughed. 'My daughter would call me a "sap", Herr Stubbendorff. "Sap" is an American expression that is fashionable among the young people in Chicago. It means a gullible idiot.'

'It's neither gullible nor idiotic to be in love.'

'Thank you, Herr Stubbendorff, for your kind words. But I can't help feeling that I have been made a fool by my love for Anna.' He sighed. 'You seem to be quite knowledgeable on the subject. Do you speak from experience?'

'No, unfortunately not. My knowledge of the subject derives from novels and the cinema, I'm afraid. I remain unattached.' Stubbendorff, wanting to change the subject, went on. 'I understand that Anna was under the impression Nils was aware of your relationship, that he died believing he had been betrayed. That could explain her despondency, her inability to commit to a life with you and Tina.'

Tina. Stubbendorff enjoyed the way the name sounded coming from his lips.

Erik's eyes widened. 'How did you come to this conclusion?'

'It was something Tore mentioned. There was an incident with Anna that had tormented him. Without his permission I don't want to divulge anything further.'

Strindberg nodded. 'Of course. So Anna believed Nils had learnt of our relationship?'

'I think so.'

Erik placed his head in his hands and sighed deeply.

'I'd like Anna to read Nils' letters,' Stubbendorff continued, regardless of his companion's obvious distress. 'The knowledge that he died holding her dear would be a relief to her. She's been under a misapprehension for thirty-three years.'

Strindberg raised his head and moved to the window and

stood, arms folded, looking to the harbour. Stubbendorff could tell he was processing this information and figuring out how these events had shaped his life.

'An unfortunate twist of fate, then?' He asked this question of no one in particular. Then he turned to Stubbendorff. 'I mistook her feelings of remorse for undying love for my brother. What a fool I was. Now it all seems so clear. Her behaviour, melancholy, her leaving . . . I was blind.' Strindberg smiled. 'The benefits of hindsight are amazing. Amazing but cruel.'

Then he turned to Stubbendorff, composure regained. 'You know, I still miss her and, although I've tried to, it's impossible to forget her. My daughter is a daily reminder. They're extremely alike in many ways.'

'How so?'

'Energetic and intelligent. Self-deprecating but also possessing a quiet confidence. Without being aware of it, Anna instructed me regularly on how to moderate my own pride. And of course, they both share the same unassuming beauty.'

Strindberg reached into his coat pocket and produced a black leather wallet. He handed Stubbendorff a faded photograph of a young woman's face against a white background. Her lightly freckled nose was crinkled and her mouth wide in speech. Her curls hung recklessly from her woollen hat and her brown eyes penetrated the camera's lens. 'I stole this from Nils and have been carrying it in my breast pocket for more than three decades. Pathetic, aren't I?'

'She's very beautiful.' Stubbendorff indicated the photograph on the mantel. 'Very similar to your daughter.'

'At times my fury with Anna, my inability to understand her, would overwhelm my reason. I employed psychiatrists and doctors and researched the field myself. I questioned her endlessly. Sometimes, at my wit's end, I'd confront her, intending to leave her or throw her out. Then I'd look into those eyes and I knew she could see right through me. Suddenly my frustration would subside.' He placed the photograph back into the sleeve.

'Anna will be here in Stockholm, Herr Stubbendorff. I know it. I don't believe she'd ever come and seek me or Tina out, but she'll be at the funeral tomorrow. That, I'm afraid, is all I can offer.'

'How can you be so sure?'

'The disappearance of my brother has shaped her life, made her the person she is. If you were in her shoes, wouldn't you want to be present for the final chapter?'

Stubbendorff understood exactly what Erik Strindberg was saying. 'You've given me much more information than I expected. Thank you for sharing your story with me. I'm sorry your life couldn't have been different. I wish you and Anna could have lived happily ever after.'

'Life is rarely black and white, as I can see now. I lost Anna but she gave me a beautiful daughter who's a constant delight. I don't have any regrets, Herr Stubbendorff.'

There was a pause.

'Will you be attending the service tomorrow?' Strindberg asked. Stubbendorff nodded.

'My family's having a small celebration here on Thursday evening, after the cremation. There's been too much sorrow over the years. Nils would never have stood for such solemnity. I'd like you to attend, as a guest of the family.' He smiled. 'My brothers would enjoy having you here, and Tina would appreciate the opportunity to speak with a like-minded individual of a similar age. What do you think?'

'If you don't think I'd be intruding on a private gathering?'

'Not at all. You seem to know more about my family than I do, Knut.' Erik laughed loudly.

FORTY

ROYAL SWEDISH ACADEMY OF SCIENCES, STOCKHOLM, SWEDEN

FEBRUARY 1895

ANDRÉE STOOD and walked to the lectern. He took a deep breath and closed his eyes briefly, taking stock. The members shifted in their seats, prompting Andrée to face their glare. He cleared his throat and took a sip of water before beginning in a stilted tone.

'The history of geographical discovery is at the same time a history of great peril and suffering, gentlemen.' He faltered and paused briefly. Looking up from his notes, he placed the glass to his lips once more then examined the pages in front of him. The words blurred for an instant. Although Andrée's hesitation would not have lasted longer than twenty seconds, the low grumbles from the audience indicated that he needed to proceed quickly. His reputation, his life's work and his greatest ambition were on the verge of collapse. He gripped the lectern firmly. His knuckles turned white. He became aware of a pain running the length of his palms. Andrée turned back to his notes. Each word lay in clear and sharp focus. He went on.

'While forcing their way through unknown regions across the vast deserts of Australia, Asia, Africa, the prairies of North America, or through the forests of South America and Central Africa, the explorers have encountered dangers, endured hardships, and been obliged to conquer difficulties, of which no clear idea can be formed by those who have never passed through similar experiences.

'However, in warm or tropical climates, nearly every hindrance can be said to contain a means of success. For example, natives frequently bar the way of the explorer, but just as often, perhaps, they become friends and helpers. Despite the harsh sun the desert may also offer a luxuriant vegetation that serves as a shelter.'

He paused again, but this time anxiety was not the reason for his hesitation. Andrée stared seriously at the men seated before him and walked purposefully out from behind the lectern, abandoning his notes.

'In the Arctic,' he went on, gravely. 'The cold only kills.'

The sentence had the desired effect. The crowd murmured solemnly to one another for a few seconds. At the precise moment, when Andrée believed the audience had had just enough time to digest his remark, he continued.

'The difficulties which meet explorers in penetrating the ice- filled Polar Sea are beyond imagination. There are no oases in the icy desert, no vegetation, no fuel, no human inhabitant, just a field of ice that invites to a journey. So far, attempts made to penetrate the central parts of the Arctic Ocean by means of vessels have failed. The sole means of travel across the pack ice towards the North Pole has been the sledge, but whether drawn by dogs or men, the form of transport has failed to carry anyone to the pole and has met with limited success.' Andrée clasped his hands at his back and strolled, casually, to the left of the stage.

'Has not the time come,' he proceeded, looking towards the spectators in the gallery,'to revise this question from the very beginning and to see if we do not possibly possess any other means than the sledge for crossing these tracts?'

By this stage Andrée's manner had relaxed. His gestures were fluid. At ease with his material, the forty-one-year-old found himself stimulated by the obvious interest evident in the audience.

'Yes!' he exclaimed, confidently. 'The time for doing so has certainly come, and we need not search very long before we find a means which is, as it were, created for just such a purpose. This means is the air balloon; not the dreamed-of, perfectly dirigible air balloon, so devoutly longed for, since we have not yet seen it, but the air balloon which we already possess and which is regarded so unfavourably merely because attention is focused on its weak point. Such an air balloon is, however, capable of carrying the explorer to the pole and home again in safety; with such a balloon the journey across the waste of ice *can* be carried out.'

'Hear, hear!' Andrée heard among the audience. He nodded in appreciation before concluding his introduction.

'These words may seem bold, and even reckless, but I ask you to suspend your judgement on the matter until you have heard my arguments. For I am assured that then your judgement will be different. We have merely to rid ourselves of preconceived opinions and then allow facts to have all the weight they may possess.'

Andrée continued to speak for over an hour, detailing with typical exactness the expedition he envisaged. From the creation of the balloon, to the supplies carried, to the most desirable wind speed and air temperature for balloon travel, to the glorious homecoming, every aspect of his proposal was explained and justified, clarified and defended.

Nearing the end of his oration, the explorer paused and wiped his brow. He was breathing hard and his throat, itchy from the smoke in the windowless auditorium, was soothed once again by water. He turned his back on his listeners momentarily, leaning one arm on the lectern. When he faced them for the final section, it was with renewed energy.

'And who, I ask, are better qualified to make such an attempt than we Swedes?' He held his arms in front of him, palms raised, an expression of complete incredulity on his face. A further chorus of 'hear, hear' echoed. Andrée moved back behind the lectern.

'As a highly civilised nation, characterised for ages by the most dauntless courage, dwelling in the neighbourhood of the polar regions, familiar with its climatic peculiarities, and by Nature herself trained to endure them, we can hardly altogether help feeling that we have a certain obligation in this matter. Are we not, therefore, called upon, before other nations, as being best fitted, to execute this great task?' A gust of mutterings sprang from the audience. Andrée waited for them to settle before delivering his final words.

'I believe I am not mistaken in thinking that, just as we hope and expect that the peoples of Central and Southern Europe will explore Africa, so they, too, expect of us that we shall explore this white quarter of the globe!'

The audience rose to its feet in applause, drowning out the protests of any nay-sayers in its midst.

FORTY-ONE

STOCKHOLM, SWEDEN

OCTOBER 1930

In the name of the Swedish nation I here greet the dust of the polar explorers who, more than three decades ago, left their native land to find an answer to questions of unparalleled difficulty. They went away – they vanished into the horizon. Their own fate but increased the number of the questions. And yet, they have come home again at last!

The country's hope, to be able to honour them in their lifetime after a successful journey, was disappointed. We must submit to the tragic result. All that is left us is to express our warm thanks to them for their self-sacrifice in the service of science.

Peace to their memory!

– King Gustav, 5 October 1930, Church of St Nicholas, Stockholm

❄

The crowd was too dense for Anna to be able to open her umbrella. Standing five deep along Slottsbacken, sodden bodies holding limp flags jostled against one another in an effort to see the road. She pushed her wet hair from her forehead and stood on her toes. Straining her neck above the thousands of heads, she saw nothing. A man in front of her relinquished his position and darted across the street in the hope of an improved view. Anna moved one step closer to the road. The mist veiling the belltower of Storkyrkan made her shudder.

The mass of heads around her turned simultaneously. Bodies leant forward in expectation. Anna heard somebody say they could see a car. She waited. Then, through the steady drum of the rain on the pavement, the low hum of an engine became audible. Next to her a father hoisted his child onto his shoulders. 'I can see them, Papa. Here they come. Three cars.'

Anna's heart thundered in her chest and her throat constricted. As the thousands of onlookers eyed the road, she stared down at the pavement, taking slow, deep breaths. Water ran to the tip of her nose and fell to the ground. She was shoved from behind as the crowd moved forward. When she looked up, the procession was directly in front of her. The open cars each conveyed an identical oak casket strewn with a wreath in the national colours. The cars were so close that Anna could see the faces of the drivers and the rain bouncing off the glistening wood of the coffins.

Behind each car walked the families of the dead. Despite her panic she could not control the compulsion to scrutinise each sombre passer-by. She hoped to recognise her daughter and Erik among the mourners. She stared intently at the dozen or so people positioned behind the first vehicle. Anna recognised no one. Andrée's body would surely be first, she thought. He had no wife or children, she remembered, and his mother had died just prior to the launch. The pedestrians, huddled beneath expansive black umbrellas, must be cousins, nieces and nephews.

The second vehicle soon reached the position where she was standing and she looked beyond it. From her angle on the pavement she could only see umbrellas. A canopy of black umbrellas cloaked those trailing the hearse. Once they were level with her, the unconscious cry she emitted made the boy held aloft on his father's shoulders look down at her in concern. Erik walked beside his two brothers. She closed her eyes and pictured him as she had last seen him, leaning against the door to their bedroom, smiling as she fixed her hair in the mirror.

'You look lovely,' he had said. 'I'm thrilled you're up and about again.' He had walked to her and nuzzled his face in her hair. 'What have you got planned for the day?'

'I thought I'd take Tina for a walk in Lincoln Park and make the most of the warmth. Winter will be on us before long.'

'Tina? Are we shortening her name already?'

'Albertina is so formal,' Anna had said. 'It will be the name we use when she is being naughty.'

Erik smiled. 'That's a good idea, on all counts! I wish I could join you. It sounds heavenly. Walking in Lincoln Park in the sunshine with my two favourite girls.' He hugged her tightly, jubilantly. 'But work beckons.'

He sat on the edge of the bed, tightening his shoelaces. When he straightened, she was looking at him earnestly. He reached his arms towards her and she walked to him and took his hands. She sat across his knees. Erik embraced her in a way he never had before. He was grateful, she thought; thankful that this whole episode was finished. That they would soon be married. Anna took his face in her hands and kissed him on the lips. It was a kiss imbued with all the love and passion in her heart.

'I love you, Erik.' This was the truth, spoken for the first time.

'I love you too, Anna.' He placed his face in the soft space between her neck and shoulder. It was in this state of momentary bliss that she heard him whisper, 'Thank you.'

He had left for work. It was the last time she had seen him until this moment. His hair had turned white in the intervening years. That was no wonder, she thought. He was already greying when Tina was born. Oscar Strindberg's white hair always amused her: it sat so thickly on his large head, belying his smooth skin. Erik's face had developed creases, she noted, but he was still handsome. His straight back and muscular frame walking between the willowy Sven and compact Tore was an impressive sight.

Behind the brothers followed Rosalie, her arm entwined with that of a much younger woman. Anna looked hard at the companion. She knew immediately it was her own daughter. Anna recognised herself in Tina's appearance and Erik's assuredness in her bearing. As the rain poured down, Anna allowed the tears to flow unheeded down her cheeks.

Welcome home! Welcome, Andrée! Welcome, Strindberg! Welcome, Frænkel! You have been many years away. And what we now receive are merely the ruins of magnificent, well-tempered instruments fitted for indomitable longing and clear-sighted achievement. When, after millions of years to come, our rolling globe shall, perhaps, tell to dumb worlds the legend of the passing amid icy cold of our vanished race, will, then, the story of the end of the last man resemble that which has made your memory glorious? All that

which passes is merely semblance. From semblance reality comes forth at last! The veil falls. The spirit lives. Jesus said: 'God is the God of the living. Amen.'

– Archbishop Nathan Söderblom, 5 October 1930, Church of St Nicholas, Stockholm

The crowd closed ranks when the third hearse passed. Somnambulant hordes followed the procession in the direction of Storkyrkan. Stubbendorff shuffled in and found a place among the sedately flowing stream. Travelling along Slottsbacken, walking shoulder to shoulder with his compatriots, he had no way to dodge puddles, and by the time they reached the cathedral, water had soaked through to his socks. The solemnity of the occasion dictated his head should remain uncovered. He wished for a hat as he wiped the water from his forehead and scanned the faces in the crowd.

He knew his mission was hopeless. The rain had not proved a deterrent to the thousands of mourners present. To find Anna Charlier here, today, Stubbendorff believed was impossible. It shocked him to realise it, but he wanted to leave, to return to his apartment, dry off, go downstairs and have a sandwich and a cup of Skarsgård's strongest brew. The thought of listening to the man's vitriol didn't hamper his intense longing to leave the scene.

It must be about ten o'clock, he thought. The service, scheduled to begin at half past the hour, was to be ninety minutes in duration. Afterwards, the coffins were to remain in the church for another three days. The numbers had shocked the organisers, so it was decided at the last minute to allow the mourners a chance to pay their respects. No one, it seemed, anticipated the level of fervour the homecoming would arouse. It was this time that would provide his greatest opportunity of finding Anna Charlier. It was a long shot and Stubbendorff would never make such a bet, but a possible seventy-two-hour vigil outside the cathedral was his only chance. Despite his deepest urgings to leave, he decided to remain. As the coffins were carried into the church, a ten-gun salute thundered, marking the beginning of the ceremony.

The downpour had petered to a drizzle by the time he caught sight of the Strindbergs leaving the church. As they were ushered into three separate cars, Stubbendorff saw Erik peruse the crowd before stepping into the vehicle behind his mother. Was it his imagination or was Erik hoping to catch a glimpse of Anna too? Stubbendorff wondered whether, after all Erik had been through, the architect still loved her and would take her back. Stubbendorff suspected he might.

When the final member of the congregation departed, police began to set up barricades to control the flow of the queue that had spontaneously taken shape. Once it was allowed entry, the sluggard serpent weaved its way closer to the doors. By mid-afternoon the sun was shining and the belltower was free from the shroud of mist. Stubbendorff looked at the clock on the steeple. It was three o'clock when he passed through the cathedral's entrance.

As the queue flowed down the centre aisle, Stubbendorff was able to see the three caskets positioned at the foot of the pulpit. They were already laden with flowers and flags. Police ensured the crowd did not cease moving, but by the time the queue reached the coffins the speed had slowed to a crawl.

The queue snaked around the three coffins in a C-shape and was then directed from the cathedral along the aisle at the far left of the pews. Stubbendorff was surprised many of the people paying their respects were crying. Most seemed to have flowers or other tokens. Stubbendorff offered nothing, strangely unmoved by the sight of the caskets. Bones in a wooden box, he thought, scheduled to be burnt on Thursday. This is not their legacy. Strindberg's bequest was secure in Stubbendorff's satchel. Andrée and Frænkel's journals and possessions were under lock and key at the Scientific Commission.

Once on the far side of the caskets, Stubbendorff enjoyed a clear view of the people in the queue until a third of the way down the aisle. He craned his neck in an effort to take everyone in. He scanned their faces carefully. There was no woman he could see who resembled Anna Charlier.

Anna took refuge in a cafe until the rain stopped. When the guns sounded, she placed her cup on its saucer and closed her eyes. To the other diners she appeared to be praying, but she was not. Anna hoped the salute signified an end. While her fiancé lay in a box, in pieces, she hoped completing this task, seeing Nils put to rest, would enable her to be whole. For decades she had been imprisoned in the past, constantly consumed by doubts and regrets and memories. Anna yearned for this to be the final labour in an odyssey that had begun thirty-six years ago. When the guns' echo stopped, she opened her eyes and calmly resumed drinking her coffee. Once the rain cleared, she planned to walk to the cathedral and view the caskets.

Stubbendorff took up a position near the entrance of the cathedral. He lit a cigarette and leant his frame, heavy with exhaustion, against the wall. He could see everyone as they passed through the entrance. His stomach gave a low grumble. After a few minutes he stamped out the cigarette and took an apple from his satchel. He hoped he would not have to wait too long.

When Anna joined the queue, she could see the cathedral in the distance. Every few minutes she would move a step or two closer. When she was about a hundred metres from the church the line began travelling more steadily. It was dusk before she finally reached the entrance.

He walked forward about twenty paces and looked up at the clock. It was a quarter past five. Stubbendorff placed his hands on his lower back and pushed his hips and chest forward. He decided to rejoin the queue. He reasoned he would have the same chance of finding Anna Charlier, and at least this way his boredom might be alleviated a little. He walked briskly towards the end of the line.

Candles gave a welcoming glow in the church. The meditative hum of whispers proved comforting. Anna had only been here once before. She and Nils had wandered in one Sunday afternoon when they were on a walk. The

Strindbergs were not a religious family and neither was she devout, but Anna recalled sitting quietly with Nils for at least half an hour taking in the grandeur of the place. It was when they had only recently begun to spend time together on weekends, so Anna had thought it peculiar when Nils took her hand and squeezed it lightly, not letting go till they left the cathedral. Despite her inexperience in such matters Anna had realised the gesture had no romantic intent. She believed Nils merely wanted to share the moment more intimately. He was like that, she remembered.

She felt no anxiety when she approached the caskets. She could barely see the oak through the shroud of flowers.

'Do you know which is Strindberg's casket?' Anna asked a policeman standing close by. He indicated the middle of the three. She nodded in thanks and took a small bouquet of daises from her bag. They were protected with a silk scarf.

Standing on the altar side of the caskets, Stubbendorff saw a woman with her head bent, a wave of chestnut-coloured curls screening her face. When she removed the scarf from the bouquet and looked up, Stubbendorff knew at once it was Anna. At the same moment he recognised her as the woman who had caught his attention outside the cafe on Lilla Nygatan. She adjusted the bouquet daintily, ensuring every bloom was at its best.

Stubbendorff studied her as she placed the daisies on the casket, closing her eyes for an instant, a lingering blink, nothing more. When she opened them and stepped back into line, he caught her gaze. Her eyes were wells.

'Anna?' he whispered. 'Anna Charlier?'

She nodded once.

Stubbendorff stepped out of place and walked to her.

'May I talk with you? My name is Knut Stubbendorff.'

She nodded once more.

'I recognise you from the cafe on Lilla Nygatan. I watched you leave a house on the street then I noticed you sitting in that cafe writing in a notebook. Are you related to the Strindberg family?'

The directness of her questions surprised Stubbendorff. He was expecting a less confident woman.

'No, I'm not.'

The sun had set and there were fewer people than before. They found an unoccupied seat adjacent to the cathedral. Both of them released an exhausted sigh when they sat. They smiled at each other.

'It's been an extremely long day, Herr Stubbendorff, and I'm not a young woman anymore. What is it you'd like to discuss? I gather it has something to do with the Strindbergs.'

'I led the second party that arrived on Kvitøya.'

'Are you a scientist?'

'I'm a journalist; *was* a journalist. At the time I was sent there by the *Aftonbladet*.'

'You found their remains, their documents, their possessions?' She articulated each word thoughtfully. 'I read about you in the newspaper.'

'That's right. You've followed the story?'

'My home is in England now. My husband found the story extremely absorbing. He filled me in daily.'

'Is your husband in Stockholm with you?'

She shook her head.

Stubbendorff was reluctant to produce the journal without first discovering more about this woman but she was accustomed to reticence, he sensed. She had fled Stockholm and then Chicago, each time leaving no clue as to her whereabouts. He wondered if her husband knew she was in Sweden. What was going to induce her to speak with him about the details of her life?

'The house, the house on Lilla Nygatan – Tore lives there now with his family,' he began.

She looked calmly to the cathedral, her legs crossed at the ankles, her hands resting comfortably on her knees.

'We were talking about you, as a matter of fact.'

Still her expression did not change. After a moment of contemplation she asked flatly, 'What do you wish to discuss with me?'

Stubbendorff produced the journal from his satchel. Handing it to her, he said, 'I found this on Kvitøya. It belonged to Nils Strindberg.'

She held the pages in her hands, her thumbs caressing the document.

'I thought you'd like to read it.'

'You've been looking for me?'

'Since I returned from Kvitøya.'

'You're a persistent man, Herr Stubbendorff. It wouldn't have been a simple task.'

'It wasn't. Today was my final hope. Erik Strindberg told me you'd probably be here, at the funeral.'

She laughed quietly.

'But I nearly missed you. I was waiting at the entrance. I didn't see you go in . . . I can't believe I nearly missed you . . .'

'May I take this with me?' Anna asked. 'I'll read it tomorrow when I'm more alert.'

Stubbendorff's eyes widened.

'Don't be concerned, Herr Stubbendorff,' Anna said. 'I won't disappear again. You can trust me.'

Stubbendorff looked at her earnest brown eyes and believed that he could.

313

'Would you like to join me for dinner at my hotel tomorrow night? I'm staying at the Berns Hotel on Väster-långgatan. At six. My surname is Hawtrey, in case you need to ask for me.'

Anna placed the journal carefully in her bag. Stubbendorff noticed the bag was otherwise empty. They wished each other a pleasant evening. He watched her figure retreat along Trångsund. He remained seated in the same position as a numbness took hold. It was over.

He had thought his response to achieving his quest would have been more extreme. He had imagined this moment and seen himself celebrating, rushing to a cafe and buying the patrons a drink. But no such urge took him. Instead he sat motionless for another hour. Was it Anna's measured reaction that had caused this inertia? Stubbendorff was expecting something grander from her. Was it that he had no one with whom to celebrate besides the nameless patrons in an anonymous cafe? When he finally began the walk home, he noticed the weightlessness of his satchel.

FORTY-TWO

STOCKHOLM, SWEDEN

OCTOBER 1930

ANNA SAT ALONE in the cathedral, staring at the caskets at the foot of the altar. She absently fingered the heart-shaped pendant hanging at her chest. The space was dimly lit with candles. Her brow furrowed and then she turned to leave.

She walked along the wide aisle to the exit. But when she turned the bronze lever, the door did not budge. She tried pushing the handle upwards. Her heart began to race.

Anna pounded on the thick door. When no help was forth- coming, her efforts became increasingly frantic. She screamed for help, then, realising it was useless, she stopped. Her fists stung. Then she heard a familiar sound. A crackle. The comforting sound of wood catching alight. Anna turned towards the altar and saw the coffins ablaze. She ran in the direction of the fire but the flames were too intense and she was forced back.

Smoke quickly filled the cathedral as the flames lapped at

the feet of the saints Nicholas and Peter. She cried out once again for help before crawling beneath a pew near the back of the church. As she was consumed by a blanket of smoke, Anna awoke from the dream.

She turned her eyes to the journal on the desk in the corner of her room. Her eyes remained fixed in that direction until, after an hour, their lids became heavy and her eyes reluctantly closed.

Stubbendorff was confounded and disappointed. He'd thought the surrendering of Strindberg's diary would be the end of it. Would he never be able to sleep again?

Half an hour later he was outside Storkyrkan. The clock beneath the belltower showed the time as just past three o'clock. Despite the hour, the darkness and the brisk air, the square was full of activity. The queue that led into the church, up the aisle and eventually to the three awaiting caskets was still long. He contemplated joining the meandering trail once again, but decided against it. Instead, he sat on the same bench he had sat on with Anna, lit a cigarette and considered the scene.

A carnivalesque atmosphere had replaced the gravity of the day before. Couples walked arm in arm across the square and families with small children stood waiting in line to enter the cathedral. Occasionally the children would race one another to the front of the queue or count the number of people waiting ahead of them. Since the afternoon, hawkers had appeared selling flowers, flags, *glögg*, pancakes, gingerbread and cinnamon buns. The scene was more reminiscent of a midsummer celebration than the aftermath of a funeral.

Stubbendorff leant back on the bench and inhaled the

smoke deeply. As he allowed his head to loll backward, exhaustion washed over him and he closed his eyes.

'Stubbendorff! Stubbendorff!' He sat up and looked to the source of the greeting. 'Fancy seeing you here. What a spectacle! Quite a sight, don't you agree?' Bergman stood directly in front of him. A lean woman and three children waited a few metres behind.

'Herr Bergman, this is a surprise.' Stubbendorff stood and stamped out what was left of his cigarette.

'Can you believe that the *Aftonbladet* is responsible for all this?' The grinning editor made a sweeping gesture with his arm.

'It's extremely impressive,' Stubbendorff said, then added, 'You must be delighted.'

'I am, I am. A better turnout than we could have hoped. This whole occurrence – finding the camp, the arrival of the bodies, the build-up to the funeral, and now this.' He shook his head in disbelief. 'The publisher is beside himself. You can't imagine sales.'

'I can, I can. I'm sure sales are spectacular.'

'What are you up to these days?'

Resigning from the *Aftonbladet* was the surest step Stubbendorff had ever taken in his indifferent life. Bergman had viewed it as a step in the wrong direction and strongly advised against such a reckless move. His litany of reasons why the young reporter would fail outside the grey doors of the newspaper was aimed at eroding Stubbendorff's confidence and humbling the upstart writer. Despite his rising ire, Stubbendorff bit his tongue and Bergman was unsuccessful. Stubbendorff had walked from his office with his spirit undamaged. But now he was unemployed and disheartened. Was Bergman more astute than he imagined?

'I have a few irons in the fire and more than a few tricks

up my sleeve. You know what they say – no rest for the wicked.'

'Right you are. Right you are.' Bergman slapped him heartily on the back. 'Glad to hear it.'

The thin woman moved forward and spoke quietly in her husband's ear.

'*Tempus fugit*, Stubbendorff. I should get these children off to sleep.'

'That seems like an excellent idea. It was good to see you again.'

Stubbendorff watched Bergman and his family depart. He envied those children, not for their father but for what was to come, the easy sleep of childhood.

Anna did not think she could stomach a full breakfast. She slept late, bathed and then took great care dressing and fixing her hair. It was ten o'clock by the time she rang downstairs for coffee and toast. She sat at the desk and fingered the pages still bound with string in front of her. When she had eaten, and drunk her coffee, she carefully unknotted the string and began reading.

FORTY-THREE

STOCKHOLM, SWEDEN

OCTOBER 1930

WHEN ANNA FINISHED READING, she carefully tied the pages together and sat for a long time contemplating what Nils had written. When the implications of his words finally struck her, she began to cry. Tears of relief, regret and sadness, coursed down her cheeks and onto the pages. When they eventually ceased, she lay down on the bed. Within minutes she was asleep.

Anna placed her hand on the knocker of the Strindberg residence on Lilla Nygatan. She lifted the brass hammer tentatively. There was laughter, mockery in the lion's eyes. It would soon be Christmas and she could avoid the family no longer. There was still no word of the expedition's where-abouts. She pounded the knocker once, then a second time more defiantly. She waited for some minutes in the cold. It was odd that no one came. When she tried the handle the door moved inwards. She stomped her feet on the top step, the snow fell easily off her boots. Anna walked into the entrance hall. The house was unusually quiet.

After removing her boots, coat, gloves and scarf, Anna checked the sitting room, pushing the door open cautiously. A fire blazed in the hearth, brightening the dark room, but the space was vacant. She pulled the door to, leaving it ajar. The gap glowed a vibrant ochre. Anna moved slowly down the hallway, stopping at the foot of the staircase. She looked up; no lights burnt. About to ascend into the black, she heard a noise in the back of the house.

She trod carefully down the hallway, attempting not to make a sound. Anna hoped the noise she heard would become recognisable. She strived to quieten her breathing, but it was impossible. Her thin, shallow intakes of breath overwhelmed her hearing. When she arrived at the door of Nils' workroom, she placed her ear against Tore's hand-painted sign, a warning to intruders. A low moan was audible through the door. Anna knocked softly and the whimpering ceased. She knocked again. The room was silent. She tried the handle and was granted entry into the dark chamber.

A figure, lying on the bed against the opposite wall, was barely visible. The curtains to the expansive windows remained open and the moon shone a column of light across the room, skimming the surface of the figure. It was Tore, huddled on Nils' bed, crying. His face was pressed into the pillow. Anna approached and sat on the edge of the bed. She laid her hand on the boy's shoulder.

'Go away,' he said.

'What's the matter? What has happened?'

'Nils is gone and he's not coming back.'

'You mustn't say, even think, such a thing. He will return. He loves us all too much.'

The boy sat up on the bed. He wiped the tears from his eyes vigorously. He snorted loudly and wiped his nose hard on the sleeve of his shirt. Then he stood and faced Anna. 'But you don't love Nils.'

'What are you saying? What makes you think that?' She attempted to stand but Tore forced her back onto the bed, his hands pressed firmly to her shoulders.

'I saw you and Erik, in the courtyard. You kissed and he said he loved you.'

Dumbstruck, Anna looked into the boy's pain until the words came. 'No. Tore, that was something that happened years ago. That was a moment of foolishness.' Her words seemed feeble in the face of her accuser's rage.

The boy did not soften. His red, critical eyes forced her to stand, to remove herself from their glare. He did not attempt to stop her. She stood by the window and looked into the darkened garden. The snow fell in intermittent waves.

'You refused to marry him before he left. That was all he wanted and you refused. You didn't love him. I hate you, Anna. Go, leave me alone.'

Anna's shame was all-consuming. She struggled to find a way of explaining everything to the boy.

'We'll marry as soon as he returns. Erik did love me but he doesn't anymore. Everything will be settled. There's nothing to worry about.' Her soothing tone failed to budge Tore.

'Nothing will be settled and you'll never marry because I told Nils everything. Before he left, I told him about you and Erik. That morning, before we left for the station.'

Nils' distraction, his disregard of her at the station was at once explained. She had laid responsibility for his behaviour that morning at the feet of the admirers and reporters who fought for his attention. Anna swallowed hard before speaking.

'But none of it's true. You can't possibly understand the complications, you're too young. You didn't tell Nils the truth, you told him a child's version of what you saw on one occasion.'

Anna's defence only served to ignite the boy's rage further. 'I know what I saw. If Nils returns, he'll never marry you and if he's dead, then he died knowing that you love Erik and not him.' His spite made him appear the child he was. 'It's all your fault, Anna. I wish Nils had never met you. I wish you were the one to die.'

He began to sob again and lay down on the bed. Anna moved towards the door. Once out of the room and in the hall, she collapsed against the wall in a tide of misery.

The pillow was wet where Anna's head was resting. Tears squeezed from her closed eyes. Then she woke in a fog of confusion. Rolling onto her back, she did not recognise the room. Unable to stop the tears, she propped herself up and looked around. Then she remembered – she was not at the Strindbergs' home; she was in her bed in the hotel room. Her weeping petered out. She wiped her eyes and blew her nose fiercely on a handkerchief then lay back down on the sodden pillow.

Anna's breathing was heavy. When she put her hand to her forehead, she felt herself perspiring. She looked at her watch. It was four in the afternoon. Despite sleeping for more than two hours, she was exhausted. But she felt stirrings of an emotion she had not been acquainted with for many years. Anna recognised this stranger as optimism.

One of the doctors Erik had encouraged her to see in

Chicago had called her dreams delusions. This term had annoyed Anna as it implied insanity or, far worse, it implied her dreams were not real. As far as she was concerned, there was nothing delusional about them. For many years they were her reality. They had become so entrenched in her psyche that a part of her worried she would be lesser if they disappeared. But as she lay on the bed staring at the ceiling, she was convinced they were at an end. While Anna genuinely hoped that the funeral, her reading of Nils' journal and the glimpse of her beautiful daughter drew a line under the distress she had carried for more than thirty years, at the same time she was concerned about what would come next.

FORTY-FOUR

STOCKHOLM, SWEDEN

OCTOBER 1930

STUBBENDORFF WAITED at the foot of the staircase. When the grandfather clock in the lobby chimed six, he turned absently to check if Anna was coming. She was already standing on the bottom stair holding the pages from the journal. In the light of the lobby Stubbendorff could see why Anna Charlier had been so admired.

She wore a sombre suit. The skirt hung to the mid-calf and the jacket was tightly nipped at the waist and sat squarely on her broad shoulders, a contrast to her slender hips. Although she did not wear heels, she stood at least two inches above Stubbendorff.

As he followed her into the dining room, he wondered how she kept such an errant assembly of locks tamed by a few pins. Through the liberal peppering of grey he was able to recognise the chestnut with which Nils had been so taken. They sat opposite each other and she smiled. Unadorned by make-up, her face was a glowing canvas for her extraordinary eyes. In their dark pupils Stubbendorff believed he could read the agony of the last thirty years. She placed the journal between them on the table.

They sat, sipping their water. Anna was the first to speak.

'Thank you for finding me. I've read the journal.' She took another sip of her water. 'It was an odd experience.'

Once again Stubbendorff felt aggravated by her lack of clarity. 'What do you mean by "odd"?'

'When you live with a certain perception, an understanding, for a number of years, it gradually becomes truth and colours your view of everything around you. When that truth is proved to be false, it's unsettling, even if the initial misperception was painful.'

She breathed deeply and picked up her glass again. 'I don't think I'm making any sense. I knew a young girl once who was extremely vain and for a very long time she hid the fact that her eyesight was extremely bad.'

'She feared the prospect of spectacles more than blindness?' Stubbendorff offered.

Anna nodded. 'When she was eventually fitted with spectacles, she complained for weeks. Not about her appearance, but that she preferred her old, skewed view of the world. It took her some time to adjust to the clarity.'

'I understand. Was that little girl your sister?'

Anna laughed as a waitress brought their starters. 'You've met Gota?'

Stubbendorff nodded.

'No, it wasn't Gota. It was a child I tutored here in Stockholm. Another vain little girl.'

When Stubbendorff and Anna had finished their meals, Anna asked, 'Does Gota know I'm in Stockholm?'

'No. She believes you're dead.'

She did not flinch. 'Good. It's better that way. But you've spoken to Erik Strindberg.'

'And his brothers and mother. They've been extremely helpful and they all remain very concerned about your well-being. Tore especially regrets the circumstances of your final meeting.'

Then Stubbendorff let go. Unrestrained, he outlined the outcomes of each interview. He spoke rapidly and with enthusiasm. Anna listened, watching him speak without commenting. How proud this young man is of his achievements, she thought, the information he has gathered. This is the moment for which he has been waiting.

Who was he to make assumptions about a situation he could never understand? It was as though, lost in the moment, he had forgotten who he was talking to. What was his aim, she wondered.

To condemn? Impress?

'You've been greatly missed by Rosalie Strindberg as well. She was deeply saddened by your departure.'

Anna folded her napkin and looked down at her hands on the table. 'It seems you've probed quite thoroughly into my life, Herr Stubbendorff. What are your intentions?'

'I have no ill intentions, if that's what concerns you. I simply found the journal, read it and it moved me. You kindled so much courage and optimism in your fiancé – former fiancé. I suppose his letters to you ignited something in me. I wanted to find you and give you the journal.' He looked directly into her eyes.

'But as my investigation went on and I learnt more about your involvement with the family, I confess to becoming quite enthralled by the story. I became rather stubborn in my determination to discover the truth. I hope I haven't pried too deeply.'

'Of course you have.' Her tone was direct. 'You must by now be equipped with the details of much of my life.'

'Up until you left Chicago,' Stubbendorff conceded quietly.

'I only wonder what you intend to do with that information. My concern is for my daughter and my husband.'

Their conversation was interrupted when the second course arrived. Anna pushed her potatoes around on her plate as Stubbendorff considered his answer.

'The piecing together of the story was purely for my own satisfaction. I don't intend to blackmail anyone or profit in any way. I simply wanted to find you and give you his journal. But I found I became deeply invested, emotionally, in the lives of everyone involved.'

'You mean you're living vicariously through those involved.'

He could not respond. Erik was correct in his assessment of those eyes. They had the frightening ability to penetrate the most hardened veneer. It was the truth and she was the first person he had met who was prepared to say it. Erik had skirted the topic but was either too polite or too flattered to comment. Tore, as well, grasped his true objective but was grateful for the opportunity to purge himself of guilt.

As soon as he had read Nils Strindberg's diary in his cabin on the *Isbjörn*, this had been his motive. Why else embark on the painstaking recovery of the documents? Why else did he invest so wholeheartedly in the project? The chance to obtain a view into another man's life, a man with dreams and ambitions far above his own, was too enticing to pass up. He hoped to eclipse his own insignificance with the glory of another.

He was jealous, he admitted. Jealous of the family, jealous of relationships that were formed decades ago. What a wretched individual he was, forcing his way into the world of a family and then becoming disgruntled when the outcome was not to his satisfaction.

'I can only apologise. It hadn't dawned on me before but yes, I suppose that's exactly what I have done, am doing. I'm really quite ashamed of myself.'

Anna saw she had distressed him. Perhaps she had been too blunt. She leant across the table and cupped his hand in hers. She smiled sympathetically. 'Don't be so hard on yourself. You said Nils' diary moved you and you wanted to find me. You just became a little side-tracked en route.' Then she laughed. It was a melodious, carefree laugh that drew the attention of the surrounding diners. 'I must admit that from an outsider's perspective the story is gripping. Now we should eat and then we can talk more afterwards, yes?'

'Will you keep the journal?'

She shook her head. 'It's yours to keep, Herr Stubbendorff.'

They strolled the short distance to the waterfront. Anna tightened the wrap she was wearing more securely about her shoulders. She breathed in heartily. 'I have missed this smell – the salt and the fish and the chill. It's probably what drew me to the seaside in England.'

'Is that where you live in England, by the sea?'

She nodded. 'First in Ramsgate – that's where I met my husband. After the war we moved to Torquay. It's very lovely there. Gil was in the navy when we met, but the war took its toll. When he came home, he still wanted to be by the sea, but his condition required a more peaceful lifestyle.'

'Was he injured?'

'He was the Chief Petty Officer on a battleship, the *Inde-*

fatigable. The ship was sunk by the Germans. Out of a crew of over a thousand, Gil was one of only three survivors.'

Stubbendorff was unable to hide his surprise.

'He found it hard to cope with the remorse that came with living.'

Two broken people drawn to one another, Stubbendorff thought. He offered Anna a cigarette. She declined and walked along the dock. When he caught up with her, he asked, 'Do you and Gil have any children?'

She shook her head.

'Do you ever think about Tina?'

She smiled. 'She is called Tina?'

He nodded.

'I think about her constantly. I saw her at the funeral. She's very beautiful. Erik's done a remarkable job. He was, is, a devoted father.'

Stubbendorff opened his mouth to speak, but Anna held up her hand. 'But re-entering her life now – it's too late. I can't be a mother to her. The three of us can't be a family. My presence would only force her to question why I left, and that had nothing to do with her. But I'm glad I saw her. It's something that had always plagued me, the uncertainty. I've wanted to know her, but until today I could never have been a mother to her.'

'She believes her mother died when she was an infant. That's what her father has told her.'

Anna nodded. 'Well, I suppose I did.'

'They're staying with Sven while they're in Stockholm.' Stubbendorff turned and indicated the house on Skeppsbron. 'In that house, the colourful one. That's Sven's house.'

She looked at the home. 'That's a coincidence,' she said calmly.

'Would you like to meet with Erik? Perhaps he could tell

you about your daughter. I have a feeling he'd like to see you. I believe he's still in love with you. He's never married.'

Anna leant against the railing, looking towards the lights of Skeppsholmen. Stubbendorff could tell she was contemplating his question, his offer. Then she said, teasing, 'You're a romantic. You want your story to have a fairy-tale ending.'

'Do you still love him?'

Anna looked at him for a moment, then clutched his shoulders firmly in her hands. 'Always!' she said. 'It's a remarkable feeling to be able to admit that freely, finally. How foolish I was. How weak I became, allowing guilt to overpower me for so long. I'd like Erik to know. Perhaps it would be a comfort, but it's all too late.'

Anna turned then and walked in the direction of the hotel. Stubbendorff followed her, but they were silent until they reached the entrance. 'Fru Hawtrey, there's one thing I still don't understand. I'm aware that I'm prying, that I've already stepped far beyond the boundaries.'

He waited for permission to proceed. She raised her eyebrows slightly.

'If you loved Erik, why did you show such loyalty to his brother?'

'That's a logical question, Herr Stubbendorff.' She thought for a moment. How could she make this young man understand?

'Erik was passion. Strong, forceful, spirited – he stirred something in me that no one else has. My compulsion to be with him was all-consuming. I know he felt the same about me.'

Stubbendorff nodded slowly as she thought.

'Nils and I were friends, great friends. I think we allowed the momentum of our friendship to push us towards romance. I know I loved Nils sincerely, but it was different from the love I had for Erik. Is this making sense?'

'Complete sense,' Stubbendorff answered quietly, although he had experienced neither form of love.

'I thought my feelings for Erik were a passing fancy. By the time I realised the level of my attachment, I was engaged to Nils. I was too weak-willed to break our engagement. I couldn't bring myself to hurt Nils; neither could I sever my relationship with Erik. In short, Herr Stubbendorff, it was a shambles of my own design.'

'But Nils writes of you with such force. You were everything to him.'

'I know. But it's strange. To be honest, it shocked me. We loved each other, but it was never as he wrote.'

'A fantasy?'

'Not exactly.' Anna sighed. 'What he wrote was the truth, but it was an embroidered truth. Perhaps, near the end, the illusion of something greater allowed him the strength to keep moving forward. I wish I had the answer for you, but I don't. How could either one of us ever imagine what he went through? But his words were beautiful. I'd like to think that the emotion behind them was genuine.'

Anna could see Stubbendorff was struggling with her disclosure. 'Nils was, he's so difficult to describe . . . He was less capable than Erik, more easily damaged. I suppose that's why I couldn't end our relationship.

'You're upset that what Nils described, what we had together, wasn't the great love you envisaged.' She could read Stubbendorff's heartbreak on his face. 'Erik was my great love, my true love.'

'Why won't you see him then?'

Anna merely shook her head.

'If you knew Tore was lying, or if that encounter had never happened, would you have married Erik?'

She shrugged her shoulders. 'It's too late to speculate.' She noticed his displeasure and said more strenuously, 'Nothing's that simple. My life has been shaped by a lie, and I can't change that.'

Anna's tone then shifted in her effort to make him understand. 'From that day, for many years, I was plagued with dreams about Nils' and my own death. After a long absence the dreams started again, just recently. As terrifying as they've often been, I saw them as a kind of consolation. A psychiatrist once called them "delusions", which I dismissed at the time. But now I see that they are delusions drawn from my own distorted perception. But I can't go back. Nothing can be altered. Events happened as they happened, as tragic as that seems to you. All that I can do is begin to see the world more clearly.'

She hugged Stubbendorff unexpectedly but not awkwardly. He melted into her embrace and listened to the final words whispered in her soft, honeyed voice. 'I'm glad you found me, Herr Stubbendorff. Thank you for your kindness. I'm leaving to go home to Gil on Friday evening – that's where my life is now. You should get on with yours.'

She released him and walked into the hotel.

He walked the streets until sunrise. Smoking, thinking, sometimes sitting, occasionally muttering to himself, Stubbendorff toured the city by moonlight, waiting for the last twelve hours to make sense. Regardless of Anna's explanations Stubbendorff remained dissatisfied and the manuscript remained in his satchel, a dead weight. Despite meeting with him, Anna had failed to appease his immense disappointment. He was shocked that their love had not been as Strindberg described in his journal. He was stunned by her acceptance of her situation and her refusal to keep the journal. She denied herself the opportunity to alter the past. The rebuff stung. In Stubbendorff's mind it was not too late for Anna and Erik.

Stubbendorff remembered a phrase Anna had used, *an embroidered truth*, and he thought it quite beautiful. He supposed everyone was guilty of this to different degrees. As he walked, a picture formed in his mind of an elaborate tapestry, with a lifetime of events combining to produce a great work of art. As the artist we're able to design the piece, he thought, colour it to our liking, just as Nils had done. In Anna's case she had been handed the wrong thread. Stubbendorff guessed this visit to Stockholm would mark the beginning of a new tapestry for Anna Charlier. Reading the journal would prompt her to begin the slow and painful task of unpicking and carefully unravelling thirty years of memory, ready for a fresh work to begin.

When he reached his apartment building, Skarsgård was opening the cafe. Ignoring his landlord's invitation to join him for coffee, he climbed the stairs to his room, shut the door and lay on his bed fully clothed. An impatient sleep received Stubbendorff almost immediately.

FORTY-FIVE

THE SUN TOUCHED the horizon at midnight. The landscape on fire. The snow a sea of flame.
   – Andrée's journal, 31 August 1897

STOCKHOLM, SWEDEN

OCTOBER 1930

On the evening of the day the remains of Salomon August Andrée, Knut Frænkel and Nils Strindberg were burnt, Knut Stubbendorff approached the home of Sven Strindberg. The journal remained nestled in his well-worn satchel. He stopped a few metres from the door. He imagined he saw the corners of the lion's mouth curl upwards into the beginnings of a snarl. The animal viewed him as an intruder, he thought. He brushed his hair from his brow in a brusque, hurried fashion and jiggled the knot of his tie, then bent his head and looked to his shoes. They were scuffed and dull. He realised he looked shabby. Panic set in and the urge to flee was overwhelming. Who would miss him? But the raw craving to see this episode concluded overrode his dread and he stepped towards the final chapter.

In the entrance hall the sounds of laughter and talk and children's shouts greeted him. Before he had even handed his coat to the maid, Erik was by his side, shaking his hand. In only a few more seconds he was pulled through the house and into a dining room. Tore rushed to him and kissed him quickly on each cheek, his hair dusted with plaster, then introduced Stubbendorff to his wife and children.

Stubbendorff remembered none of the names of the children, of whom there were four. Sven soon approached, offering a glass of champagne. His suit was an eye-catching indigo and his waistcoat the colour of butter. Rosalie led Stubbendorff to a seat away from the table, by the window, where the adults were conversing. Here he met Sven's wife who, in turn, pointed out her children, seated on the opposite side of the room playing jackstones. Later that evening Stubbendorff could not recall their names either. There was a burst of laughter provoked by something Erik said and then the crowd became more reflective. 'My granddaughter has not yet come down, Herr Stubbendorff,' Rosalie said. 'She's the only person we're waiting on.'

'When I told her a young gentleman would be joining us, she panicked, fled to her room and has not been seen since – lost in a flurry of powder and perfume,' Erik said.

'Don't tease, Erik. It's a young woman's prerogative to make an entrance,' Rosalie said.

After only a few seconds, she said, 'And here she is now.'

Erik walked to his daughter and, after kissing her on the cheek and speaking softly in her ear, led her over to the group.

'Herr Stubbendorff, I would like you to meet my daughter, Tina.'

Stubbendorff stood and the young woman held out her hand. When they shook, he noticed she stood two inches taller than he. Glancing down at her feet, he felt a pang of disappointment. She was not wearing heels.

'Can you speak English, Knut?' Erik asked.

Stubbendorff nodded.

'My daughter's Swedish is abysmal, unrecognisable. She only speaks American.'

'Papa! My Swedish is first-rate. He's teasing, Herr Stubbendorff.' Then she added quietly, 'But do let me know if you would prefer to speak English.' She smiled coyly and the group laughed. He couldn't remember ever hearing an American before, other than on the cinema screen.

Stubbendorff thought she was beautiful. She wore a violet dress the likes of which he had never seen. He could only guess at the fabric. It would have to be silk, he thought. It fell elegantly over her hips and stopped in its flow six inches from her ankles. From the front the dress was understated, sleeveless with a plain bodice. But when she turned, the back of the dress plunged to just below her shoulder blades. A sumptuous bow sat at the base on the vee in the small of her back.

He could not be certain, but Stubbendorff believed her face was unadorned by make-up as a scattering of freckles was visible across her cheeks and nose. The only embellishment to her otherwise simple refinement was a silver, heart-shaped pendant that nestled just beneath her collarbone.

The young man suddenly became aware of his wordless gawking. He cleared his throat. 'I will speak in whatever language you please, Fröken.'

Erik shook his head and joined the rest of the group.

'You're multilingual then?' Tina enquired seriously.

Stubbendorff merely nodded, hoping she would not push any further. He didn't want to appear immodest. But she was not satisfied.

'Well?'

'English, French, Italian and German . . . and a little Russian.' He was glad the rest of the party had by this stage begun to speak among themselves.

Stubbendorff was confounded as to how he had managed to embarrass himself before he had even consumed one sip of the champagne he gripped in his sweating palm.

'Oh, is that all?' Tina laughed and touched his arm lightly as she did so. 'That's remarkable. I envy you, Herr Stubbendorff. What a fantastic talent to have. You must have travelled often?'

'No. Not at all. I'm ashamed to admit I have only left Sweden once.' He was too embarrassed to add that it had been recently, when he made his voyage to Kvitøya.

When she smiled, Stubbendorff strived to locate a sign of condescension in her expression. There was none. He was amazed at what a perfect blend of her parents she was. In her appearance he could see Anna everywhere – in her body, hair, mouth and especially in her warm eyes. But her mannerisms and expressions were mainly her father's. When her mouth curved into a smile, it was Erik's personality that shone through. When her eyes searched his face in enquiry, it was with her father's determination and curiosity.

Rosalie assembled the group for dinner. The table was laid lavishly with flowers, china, silver and crystal. Stubbendorff was seated between Tore and Tina. He was pleased by the arrangement. The children were seated at a smaller but equally splendid table at the foot of the larger one. After a brief but heartfelt toast by Erik the meal began.

Memories of Nils were shared heartily among the brothers. Stubbendorff listened greedily to the lighthearted chat, the friendly mockery and the moving reminiscences. The voices were loud and animated. For Tina's benefit what they spoke was a convivial medley of Swedish and English. It was a controlled commotion. The women at the table were equally energetic. Stubbendorff wondered if this was the nature of all families and his muted relationship with his mother was an anomaly. He hoped so.

'Tell me it's not so, brother,' Sven directed his question to Erik. 'Mama tells me you may be staying in Stockholm permanently.'

'It is so,' Erik said, holding his glass aloft. 'Champagne, beer and schnapps have reminded me what an abomination is prohibition.'

'Your love of liquor is driving you home. There have been less noble reasons I'm sure. Although they don't come to mind.' The gathering laughed.

'My daughter's mishandling of the Swedish language is also an abomination. What she needs is to come home and be Swedish. In truth, I need it too. We have been away too long.'

'Perhaps Herr Stubbendorff could help you with your Swedish, Tina?' Sven raised his eyebrows and twisted the ends of his moustache theatrically. Stubbendorff felt the blood rise in his pallid cheeks.

'I'd be extremely thankful for any help Herr Stubbendorff could offer, Uncle,' she retorted firmly.

'Well, Herr Stubbendorff.' Tore leant towards the writer. 'Tell me, did you find Anna? That's what we all want to know.'

The table hushed. Stubbendorff looked towards Erik, who gave him a barely noticeable nod. He cleared his throat and addressed the group.

'Yes, I'm happy to say I did. By chance, I saw her after the funeral in Storkyrkan.'

'How is she? Is she well? Has she kept well?'

'Hush, Mama,' Tore said. 'Let him finish his story.'

'She's extremely well. We had dinner together on Monday evening after she'd read the journal. From my perspective it was a remarkable night. To finally meet her and speak with her . . . she was slightly annoyed by my meddling but when she realised I had no sinister motives she spoke candidly about her life.'

For the next hour Stubbendorff fielded a barrage of questions from the family. He answered as selectively as possible. Erik did not say a word, piecing together the story of her life, from which he had previously been exiled. Stubbendorff could see him turning over the facts in his mind.

'It's a pity she never had children,' Rosalie said. 'Anna would have been an excellent mother. She was a wonderful governess.'

The table agreed with the matriarch's assessment. Stubbendorff was relieved when the arrival of dessert interrupted the direction in which the dialogue was heading.

Distracted by the cloudberries and cream placed before them, the gathering gradually began to banter about topics unrelated to Anna Charlier. When the volume was at a suitable level, Tore whispered to his neighbour, 'Do you think she forgives me?'

Stubbendorff placed his spoon in his bowl and nodded. A tiny white spot dotted Strindberg's moustache. Stubbendorff was unsure whether it was cream or perhaps plaster from his studio. He looked into the artist's eyes, which were luminous with tears.

'She understands. Although much of her life she has been troubled by the past, she doesn't hold a grudge. I believe she spoke honestly.'

'Thank you for your honesty. I'm happy Anna feels this way but it will be more difficult to forgive myself.' Strindberg's gaze returned to his dessert.

Stubbendorff noticed Tina was the first to finish her plate. He looked from his bowl upwards in a surreptitious attempt to glimpse her pretty face. He was embarrassed to find she was unashamedly looking directly at him.

'Herr Stubbendorff, it's been a remarkable journey you've undertaken. You must be gratified to have finally met her, given her the journal. What a wonderful thing you've achieved,' she said.

He smiled. That was not his experience at all, but he nodded nonetheless.

'For her to be granted access to her lover's private thoughts and feelings. It was by your hand that my uncle's legacy was fulfilled.'

'Thank you for your kind words, but I fear you might be overstating my involvement.'

'Nonsense!' she reprimanded. 'You have every right to be extremely proud of what you've achieved.'

Stubbendorff turned back to his dessert.

'Did Anna keep the journal?' Tina asked.

He shook his head thoughtfully.

'May I read it?'

Stubbendorff pondered the consequences of this. Her question was surprising. Tina was the one possible recipient he had not considered.

Noting his hesitation, she pressed. 'My father talks about Uncle Nils a great deal. When he disappeared, Papa lost not only a brother but a best friend as well. I would appreciate the chance to try to get to know him better, to meet the man my father remembers.'

In an instant it was blindingly obvious to Stubbendorff that Tina was the single and only person to whom the journal should be given. She was the only one who would be able to read Nils' words with vision unsullied by the past. Her perception was clear and uncorrupted by context. It would be possible for her to glean from the diary its author's original purpose. Moreover, this was the only foreseeable way she would ever be able to get to know the woman who was her mother.

'Of course. I have it with me.'

Her hands closed over his own. They were warm and the gesture forced a hasty, shallow intake of breath into his lungs. The moment was interrupted by Rosalie moving the group into the parlour. Tina was going to perform for the party.

'That's when I see it most vividly,' Erik said. 'When she plays. The control of her hands. The passion with which she commands the keys. The manner in which her eyes close and her head and body sway to the music. That's when she most resembles Anna.'

Following Tina's recital Stubbendorff had asked Erik if he could speak privately. Erik indicated the sitting room then took a seat in the same armchair he had occupied during their previous meeting. He rubbed his forehead then leant back into the chair. As his long legs stretched out before him, a contented, sleepy, slightly inebriated grin transformed his face. He closed his eyes.

Stubbendorff was unsure of how to begin or of what he hoped to achieve by telling Erik that Anna loved him. Anna had made her intentions clear. She was leaving Stockholm the following evening. Was it true? Was he jostling for a happy ending? Erik began to speak.

'You no doubt wish to talk about Anna, Knut.'

Stubbendorff nodded.

'Tell me how she is faring. I could see you were being cautious with your answers during dinner.'

Stubbendorff gave a thorough account of his meeting with Anna Hawtrey. No detail was concealed. Erik's eyes remained closed through the entire monologue.

'She wouldn't keep the journal but she was glad to have read it, I think.'

Erik opened his eyes.

'She explained that she was now able to view the world more clearly.'

'Tore confessed to me today, after the cremation,' Erik said. 'After everyone had left, I found him sitting alone in the chapel, weeping. I thought it was because of the memorial, but that was only partly true. He told me of what he'd told Anna, what he'd seen in the courtyard. He apologised endlessly, believing he'd ruined my life and Anna's.'

'He feels very deeply.'

'We all do, Knut.' He straightened in his seat.

'I believe my family – well, Tore and Sven – have their suspicions about Tina's mother. Seeing her now at twenty-three, the same age as Anna when she was introduced to the family, they can see the similarity. I've witnessed both of them examining her face, scrutinising her behaviour. I trust them to be discreet, but I must admit it's comforting that they know my secret, even if we never speak of it.'

'She still loves you.'

Erik's face was expressionless.

'Anna told me she'll always love you, and I got the impression she'd like the opportunity to explain her behaviour to you in person.' Stubbendorff's final attempt to bring the two together provoked no response from Strindberg.

Stubbendorff persisted.

'As I said, she doesn't want to disrupt Tina's life, but she does still love you.'

Erik stood and moved to the mantel. He took his daughter's photograph in his hand.

'She's staying at the Berns Hotel on Västerlånggatan until tomorrow evening.'

When Erik turned, Stubbendorff could see he was smiling. 'We'll see,' he said. 'We should return to the party.'

When they re-entered the parlour, Sven was waiting, arms open. He held a bottle of schnapps in one hand, two glasses in the other. Tina was still seated at the piano, casually picking out notes to a tune that Stubbendorff did not recognise. Her grandmother sat behind her, glass in hand, gently humming. The children and wives were no longer in the room. He guessed the young ones were being put to bed. As Sven filled both glasses, he began.

'We've been discussing you, Knut, in your absence. We've decided that the family owes you a gift. A gift for keeping our dear brother's journal out of the hands of the Scientific Commission and for bringing it home.' Erik and Tore shouted a lively 'Hurrah!'.

Stubbendorff, stunned, looked to Erik.

'I know nothing about this,' Erik said, 'but I agree. We do owe you our appreciation.'

Sven explained. 'So, Tore and I have assembled a list of people, influential people, throughout Europe who, we are confident, will give you a helping hand if you choose to contact them. We believe your many talents could be put to good use abroad. Use them to broaden your horizons and experience the world.'

Stubbendorff opened his mouth to speak, but Sven cut him off.

'Erik, will you add any names that come to mind in America? So far the list is mainly people in the art world.

Your acquaintances in architecture and Chicago society will expand the list very nicely.'

Erik took the paper and removed a pen from his coat pocket. He sat down and immediately began adding to the catalogue of names and addresses.

Tina walked to Stubbendorff and put her arm through his as she led him to the settee.

'I hope we don't seem presumptuous,' she said. 'We simply believe you could achieve great success if you allow yourself the opportunity. We just ask for one thing in return.'

He lifted his head in enquiry.

'That you write regularly to keep us abreast of your travels, triumphs and travails.' She smiled warmly and a lively flutter of butterflies took flight in his stomach.

'I don't think you're presumptuous at all.' He cleared his throat in preparation for an impromptu toast. He was typically nervous in situations such as this, but tonight he was not. He stood.

'I'd like to thank you most sincerely for this generous gift and for your assistance in my efforts to find Anna Charlier.' He took in each person at the gathering. 'Mostly, I'd like to offer my thanks for your honesty. It's been an honour and a pleasure to meet all of you. Finally, I believe a salute to Nils is appropriate.'

The group raised their glasses and together shouted a second 'Hurrah!'.

His cheek tingled in the spot where Albertina kissed him goodbye. He touched his face lightly as he ran his eyes down the list of names. None of them he recognised. Stubbendorff lay back in his bed and thought about the future. Seventy kronor remained from Bergman's bonus. He was also hoping

Skarsgård would refund the rent he had already paid. This endeavour would be fraught with danger. He would have to catch Skarsgård in the right mood. The amount was enough, he reckoned, to see him to Paris. The first name on the list was the director of Musée Rodin. As good a starting point as any, he thought. Uncertain of the time, he closed his eyes and dropped into a peaceful sleep.

FORTY-SIX

STOCKHOLM, SWEDEN

OCTOBER 1930

WHEN ERIK APPROACHED the Berns Hotel, it was ten o'clock in the morning. He stood outside for a moment and tapped his cane on the ground before looking up and down Väster-långgatan. Tina had enquired about his plans for the morning as he was leaving the house. Erik had said he was meeting an old friend. She had complimented him on his suit, told him how handsome he was looking, then said she had never realised how much Stockholm agreed with him.

A porter outside the hotel asked if he needed help. He replied in the negative then crossed the street hurriedly and took refuge in a cafe. Sitting by the window, he could see the hotel clearly. He ordered a cup of coffee from the pretty waitress and removed his hat.

To passers-by and patrons of the establishment he seemed, as he calmly sipped his coffee, like a man waiting. With his eyes fixed on the building opposite as they were, one assumed he was waiting for a resident of the Berns Hotel to join him. But he was not.

When the same waitress approached and placed a second cup of coffee on the table, Erik looked at the time. He had been sitting, waiting, contemplating how he should proceed, for forty-five minutes. He thanked the waitress and removed the photograph of Anna from his pocketbook, examined it thoughtfully, then held it to his cheek briefly before replacing the dog-eared image into its sleeve.

He leant low across the table and tilted his head in order to view the entirety of the hotel. When he straightened, his lips were curled in a wry smile. He leant back in his chair.

'Would you like to order some food, sir?' the waitress enquired.

'No, thank you.'

It was a large hotel and many people entered and exited through the vast glass doors. Many of those who left the building, Erik noted, came into the cafe. He asked the waitress for a menu, which he read but ordered nothing.

Time slipped by as he sat watching the hotel. When he checked his watch, it was five minutes to twelve o'clock. The cafe was quickly filling with people hungry for lunch. Standing, he searched in his pocket and placed a five kronor note on the table. After putting his hat on, he departed.

He lingered outside for a moment and looked into the sky. It was a warm, brilliant day. When he directed his gaze towards the hotel, his vision was still obscured from the sunlight. His eyes cleared and he allowed them to run from the roof of the building down to the entrance. After a minute or so Erik firmly planted his cane on the ground, a final punctuation point. He walked away.

BONUS EPILOGUE

THE ICE BALLOON

Get a free copy of the epilogue, *The Swedish Cottage* when you
for my newsletter at https://BookHip.com/HMZHWVZ

You'll also be notified of giveaways and new releases and
receive updates of my author journey

ENJOYED THE ICE BALLOON?

Thanks for reading *The Ice Balloon*. If you enjoyed the story, share a review where you bought the e-book, on Goodreads or contact me at jennybondbooks and share your thoughts.

AFTERWORD

This novel was first published in Australia and New Zealand as *Perfect North* in 2013 by Hachette Australia. Recently, I had the rights returned to me, and I decided to publish the same story under the original working title, *The Ice Balloon*. The reason I did not use this title in 2013 was because another book called *The Ice Balloon* had recently been published. I believe enough time has passed to return to my first-choice title.

You see, the idea for this novel first came to me when reading an article in the *New Yorker* magazine. The piece was titled 'The Ice Balloon' and it was written by Alec Wilkinson. It was an extract from his non-fiction book. I found it extraordinary that I had never heard of S. A. Andrée and his 1897 expedition to the North Pole. What an absolutely daft scheme, I thought. Prior to 1900, over one thousand explorers had tried and failed to reach the North Pole. The only man to attempt the exploit in a balloon, Wilkinson wrote, was S. A. Andrée.

Andrée made two attempts to reach the top of the world. The first, in the summer of 1896, never left the ground.

Conditions in Spitsbergen were not conducive to launch. The second, the following year, ended in tragedy. Until 1930 the world didn't know how the lives of Salomon August Andrée, Nils Strindberg and Knut Frænkel ended.

In August 1930 a Norwegian scientific expedition discovered the bodies of two men on Kvitøya (also known as New Iceland or White Island), a small, ice-bound island in the Arctic Ocean. For decades it had been known among sealers and whalers as 'the inaccessible island'. An unusually warm season had made the journey possible.

As well as skeletal remains, the remnants of the explorers' final camp were unearthed. Several of the objects found had been stamped with the words 'Andrée's Pol. Exp. 1896'. Finally, after thirty-three years, the fate of Andrée, Strindberg and Frænkel became known. A few weeks later Knut Stubbendorff, a journalist, was sent on assignment to Kvitøya to cover the story. By this time more ice had melted and Stubbendorff discovered the remains of the third man, as well as the scientific logs and personal journals of the adventurers. The entries in the journals did not go beyond the first week in October 1897, an indication of when the men had died. The trio kept rigorous notes during their three months in the Arctic that enabled the authorities to determine their exact path through the air and their route across the ice.

The balloon had lost altitude soon after launching and Andrée was forced to anchor on the ice. The explorers then set off across the frozen wasteland on foot, pulling their supplies on sledges. Inadequately clothed, ill-equipped and underprepared, the men could not reach the supply depots on Franz Joseph Land and Seven Islands. They suffered a harrowing drift southwards, ending their journey on Kvitøya.

While the team's journey by balloon into the polar wilderness was gripping, I was more fascinated by the relationship between Nils Strindberg and his fiancée Anna Charlier. Strindberg's personal diary contained many letters written to Anna. Many of these were written in shorthand, doubtless so no one else could read them. Explorers of that era kept scrupulous diaries. If they returned, the individual would have them published. If not, the hope was that the documents would be discovered and subsequently published. It seems likely that Strindberg believed Anna would read the correspondence one day.

As I researched the expedition and the people involved, I discovered that Strindberg, second cousin and godchild of playwright August Strindberg, came from a family of well-to-do high achievers, all of whom had an artistic leaning. His father, Oscar, a businessman, wrote poems under the pen name 'Occa'. His brothers' occupations were as in the novel. Nils played violin and practised photography. It was a remarkable family, I thought.

Not a great deal is known about Anna. She was a governess who played piano and she seems to have been quite a free spirit. It is said Nils' first sight of Anna was of her swimming naked in a lake! What is known is that she was never able to reconcile the loss of her fiancé. After his disappearance she drifted in and out of hospitals and sana-toriums and sometimes resided with the Strindberg family. She eventually married Englishman Gilbert Hawtrey but was forever obsessed over the memory of Nils. She instructed her husband to have her heart's ashes buried next to those of Nils. Hawtrey, who must have been the most devoted of partners, sent a small silver box to Tore Strindberg in Sweden. Tore fulfilled Anna's request in 1949.

The box was engraved:

Ashes from near the heart of

Anna Albertina Constancia Hawtrey (nee Charlier) To be placed near the grave of Nils Strindberg

To whom she was engaged in 1897

– and may the Great Conductor allow them both to share in the Music of the Spheres.

While this story of overwhelming love intrigued me, I didn't think a reader would find it a convincing explanation for Anna's breakdown. Consequently, as the book progressed, I found myself creating a relationship between Anna and Nils' brother, Erik. Guilt and regret are far more realistic motivators, I thought. It's Stubbendorff's unravelling of the mystery of this relationship that ties the novel together. His role as detective in the story, and his personal journey from uninspired hack to globe-trotting writer, are concoctions.

Apart from the diary extract where Nils describes his night of camping with Tore in chapter nine, the birthday letter to Anna on page 116, and the peppering of quotes that strike Stubbendorff when he is reading Nils' journal in chapter three, those that I have quoted in *The Ice Balloon* are authentic, first-person accounts that I sourced from *Andrée's Story: The Complete Record of his Polar Flight, 1897* (1930). Likewise, except for the newspaper article headlined 'Andrée's Daring Voyage' at the end of chapter sixteen, all news features are genuine.

I found Alec Wilkinson's non-fiction book on the subject, *The Ice Balloon: One Man's Dramatic Attempt to Discover the North Pole by Balloon* (2012), a brilliant and exacting study of the Andrée expedition and Arctic exploration in general. Two other books that helped me get my bearings in regards to the flight of the balloon and the explorers' journey to Kvitøya were Per Olaf Sundman's *The Flight of the Eagle* (1970) and John Grierson's *Challenge to the Poles – Highlights of Arctic and Antarctic Aviation* (1964).

The Ice Balloon is a work of fiction, a dramatic reconstruction of real events, woven around the relationship between Nils Strindberg and Anna Charlier and an astonishing, ill-conceived expedition to the North Pole. Although many of the characters' names are real, and although they may embody qualities of people who existed at the time, the book is essentially a work of the imagination.

ACKNOWLEDGMENTS

I would like to express my gratitude to the team at Hachette Australia who took a chance on a first-time author and decided to publish my debut novel. However, neither *Perfect North* nor *The Ice Balloon* could not have been written and revised without the untiring encouragement of my husband, Chris, an extremely busy journalist who afforded me the time and support to complete my first novel.

ALSO BY JENNY BOND

HISTORICAL FICTION AVAILABLE AT ALL ONLINE BOOK STORES AND AT WWW.JENNYBONDBOOKS.COM

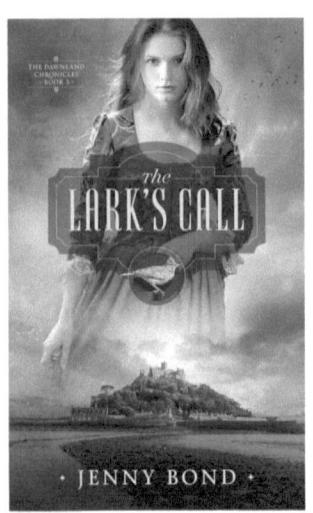

THE DAWNLAND
CHRONICLES
BOOK 1

the
LARK'S CALL

· JENNY BOND ·

A
Will a chance
encounter change her
life forever?

A DAY in MAY

A compelling story of politics and
power, love and loss, set in one
of the most exciting and
cataclysmic periods of history.

· JENNY BOND ·

ALSO BY JENNY BOND

CONTEMPORARY FICTION AVAILABLE AT
ALL ONLINE BOOK STORES AND AT
WWW.JENNYBONDBOOKS.COM

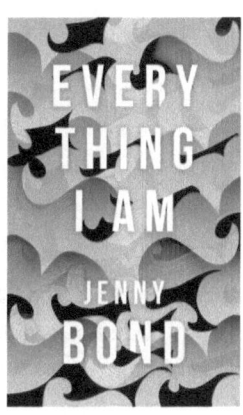

FLY FURTHER INTO THE WORLD
OF THE ICE BALLOON

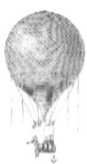

Check out my Pinterest board for *The Ice Balloon* - images
that provided inspiration and information during the
writing process.

To access the above search 'jennybondbooks'.

ABOUT THE AUTHOR

I'm an author of contemporary fiction, historical fiction and non-fiction. I have published my books in Australia, New Zealand, USA and Europe.

I'm also an English teacher and I've been lucky enough to introduce the love of language to many students around the world.

I guess this also planted the seed of an idea that I should give writing a go myself

Sydney, Australia, is where I was born and raised, but prior to my reinvention as a writer (which had something to do with a friendly argument with my husband!), I held the position of Head of English at Eaton House The Manor in London's Clapham Common. I also taught English and Drama for eight years at a selective high school in Sydney, and for five years at a private girls' college in Canberra.

Whether I've been at home, living and working in another country, or travelling for the sake of adventure, I have never spent a single day without a book by my side. This meant slipping from the act of reading into the act of writing didn't actually seem that much of a change.

I've long been a fan of great historical fiction writers such as Hilary Mantel, but I also spend quality time with books by authors from other genres, such as Margaret Atwood, Kate Atkinson, Karen Brooks, Tim Winton, Ian McEwan, Jane Austen, John Irving and E. Annie Proulx.

I live in Canberra, Australia with my husband, two sons, and a lively Staffordshire Bull Terrier named Mick.

I enjoy running, swimming and yoga daily, as I believe staying active is an integral component of a happy writing life. You can visit me at www.jennybondbooks.com.au.

Jenny